ROGUE NATION

Alan Clements is the director of content at Scottish Television and the co-author of *Restless Nation*, which accompanied the BBC Scotland television series on Scottish politics. He is married to Kirsty Wark and has two children, Caitlin and James.

ROGUE NATION

ALAN CLEMENTS

MAINSTREAM
PUBLISHING

EDINBURGH AND LONDON

For my family

This edition, 2010

First published in Great Britain in 2009 by
MAINSTREAM PUBLISHING COMPANY
(EDINBURGH) LTD
7 Albany Street
Edinburgh EH1 3UG

ISBN 9781845965808

A catalogue record for this book is available
from the British Library

Typeset in Garamond and Headline

Printed in Great Britain by
CPI Cox and Wyman, Reading, RG1 8EX

1 3 5 7 9 10 8 6 4 2

*Those who would give up essential liberty to purchase
a little temporary safety, deserve neither liberty nor safety.*

Benjamin Franklin

CHAPTER 1

FRIDAY, 2 MAY 2014

THE WHITE HOUSE, WASHINGTON DC, 00.10 A.M.

President Todd MacFarlane strode the short path from the Oval Office along the side of the Rose Garden into the residence. As soon as he was out of view of the Secret Service agents, his body relaxed and he wearily made his way up the short flight of stairs to his bedroom. He was relieved to see that Janice was sleeping in her own room again tonight.

Shrugging off his jacket, he slumped onto his bed and turned on CNN to catch the headlines. He gave a low whistle at the breaking story leading the news. It looked like the political briefing he had been given that afternoon had been totally wrong and, from the way the two TV anchors were struggling to catch up, he clearly wasn't the only one who had been misinformed.

'Well, I'll be fucked,' he muttered to himself. 'Who would have thought the old country would have the balls. Goddamn polls never get anything right.'

He picked up the phone. 'Put an early morning call to Prime Minister Jones into the diary, please.'

Still, he mused, there surely must be some political advantage in this for a man called MacFarlane.

NORTHUMBERLAND STREET, EDINBURGH, 5.15 A.M.

George Wallace, the senior special adviser to Ross Johnson, Scotland's first minister, was wide awake, lying on the bed fully clothed. There was no point in trying to sleep now. He had to be with Ross at the studios in an hour. Radio first – *Today* and *Good Morning Scotland* – then breakfast TV, then he would have to start with the foreign press. And all the dignified concession remarks he had prepared for the first minister would have to be ditched and new words of triumph written.

Beside him, Clare stirred and turned over. He smiled at her pixie features and cascade of brown hair, then swung his legs off the bed. He had secretly hoped she would wake up when he had lain down ten minutes before, but she had stayed resolutely asleep. He longed to share that morning's amazing news with the woman who had restored his life to happiness. That pleasure would have to wait.

George padded quietly to the kitchen and set the coffee machine to brew. Grabbing a mug, he wandered to the drawing-room windows to watch the sun rising over Edinburgh's New Town. He turned over some phrases to use on the press that morning, wondering if 'new dawn' was just too clichéd. Deciding that the new Scotland deserved better, he headed to the shower to clear his head of the two ill-judged celebratory whiskies he had downed when the result had finally been announced at 4 a.m.

NUMBER 10 DOWNING STREET, LONDON, 8 A.M.

Tony Hodge, the prime minister's chief of staff, knocked firmly on his boss's bedroom door. Barely waiting for the invitation, he strode in. After ten years working together, they no longer bothered with pleasantries. And the chief of staff had to talk urgently to his boss about the email the prime minister had sent him ten minutes after the referendum result had been announced.

'Are you sure you want to do this?' asked Hodge. 'It's all a bit Churchillian by your measured standards, isn't it? And those lefty ponces at the BBC are kicking up hell about balance . . .'

'I've made up my mind,' the prime minister replied, characteristically soft-spoken but decisive. 'It's the only way. It has to be a direct address to the nation. Christ Almighty, it's not every day the United Kingdom falls apart, so the masses will just have to wait ten minutes for *EastEnders*. Remind the director-general the licence fee is up for renewal in two years and that I am minded to share it with Channel Four. That should concentrate his mind. And make sure the whole Cabinet is here for nine sharp. This is definitely a day for collective responsibility. Now, if you don't mind, I'd like to get dressed.'

Tony Hodge's brief nod of his head was an acknowledgement of both the prime minister's decision and his own subservient position. He closed the door quietly behind him.

THE PRESIDENT'S OFFICE, THE KREMLIN, MOSCOW, 6.30 A.M.

Colonel Sergei Karimov nervously entered the Senate building and athletically climbed the polished steps to the president's personal office two at a time. He knew in the short term this was not going to be a pleasant experience, but he also knew it was potentially the greatest opportunity in his career.

President Igor Churov was notoriously short-tempered and would not be best pleased that his top British specialist had got his intelligence briefing so spectacularly wrong. As an ex-FSB operative himself, President Churov took these things to heart.

The secretary seated at a desk outside the president's office waved him forward as soon as she noticed him at the top of the stairs. Colonel Karimov took a deep breath and knocked.

'Enter.'

Sergei Karimov's gaze swept quickly over the books adorning the oak-lined walls and rested on the burly figure seated behind the desk that dominated the room. 'Sir, as requested, I have brought the latest figures. There is now no doubt that the "Yes" vote was victorious. It was incredibly close, but—'

'But not the significant "No" vote you were predicting.'

All of Karimov's training had drummed into him that calmness was the most effective response to aggression. 'Unfortunately, the analysis of our political operatives was wrong. But to be fair, sir, not one political analyst predicted a "Yes" vote.'

President Churov's face tightened with annoyance. 'That's hardly an excuse, Colonel Karimov. I expect the FSB's intelligence officers to deliver me more insight than I can read in the newspapers.'

The president paused, torn between the desire to continue the dressing-down and the need to get on with the day's business. The latter impulse won. 'In any event,' Churov continued, 'we have more pressing matters. Obviously, this changes everything and grants us the opportunity we have been seeking. I want you to immediately begin Operation Braveheart.'

Karimov struggled hard not to show his delight. He kept his voice neutral and properly deferential. 'Of course, sir. At once.'

'And, Colonel.'

'Yes, sir?'

'I'm holding you personally responsible for its success. Don't let me down . . . again.'

THE WHITE HOUSE, WASHINGTON DC, 8 A.M.

President MacFarlane's private secretary put his head round the connecting door to the Oval Office. 'The prime minister of the United Kingdom on line one, sir.'

Not for much longer he isn't, thought Todd MacFarlane as he swung his legs off the desk and reached for the receiver. He hadn't warmed to Nick Jones in the year since he had become prime minister, resenting his superior tone and earnest, pointy-headed intellectualism. But this was duty. 'Prime Minister, a great pleasure to talk to you again. Even though my family are Scottish through and through, I would never have believed it would come to this and I'm deeply saddened for y'all in the United Kingdom.'

Nick Jones's response was surprisingly brisk and upbeat in response to MacFarlane's sympathy. 'Well, that is very kind, but don't be too downcast. The Scots have made their bed, so let them lie in it. This offers a great opportunity for England to flourish and I am determined to grab it. I've no intention of resisting this decision. Let's see how the Scots deal with the big bad world on their own. There may well be teething troubles between England and Scotland but, given the history of the special relationship between our two countries, I take it I can count on your support for us?'

'Of course,' MacFarlane replied, 'but you have to understand my position. The Scots-Americans are not an obvious lobby like the Irish or the Jews, but they are real powerful behind the scenes. As I speak, there will be a dozen senators burnishing their Caledonian credentials and welcoming the 193rd member of the United Nations. And the presidential primaries start in nine months, so I need to be balanced. It's just politics, you understand. Nothing personal.'

The prime minister bristled. He hated being patronised at any time, but to be offered lessons in political tactics from this jumped-up redneck was truly insufferable. 'Of course, Mr President, I understand. I'll keep you posted on our progress.'

THE BALMORAL HOTEL, EDINBURGH, 11 A.M.

George Wallace had always thought Jessica Schwartz, the *New York Times'* UK correspondent, was a bit special. She combined good looks and glamour with the self-confidence and sense of entitlement that only an expensive Ivy League education can bring. How he envied that, he thought, as he watched her toned body cross the hotel lobby towards him.

And besides, she had been a great finisher as a centre-forward.

She kissed both his cheeks, then sat down, leaving a lingering scent of expensive perfume.

They were both experienced players in this game. George knew what she wrote carried weight with the American opinion formers who would be so important to the new Scotland and had expended no little effort wooing her over long lunches in London.

Jessica knew that George and Scotland's first minister Ross Johnson had been friends since their university days thirty years before and that therefore he spoke with the full authority of his boss, unlike so many other arrogant and overpaid 'spin doctors' in the other parties, who hinted at access they never truly enjoyed.

As important, George had studied and worked in the States and shared none of the juvenile anti-Americanism so common in the United Kingdom. Jessica liked the adage that the relationship between a journalist and a politician should be akin to that of a dog and a lamp post, but she knew the reality was more complex. She really enjoyed the intellectual flirtation with George.

And besides, George had been the nicest high-school history teacher she had ever had. 'So, my dear George, how does the first day of freedom feel?'

'Wonderful,' George replied. Then he added with a smile, 'Obviously, I never doubted for a moment it would happen.'

Jessica snorted at the obvious fib. Unabashed, George took a sip of coffee and continued. 'So, how do you want to begin? On or off the record?'

Jessica laughed and tossed back her long brown hair. 'Off, of course. But tell me first, how is that lovely young girlfriend of yours?'

SHEREMETYEVO INTERNATIONAL AIRPORT, MOSCOW, 11 A.M.

Colonel Karimov settled back in his seat on the flight to London and tried to focus on the editorials in *The Economist*, but his mind kept drifting to the task ahead. Russia had come so far since the dark, desperate days of Yeltsin's presidency when the nation he loved had been reduced to an international laughing stock: an impoverished banana republic presided over by a drunken oaf.

Driven by Vladimir Putin's steely determination and fuelled by record oil and gas prices, Russia had slowly clawed its way back to power and respectability. Now, this surprise referendum result in a tiny, unimportant country had finally given Russia the chance to become the equal of America for the first time since the Cold War ended in the 1980s.

And he was the man who was going to make it happen: a player at last. He finally had a chance to expel the nightmare of East Germany from his mind for ever. It was a chance he would not allow to slip.

BBC BROADCASTING HOUSE, LANGHAM PLACE, LONDON, 8 P.M.

The BBC had grumpily assented to a live prime-ministerial broadcast with much muttering about editorial integrity and the need for the leader of the opposition to have a right to reply. But Nick Jones had been correct: the arm-twisting on the licence fee had ultimately worked.

As he polished his spectacles, the prime minister looked round the bare walls of tiny Studio C, empty apart from a single cameraman and a floor manager. It seemed an oddly inauspicious setting for such a historic announcement.

Jones disliked live TV, but he couldn't deny that it got the adrenalin pumping. And he knew he was a lot better at giving speeches than he was in the brutal cut and thrust of TV debate.

The floor manager started the countdown at ten. Nick Jones took one last sip of water, moistened his lips and turned his focus to the autocue in front of him.

'Three, two, one . . .'

The light on the wall glowed red, accentuating the black letters spelling out 'Microphone Live'.

'My fellow citizens, as you will all now be aware, last night the people of Scotland voted to leave the United Kingdom. It is true that the margin was incredibly close, fewer than 2,000 voters in the end. However, in a democracy, a winning margin of one is sufficient and I fully respect that decision.

'The question the Scots said "Yes" to was unambiguous. They agreed that the Scottish Parliament should negotiate a new settlement with the British government so that Scotland becomes a sovereign and independent state. I have today spoken to the king and can announce that my government will not put obstacles in the way of Scotland as it seeks that independent future. We will work towards a painless "velvet" divorce, as the Czechs and Slovaks managed in the early 1990s and the Flemish and French-speaking parts of Belgium achieved last year. I believe that, with goodwill on all sides, that objective can be successfully achieved.

'However, I will not countenance these negotiations being protracted and potentially destabilising. Our respective civil servants in the Constitution Unit in Edinburgh have already drawn up fairly advanced plans in the White Paper and these will be implemented quickly. As of midnight on the thirty-first of

July this year, Scotland will be a fully sovereign nation, taking full responsibility for its own economy, foreign affairs and defence. A Scottish pound will neither be tied to, nor supported by, the Bank of England. Also, a process of military disengagement will commence with immediate effect, beginning with the withdrawal of the nuclear submarine fleet from the Royal Navy base at Faslane.

'I wish the people of Scotland well, but I must say that I hope and expect that, freed from the drag of subsidies to Scotland, the people of England, Wales and Northern Ireland will continue to progress and I look forward to leading them to further prosperity. Thank you for taking the time to listen. Goodnight.'

Tony Hodge walked down from the studio gallery and joined his boss in make-up as he wiped off the last of the foundation. 'Very positive and direct, Nick. That should put the wind up the Jocks. Our people in Edinburgh are saying that they are already getting cold feet and would probably settle for a federal solution. I could speak to George Wallace about a conference at . . .'

The prime minister stood up and closed the door. 'Don't you get it, Tony? This is not a bluff. I mean it. I was always a Unionist. I always thought of myself as British, but these people have chosen to make me English. Well, so be it. And it's unquestionably in our political interests. Even when Blair won the election comfortably in 2005, the Tories won the popular vote in England. By removing Scottish MPs I have just guaranteed a Conservative government in England for the next fifty years. Not even your heroine Mrs Thatcher could do that.'

Tony Hodge was taken aback by his boss's sudden, out-of-character passion. 'But what about our support for the Scottish Unionists? What'll happen to them?'

'Let the brightest and best come south, and tough for the rest. Their unsettling presence in Scotland will mean the SNP will have to focus inwards and thus be less demanding on us.'

Nick Jones remembered an appropriate phrase from that morning. 'It's just politics, Tony, nothing personal.'

THE IRON DUKE BAR, DENNISTOUN, GLASGOW, 8.10 P.M.

As the prime minister's address ended, Sammy Wilson slammed down his pint glass on the scratched and sticky table in disgust. 'Well, that's us fucked, then. Another fucking sell-out. First Ulster, now us.' He turned his shaven head from the television screen to his five drinking companions. 'Boys, it's time for us to get active again. This is our last chance to save Britain. Remember our oath of "No Surrender"? Well, it's time to live up to that. Are you wi' me?' he demanded.

Sammy's five mates looked at his cold killer's eyes and the long scar that disfigured his face, and nodded their assent one by one.

Sammy wasn't the kind of man you disagreed with lightly.

KNOCKAVIE HOUSE, STIRLINGSHIRE, 8.10 P.M.

Robert Cowan switched off the television and turned to face the twenty stony-faced senior financiers, politicians and entrepreneurs in his drawing room. He surveyed the dinner-jacketed men clutching their pre-dinner gin and tonics. This planned victory party for the 'No' campaign had turned into a wake.

But Cowan had a surprise for them. He knew this was the moment to seize the initiative – the moment to show he could lead from the front. 'Gentlemen, you have heard the prime minister. Though hardly surprising, it is nevertheless deeply disappointing to hear this message of surrender from a man who promised us his full support in this very room just a year ago. We have been abandoned by the British Conservative Party.'

Scotland's business elite murmured their agreement. 'However, we are where we are, and the defence of the Union now falls on our shoulders – and wallets. Some, of course, more ample than others.'

He waited for the laughter to subside, then grew serious. 'The "Yes" vote was unquestionably a devastating blow. Our beloved nation faces the greatest peril since the Battle of Britain in 1940. As we did then, we must stand firm. We cannot allow three hundred years of glorious history to be tossed aside on the basis of one snapshot poll. Therefore, I suggest tonight that we put aside our sadness and disappointment and rededicate ourselves to the task. I propose that we establish a political movement to fight for Unionism the way that the spineless Labour Party, Liberal Democrats and Conservatives have singularly failed to do. I believe we should call ourselves the Scottish Unionist Resistance, and then do what it says on the tin and defend our nation.'

Cowan relished the growing excitement in the room. 'Gentlemen, I ask you to raise your glasses to toast the birth of the Scottish Unionist Resistance. The SUR!'

'The SUR!' chorused twenty voices in unison.

A satisfied smile crossed Cowan's face. 'Now, if you would like to head through, dinner is served. We have much to discuss.'

THE BALMORAL HOTEL, EDINBURGH, 8.10 P.M.

As Prime Minister Jones finished his last sentence, Colonel Karimov switched off the television set in his hotel room. He was going to have to move faster than anticipated. Three months from a vote for independence to a complete severing of the two nations was less than a quarter of the time anticipated in Operation Braveheart's blueprint. He would need to see Ross Johnson as soon as possible.

In the hotel bar below, George Wallace punched Clare's number on his speed dial. 'Did you see the broadcast, sweetheart? Yes, I thought you might be watching. Three months will be really punishing. I'm afraid our celebration dinner is going to have to wait. I'm off to see Ross to discuss what this means. Don't wait up, I'll try to be quiet when I come in.'

As he hurried out to the taxi rank, George felt a wave of tenderness toward Clare. Her love and tolerance made all of this bearable. Then a stab of tiredness made him realise that this was likely to be another sleepless night spent with political apparatchiks instead of in Clare's sweet embrace.

Not for the first time that day, in spite of his elation at the referendum result, George felt just a little sorry for himself.

THE SITUATION ROOM, THE WHITE HOUSE, 4.10 P.M.

As President MacFarlane entered the room, the political and military elite of the United States rose as one to their feet. He waved them to sit. 'Gentlemen. Sorry, lady and gentlemen. The prime minister's decision to accelerate the road to Scottish independence raises some interesting issues for us. A situation report, please. Military first. Carl?'

The head of the joint chiefs of staff, Admiral Carl Butterworth, cleared his throat. 'The most immediate issue is the nuclear base at Faslane on the Gare Loch in western Scotland, where our new nuclear missiles are on Royal Navy subs. That is not hardware we want to be sharing with anyone but London. Working with the English government, we will have those out within the month.

'We have the fast reactive Marine battalion based at RAF Forres near Inverness, but that can be easily shifted to England. Then, of course, there are Special Operations forces which don't appear in the official number. I reckon no more than a hundred across Scotland. Militarily, the situation is difficult, but by no means insurmountable.'

'Politics, Chuck?'

Charles Sands, the White House chief of staff, had never had the nerve to tell his boss how much he hated that abbreviation of his name, which reminded him of years of abuse at his prep school at Andover at the hands of pupils less academically gifted than himself. However, at least when the president called him Chuck he felt less of what he in reality was – the only East Coast intellectual in an administration of Southern populists.

Sands was his usual crisp self; he knew how much his boss hated unnecessary waffle. 'The SNP is a mainstream political party and leader Ross Johnson a convinced social democrat. The only political danger is a Unionist backlash, given the tightness of the vote, and thus the potential for some form of civil disorder, but I reckon that is remote. There's no tradition of violent protest in modern Scottish history.

'The SNP is committed to removing nuclear weapons from Scotland and is traditionally pretty hostile to America. However, Johnson's senior special adviser – effectively his chief of staff – is a guy called George Wallace, and he's friendly to the United States. He and Johnson are the tightest pair in British politics since Tony Blair and Alastair Campbell. Wallace studied at Penn and worked in LA. He should be our entry point for exercising some influence.'

Sands looked pointedly at the director of the CIA, as if inviting a challenge. 'I think it is time for a charm offensive. My team is already on it.'

'Intelligence?'

Jane Chalmers, the director of the CIA, shifted uncomfortably in her seat. As the president's awkward introduction had illustrated, it was a tough enough job to be the first ever female director of the Agency, without presiding over yet another intelligence failure. 'Well, Mr President, I'm afraid we clearly called this one wrong. All our analysts thought the Unionists would win comfortably, so we are playing catch-up here. We have no agents inside the SNP hierarchy, though I understand MI6 does have one who is well placed.'

Chalmers then played a card which she hoped would take the attention off her Agency's mistake. 'However, I don't agree with Charles that the most pressing issue is the danger of civil disorder in Scotland. For me, the real big issue is what the Russians do.'

Chalmers was aware that she suddenly had the undivided attention of a dozen pairs of eyes. She chose her next words carefully. 'Under President Churov, the Russians have returned to the hardline policies of the Putin era and the Communist regimes before that, effectively seeking to restore the influence the Soviets had in Europe during the Cold War. They are furious that we have extended NATO to their borders and even angrier about our new missile defence system in Poland and the Czech Republic.

'The Russians control major politicians in Hungary and the Czech Republic and have been funding separatist movements in Catalonia and Flanders in order to destabilise the European Union.'

'Any evidence they are behind the SNP?' interrupted MacFarlane.

'No, Mr President, but independence could give them an opening. And control of an independent Scotland gives power over the North Atlantic's shipping lanes.'

'OK, thank you all. Let's gear up the political and intelligence effort – and let's find some friends in the SNP. Chuck, let's get this guy Johnson over here real soon. The last thing we need is more Russian influence in Western Europe. They already control half its gas and oil supplies.

'That's it, gentlemen. Sorry, Jane. I mean, y'all get to work.'

CHAPTER 2

FRIDAY, 6 JUNE — FIFTY-FIVE DAYS TO INDEPENDENCE

SNP REGIONAL HEADQUARTERS, ARGYLE STREET, GLASGOW, 4 A.M.

Sammy Wilson sat in a battered old Ford Fiesta with his brother Billy and his second cousins, Jack and Gordon Williams. He hadn't felt this excited since the Scottish brigade of the UVF – the Ulster Volunteer Force – had gone on ceasefire eight years earlier. Now he was back on active service. The head of the Glasgow East Battalion of the new British Loyalist Army. Someone again. A leader.

Sammy had been just twenty-one years old when the ceasefire had been ordered in 2006, a junior player, muscle for the leaders, but at least a part of something. Since then, he had felt his life drained of real purpose. He led the Dennistoun Young Team, the toughest Loyalist gang in Glasgow's East End – significant, but a poor substitute for the good old days of the UVF. Now he was back in the big time.

Sammy only truly felt alive when fighting. He was aware the boys followed him not because he was the biggest, or strongest, or even the best fighter, but because they feared him. He knew that the winner in a fight was always the person who could take most pain and cared least what happened to him.

If Sammy had been a little better read, he would have also known that was one of the classic signs of psychopathy.

Sixteen years living with his dad had taught him how to take pain, weekly beatings with a buckled belt, whether he deserved them or not. He had endured it until the day of his sixteenth birthday, when he had used a baseball bat to put his dad in intensive care.

His father had never touched him again, leading Sammy to the conclusion that violence worked and absolute violence worked absolutely.

Leading his battalion of the BLA gave him a renewed reason for being – the only thing in his life of which he was remotely proud. And, most important, it made him someone on the mean streets of east Dennistoun. He hated the fact that any criminal and crackhead now got respect. It made him furious. He wasn't scum like that. He was a soldier in the king's service.

The old guys had hung up their balaclavas and he was now in charge. Like all psychopaths, Sammy saw himself as a victim and loved nothing more than feeling righteous as he inflicted violence.

Sammy also relished his physicality. He had the defiant, wiry muscularity of the classic Glasgow hard man. Running his right hand across his shaved head, he fingered the long ugly scar that Sean Kelly's hatchet had left.

He was always really pleased with his rehearsed response when people asked him about it. 'Aye, it's bad, right enough. But you should see the other guy.'

He was right. Sean Kelly was dead. Killed with his own hatchet.

Sammy looked down at the mobile phone and carefully punched in four digits. The blast ripped the door off its hinges and sent shards of glass cascading across the tar of the empty street.

Sammy tucked the mobile into his leather jacket and gunned the car into action. 'Good practice, lads. I think we're ready for bigger things,' he said to his companions.

The others nodded. But Gordon Williams kept his eyes fixed on the glass reflecting in the orange glow of the street lamps.

OFFICE OF THE SENIOR SPECIAL ADVISER, SCOTTISH PARLIAMENT, EDINBURGH, 7 A.M.

George Wallace's head lay still on his desk. He was fast asleep.

He was woken by his PA, Morven, rapping her knuckles on the glass door. She carried a steaming and very welcome cup of coffee. 'Morning, George. Thought you might need this. By the way, another bomb in Glasgow this morning. That's the fourth this week.'

George stretched and rubbed his eyes. He had always considered himself a hard worker – a fit, energetic man. He had been an exceptionally diligent student, attending lectures while others propped up the bar. He had built up and sold a successful public relations company, spending late Friday nights trying to spike stories about his clients in the Sunday papers and late Sunday nights struggling to work out the VAT in an old pencil ledger.

Returning to his first love of politics in his mid forties, he had revelled in the 24/7 news cycle, the addiction, the sheer exhilaration of being in government keeping him going.

But nothing, *nothing* had prepared him for the last month. The intensity of negotiating the unravelling of a major nation in the full glare of the world's media had drained him to the core.

When he had had two kids under two, George used to joke that people without sleepless infants should be banned from using the word 'exhausted'. But this was worse even than that.

The negotiations had been excruciating. The English side held all the trump cards and hadn't been slow to let their Scottish counterparts see the brutal side of power politics. What couldn't be agreed was imposed.

And how could the Scots respond? As one of his English opponents put it to him: 'What are you going to do, George? Invade Carlisle?'

On top of the constant pressure of the independence negotiations, every day brought a steady stream of bad news. In a major public-service brain drain, many senior civil servants and military personnel had already voted with their feet and headed south, wanting nothing to do with the new Scotland, their insistent complaints filling the newspapers and the airwaves.

Almost immediately, the opinion polls suggested that the Scottish people regretted the choice of independence. Post-referendum surveys showed that many Scots had voted 'Yes' to put pressure on the Westminster government to give Scotland more powers, or just to show their disgust at the UK Conservative government which had been elected in 2010, expecting that other voters would produce a 'No' vote overall.

The result had been a complete shock.

The poll in that morning's *Scotsman* showed that, four weeks after the vote, only 35 per cent were now in favour of independence, with 65 per cent opposed.

The economic news was even worse. Part of George's role in the party had been to liaise with the business community and he had worked hard to bring many over to the cause of independence, especially after the credit crunch of 2008 had wrecked Scottish banking.

Now that independence was a reality, the hard core of refuseniks were making good their promise to take the first shuttle down to London and making very public their disdain for the new Scotland and its economic prospects. Those that remained were pouring money into the nascent Scottish Unionist Resistance.

This flight of capital and talent was in danger of making their dire predictions of economic collapse a self-fulfilling prophecy as it further rocked Scottish confidence. In just a month's time the new Scottish pound would float on the world's markets and potential disaster loomed.

The Scots' cold feet were now getting positively icy.

Of course, the opposition were making his life hellish. Despite only being a month old, the SUR were winning support from across the political spectrum. The rump of the Scottish Conservatives had joined en masse, as had disaffected members of the Labour Party, who felt their leadership had been less than robust in its defence of the Union and hated their party's acceptance of the inevitability of independence.

Most worryingly, an organisation calling itself the British Loyalist Army – or BLA – had embarked on a series of low-level acts of terrorism against the very idea of an independent Scotland. There had been nothing serious yet: a couple of letter bombs to left-wing members of the SNP; blasts in the middle of the night with no casualties. So far.

The SUR leader Robert Cowan had condemned them, following up with the usual 'but you have to understand the frustration of young men in difficult circumstances' bollocks. It reeked of hypocrisy.

Both the SUR and the BLA had been able to rally people round the Scottish government's decision not to have the king remain as head of state in Scotland. How George cursed the republican left of the SNP for pushing through a meaningless gesture which had alienated many people in Scotland just when they needed friends the most.

This was one of the actions that fuelled George's deepest and most secret fear, one he had so far only dared to share with his girlfriend Clare. What if independence wasn't the best option, after all? Maybe it was all a big mistake that would condemn Scotland to impoverishment and political irrelevance.

Christ, if *he* was starting to think like that, what hope was there for everyone else?

George's reverie was broken by Morven popping her head round the door. 'Remember, you have the first minister in five. And the White House chief of staff's office would like an advance copy of your American speech. Do you have it on the laptop so I can email it?'

George muttered his assent and went to freshen up. He splashed his face in the staff bathroom, the cold water cutting the tiredness from his eyes. He stared intently at the mirror.

Not bad for forty-nine, he mused, surveying a greying but full head of dark brown hair and only the slightest swell of a beer belly. Though he never discussed it,

George took a secret pleasure in having aged so well and was quietly horrified at his rotund peers in the parliament building. He loved the physical challenge of sport almost as much as he loved the intellectual challenge of history and poetry.

He still had the classic male V-shape, broad shoulders and thin waist, accentuated by his single extravagance since he had made some money: beautifully cut, bespoke suits from the little Italian tailor on the south side of Glasgow.

George had kept himself fit playing amateur football with Dennistoun Villa until he had left Glasgow three years before and he still played five-a-sides twice a week in an MSPs-against-advisers match, topping it up with stress-busting visits to the gym.

His pleasant, regular features were spoiled by a nose broken by an over-eager centre-half during a particularly brutal game of football, and which now appeared to be trying to colonise the rest of his face.

A distinctive anger vein ran down his right temple. It pulsed disconcertingly when he was furious, which was more often than was healthy for him. And now, of course, he had massive greyish bags under his intelligent dark brown eyes.

George knew he needed to harness all his energy and acumen to steel himself once more for the stressful day ahead.

OFFICE OF THE FIRST MINISTER, SCOTTISH PARLIAMENT, EDINBURGH, 7.30 A.M.

As he sat in Ross Johnson's outer office, George reflected on the twisted path that had brought them together. They had been students together at the University of Glasgow in the mid 1980s, at the high point of Thatcherism. They had been rival debaters in the old University Union – Ross, the charismatic opener for the student nationalists; George, the tenacious closing debater for the socialists.

They had bonded over heroic drinking sessions and had stayed friends since, despite their political and personal differences. Ross was a glamorous, commitment-phobic womaniser; George, more cautious and hardworking. Ross was an expansive but slipshod thinker; George, a logical pedant with a passion for detail. Though neither was classically handsome, both had been big social and intellectual presences on campus.

Like many modern politicians, Ross Johnson had never really had a proper job. After student politics, he had taken various research roles in the party. He had won a Westminster seat for the SNP at a by-election in his mid thirties and had progressed rapidly up the ranks of a party short on glamour.

Over the years, George had admired Ross's unfailing capacity to work a room.

He was equally at ease with charladies and chairmen, and shared with Bill Clinton the invaluable ability to make whoever he was speaking to at the time feel he or she was the most important person in the world to him. Ross knew as a politician that if people liked you, they would forgive you anything; if they disliked you, they would forgive you nothing.

And people definitely liked Ross. Unlike George, they had not seen that his charm could be switched on and off at will, or witnessed the cold wind of his disapproval.

Disillusioned with New Labour from the start of the century, George had grown closer to Ross politically over the years. Working in the PR business in London, he had seen at first hand how little Scotland mattered to the capital's press and power brokers. He had slowly become convinced that Scotland would only prosper as an independent nation, a feeling Ross had encouraged over late-night whiskies when they met on the sleeper north.

Like many male friendships, theirs made few demands. Neither felt the need to nurture it or, indeed, examine it in any way. They met once every few weeks for dinner, played the odd game of poor golf and travelled to Scotland football games together. They talked sport and Ross offered political insight in return for media gossip. For George, their ties had become looser, but deeper, as they had grown older. They didn't need to work on their friendship. It just was. And every time they met, they seamlessly picked up where they had left off.

When Ross became first minister after the 2011 Scottish election, he had shocked George by asking him to come to work for him as his senior special adviser, flattering him by saying he needed someone who would tell him the truth, not a party hack who would tell him what he wanted to hear.

In all honesty, George hadn't needed much persuasion. His wife, Bridget, had died two years before, he had sold his PR company and was itching for a new challenge. After years of explaining and defending the actions of others, it was so tempting for him to be able to make decisions that actually made a difference. To be a doer, not a viewer. To be an insider. Finally, a player.

Ross's clinching argument over a fine Arran malt was to remind George that he had a chance to overcome Schopenhauer's observation that the first forty years of life were text and the rest commentary. George had said yes that same night. He had never regretted that decision.

Though it was not an elected post, everyone knew the power that George wielded. He was Ross's eyes and ears in the party. He controlled access to him. He had his attention night and day.

George knew that many in the SNP resented this position, particularly as he had been in the Labour Party for years and hadn't suffered with the party faithful through the decades in the wilderness. This was compounded when *The Scotsman* named him the second most powerful man in Scotland after the first minister. George knew that was rubbish, the product of lazy journalism – an obsession with lists instead of writing proper analysis – and no more a compliment than being the second-best downhill skier in Jamaica.

He was also aware that he lacked an independent power base in the party, which meant that his future was completely tied to that of his boss. And Ross liked that. George's dependence guaranteed his absolute loyalty, a rare quality in politics.

Of course, George sometimes idly wondered if it could have been him at the top instead of Ross, but he knew he could have no real regrets. He had two great kids, money in the bank, the house in the Algarve, and now Clare. He would still have a life if this all fell apart. And he knew that, one day, it all would. All political careers do.

Ross, by contrast, had nothing but politics. He was married only to the party. He had spent the best years of his life doing the 'rubber chicken' circuit of dinners with local party branches to shore up his position, trailing a series of increasingly short sexual relationships in his wake. George admired lots of things about Ross, but found it hard to envy him.

George had also realised in the last three years, as he watched Ross defeat rivals and friends in equal measure, that he didn't have the requisite ruthlessness, the constant cynicism, that winning at politics requires.

He occasionally wondered if that political ruthlessness and Ross's cynicism in his relationships with women extended to his friends, but always pushed that uncomfortable thought to the back of his mind.

George trusted Ross, but sometimes had a sneaking suspicion that that trust was not repaid in full. There was nothing concrete he could point to. No other close adviser he feared. But it was there in the occasional hesitation in sharing secrets; an odd silence in conversation; a quizzical look in a meeting. He was starting to think Ross was like that old saying about a bikini – what he revealed was suggestive, what he hid was vital.

However, George couldn't deny that he absolutely adored his advisory role. Being an insider stroked his vanity. He had access to power, without having made the sacrifices that Ross had. He had power without responsibility, the prerogative of the harlot throughout history.

And now Ross had made him head of the seven Scottish Commissioners negotiating independence. A front seat in history. He was exhausted, but fulfilled.

'Penny for them?' Ross's smiling, fleshy face appeared round the door of his office.

'Sorry, Ross, I was miles away. Actually, I was thinking about us, reflecting, as my old hero Benjamin Franklin put it, "We either hang together or we will hang separately."'

'Well, the way things are going, it looks like we will both soon be swinging in the wind. Come on in.'

As Ross settled his ample frame into the leather armchair behind his desk, George looked at his friend. The three stone he had put on since university sat comfortably enough on his tall frame, though the endless round of official lunches and dinners were starting to strain his suit jacket across the middle. His strawberry blond hair – a description he always preferred to ginger – was thinning, but swept back and still distinguished.

Ross's restless, laughing, piercing blue eyes stared, amused, at George. 'Well, if you have quite finished eyeing me up, could we begin?'

George reviewed the grim political and economic situation for him. Ross nodded gravely, then asked him what he thought of the BLA, adding, 'After all, they are your people.'

George took the jibe in good part. Ross knew George's working-class family had all been in the Orange Lodge in the East End of Glasgow, and that he knew the outer fringes of the Protestant world well. George had been a regular Rangers supporter as a kid and had continued his allegiance when it was terminally unfashionable on the political left at university.

Before Rangers cracked down on the extremists at the turn of the century, the people he travelled to games with revelled in the team's Protestant identity. Their loyalty was not to Scotland, but to the Crown and the United Kingdom. Most emotionally, it was to their fellow Protestants 'across the water' in Ulster. For most, it didn't go beyond sentimental songs sung late at night in pubs. For others, it had hardened into action.

For George, it was a world he was glad to have left behind. He had found the ideology increasingly distasteful as he had seen more of the world. He now much preferred the joyful exuberance of the Tartan Army to the bigoted chants of the Rangers support. The last straw was being caught up in the disgraceful organised violence at the UEFA Cup final in Manchester six years before. There was no place for him in a support that included Ulster Loyalists and English fascists, as well as Scottish thugs. He hadn't been to a Rangers game since.

His intellectual journey from working-class Unionism was accelerated when he had done the unthinkable and married Bridget Kelly. A Catholic. A *Fenian*. George thought he had got off lightly when the wedding reception had been punctuated by only two fist fights. Since his father's death, it was a world glimpsed only occasionally when he returned to see what was left of his family in Dennistoun. George still fancied himself part of the working class, but in his heart he knew it was a world he had left behind a long time ago.

He looked back at Ross, dwarfed at his desk by the huge, socialist-realist painting of Scots on the march which dominated the wall behind him and which had hung there since the Salmond years. 'These young guys haven't had a cause since the UDA and UVF laid down their weapons in 2006,' George told the first minister. 'I would say there is a hard core of maybe five hundred guys and a couple of thousand fellow travellers. The big fear is that it opens deeper, older wounds.'

Ross nodded. He recognised the danger. Scotland had made great strides in ending the traditional sectarianism between Catholic and Protestant and in forging a new Scottish identity that embraced everyone. More than anything, Ross didn't want to throw that away.

George couldn't have agreed more, but felt they had more pressing matters. 'Anyway, let's leave that to Special Branch. More important, Ross, what the hell are we going to do when the Scottish pound floats in a month's time?' George leaned forward as if to take Ross into his confidence. 'I talked to Sir Michael at the Royal Bank last night and he thinks there could be meltdown. There could be a flight of people and capital we haven't seen in Europe since the fall of the Berlin Wall.'

'I have been thinking about that a lot,' Ross replied. 'And I think I may have a solution.'

Ross gestured to a tall, handsome, athletic-looking man who had just appeared in the doorway. Under a tidy square-cut head of fair hair sat a pair of classic Slavic prominent high cheekbones and the most piercing light blue eyes George had ever seen. 'George, I would like you to meet Colonel Karimov, the new Russian ambassador to the Republic of Scotland.'

CHAPTER 3

WEDNESDAY, 11 JUNE — FIFTY DAYS TO INDEPENDENCE

THE KREMLIN, MOSCOW, 10 A.M.

The limousine swept through the vast gates on the edge of Red Square and into the main courtyard. The guards saluted Ross and George and an aide ushered them up the stairs of the senate building.

When George had first been here, in 1989, it had still been called the Soviet Council of Ministers Building and had been at the heart of the old Communist apparat which had controlled the country. Not for the first time, George wondered if the names in Russia had changed, but the reality had not.

He looked around the imposing entrance hall and smiled at the memory of his first guided tour of the Kremlin. After Glasgow University, George had spent three years in America, first as a scholarship student at the University of Pennsylvania, where he had studied Russian history, Soviet politics and colonial American history. Then he had taught history and coached soccer at an all-girls school in Beverly Hills, a job which brought the same knowing laugh every time he revealed it.

In 1989, he had brought a group of twenty Californian sixteen- and seventeen-year-old girls – one of them Jessica Schwartz – to the Soviet Union, just as the full impact of President Gorbachev's twin policies of perestroika and glasnost – 'restructuring' and 'openness' – was beginning to be felt.

Then it had been a nation in the midst of an identity crisis. His student group still had to have the compulsory meetings with Young Communists extolling the benefits of state planning, but they also went to Moscow's first McDonald's.

He hadn't had too much time to enjoy the irony, as most of his energy had been devoted to fending off the attentions of Soviet sailors, who had their own particular version of glasnost in mind for his young charges. But it was fascinating nonetheless.

Since then, the country had changed beyond recognition – the mad gangster capitalism of the 1990s under Boris Yeltsin, the brief flowering of democracy then the restoration of the old order under Vladimir Putin, whose potent mix of personal rule, economic nationalism and ruthless restoration of Russia's international position had been eagerly followed by his hand-picked successors, President Medvedev and the most recent, their host today, Igor Churov.

President Medvedev had toyed briefly with liberalisation and co-operation with the West between 2008 and 2010, but President Churov had regarded that as wasteful, pathetic weakness and reverted to a much harder line of straight power politics, using Russia's massive oil and gas reserves as his major weapon.

George's previous visit had been in the company of a tour guide whose natural authority had been somewhat undermined by a shaky grasp of English and a shocking lack of teeth. This time, he was going beyond the red ropes, where the tourists never ventured. An insider, at last. These meetings were the real reason George loved politics. And put up with all the shit.

President Churov was all smiles as he welcomed Ross and George into his office. He gestured to the meeting table by the window. George was surprised to see both of the president's aides slip quietly out of the office. 'Gentlemen, please sit. Some tea?' The president's English was heavily accented but perfectly clear.

George suppressed his historian's desire to look at the hundreds of leather-bound volumes which lined the walls and took a seat. But he couldn't ignore the vast Second World War recruiting poster for the Soviet Army which sat behind the president's desk. Square-jawed heroes demanded sacrifice for the Motherland in the Great Patriotic War. The symbolism could not have been more obvious.

As the president personally sorted out the refreshments, George admired the physical assurance of the man, who had been a wrestling champion in his youth, his muscular frame still clear under the dark suit. A shaved head completed the air of underlying menace, despite all the smiles.

George and Ross had met him twice before, at the annual Russian–Scottish celebrations the Scottish press had inevitably dubbed 'Tsartan Week'.

'I have been so looking forward to seeing you both again. Our nations share so much. A passion for equality and perhaps an overfondness for drink. And, of course, a shared admiration for your national bard, Robert Burns. Were you aware that Russia has more Burns appreciation societies than Scotland? No? In

fact, I recited his famous poem at our official Burns Supper in Moscow this
January. Who could fail to be moved by the lines:

> For a' that an a' that.
> It's coming yet for a' that
> That man to man, the world o'er
> Shall brithers be for a' that.

'An inspiration to us all. Don't you think?'

'Indeed, Mr President, and very eloquently put, if I may say so,' George heard
Ross reply.

George suppressed a laugh. He wondered what the student radicals whose
testicles had been attached to electrodes by Agent Churov in the 1990s would
have made of that sentiment.

'However, I have not asked you here simply for small talk and friendship,'
President Churov continued. 'As I believe Colonel Karimov has outlined to you,
I have a proposal to make. And one I wanted to make in person.'

The Russian president then launched into what was clearly a carefully prepared
pitch. 'We know Scotland will face huge economic problems when you declare
independence in just seven weeks' time. Russia will offer the new Republic
of Scotland unlimited supplies of natural gas at half the market rate and an
unlimited line of credit over the next year to support the new Scottish pound and
maintain its parity with the English pound. Put simply, we will acquire as many
Scottish pounds as necessary to maintain the price.'

'That's very generous,' Ross Johnson responded. 'And in return?'

'In return, we ask one small favour. Let me explain. The United States
is determined to have a monopoly of world power and to achieve this by
overwhelming superiority in armaments. As you know, the US has lavished vast
resources on her Airborne Laser and Kinetic Energy Interceptor programmes and
then, finally, installed missile defence systems in Eastern Europe early in 2012,
despite massive local opposition.'

George knew the story well, as it had dominated international politics in the last
two years the way the Iraq war had dominated the early years of the century. The
Americans had installed a mobile tracking system based at the Brdy military base
near Misov in the Czech Republic and a series of interceptor missiles on Multiple
Kill Vehicles in Poland. They both linked electronically to the British advance
warning system located at the military base at Menwith Hill in Yorkshire. The
Czech, Polish and British governments had all faced huge demonstrations against

the system, as well as widespread international criticism, but had still activated the system in 2012. The Russians had been incandescent, but impotent.

President Churov was warming to his theme. 'The Americans claim this system is to warn them of potential missile attack from a rogue state like Iran and then allow them to take that missile out before it threatens either the US or Western Europe. But we know it is really aimed at Russia. They promised us it would be small and limited. They promised we could have observers at the sites. They promised the system would not be activated until there was positive proof that Iran actually had nuclear weapons. All lies. The system is five times the size it needs to be to detect Iran's puny missile fleet.'

Churov was now genuinely animated and angry. 'The truth is that they cannot stand that we have restored our strength since the disaster of the Yeltsin years. Their aim is to know if we plan to attack, but keep their own activities a secret. Let me be clear. This is not, and never will be, acceptable to Russia.'

Sensing a pause, the first minister interrupted. 'But surely there is a response you can devise with your own armed forces?'

Churov nodded. 'We have, of course, improved our own defences, at the Lethuski missile facility in the north and at Armavir Air Base in the south. But the fundamental issue of imbalance remains. We cannot detect American Intercontinental Ballistic Missiles until they are over Germany. They can detect ours when they are barely out of their silos. No amount of Russian technological progress can disguise that fact.

'Therefore, to correct that dangerous and destabilising imbalance, we propose to put the same tracking and interception system in Scotland. As the system will *exactly* replicate those the Americans have in Eastern Europe, there can be no genuine complaint from the United States. This installation is, of course, purely defensive. Of course, First Minister, your new nation of Scotland will fall under its protection.'

George had heard the outline from Colonel Karimov, but the boldness of the plan still staggered him. It was the lifeline they desperately needed, but at what cost? Once the Russians held that level of economic sway over Scotland, would the price be only this one favour? What would the English think? What would the EU say? And what the hell would the Americans do?

In the early 1990s, George had turned his Master's thesis on his hero, Benjamin Franklin, into a well-received biography. This situation made him think of that philosopher's sage advice: 'Those who would give up essential liberty to purchase a little temporary safety deserve neither liberty nor safety'.

Knowing he could not give voice to such a thought here, all he said was, 'Mr President, aren't you worried about the reaction of the Americans?'

President Churov spread his hands, palms facing upwards, and looked heavenward. 'Who knows, Mr Wallace? I think they can be won over, especially as we'll have the backing of the international community. This is only equality, after all. Many nations feel we've had a bad deal. At the end of the 1980s, we pulled out of our bases in Cuba and the Middle East and disbanded the Warsaw Pact. The American response? To expand NATO to our very borders by admitting the Ukraine and Georgia into membership. This is merely a correction. We are not trying to replay the Cold War, just slightly rewrite the ending.'

Ross's eager face stopped George from pushing the issue further, so he relented. Taking silence for agreement, President Churov resumed. 'Gentlemen, because of the timescale imposed by your prime minister, speed is of the essence. We believe it is better to have the system in place before this becomes public. To create what our friends the Israelis call "facts on the ground". Once it is in the public domain, the so-called peace movement may pressure us to retreat. But it's so much harder to remove something than to stop it being installed in the first place, don't you agree?

'Now, if you will excuse me, Mr Wallace, I would like to speak briefly to the first minister alone. My aides will show you the Fabergé collection in the main building, the eggs are well worth a visit, I can assure you. The tsars may have been ruthless but they had exquisite taste.

'Mr Johnson, please walk along the corridor a little with me. I would love to show you the Catherine Hall, where we hold our official receptions.'

As President Churov finished his sentence, in the basement of the United States embassy a mile away, Lieutenant Gerry Morrison slipped off his earphones and picked up the receiver by his side. 'Get me the CIA duty officer. Yes, immediately. We have a Code Red situation.'

CHAPTER 4

SUNDAY, 15 JUNE — FORTY-SIX DAYS TO INDEPENDENCE

KNOCKAVIE HOUSE, STIRLINGSHIRE, 4 P.M.

The perfectly maintained Robert Cowan stood at the large bay window of his drawing room and gazed out at his perfectly maintained estate. He was a satisfied man.

In fact, everything about Cowan's life gave him satisfaction. Every time he hit a ball on his tennis court, or picked an apple in his orchard, or swam a length in his indoor pool, he was reminded of how much he had achieved. Of how far he had climbed.

When he admired his chiselled features and coiffed grey hair as he shaved in the morning, his feelings were always of satisfaction. Satisfaction that he had kept in shape through disciplined exercise. Satisfaction with his trophy wife and trophy children. Satisfaction with his business success. And satisfaction, above all, at the length of the road he had travelled. Self-satisfaction had pretty much driven every other sentiment out of Robert Cowan's mind, apart from one: ambition.

Cowan's father had been a working-class Tory who had been a foreman in McDonald & Mason, Glasgow's leading building company, and he had grown up in Dennistoun just three streets away from where George had lived, just around the corner from The Iron Duke where Sammy drank.

But there the similarities ended.

They had all sought power in their own way. Sammy through control of the streets, George through education, Robert through sheer hard graft.

Cowan had hated his comprehensive school, where he had been bullied because his father was seen as a scab, a boss's lackey. His family had put him in the awful position of being too rough to be accepted by the middle classes and too snobby to be accepted by his own community. On one occasion, three boys had forced his head down a toilet and flushed it over and over again because their fathers had been laid off by his father.

They had believed it would humiliate him. Destroy him. They were wrong. It made him stronger. He took all the bitterness and anger and forged it into pure, shining ambition. And he had never forgotten or forgiven. Years later, he traced them all and made sure they were blacklisted from the building trade as 'troublemakers'. It was never wise to cross Robert Cowan.

Cowan had joined his father at McDonald & Mason as an apprentice at fifteen and had rapidly worked his way up. With a natural aptitude for numbers, he was finance director within ten years and, after backing the right side of the family in a boardroom battle, chief executive two years after that.

His attitude to sport reflected his personality too. Not for Cowan the fun of team games like rugby and football – he loved swimming, skiing and, above all, long-distance running, all sports where he could push his own personal limits. All sports where he didn't have to rely on others. All sports where he could spend endless hours thinking and plotting, planning his way to the top.

Noting how few got rich on a salary, Cowan set up his own business, took the management team and some key accounts with him and ruthlessly set about destroying McDonald & Mason's dominance of the market. By the time he was fifty, Cowan Construction had made him a multimillionaire and a laird in his expansive, and expensive, Stirlingshire estate.

There had been some dodgy dealings, the greasing of a few town council palms along the way. But nothing had been proved. Now, his success was undeniable and, what was more important to Cowan, there for all to see.

Cowan Construction had no real rivals in the building business and he was getting restless again, he needed a new task, a new challenge – one worthy of his talents.

He hated the worthless Scottish political class, who had never worked a day in their life; he had total contempt for the Edinburgh lawyers and Glasgow trade unionists who had driven the campaign for Scottish self-government, another layer of unnecessary bureaucracy slowing down the true wealth creators, like himself.

He had campaigned for a 'No' vote in the 1997 referendum, believing, as Tam Dalyell put it, that devolution was a motorway to independence with no exits. As in the rest of his life, it gave him a grim satisfaction to have been right.

Now, as he poured tea for his guests, the organising committee of the SUR, he knew that the decisiveness, the single-minded determination, he had shown throughout his life was needed once more – this time in his nation's service.

Cowan had always known he was capable of more than making money, he knew he could lead. Like many rich men, the money itself no longer interested him – the millions in the bank was just a way of keeping score when the *Sunday Times* annual Rich List was published. What obsessed him now was power.

Cowan smiled at his guests. 'Gentlemen. The news is all good. We have raised over £10 million in the last six weeks. The opinion polls show that the Scottish people are behind us two to one. As I predicted, the financial realities have washed away the romantic mists of nationalism. The traditional Unionist parties are disintegrating as their members flock to us. It is now time to push home our advantage.'

MONDAY, 16 JUNE – FORTY-FIVE DAYS TO INDEPENDENCE

ANNENBERG CENTRE, UNIVERSITY OF PENNSYLVANIA, PHILADELPHIA, 10 A.M.

As he surveyed the largely balding and greying heads of the audience in front of him, George tried to shake off the tight metal band that only a whisky hangover brings. It had been a slip for him to drink too much, but one that was becoming more common as the political pressure mounted. Coming from a long line of men who drank heavily and died early, George recognised the dangers. After Bridget died, he had promised his daughter that he would not have any alcohol at least four nights a week. He had stuck to that regime faithfully for three years, replacing the alcohol with the natural high of exercise. The plan had started to crack in the last month, but last night's excesses had been the product of happiness, not stress.

It had been wonderful to be back on the campus this weekend, especially in June, when the Philadelphia sunshine had not yet given way to the torpor of high-summer humidity.

George had spent some of his happiest times here as a graduate student in the mid 1980s and had relived many of them last night, sneaking off with Clare after the official function to meet Alan and Steve, his two former room-mates from the tiny wooden row house in Samson Street, and laughing over the old days. They had talked politics and families and, when Clare had repaired to the toilet, his luck in securing such a wonderful woman after Bridget's death.

He hadn't felt so relaxed in months and this had led to his unfortunate over-indulgence. George had won many of his battles with alcohol, but still struggled to stop drinking when the atmosphere was great and he was having a good time.

George had been delighted when Clare had managed to swing some time off to join him on this trip, although, as she was a civil servant not servicing the trip, protocol dictated she had to travel separately from the political mission. But at least she was here.

As the provost finished her introduction of him as a distinguished alumnus, George repressed one final memory of the night in 1987 when his team had danced on the tables of Murphy's Irish Tavern on 44th and Walnut, after winning the graduate soccer league, and stepped to the podium as a respected senior politician to address the university's World Affairs Council.

George had been comfortable with public speaking since his school days. He knew the twin secrets were confidence and knowing your audience. This one clearly needed its intellectual tummy tickled. But he also had to provide a sound bite for the watching news cameras for the forty seconds he might get on CNN. 'Lord Provost, distinguished professors, ladies and gentlemen. Thank you so much for such a kind and, I must say, thoroughly undeserved introduction. Actually, I spent so much time in the bars of Philadelphia when I was here that I convinced at least a dozen students I was on a Guinness rather than Thouron scholarship!

'As some of you may know, I was a student of both Russian and American history, then went on to write a biography of one my heroes, Benjamin Franklin: a patriot, politician and philosopher, and the founder of this great university. Even if we don't always acknowledge the source, we all use his pearls of wisdom. Hardly a day goes by when I don't hear Franklin being quoted. "Time is money." "In this world nothing can be said to be certain, except death and taxes." And that great Protestant slogan which has driven my nation and yours: "Early to bed and early to rise, makes a man healthy, wealthy and wise." Advice, I admit, I should have heeded more often when I studied here. Though, I have to say, as you would expect from a Scotsman, that my personal favourite attributed to him is: "God made beer because he loves us and wants us to be happy."'

George waited for the laughter to subside. He had made his joke, softened up the audience, now it was time to get serious. 'I'm delighted to be back on this beautiful campus, where I learned so much about history and politics and made such firm American friends. It's particularly appropriate that I should be here at this time. Scotland, one of Europe's ancient nations, is about to take its rightful

----

place in the world – a fully free, sovereign member of the family of nations. Nowhere will that sentiment be better understood than here in Philadelphia, the cradle of American liberty. When the American patriots gathered in Independence Hall to express their determination that they would live free or die, they drew deep inspiration from David Hume and Adam Smith, philosophers of the Scottish Enlightenment. Fully one quarter of the signatories of the Declaration of Independence were of Scottish stock, seeking a freedom denied to them at home. Who could forget their words as they sought liberty, words that have echoed down the centuries: "When in the course of human events it becomes necessary for one people to dissolve the political bands which have connected them with another . . . We hold these truths to be self-evident, that all men are created equal, that they are endowed by their Creator with certain inalienable rights, that among them are life, liberty and the pursuit of happiness."

'That philosophy – your philosophy – will be the guiding principle of the new Scotland as it dissolves the bands with England. And, of course, your Declaration in turn drew inspiration from our own Declaration – that of Arbroath four hundred and fifty years previously. In the year 1326 the Scottish nobility wrote to the pope. Let me share a quote with you: "For, as long as but a hundred of us remain alive, never will we on any conditions be brought under English rule. It is in truth not for glory, nor riches nor honour that we are fighting, but for freedom – for that alone, which no honest man gives up but with life itself." Stirring stuff, I trust you will agree.'

Sensing he had won the audience over, George continued in the same vein, praising the shared history that had shaped both Scotland and the United States in their long struggle to uphold freedom.

Knowing the power of flattery, he reminded his audience that they were the key opinion formers that Scotland needed as friends. George was now in full flow, in command of his brief and his audience; thoroughly enjoying being centre stage.

In the front row, the White House chief of staff listened intently to the speech. In Sands' jacket pocket was a deeply troubling note from the director of the CIA. After a series of scandals and hacking disasters, the intelligence elite had returned to the nineteenth-century practice of sending handwritten notes. Easy to deny and destroy, and hard for prying journalists to find under the Freedom of Information Act.

Sands had thought he had been making good progress with the putative Scottish government. He had worked in partnership with George to set up a series of positive events, this speech today for him while the first minister was doing the main TV networks in midtown New York, a breakfast with top newspaper editors and a barbecue with the congressmen of the House Foreign Affairs Committee on Tuesday. All topped off with a personal meeting with the president on Wednesday. Red-carpet treatment.

And then, last week, this bombshell, in Chalmers' own handwriting, which had rendered all his careful courtship meaningless.

His team had worked through the weekend on solutions and agreed it had to come from the very top. But it was a risky strategy.

He forced his mind back to George's history lesson. As a Yale history graduate, he knew the material well already and was irked by George's over-the-top praise for Penn, a big Ivy League rival. And, God, he didn't half like the sound of his own voice.

Perhaps George should have reminded himself of another of Benjamin Franklin's observations: 'He that falls in love with himself will have no rivals.'

WEDNESDAY, 18 JUNE – FORTY-THREE DAYS TO INDEPENDENCE

THE RESIDENCE, THE WHITE HOUSE, WASHINGTON DC, NOON

Todd MacFarlane was very proud of his Scottish roots. His mother's family were McGregors who had fled to the Blue Mountains of West Virginia after the Jacobite defeat at Culloden to avoid the brutal Hanoverian retribution that was sweeping through the glens.

The MacFarlanes on his father's side had settled in Georgia in the 1820s, handloom weavers thrown into unemployment by industrialisation in Scotland, who had headed to the New World to forge a new life.

Both families had lost sons at the battle of Gettysburg when the Confederacy reached its high-water mark in the bloody carnage of Cemetery Ridge.

Given this background, he was reading George's speech with great interest. Mostly, it made him laugh. Just goes to show the Scots were as susceptible as any other nation to rose-tinted spectacles, he thought.

It wasn't that what George was saying was wrong, just very incomplete. MacFarlane wondered what those achingly liberal types at Penn, with all their talk of the Enlightenment, would have made of his own particular Scottish–American history, of white struggle against advancing black rights. It was not by accident that the Confederate flag was a St Andrew's cross, or that the men in white robes called themselves a Klan.

Their descendants, those same white, working-class Southern males who would not know Adam Smith from Homer Simpson, had propelled him – one of their own – to the White House to look after their interests. Jim Webb, the Democrat senator from Virginia, had been right to point out these Scots-Irish were the Republicans' secret weapon. In the crucial swing states from central Pennsylvania to northern Georgia, these white men dominated politics. They were evangelical Christians who had hated having John McCain as the Republican candidate in 2008. And MacFarlane's greatest political skill was knowing how to reach them.

MacFarlane reflected that it was just as well they were voting for the facade rather than the man. He pulled on his jacket and, as he always did, drew once more on the inner strength that came from that terrible day in North Carolina.

He was going to show these upstart Scots some of the Southern steel he pretended to have inherited from his great-grandfathers.

THE OVAL OFFICE, THE WHITE HOUSE, WASHINGTON DC, 12.15 P.M.

'It's a bit small,' had been George's overwhelming sense of the White House. Like most political junkies he had been a huge fan of *The West Wing* at the turn of the century and, as he was shown around by one of the president's staff, he was amazed at just how tiny the press briefing room was, with star network TV reporters crammed into a cupboard at the back which must have breached several health and safety regulations.

Given the American love of all things big, George couldn't help thinking that the contrast with the sweeping grandeur of the Kremlin was stark.

However, the Oval Office itself did not disappoint. As he and Ross waited for the president, he couldn't help reflecting on what these walls must have seen – the devising of the New Deal, the decision to drop the atomic bomb on Hiroshima, the resignation of President Nixon.

George wondered what his dad, a classic working-class intellectual, would have made of his son being in the Oval Office. He hadn't much cared about the money George made, but he would truly have loved this. He would have squeezed every last detail out of George, to boast about to his friends in the pub.

As he closely examined the presidential seal on the carpet, George could sense Ross fidgeting nervously beside him.

'Ross, do you remember the anti-MacFarlane bumper sticker, "The Christian Right is neither"? I wish I had been clever enough to have written that.'

Their laughter was interrupted by the president's voice. 'So, Mr Wallace, Chuck here tells me you are a bit of a historian of our great nation. I was just admiring the erudite speech you gave at Penn.'

Todd MacFarlane and Charles Sands entered the Oval Office through the glass door which led directly out to the Rose Garden.

'I dabble, Mr President,' was George's modest reply. 'And a long time ago I wrote a reasonably received biography of Benjamin Franklin. Being in the office he graced is a real treat.'

Todd MacFarlane crushed his hand in greeting, a reminder of the University of Georgia football player he had once been. He was well over six feet tall and carried his fifty-five years very lightly, from the top of his regulation crew-cut to the tips of his hand-made Allen-Edmonds shoes.

His face was square-set, symmetrical and handsome. It reminded George of an older version of the faces that used to appear in Gillette razor adverts.

George couldn't decide whether it was his physical presence or the aura of the office that made him feel so impressive. Though MacFarlane did seem to be trying harder than he needed to impose himself on the room.

The president gestured to Ross and George to sit, but focused most of his attention on George, which seemed odd, not to mention a breach of protocol. He felt Ross shift uneasily in his chair. 'So, how long did you live in the States?'

'Three years, a year doing a Master's in history at Penn, then two years teaching history and coaching soccer at a girls' school in Beverly Hills.'

The president smiled knowingly. God, even the leader of the free world does it, thought George. 'A dirty job but someone had to do it, I guess!' laughed MacFarlane. 'And were you well treated?'

'I will always be indebted to the people of America for their warmth and generosity, Mr President.'

MacFarlane turned to Ross. 'Now, First Minister, let's talk turkey. Tell me your plans.'

George watched Ross admiringly as he outlined the countdown to independence in six weeks' time and his desire to remain a close ally of the United States. He really was a smooth performer, even in the most intimidating of environments: a charmer, a class act.

MacFarlane listened in silence. 'That's all real interesting, First Minister. You've certainly set yourself a challenging timetable. We've only a few minutes before the photographer comes in for the official portraits, so let me speak plainly.

'It is in my political interest to have a close relationship with the new Scotland.

I am the product of MacFarlanes and McGregors and that plays well for me in the South. There are nineteen Scottish–American Associations in the States and they all endorsed me for president. By way of contrast, no one particularly cares for the English, especially since Princess Diana died and Tony Blair left office. There is no English–American lobby. And it's no accident that a lot of Hollywood villains are posh English guys.'

George and Ross both smiled with pleasure and relief.

'I am on your side, Congress is on your side and the American people love the little guy winning.'

George felt himself relaxing in the deep armchair as MacFarlane paused.

'But, bluntly, there is a huge smell of bullshit here.'

Both Ross and George immediately stiffened, their eyes fixed on the president. His deep green eyes surveyed them impassively. 'We know the Russians are planning to put a missile defence system on the west coast of Scotland. If your government goes along with this – as we know you plan to do – then it cannot possibly be a friend of the United States.'

Ross struggled to recover his composure. Looking at MacFarlane's implacable face, he realised there was no point in denying the story. 'But Mr President, you have similar systems in the Czech Republic and in Poland, much closer to the Russian missile bases than the one in Scotland will be to you. And, as a sovereign nation, it is our right—'

'Sovereign, my ass,' sneered MacFarlane. 'In this globalised world, we are all interdependent. None more so than a nation on the tip of north-western Europe, which has poor land, declining oil resources and an economy mostly owned by others. Mainly by us, I should point out. How long would your shining new nation survive US economic sanctions? We destroyed Chavez in Venezuela despite all his oil wealth. And we caused revolution in Cuba after Castro's death. What chance would you have?'

The question hung in the air, menacing and unanswered. The silence was broken by a gentle knock at the door. 'Ah, this is Greg, the White House's finest photographer. Come over to the desk, First Minister, he always loves the light from the garden here.'

As the photographer fiddled around, MacFarlane whispered threateningly to Ross, 'First Minister, your choice is clear. And may I remind you that the US is a good friend, but a terrifying enemy. Choose wisely.'

Three bursts of the flash later, the president was back to his charming self.

'Thank you for coming,' he said as he ushered them out. 'Y'all have a great day. And, Mr Wallace, as you are a historian, keep in mind one of the constant and binding lessons of history: friends of the United States prosper, enemies wither. In politics, don't ever mistake what you *can* do for what you should do. Please keep my chief of staff informed of your decision.'

Todd MacFarlane walked back to his desk a relaxed and satisfied man. He knew he had Ross where he wanted him and that George was a friend at court, easily impressed and flattered – out of his depth at this level.

He remembered the golden rule of politics: when you have them by the balls, their hearts and minds tend to follow.

CHAPTER 5

WEDNESDAY, 18 JUNE – FORTY-THREE DAYS TO INDEPENDENCE

DULLES INTERNATIONAL AIRPORT, WASHINGTON DC, 4 P.M.

Ross hadn't spoken a single word to George in the limousine to the airport, both men being acutely aware of both the driver and the Secret Service agent within earshot in the front of the car.

George didn't need words. He knew the signs. He had seen Ross furious before. Beneath his affable charm, Ross Johnson was a man who liked to get his own way. Once he had mapped out the path he intended to take, he was deeply intolerant of people who didn't share his vision. When crossed, he was capable of titanic rages.

As the landmarks of DC slipped past, the Washington Monument and Lincoln's brooding statue, George watched the inner fury being worked out in the clenched cheekbones, clear even in the first minister's chubby face. The explosion wasn't long in coming. They had the first-class cabin of the British Airways 747 to themselves.

'The cunt, the absolute fucking cunt. Who the hell does he think he is, threatening me like that, the jumped-up fucking cowboy?'

'Calm down, Ross,' George soothed. 'We need to work out some kind of compromise.'

Ross was not in a mood to be mollified. 'There will be no compromise. Not on my watch. I have not struggled for thirty years for Scottish independence to have my authority undermined by some clown who thinks the theory of evolution is a mistake. He thinks he's so tough. Well, I've a surprise in store for him.' Ross paused in his tirade as a thought struck him. 'How the fuck did he know about our plans in the first place?'

George shrugged. 'Search me.'

George knew it must be a leak from the Russian side. Only he and Ross in Scotland knew. After much soul-searching, he had decided to share the burden of knowledge with Clare, but had only told her late the previous night, after they had made love. Anyway, she had never been to the States before and didn't know a soul there.

They argued for another hour but with no resolution. Ross was adamant. His brave new Scotland would not bend the knee to Washington. He kept hinting he had another card up his sleeve, but would say no more about what it might be.

Like many men with power, Ross loved hinting he knew more than the person he was talking to and had inside-track knowledge available only to the chosen few. He knew how deeply that unsettled people, especially a man like George, how much it made him desperate to share the knowledge. Ross knew it kept him in control.

Even worse for George than the frustration of ignorance was the nagging fear that Ross might be bluffing, the card up his sleeve a deuce.

Not for the first time, George was acutely aware of how guiding Scotland to independence and becoming its first leader had become the only thing that mattered to Ross. The only thing he had in his life.

As Ross had grown in power, he had shrunk in humanity. The young man interested in art, music and travel had diminished in front of him. It may have been necessary to achieve success but that did not make it any less painful for George to watch.

Yet again, he felt the growing distance between them.

Ross went to the front of the cabin to make some calls. George tried to nap. Sleep would not come. He felt worries pressing on him from all sides, as the happiness of Philadelphia seeped away over the Atlantic.

FASLANE NAVAL BASE, THE GARE LOCH, SCOTLAND, 11 A.M.

As Ross and George bickered in the plane, one hundred and fifty soldiers of the Russian 3rd Special Operations Battalion made their way meticulously through the offices abandoned by the British Navy two weeks previously, checking for booby traps and listening devices.

Their commander, Major Andriy Gustov, stepped outside and lit a cigarette. He sucked the sweet smoke deep into his lungs and surveyed with pleasure and excitement the beauty of the calm loch stretched out in front of him. Finally, he was in charge, on a real, grown-up operation. This was why he had joined the Special Forces.

Mercifully, he had been too young to have been involved in the humiliation of the retreat from Kabul and the Soviet Union's subsequent collapse. He had been part of the restoration of Russia's strength, though personally he had had his fill of the Chechen mess; too much torturing of peasants for his taste. But this was different. This was amazing.

To his right was the massive grey shed which had housed the nuclear submarines. Behind that was the picturesque village of Garelochhead, nestled at the foot of the hills. To his left stood the row of tall, dun-coloured brick accommodation blocks. Before him, a massive, black boom protected the base from attack from the water. And behind him, the whole complex was enclosed in a three-metre fence topped with razor wire.

Andriy Gustov liked what he saw. His role in Operation Braveheart could not have been clearer, or more satisfying.

'This will do perfectly,' he told his sergeant. 'Get the men settled in.'

THE OVAL OFFICE, THE WHITE HOUSE, WASHINGTON DC, 4 P.M.

As the Russian soldiers began to unpack their kitbags, President Todd MacFarlane placed a call to Nick Jones in 10 Downing Street. 'Good afternoon, Prime Minister. I believe your team have briefed you on the extremely worrying intelligence we have received from Russia. This comes from the top and is completely reliable.'

Before he could continue, the prime minister came back smoothly. 'It was very kind of you to think of us, Mr President. I did get the message, but MI6 already had that information.'

Nick Jones could almost physically hear MacFarlane trying to work out how that was possible. Unlike most of the conversations he had with the US president, he was starting to enjoy this one.

'Well, that's just great,' replied MacFarlane after a pause. 'But the question remains: what are we going to do about it?'

'With all due respect, Mr President, the question is: what are *you* going to do about it?'

This time, there was no pause. MacFarlane said coldly, 'I am astonished, Nick, that you can be so casual about this threat to the free world.'

'Well, I have to say I struggle to see how a Russian defence system against US missiles is any threat to the vital national interests of England,' Jones said evenly.

'Besides, we need to be practical. In six weeks, we lose our automatic access to the Scottish oil of the North Sea. The way the negotiations are proceeding, I can't imagine the Scots will be rushing to give us preferential terms in the near future. We're already reliant on Russian natural gas and will become more so until our new nuclear power stations come on stream in 2020. And, I might add, we can't rely on Arab oil since the pro-Iranian coup in Iraq two years ago – the result of disastrous decisions by the American government. Therefore, it is not in my country's interests to make an enemy of Russia.'

Jones paused to let the full implication of his words sink in, then continued. 'I would love to help, Mr President, but it is very difficult.'

The prime minister chose his final words with relish. 'It's just politics. Nothing personal.'

As soon as he finished the call, Jones phoned his chief of staff, Tony Hodge. 'Hi, Tony, I need to see you and the head of MI6 in the office at six. Yes, Tony, of course six tonight.'

THE SITUATION ROOM, THE WHITE HOUSE, WASHINGTON DC, 5 P.M.

Normally, Todd MacFarlane immensely enjoyed sitting at the top of the table in the Situation Room, with its giant screen at one end and blinking computer monitors dotted everywhere. He hadn't felt such power since he was a star quarterback on the all-conquering University of Georgia team of the early 1980s. Now, he was the world's quarterback, calling the plays to a massive military team.

Only, today he didn't feel so omnipotent. He dispensed with the good-old-boy charm he usually deployed on his top team and surveyed the grim faces around the table. 'Let's get to it. Carl, a military assessment of the threat?'

Admiral Carl Butterworth didn't sugar-coat the news. 'I've spoken to the heads of the air force and army and they share my assessment. If the Russians successfully install a satellite system on the west coast of Scotland, they wipe out at a stroke the military and technological advantage we have enjoyed over them since the fall of the Berlin Wall in 1989 and the massive advantage we have enjoyed in the last two years since our systems went into Eastern Europe.

'The current Russian missile defence system operates from Lethuski missile base in the north and Armavir Air Base in the south. Our military intelligence reckons the earliest it can detect our missiles is when they reach Belgian airspace, so the Russians would have under five minutes to launch their defensive missiles or to scramble squadrons to attack the incoming warheads – too little time to be truly effective.

'By way of contrast, our tracker and interceptor systems in Poland and the Czech Republic, although they are primarily focused on the threat from Iran, also let us know within three minutes of any Russian launch and would take out one hundred per cent of their missiles before they even reached Central Europe. This means that the Russians could never take us by surprise, where we could do so to them, if we chose.

'This situation completely destroyed any remaining semblance of the theory of Mutually Assured Destruction by giving the US first-mover advantage. It cemented America's supremacy in a unipolar world. Basically, we could nuke them without any fear of a response.'

Butterworth was clear and confident, in command of his brief. 'We reckon any Scottish early-warning base which was roughly equivalent to what we have in Eastern Europe would detect any US warheads by the time they reached Iceland and would be able to launch missiles to destroy them as they flew over the Hebrides, the islands off the north-west coast of Scotland. We have our submarine-based nuclear missiles around the globe but not enough to disable all of Russia's nuclear forces in a first strike. I have a team of specialists at Cheyenne Mountain Air Base working on the exact logistics at the moment and I would hope to have a full report for you, in forty-eight hours, on what percentage of their missiles we could guarantee to destroy.'

He paused, then concluded emphatically, 'But in layman's language, Mr President, it makes us equal. We're all-square again, just as we were in the 1970s.'

The president sighed deeply. 'I have just come off the phone with Prime Minister Jones. I have to report that those devious English bastards have let us down once again. They won't lift a finger to help us. So much for the special relationship.'

MacFarlane looked hopefully at his chief of staff. 'Chuck, any chance of other political support?'

Sands was gloomy. 'I can't see it, Mr President. As the system is based on the west coast of Scotland and is monitoring us only, it is no direct threat to Western Europe. For example, it can't detect or destroy France's *force de frappe*, its independent nuclear capability. Also, Russia now supplies sixty per cent of Germany's power requirements, so it could put the German economy into recession overnight, an economy which is only now recovering from the big downturn of 2009. There's not much warmth towards the Russians in Western Europe but, to be honest, Mr President, there isn't much for us either since the decision to invade Iraq over a decade ago, especially now that Iranian-backed Shias are in control there.

'As you know, our decision to put our early-warning systems in Eastern Europe was incredibly controversial. A lot of the European left swallowed the Russian line that it was aimed at them and will see the Scottish system as a reasonable quid pro quo for our systems in Eastern Europe. It will be hard to repudiate that publicly. As for the rest, the Latin Americans are neutral, the Africans indifferent and the Chinese . . . well, let's just say that anything that sets America against Russia is welcome in Beijing. In summary, no one is going to spend any political capital keeping us in a pre-eminent military position. We're on our own.'

'So, how do we remove it? Carl?'

Butterworth's brow furrowed in concentration. 'We could take it out from the air, using our tactical strike squadron based in England, but that would be inconceivable without English permission and, as you say, they show no inclination to help us. Plus, it is hardly going to go down well with the half-million Scots who live in England. The issue is more political than practical. Are we willing to risk worldwide condemnation for what would inevitably be seen as an act of aggression?

'More crucially, it would be seen as a clear act of war by Russia, opening us up to the danger from submarine-based warheads. You may recall that President Putin ordered four new Borei nuclear subs before he left office in 2007. We believe that at least three are currently at sea and, obviously, are not monitored by the early-warning systems in Eastern Europe. The one in the Pacific, for example, could penetrate our defences and take out San Francisco. Can we risk that? And all for a defensive missile system that only mirrors what we already have?'

'What about Special Operations?'

'Possible,' replied the admiral thoughtfully. 'I can put together a series of plans, Mr President. We could certainly sabotage the system in Faslane once they put it in, but what do we do when the Russians rebuild it with Scottish government help? And, again, we have to consider world reaction to an act of aggression against a tiny nation like Scotland, a traditional Western ally, not a rogue state like North Korea. I think our reputation is only now recovering from the assassination of Chavez and the toppling of his government in Venezuela.'

Everyone in the room looked at Jane Chalmers. They all knew that had been her call, against the overwhelming advice of the people seated round the Situation Room table, especially Carl Butterworth.

'Jane?'

'I will happily work with Carl on those Special Ops plans, Mr President. But I agree that the key is securing a compliant government in Scotland. I think the growth of support for the Scottish Unionist Resistance gives us some openings. We urgently need some friends in Scotland.'

MacFarlane sighed for a second time. 'OK. Carl and Jane, put together those Special Ops scenarios and investigate what realistic support we could get on the ground from the Scottish Unionists. And, Chuck, draw up plans for economic sanctions against Scotland, both an export ban and restrictions on their financial services industry. If we can't bomb them, then let's starve the bastards.'

THURSDAY, 19 JUNE – FORTY-TWO DAYS TO INDEPENDENCE

EDINBURGH INTERNATIONAL AIRPORT, 6 A.M.

As George and Ross disembarked, bleary-eyed, from their transatlantic flight, George was surprised to see Colonel Karimov waiting in the VIP reception lounge along with Ross's assistant, Jean. It had troubled George to see that Karimov had taken up what felt like permanent residence at the Scottish Parliament. He was amazed to see him at the airport at this time in the morning.

Ross and Karimov walked ahead, deep in conversation, as George caught up on the office gossip with Jean. Two Scottish government black Jaguars awaited them on the concourse. Ross and Karimov headed to the first. George made to follow.

Ross turned to him and spoke firmly. 'No, George, I need to talk to Colonel Karimov alone. Would you mind going with Jean in the other car?'

Ross added 'thanks', without waiting for George's answer. The snub could not have been more calculated or have wounded more.

The half-hour that the car took to arrive at the entrance to the Scottish Parliament building was the longest George had endured in his political life. He was supposed to be Ross's closest adviser. His friend. What could Ross have to talk to Karimov about that he couldn't share with him? What the hell was Ross keeping from him?

THE RUSSIAN CONSULATE. EDINBURGH. 3 P.M.

Colonel Karimov was deep in conversation with President Churov over a secure line. It was a conversation of troubled men.

'Sir, Operation Braveheart is definitely compromised. I have spoken to the first minister directly and the Americans know everything – well, everything so far. He claims the leak must be at our end, as only he and George knew. No one else in the Scottish Cabinet had been consulted. May I respectfully suggest another sweep of your offices? And another thing, sir, could you order our MI6 source to contact me and tell me who British intelligence have working on the Scottish question? That would be very helpful for me.'

President Churov was his usual no-nonsense self. 'I will order both right away, Colonel Karimov. And, Colonel, given the changed circumstances we must accelerate our plans. Implement phase two of Operation Braveheart without delay.'

NUMBER 10 DOWNING STREET. LONDON. 6 P.M.

Prime Minister Nick Jones, his chief of staff Tony Hodge and Helen Fairbairn, the tough new head of MI6, all came from the same social class, so instinctively knew that six o'clock meant that having a sherry was now acceptable. The three took chairs around the fireplace in the prime minister's study.

As they sipped their drinks, Helen expanded in detail what she had learned from her agent about the Russian plans for an early-warning system in Scotland.

Jones listened very carefully, then spoke. 'I think we face a major crisis here. The Americans are furious and MacFarlane's administration has a habit of shooting first and asking questions afterward. And, no matter how careful we are, some stray bullets may hit us. I don't relish being the victim of some American friendly fire.'

He carefully polished his glasses, his usual tactic to buy time to think, then looked directly at the head of MI6. 'Helen, I know you don't like using your deep source inside the Kremlin unless it is a matter of critical national security, but I really need to know what the Russians are up to. Something in my water tells me it may be even more complex than your Scottish agent thinks. Before I act, I need to know.'

Helen was reluctant. 'Well, if you insist, Prime Minister, but he is fearful for himself and his family, and our money only buys so much—'

Jones cut across her, 'I am sorry, Helen, I do insist.'

After Hodge and Fairbairn left, Jones sat back in his ample desk chair, took off his spectacles again and gently massaged his brows. Jones had only been prime minister for a year, a compromise candidate when David Cameron had mysteriously resigned to 'spend more time with his family'. He was well aware he had been selected as the candidate MPs disliked the least rather than the one they loved the most. Many of the big beasts of the Cabinet thought he was living on borrowed time. They were just waiting for a major failure so they could take what a number of them believed was their rightful place in his office.

Mild-mannered and erudite, he had initially struggled with the switch from the sedate pace of school reform as Secretary of State for Education to the constant activity of Downing Street. Slowly, he had got his bearings, discovering his voice and authority, and had actually started to enjoy himself.

Jones found the dumbed-down, sound-bite culture of modern politics distasteful and depressing but loved working on the long-term, strategic policies. Few politicians could match his clear, logical thinking. An instinctive Unionist, Jones had felt initially hurt and troubled by the break-up of the UK, but once it had become inevitable he had been first to grasp the real benefits to his party.

As President MacFarlane had discovered earlier that day, there was a steely sense of purpose underlying his mild-mannered exterior. So far, he had handled the Scottish issue cleverly. It now threatened to blow up into a full international crisis that would stretch his abilities to the full and be his first real test as prime minister.

As he drained his sherry glass, he hoped his inner strength would be enough to see him through. One thing was for certain: the stakes could not be higher. There would be no second chances for Prime Minister Nick Jones.

CHAPTER 6

- -

SUNDAY, 22 JUNE — THIRTY-NINE DAYS TO INDEPENDENCE

NORTHUMBERLAND STREET, EDINBURGH, 8 A.M.

As was his habit on a Sunday, George sat propped up in bed, speed-reading the newspapers, a freshly brewed mug of coffee by his side. He was relieved that the story of the Russian defence system hadn't broken in the press, but that was the only piece of good news that morning.

The *Sunday Times* led on the latest poll, which suggested support for independence had dropped to twenty-seven per cent, the lowest in five years. *Scotland on Sunday* went with the looming banking crisis and the *Sunday Herald* quoted an 'inside source' at the independence negotiations describing George's leadership of the team as 'insipid'.

Recalling Tony Blair's description of Scottish political journalists as 'unreconstructed wankers', he sighed and heaved the papers off the duvet. More than ever, he agreed with the old adage that journalists never took part in battles, they just came down from the hill and bayoneted the wounded when they were over.

Clare stirred softly as he snuggled into her back. George savoured her silky, warm, downy skin as he cupped his hand round the swell of her naked bottom. He marvelled again at his good fortune at having such a partner and achieving a happiness he hadn't thought possible after Bridget's death from cancer five years previously.

The daughter of an English father and a Scottish mother, Clare had grown up in the prosperous Glaswegian suburb of Bearsden, a classic outpost of middle Scotland. She had come back home from London in 2011 after the SNP's second successive win in the Scottish parliamentary elections. After that victory, the

----

UK government had set up a Constitution Unit in Edinburgh to look at the implications for the UK of further political change, whether more devolution, federalism or independence, and to draw up detailed legislative plans for each of those possibilities.

Clare had been seconded to the new unit from her job at the Ministry of Defence. She told anyone who cared to listen how much she loved swapping her three hours a day of commuting in London for a fifteen-minute stroll from George's flat to her offices on Calton Hill.

George's relationship with her had begun eight months earlier in clichéd fashion, at a works night out for a colleague who was leaving to work in Brussels. Previously, they had bumped into each other a few times as George had outlined the Scottish government's policy in briefings to the Constitution Unit. He had thought her charming, smart and beautiful but out of his league. And too young.

That night, after a few beers in The Tun, the local bar for the Scottish Parliament, he had risen to make his excuses but Clare had asked him to join her and the others going clubbing. Given that his tenuous links with contemporary music had finally been severed when Bruce Springsteen retired from touring in 2010, George had been reluctant but had been persuaded by her exciting insistence.

They had danced at the club, he awkward, she encouraging and flirtatious. They danced for four tracks. As they left the floor she slipped her arm in his. As they waited to collect their coats, much to his astonishment, she kissed him for the first time.

George found the relationship intoxicating and completely addictive. He savoured every moment they had together. Like a teenager in love, he was thrilled every time the text pinged on his phone, disappointed every time it wasn't her.

The fifteen-year age gap provoked glances and even some comments when they were out together, but didn't bother him – or, she assured him, Clare. They shared so much in common: a love of history, a fascination with politics. They never seemed to run out of things to say on their long Sunday walks up Arthur's Seat.

He loved so many little things about her: the bobbed haircut that fell across one eye when she laughed, the shape of her right calf when she put on high heels, the way she tucked her right leg under her when she sat in his old leather armchair, the enticing hint of cleavage in her favourite black dress at the Christmas party.

George knew he was playing out of his league but it felt to him like Premier

League against First Division rather than Third Division. He had always had reasonable success with women before he met Bridget. He put it down to what one of the women clients of his public relations company had once called his smouldering, Celtic good looks – a phrase he took pleasure in repeating.

Ross thought otherwise. He claimed to be amazed George attracted any women at all and used to tease him by saying his puppy eyes had an appealing helplessness and that women slept with him because they wanted to look after him.

The truth lay somewhere between those two points of view.

Clare had moved into his New Town flat just before Christmas, twelve weeks to the day after they had first kissed. Given his propensity for grumpiness, George was surprised to find this interference with his set, bachelor ways endearing rather than irritating. He knew he was a changed man when even her female clutter did not exasperate him.

They had struggled to find time together in the frantic run-up to the referendum in May, but that just seemed to make every stolen moment even more precious. George was a walking cliché of a man in love: light-hearted, good-tempered, rejuvenated.

As a civil servant, she couldn't, of course, express publicly any view on the constitutional question, and she was even quite guarded at home, but George could tell she was sympathetic by the way she listened attentively to his description of every twist and turn in the campaign. Given the sensitivity of both their positions, George had raised the relationship with both the permanent secretary, the most senior civil servant in the Scottish government, and the first minister. The permanent secretary had raised one of his huge eyebrows quizzically and assured George he was officially breaking no rules. Ross merely remarked it was about time he got a good shag and hoped that it might make him less bad-tempered.

And Clare had even passed the toughest test of all. His daughter, Catherine.

Two months after she moved in, George knew, as you always do, that this was really serious and took Clare over to meet Catherine in Glasgow.

Catherine had followed George and Bridget into the media and was already, at the tender age of twenty-three, the youngest producer in the News and Current Affairs department at BBC Scotland. She had settled with her husband Geoff, a graphic designer, in a mansion flat in Glasgow's West End.

Catherine had been away from home in her first year at the University of Edinburgh when her mother died so hadn't had the day-to-day agony of watching

Bridget deteriorate that had so consumed George and her brother John. George was glad she had been spared that ordeal.

Catherine had accelerated her marriage plans with Geoff, so that her mother could see them wed. The ceremony was held three weeks before Bridget died, with her in a wheelchair in the front row, with a morphine drip. It had been a day of tears of pain more than tears of joy, simultaneously both the happiest and saddest day of George's life.

Bridget's death had brought George and Catherine even closer together and fundamentally changed their relationship. Her father's grief had accelerated Catherine's emergence from the all-consuming self-absorption of her teenage years. She found herself taking on the role of surrogate mother to him and he leaned on her in a way he would never have believed possible.

The day George brought Clare over to meet Catherine and Geoff, the four of them enjoyed a wonderful, relaxing, boozy lunch at The Ubiquitous Chip, with only Catherine holding back on the wine, and then went for a stroll in the low, winter sun in the Botanic Gardens, along the same path George had pushed Catherine on her first bike.

Catherine linked arms with her father as they walked. She had always known just how much she meant to him. He had indulged her as a child and she had exploited that ruthlessly in her teenage years; it was now a power she was determined to use responsibly.

They could hear Geoff and Clare, fifty feet behind them, jokingly discussing the respective merits of Glasgow and Edinburgh – Geoff, an Edinburgh boy who had reluctantly moved to Weegie-land; Clare, a Glasgow girl adjusting to the more rigid social stratification of Edinburgh.

'She seems lovely, Dad, I'm so delighted to see you happy again,' Catherine enthused. 'I know you love your work, but there needs to be more to life than that. Trust me.'

George smiled fondly down at his daughter's blonde head. 'Thanks, sweetheart, that means so much to me.'

'Well, I guess I owe you, given you were there for me during the wild years.'

'Yeah, thanks for turning my hair grey. When I think of some of those guys you dated. Do you remember that guy Euan, the Goth with the nose ring?'

'Yes, and believe me, that wasn't his most unusual piercing.'

George winced. 'That definitely gets filed under the heading "Too Much Information". You were lucky I was so understanding.'

Catherine playfully punched her father. 'I might have been more impressed if the philosophical underpinning for all your parenting hadn't been a line from *Grease.*'

Together, they laughed as they remembered, 'The only guy a girl can trust is her daddy.'

Catherine's intelligent blue eyes scanned her father's face. 'Do you worry about the age difference with Clare at all? I mean, she's only eleven years older than me.'

'Not really, no. I don't really appreciate the "How old is your daughter?" stuff I get in the office. But, hey, I've been through a lot worse.'

'I wasn't really meaning did you feel like some kind of a paedo, Dad, I meant . . .'

Catherine hesitated, then blurted out her thought. 'Look, Clare is only thirty-four, what if she wants a family?'

Because he was an anally retentive planner, it was a conversation with Clare that George had already foreseen and had rehearsed in his mind. He had never understood those men who tried to recapture their lost youth by having a second family. The prospect of having a child who would be twenty as he was contemplating his seventieth birthday was one that filled him with dread. But he knew the answer would have to be yes. Even after two months living together, he loved Clare so much. She made him so happy. He could not deny her that.

Sometimes, you just knew.

That was not a feeling George felt he was ready to share with his daughter. 'Let's cross that bridge when we come to it, darling. We've only been living together for two months.'

'If you hurry up, you could make it on to one of those daytime chat shows.'

'What do you mean?'

'Well, I'd watch *The Man who has a Child and Grandchild in the Same Year.*'

'You mean . . . Oh, sweetheart, that's fantastic news! When are you due?'

'I'm only eight weeks gone, so we haven't been telling people yet. Dad, it looks like a baby at the end of September.'

'My goodness, that is amazing, I mean you are so—'

'Young?' Catherine cut across him. 'I had noticed, Dad. What happened to your famous tact? If you must know, it wasn't exactly what we had planned, but now that it is here . . .' Her voice trailed off.

George recovered quickly from his mistake and gave his daughter the silent reassurance she needed in a massive hug, then turned to embrace his son-in-law.

THE IRON DUKE BAR, DENNISTOUN, GLASGOW, 5 P.M.

The Iron Duke bar stood like a squat, white molar in an otherwise toothless mouth in the urban wasteland where the tall sandstone tenements of Duke Street gave way to the deeper deprivation of Glasgow's East End.

All the surrounding buildings had been demolished to make way for a promised but as-yet undelivered bout of regeneration. The Iron Duke's whitewashed walls and grilled windows spoke silent defiance to the very concept of progress. As it always had been, it was a place for men to drink, without interruption.

Inside, Sammy Wilson was getting impatient. 'OK, boys, I am going to go through this one more time for the hard of understanding among you set of useless cunts.'

Sammy glared round the table, making sure he had their full attention. 'She will be alone in the house. The nanny will be out taking the daughter to nursery. We go in quickly and take her. Billy injects the sedative and she goes in the back of the van. No one gets hurt. Is that clear?'

Three intense faces nodded back to him.

'Right, Monday it is,' said Sammy, before adding with his trademark menace, 'and, boys, don't fuck it up.'

WESTMINSTER BRIDGE, LONDON, 9 P.M.

'You make one mistake and . . .' Paul Richmond reflected bitterly for the thousandth time as he hurried to his rendezvous with another bloody Russian.

These bastards had him by the balls and just kept squeezing.

Yet again he asked himself why he had done it. He could close his eyes and picture the scene now, his mouth dry, his hands at the computer nervous and sweating despite the December cold, Joanne and the girls at the local pantomime. A chance to download those pictures: disgusting, loathsome, wonderful.

His briefcase with his laptop had been stolen from his side as he dozed on the long commute home to Kent. Then the phone calls began – cajoling at first, then increasingly threatening.

Now he was a traitor to his country. The finance director of MI6 helping the Russians in order to avoid an even greater disgrace.

'You make one mistake . . .'

This Colonel Sergei Karimov was a new contact to him, but he was in exactly the planned place, at the third light on the left, carrying a folded *Financial Times*, like someone from a John Le Carré novel.

Richmond launched right in as he approached him. 'Listen, this has to stop, people at work are getting suspicious. And—'

Karimov cut across him cruelly. 'Your personal circumstances are of no interest to me at all, Mr Richmond. All I require from you is the name of the MI6 agent inside the Scottish government. And I require it now.'

'But this could destroy me completely!' Richmond persisted.

'Then I suggest you should have chosen your hobbies with greater care,' replied Karimov with a cold smile.

Chastened, Paul Richmond blurted out the name.

Despite his surprise, Karimov's face showed no emotion. In another life, he would have made a great poker player.

KNOCKAVIE HOUSE, STIRLINGSHIRE, 9.30 P.M.

Thomas Atkinson stretched contentedly. The UK bureau chief of the CIA had immensely enjoyed his meal of smoked salmon followed by rare roast beef. The rich and intense 1964 Château Latour Bordeaux had been the perfect accompaniment to the main course, as had the fetching Mrs Cowan, the living definition of a yummy-mummy.

Even though he had been through all the CIA's finest psychological training, he couldn't deny the appeal of a good-looking woman paying attention to everything you said. Men were so vain, they never questioned why a woman might be interested in them. That was why the honey trap was always the most effective tool in the intelligence agent's box. Even knowing this hadn't dulled Atkinson's pleasure one iota.

But now it was time for business.

Robert Cowan reached for the whisky decanter as his wife Mary made her excuses and left. As ever, she had been the perfect hostess for Cowan. Impeccably educated at St Leonard's School for Girls, then the University of St Andrews, she knew how to carry on the perfect level of polite, but completely pointless, conversation, with just the right hint of flirtation.

Cowan marvelled at how well they both understood the Faustian pact. Charm and discretion in return for unlimited access to the credit cards. He hoped she enjoyed the sex as much as she appeared to, although it didn't really matter, in the end. Cowan's sense of satisfaction didn't rest on something so trivial.

The two men settled into their armchairs in front of the large, stone fireplace, set with logs but unlit. They felt comfortable with each other, each recognising power and success in the other. Both doers rather than thinkers.

Cowan liked Atkinson's direct language and correctly thought his well-maintained, if now slightly fleshy, physique suggested a man who had seen lots of action. Atkinson found Cowan straightforward, a businessman without the fussy moral complexities of many politicians.

Atkinson knew this had to be a delicate but decisive conversation, the trickiest since his promotion to UK bureau chief in 2011. Atkinson had to get what he wanted from Cowan without committing the USA irrevocably to any particular course.

Now in his mid fifties, greying and slightly paunchy, Atkinson was a time-served CIA veteran. He had cut his teeth supplying arms to the UNITA rebels in southern Angola in the early 1980s, working alongside the white South African Defence Forces. Then he spent ten years in Eastern Europe, first hunting down and eliminating Soviet spies, then helping the newly emerging democracies of the Eastern bloc to purge their bureaucracies of communists. That had been followed by gruelling tours in both Iraq and Afghanistan.

The London posting was always considered a soft one within the CIA, a reward for long service and a job to see you into a comfortable retirement. Until now. Who could have predicted that the United States' oldest and most stable ally would find itself in the middle of the biggest international crisis since the 1960s stand-off over Cuba? Part of Atkinson resented this intrusion into his routine and comfortable life, but a bigger part of him relished a return to frontline action.

The two men sipped their twenty-four-year-old Old Pulteney appreciatively. Atkinson spoke first. 'Robert, I'm not at liberty at the moment to give you full details of the intelligence we have – or, indeed, of all our contingency planning. I can tell you we have reason to believe the current Scottish government is working with a foreign power against the interests of the United States.'

Atkinson was aware he had Cowan's full and undivided attention. Cowan's business nose had smelled an opportunity. 'If we chose to act against this conspiracy, in our interests but also in the true interests of Scotland, it would be crucial to have friends here we could rely on. I'm assuming we could put our faith in the leadership of the SUR?'

'Absolutely,' Cowan replied emphatically.

'And would extra funding aid your task?'

'We have significant backing, Thomas. But, as any businessman will tell you, there can never be too much income on any balance sheet.'

'If you give me the account details, I can arrange the deposit of ten million dollars tomorrow, channelled through a friendly think tank in DC we use as a front organisation. That should buy a few poster sites and radio ads in the Unionist cause.'

Cowan worked hard to disguise his excitement at the amount and continued, with the merest pause, 'It should, indeed. That is very much appreciated.'

Atkinson moved quickly to take advantage of his largesse. 'I am delighted we can help. However, there are a couple of delicate matters I need to raise with you.'

'Please be my guest. If we are going to work together then we need to be completely open with one another.'

Atkinson took up his offer immediately. 'How well do you know the leaders of the army and the police in Scotland?'

'I have met Major-General Rory Stewart, the commander of the Royal Regiment of Scotland, a few times and golfed with him at Gleneagles. Very adept with a sand iron in those hellish bunkers, I recall. And Alistair Stroud, the chief constable of Strathclyde, is a close friend. What your Founding Fathers would have called a brother.'

Thomas smiled, recognising the reference to the importance of Freemasons in the establishment of the American republic, a contribution still celebrated in the symbols on the dollar bill in his wallet – the pyramid and the eye that cannot see. 'So he should be easy to "square off" – I believe I have the correct expression?'

'You do, indeed.'

Atkinson then asked the most delicate question of all. 'I also need to know how close your links are to the British Loyalist Army.'

Cowan shifted uncomfortably in his leather armchair. 'Well, obviously, while understanding their frustration with the undemocratic dash to separatism, we completely condemn their use of violence,' he replied cautiously. 'Why do you ask?'

'It may be of use to us to have a channel of communication to their leadership. Not for immediate use, just in case we need some operatives on the ground. Do you think you could organise that?'

'Of course,' said Cowan, reaching once more for the decanter. 'Anything to help our American friends.'

Atkinson leaned back, relaxed. Mission accomplished.

NUMBER 10 DOWNING STREET, LONDON, 11.30 P.M.

Helen Fairbairn enjoyed the fact that, as head of MI6, she was one of only three people entitled to direct access to the prime minister, whatever the day or time.

Sometimes, she had to accept, that privilege had been abused by her predecessors. But this Sunday night, it was needed more than at any time in the four years she had headed the Secret Intelligence Service.

Nick Jones met her in his pyjamas and dressing gown in his private office. Tony Hodge joined them direct from a fund-raising event, still in his formal dinner jacket. They were both completely shocked by her news.

Fairbairn gave a complete briefing on the stunning information the MI6 source in Moscow, a deputy minister in the Energy Ministry, had revealed to her. He had been very reluctant to tell her, fearing the leak could be traced back to him, which would have been literally fatal. She had assured him that the English government would use it carefully and promised it was the last favour she would request for at least a year.

When she had finished, Fairbairn and Hodge both looked at their boss for orders. Nick Jones tried to swallow the panic in his throat and bought some time. 'What do you think I should do?'

Hodge spoke first, urgent and direct. 'I think you need to tell the Americans and then go public. When this is revealed the international community will be furious and will force the Russians to retreat.'

'Helen?'

'I agree, sir. I don't think there is any advantage on sitting on this. Plus it will help in the propaganda war. I don't think there will be much more talk of plucky little Scotland battling against its overpowering southern neighbour once this comes out.'

Nick Jones could think of no alternatives and drew comfort from the consensus. 'I'll talk to the president right away.'

Once Fairbairn and Hodge had left, the prime minister placed an urgent call to the president of the United States, using the code E428, which mandated person-to-person only, with no staff on the line.

If it was possible, Todd MacFarlane seemed even more shocked than Nick Jones. Once he had recovered his composure, he asked, 'What do you think we should do?'

The prime minister was decisive. 'I think we should leak the information, get it into the public domain as soon as possible before it actually happens. I think that would both force the hand of the Russians and get them to retreat and also ensure that our source inside the Kremlin is not compromised.'

That made sense to the president. Like the prime minister, he couldn't think of a coherent alternative. 'OK, let's do that.'

'Also, for this plan to work we need to keep it completely secret. No staff here know, apart from the head of MI6 and my chief of staff. We need to act completely surprised when the story breaks. Are you OK with that?'

'Yes, of course,' responded MacFarlane. 'Thank you once more for the heads-up, Prime Minister. Goodnight.'

As he hung up the phone, the president automatically, instinctively, touched his penis. The one thing in the world he knew for certain was that he could keep a secret.

THE PRESIDENTIAL OFFICE, KREMLIN, MOSCOW, 8 P.M.

The adjutant saluted smartly and handed the folded piece of paper to President Igor Churov. On it was written: PHASE TWO ACTIVATED. KARIMOV

CHAPTER 7

TUESDAY, 24 JUNE — THIRTY-SEVEN DAYS TO INDEPENDENCE

PRINCES STREET GARDENS, EDINBURGH, 1.10 P.M.

The beautifully kept Princes Street Gardens ran the length of the Scottish capital's premier shopping street and covered the dip which separated the street from the base of the castle. In the heart of the gardens, among the neat flowerbeds, lay a stage where the bands performed at the annual Hogmanay celebrations and which would host the concert to celebrate independence in five weeks' time.

The gardens were one of George's favourite spots in the city: a slash of green in the mass of grey stone; a place to think. Today, George sat alone on the third bench along from the gate to the gardens that faced the National Art Gallery, instinctively tut-tutting at the scruffy graffiti scratched on it.

If he hadn't felt so anxious, George would have enjoyed more the sunshine playing across the face of the imposing basalt rock on which Edinburgh Castle sat. Something elemental within him was always awed by the power of the eruption which had thrown up this massive volcanic rock, with its long sloping tail that now formed the Royal Mile, extending from the castle down to the Palace of Holyroodhouse.

It was the kind of summer day in which the New Town looks its best and you actually felt, for once, a warm breeze blowing in from the Forth. Even the Princes Street shoppers looked positively jovial without their shoulders hunched against the cold wind which usually swept down the street.

In the four years he had lived in Edinburgh, George had grown to love the cold beauty of the New Town. He enjoyed the irony that he had moved to Edinburgh to destroy the British state and yet lived in the most visible living legacy of the enduring Union – the Georgian New Town. With its praise for the conquerors of the Jacobites in the names of Hanover, George and Frederick streets, and its original design as a Union Jack, the New Town represented the high point of Britishness, when many in Scotland had proudly called themselves 'North British'.

Well, no more. He had helped consign that feeling to history.

But today, George's mind was on other matters. Clare had called to say she needed to see him immediately, neither at their respective offices nor at the flat. For a split-second, his hand holding the phone grew clammy and he feared she might be leaving him; the wave of apprehension receded when she added that they needed to meet in the open air, where no one could listen in.

At the lunch break, George had hurried from the independence negotiations at the Great Hall in the complex of buildings at the top of the castle, down past the lovely Ramsay Garden, over the railway lines snaking into Waverley Station and into Princes Street Gardens.

As he waited anxiously for Clare, he studied the plaque on the faded and scratched wood of the bench. *In Loving Memory of Angus and Martha McPhee. Presented by their daughters. 'As life goes swiftly past, rest awhile in quiet meditation.'*

George was reflecting that this was pretty sound advice, when he noticed Clare hurrying along the path towards him. She met his hug with a perfunctory squeeze. Brushing aside his suggestion of a sandwich, Clare looked him directly in the face. 'Darling, I need to talk to you about Faslane.'

Now he understood the need for secrecy. As far as George knew, still only three people in Scotland knew about the Russian plan for an early-warning system at the naval base: Ross – and the two of them.

'Honey,' George protested, 'we're all concerned about the ramifications of letting the Russians install this system, but we are in an impossible situation. We need the Russian natural gas and money. Scotland faces financial collapse in just five weeks' time. I'm sure we can deal with the political fallout in Europe and America. After all, it's only a defence system which mirrors what the US already has in Eastern Europe.'

Clare completely ignored what George was saying. 'Do you remember my best friend Judy from the MoD? You know, the one who came up for the Christmas party at the Constitution Unit?'

'Yes, of course. To be honest, she seemed a little flaky for someone in such a senior position, but otherwise very nice. Good legs, too, I recall.'

'For Christ's sake,' Clare snapped, 'this is serious. She called me this morning.

She has come to me because she wants me to warn *you* what the Russians are really planning.'

Clare's lovely face was pale and strained. 'The Russians are not just planning to put a defensive missile system into Faslane. They are going to put offensive missiles there, pointing straight at the USA. Intercontinental Ballistic Missiles, George. Fucking nuclear warheads.'

The shock of hearing Clare swear for the first time helped drive home to George the enormity of what she was telling him. Still, he could not believe it. 'That can't be true. Come on, sweetheart, don't be ridiculous. I would know if Ross was risking a Third World War.'

But Clare was implacable. 'I promise you it *is* true. Judy has seen the intelligence reports for herself. They've been leaked to the Ministry of Defence. She says the Topol-M missiles will arrive by boat in Rosyth on Thursday afternoon, disguised as agricultural equipment. The Russians are taking advantage of the fact that the navy has scrapped its activities in Scottish territorial waters since the referendum and the RAF is also no longer flying patrols. Then they are travelling in a convoy overnight in order to avoid detection. The Russian advance team are already at Faslane and the warheads are arriving at dawn on Friday. They are avoiding the main road through Helensburgh and Rhu and, instead, are bringing them along the single-track road through Glen Fruin.'

Clare's face creased in frustration at George's incredulous look. Her voice took on a pleading tone. 'Darling, I swear to you Judy is right. I would trust her with my life. You must believe me.'

There could be no doubting Clare's urgent, driving sincerity. George rose unsteadily to his feet. 'I must talk to Ross. This would be a disaster, the Cuban Missile Crisis all over again. Jesus, what's he thinking?'

He gave Clare an absent-minded kiss as they parted by the imposing equestrian statue to the Royal Scots Greys on Princes Street. George waved down a taxi to take him to the Scottish Parliament at Holyrood. Clare turned the opposite way down Princes Street.

As they left, neither of them noticed the two figures simultaneously rise from the bench three along from theirs and follow them on their separate paths.

OFFICE OF THE FIRST MINISTER, SCOTTISH PARLIAMENT, EDINBURGH, 1.45 P.M.

George barged through the door and swung it shut in the face of a protesting Jean.

'Is it true?' he demanded.

'Is what true, George?' replied Ross calmly.

'You know fine well what I mean. Are the Russians really going to put nuclear weapons in Faslane?'

Ross's cheekbones clenched and unclenched, but he said nothing. He didn't need to. George knew Ross too well to need to ask further questions. His mind raced through the implications of this fact. 'Christ, you knew. You knew all along. That's what Churov and you were talking about in the Kremlin when you were alone together. That's why you and Karimov needed to be alone in the car at the airport. It never was simply a defensive system, was it? That was a lie from the start.'

Ross was cold and clipped. 'I need to ask you formally, George, how you came into possession of this information?'

His calmness infuriated George. 'Answer my fucking question!'

'No. But I must insist you answer mine.'

George felt his anger swell. The vein on the side of his forehead pulsed. He had often argued with Ross about politics. But they had never fallen out as friends. Nothing prepared George for this new cold, hard fury toward his friend. He struggled to control his emotions. 'With all due respect, *First Minister*,' George spat out, 'I don't think I am the one who needs to be answering questions here. What the fuck are you thinking? We could maybe have got away with a defensive missile system on the basis of Russian–American parity, but nuclear warheads, Ross? Are you insane?'

Ross's voice started to rise to match George's. 'Beggars cannot be choosers. I have no choice, in order to safeguard Scottish independence.'

'But how the fuck could you do this without telling me? Without asking me? Jesus, I'm your closest adviser. I'm supposed to be your friend.'

George couldn't tell whether he was more furious about Ross's stupidity or the fact that he had been deliberately kept out of the loop but suspected it was the latter.

Ross stood up and walked round to the front of the desk. 'I have to remind you that I am first minister, not you, George. And that what I say goes. You work for me. If I want your advice, I will ask for it.'

Something in George snapped. Of course, he had always known that technically this was the situation. Ross was his boss. But to know is one thing, to have it thrown in your face quite another. They had always spoken, always acted, as equals. Ross's remark shattered that pact.

He hadn't been spoken to like that in thirty years and to hear it from Ross of all people was just insufferable.

He moved toward him, snarling, 'You pompous, arrogant bastard!'

Like most fights, it was swift and untidy. Ross was taller, but George fitter. They grappled briefly until George caught Ross in his fleshy stomach with his strong right fist, forcing him to slump back against the desk like a slowly deflating balloon. Ross groaned, his face flushed under the ginger hair.

The two men stared at each other, breathing heavily. George's head was spinning. He hadn't been in a physical fight since he was eighteen. He didn't trust himself to say anything more. He needed to think. He turned to the door. Ross panted, 'George, I need to remind you of your obligations to this government. To me. This must remain totally confidential. You owe me that. In fact, you owe me everything.'

George didn't look round.

As he hastened down the corridor, a smiling Colonel Karimov was heading the opposite way, towards the first minister's office. 'Good afternoon, George. In a hurry?'

'Go fuck yourself, Karimov.'

WEDNESDAY, 25 JUNE — THIRTY-SIX DAYS TO INDEPENDENCE

THE TOUCAN BAR, SOHO, LONDON, 8 P.M.

George sat alone at the table, nursing a pint of Guinness. In spite of all his years commuting to London, he had never managed to shake off his Scottish aversion to warm beer, even though he knew cask-conditioned ales were supposed to be superior.

After he had left Ross's office, George had forced himself to return to the negotiations in the Great Hall at the castle, knowing his absence would be difficult to explain away. As the debate on fisheries had washed around him in the ancient chamber, he had simply stared at the wood-lined walls and the fearsome array of weaponry displayed there, desperately trying to think of some solution to this disaster.

At the end of a long day of debate, George had joined the rest of the team on the sleeper from Waverley to Euston. Public relations and national pride demanded that the negotiations be split between Scotland and England, so the teams shuffled en masse between the two capitals.

He had spent the next day at the talks, which had been as brutal as usual, with a heavy heart. The London end of the talks was based in Lancaster House, where the negotiations for Zimbabwean independence had taken place. No one on the Scottish negotiating team had missed the irony that a catastrophically failed state had been born here.

Despite the magnificent setting in the vast upper hall of Lancaster House, George couldn't focus on the discussion with the weight of this secret constantly pressing on him. The heated debates on agricultural tariffs and control of the coastline that raged around him seemed so completely trivial compared to the looming arrival of nuclear missiles. He felt he was an unwitting midwife to a policy that was going to destroy the country he loved.

As the session broke up, he turned down the offer of dinner with the Scottish delegation and returned to his old haunts in Soho's narrow lanes, where he had conducted much of his old public relations business, and where old-fashioned pubs could still be found among the trendy wine bars. He particularly loved the extra-cold Guinness served in The Toucan.

He recalled sitting at this same table, frantically worried that a pitch hadn't gone well or that a key client might desert. What he would give for problems like that now. Given what he knew, he couldn't have faced an evening of political gossip with his fellow Scottish commissioners, the seven men and women who were leading the negotiations on the Scottish side and had been given the same title as their predecessors who had negotiated the Union in 1707. He didn't want them sensing his unease.

Besides, there was someone he desperately needed to see.

'Hi, Dad.'

George surveyed his son's handsome young face, still framed by the floppy hair that had annoyed him since John was thirteen. He certainly had the looks to follow his chosen career as an actor.

'Hi. What do you fancy?'

As George carried his pint of Guinness and John's overpriced bottle of continental lager to the table, he reflected that their respective choice of drink said something about the uneasiness at the heart of their relationship.

Despite his wealth, George still liked to play the proletarian – beer over wine, football over rugby, steak pie over nouvelle cuisine. His son found this amusing and pretentious in equal measure. He used to tease him that his accent changed depending on whether he was pitching to Unilever or playing amateur football in Govan, a criticism George publicly rejected but secretly feared might be true.

Their traditionally jokey, but edgy, father–son relationship had been fundamentally changed by Bridget's death. John had been incredibly close to his mother and had coped the least well in the family with her loss. Unlike with Catherine, it had driven them further apart and George had compounded John's grief by selling the family home in Glasgow when he moved to Edinburgh to start working for Ross. He had hated rattling around its three floors on his own, feeling a stab of pain every time he walked into the kitchen that had been so much Bridget's domain.

Catherine had backed his decision, but, for John, the house was a precious source of memories, a place where his mother's spirit lived on. He had vehemently and vocally opposed George's decision and had barely spoken civilly to him since. To him, the sale was a betrayal.

Those fissures were deepened by politics. As George became more committed to the nationalist cause, John stood up for the Union, a divide replicated in families throughout Scotland, but one that still hurt George deeply. By rejecting his politics, he felt John was rejecting him.

They struggled through some small talk, tiptoeing around the chasm that lay between them, at least sharing pleasure in the news of Catherine's pregnancy, though both wondered if she was too young to have the responsibility of a baby.

Then it began, as ever. This time, John started it. 'So how is young Lolita, then?'

'Clare is fine, thank you very much. And there's no need to be so sarcastic.'

'I guess it runs in the family.'

John had only come to Edinburgh to meet Clare once and had not gone to any trouble to hide his disapproval of the relationship – and of Clare herself. George had been both wounded and completely mortified by his son's attitude.

'Jesus, John, what would you have me do? Your mother has been dead for five years. All our lives were ripped apart by that. But it wasn't my fault.'

'No one is saying it was your fault, it's just . . .'

'Just what? Live like a monk to make you happy? Pray every night at the altar of her memory?'

'Please don't talk about her like that. I hate it,' John snapped back.

'I'm sorry, son, but you have to cut me some slack. It has been five years.'

'You think I don't know exactly how long it has been?'

They simultaneously noticed that a young couple at the bar had turned round at the raised voices. They slumped into silence.

Bridget's sudden death had been a huge blow to them all. She had been first diagnosed with breast cancer in January 2009. By May she was dead – an inexorable, hideous progress.

George had worn the ribbons, raised money for the Maggie's Centres that treated his wife and explored all the radical new treatments. But still Bridget had died.

John, who had been doing his Highers that year, effectively abandoned his studies to be with his mother. His parents had urged him to keep studying, advice he resented to this day. He had wanted to spend every possible second with his dying mother, even if it was only fetching her some water, reading to her from the newspapers or simply sitting silently, holding her hand.

He had tried his exams again in his sixth year but his heart wasn't in it. He just scraped into the Royal Scottish Academy of Music and Drama in Glasgow then, on graduation, like so many others, headed to London to further his career. It had been fruitless so far. It hadn't escaped George's notice that London was about as far away from his father as John could currently afford.

George tried another tack. 'So, how's work?'

'I've had a couple of theatre auditions, but the ad and voice-over work has dried up. For some reason, a Scottish accent isn't flavour of the month at the moment. Can't think why.'

'I always said the secret of happiness was low expectations.'

'Well, that's you, Dad, a merry quip for every occasion.'

'I'm just trying to be helpful.'

'You're failing, then.'

George could feel them sliding into open hostility, but couldn't stop it. To be more accurate, he didn't want to stop it. He really resented being talked to like that. Although he knew it was wrong, he couldn't help but compare it with the automatic deference he had offered his own father. His voice took on a harsher tone. 'So, once more, your unhappiness is due to my failings. Fancy a passport to the world of self-reliance, John?'

'Funny you should mention passports, since you are the one who wants to make me a foreigner in my own home. Just as the world is shrinking, you want to break it into parochial parcels.'

George heard his own voice rising with anger. 'Forgive me for righting three hundred years of historic injustice and seeking freedom for my people.'

But John would not be browbeaten: he had learned to argue on his father's knee, and he had learned well. 'Spare me the crocodile tears, Dad. You think we have difficult neighbours, try being Polish. You're so full of shit.'

The couple at the bar looked round again. George was beyond caring. His debater's desire to win every argument took over, bolstered by the knowledge that, if he had ever spoken to his father that way, he would have felt the back of his hand. 'I'm just trying to do what is right,' he insisted.

'Huh. Reminds me of what Mum used to say: "When I married Mr Right, I didn't know his first name was Always."'

'Now who's using memories as a weapon?'

Having reached a score draw in pain, they paused, reluctant to inflict further punishment, aware that one day it would go too far and there would be no going back. Instinctively, both knew they didn't want that. George took a deep breath. 'I'm sorry. I don't want to fight. Honestly. I have enough going on in my life without this.'

John responded to the olive branch. 'Me too, we just go over the same shit every time. What's the point? We are never going to be the Waltons, just your everyday, average, fucked-up family.'

George smiled, despite himself.

'Good to see you smile, Dad. You seem really stressed. What's up? Is Ross the Boss driving you mad?'

George knew Ross loved that particular nickname. 'Things are hectic, yes. It's not just that. I can deal with the hard work.' George hesitated. 'I'm not really free to reveal what it is . . . to be honest, sometimes I'm not even sure we are doing the right things, despite all I say.'

'I don't know what the big secret is, Dad, but I do know you will do the right thing. You may have been self-important and self-righteous, but you did teach us that. Do you remember I used to joke that your answerphone message should say, "Please leave your message after the high moral tone"?'

'Cheers, John, I guess I'll take that as a compliment. You know what, you were no angel yourself growing up and—'

George stopped abruptly and looked at his son. Suddenly, it was completely clear how he must resolve his dilemma. The right, moral thing to do could not have been clearer.

'Actually, thanks, son. You have really helped me. More than you can imagine.'

An hour later, George hugged John goodbye and stepped into the light from the street lamp at the corner of Soho Square. He smiled at the faded and pockmarked statue of King Charles II in the park, thinking to himself, 'Well, you certainly wouldn't have done the right thing, would you, you old bastard? You wouldn't have known decency if you had fallen over it.'

Hesitation over, he stabbed in a number on his speed dial. 'Jessica, it's George. Listen, I need to talk to you.'

'George, it's ten o'clock. What the hell can be so important?' Jessica stepped away from the noise of a bar and whispered, 'And I am out on a pretty hot date.'

'Well, ditch him, Jessica, this can't wait.'

'You sound drunk. You sure it isn't Clare you need to speak to?'

'No, it's you. And it needs to be now.'

JESSICA SCHWARTZ'S FLAT, REGENT'S PARK, LONDON, 10.30 P.M.

Jessica was pretty ticked off with George, not a common feeling for her. She had always liked him, ever since he had desperately tried to instil a passion for Bismarck and the Franco–Prussian war of 1870 into her tenth grade, gum-chewing class. She had also been the star striker in his soccer team, leading them into the Southern California play-offs for the first time in a decade.

They had kept in close touch over the years, first when she was a graduate-student Rhodes scholar at Oxford, then when she had worked in his London office on a couple of the American accounts.

Ten years ago, she had joined the *Philadelphia Inquirer* as a politics reporter, before joining the *New York Times* three years later and being posted back to London in 2011 as UK correspondent. George kept her up to date on Scottish affairs and was the only person in British politics she completely trusted.

On at least two occasions, they had nearly started a relationship. Once, before he met Bridget, when Jessica was at Oxford, and after Bridget's death, when she had tried to comfort him. On both occasions they had drawn back, content with the flirtation and fearing the consequences of a failed relationship on their friendship.

He was certainly the only person in British politics for whom she would have ditched a hot date.

'This had better be worth it,' she said as she opened the door. She looked wonderful, in a low-cut red cocktail dress slashed to the thigh on one side. 'I spent ages – and a fortune – to look this good.'

George followed her splendidly gym-toned body into the living room, wondering why, no matter the level of crisis, men could always have their

----

attention diverted by an attractive woman. 'Aye, no question, you're not bad for an old doll,' he acknowledged.

She laughed. 'Listen, you cheeky bastard, we are not all blessed with young lovers. When you get to my age, exciting dates are rarer than genuine scoops. So, don't disappoint me.'

When George left her flat an hour later, he most definitely had not done that.

CHAPTER 8

FRIDAY, 27 JUNE — THIRTY-FOUR DAYS TO INDEPENDENCE

FASLANE NAVAL BASE, THE GARE LOCH, SCOTLAND, 4 A.M.

Jack Ashton edged himself forward on his elbows, silently cursing the dew-soaked clumps of heather that dogged his every forward movement. How the fuck could this godforsaken country be freezing even in the summer?

He and Jessica had parked the car an hour before across from the stark, whitewashed parish kirk in the village of Garelochhead and set off, passing the main gate of Faslane Naval Base and mounting the hill. Jessica had stopped at the first lay-by. Jack had continued up the hill, past the croft abandoned in the clearances of the nineteenth century and the odd curious Highland cow, then found a vantage point near the gate at the top of Glen Fruin, just before the road began its winding descent down to the loch.

After making himself as comfortable as possible, he unpacked his trusty Nikon and peered through the mist at the rising dawn. He had worked with Jessica for four years and she had never let him down before. Even so, this seemed the wildest of goose chases, the product of the fevered imagination of some crazed political conspiracy theorist.

Then, as the sun broke over the hills framing the glen, he spotted them.

'Well, I'll be fucked.'

Thanks to the wonders of digital photography, Jack shot over a hundred stills as the thirty trucks thundered noisily over the metal squares of the cattle grid at the gate, before disappearing over the brow of the hill.

Instinctively he knew these would be the pictures that would make him famous. No longer a press snapper. A proper, named photographer. Famous.

Breathless, he greeted Jessica, who was waiting at the lay-by. She had seen them pass too and shared every inch of his excitement. 'No bullshit, Jess, the best tip-off ever. The Russian writing on the trucks couldn't have been clearer. Let's go.'

Within fifteen minutes Jack was wiring the photographs from his laptop in his room at The Anchor Inn to the editor's office at the *New York Times*.

THE OVAL OFFICE, THE WHITE HOUSE, WASHINGTON DC, 1.30 A.M.

As they awaited the arrival of the president, Admiral Carl Butterworth, Jane Chalmers and Charles Sands all kept their own counsel. Each was trying to fathom why they had been summoned from their beds – or, in Sands' case, someone else's bed.

Chalmers, lost in her own thoughts, alternated between twisting a strand of her dyed black hair and silently stroking her right index finger down her long, aquiline nose. Two hours previously, she had been informed that the CIA had lost its electronic bug and agent inside Churov's office. The president's principal private secretary had been arrested and his apartment ransacked.

She was in damage-limitation mode. The two CIA officers he could name under torture were already on their way home. Wherever her mole was, he was now paying a heavy price for his weakness for cards and high-class hookers.

Chalmers did not like losing and this was the latest in a long list of CIA fuck-ups. Neither of the men there with her was a natural ally. Sands thought she was uncouth, Butterworth that she was consumed more by her own interests than those of the United States.

To her close staff, she put their resentment down to her being a successful woman in a man's world. In private, unshared moments, she did acknowledge there was some truth in both criticisms. The more brutal truth was that no one in the White House liked or trusted her.

Despite her outward charm, her colleagues and both ex-husbands were now aware that the only person Chalmers really cared about was herself, and she would lie and cheat as much as necessary. One embittered husband had divorced her, having discovered she had been secretly taking contraceptive pills while professing the desire to have a baby. The other, faced with her chronic indifference, had become an alcoholic.

Chalmers, an absolute master at emotional blackmail, used the fact that many old-fashioned men were reluctant to be brutal to a woman in a power struggle, then knifed them when they were least expecting it. She was equally adept at wielding tears and smiles, sometimes within a single argument.

She had heard that Butterworth had once described her as a woman without a single redeeming feature. But she knew that wasn't true in the eyes of the president. To him, she had at least one: her absolute, binding loyalty to Todd MacFarlane and his family.

Her father and Todd's father were old friends in the cosy world of Southern business. She had been the treasurer of MacFarlane's campaign in 2012, using her father's business leverage to raise the money to fund the most expensive presidential race in American history.

Much of the cash had come from the defence industry. In return they wanted one of their own in charge of the CIA. One of the new president's first acts had been to grant their wish and appoint Chalmers.

Successfully raising all that money for MacFarlane could buy her the position but not keep her there. After a failure in Iraq and a PR disaster in Venezuela, she knew the United States and she, especially, had to get Scotland right. But if she did get it right, her ultimate ambition would be one step closer.

The door from the garden swung open and everyone rose as the president entered. As was becoming more common as his term wore on, MacFarlane wasted no time on small talk. 'I apologise for summoning you so late. Half an hour ago, I had a phone conversation with Frances Copeland, editor of the *New York Times*. Unfortunately, she was not calling to announce her conversion to the Republican Party but to tell me that she is going to break a story later this morning that affects every one of us. It is my duty to inform you that, as of this morning, the United States faces a clear and present danger to her national security.'

The president quickly outlined what the editor had told him to his three astonished colleagues. It was testimony to Todd MacFarlane's gifts as an actor that none of the three of them doubted for a minute that this story was news to him, too.

OFFICE OF THE FIRST MINISTER, SCOTTISH PARLIAMENT, EDINBURGH, 8.30 A.M.

Ross's assistant, Jean, was completely flustered. 'First Minister, I have the president of the United States on the phone. He says it's urgent and confidential.'

With a flick of his eyes, Ross dismissed the two aides sitting with him. He glanced at his watch. 'Mr President, good morning, you're having a late night.'

'I am indeed, First Minister, and I have to say it is pretty much all your fault. I am calling you from the Oval Office in the White House, where I have spent the last two hours locked in discussion with my senior military and intelligence advisers regarding your decision to let the Russians install offensive nuclear weapons in Scotland. The *New York Times* is running the story on its front page.'

'Mr President, let me say . . .' began Ross, in a conciliatory tone.

The president, in talking, not listening, mode, was determined there would be no hint of wimpishness in his attitude. 'I have to tell you, First Minister, that the United States will never, and I mean *never*, countenance hostile nuclear weapons in Scotland and would consider any attempt to site them there as an act of aggression against the United States.

'Let me be blunt. I will be making public that I am giving you twenty-four hours from now to announce the immediate and complete withdrawal of those weapons from Faslane Naval Base. Failure to do so will result in automatic and complete economic sanctions and a series of escalating measures as and when we see fit until this is achieved. By the end of the summer, there will be no Russian nuclear weapons in Scotland. On that you have my word. Goodbye.'

As he hung up, Ross Johnson closed the tips of his fingers on the end of his nose and drew a deep breath though his cupped hands. He realised he was engaged in an unprecedented political high-wire act. There could be no turning back now. At least he had been right about one thing – he had known exactly what George would do with the information, the stupid, vain, weak bastard.

He picked up the phone to his assistant. 'Get me President Churov on the line. Yes, Jean, of course *now.*'

As he replaced the receiver after talking to Ross Johnson, Todd MacFarlane glanced at the grim faces of the three other occupants of the Oval Office. 'OK, let's summarise our contingency planning one more time before we call it a night. It is going to be a hectic day tomorrow, so let's get some beauty sleep. We're agreed that we keep this situation tight – just the four of us in this room on the political side. No written minutes of meetings. No other staff involved, unless operationally essential. We need to keep it to those we absolutely trust.'

Chalmers, Butterworth and Sands all nodded their assent. Each was sure of one thing: 'trust' was not a term they would have chosen to describe their relationship with any of the other current occupants of the Oval Office.

PRESS CONFERENCE, THE BALMORAL HOTEL BALLROOM, EDINBURGH, 4 P.M.

George's head ached and the vein in his temple throbbed. He had been on his mobile non-stop in the eight hours since the story had broken. The right side of his head was now actually hot to touch and he hated to think what all that radiation was doing to his brain. He briefly wondered if dying of a media-induced brain tumour could be classified as poetic justice.

The massive international media demand provoked by the *New York Times* story had completely overwhelmed the Scottish government's media relations team and its facilities, so he had authorised an emergency press conference in the ballroom of the Balmoral. Even this huge room was packed to the rafters with film crews, radio reporters and press hacks.

And now George had to face them. Alone.

He felt like one of those police inspectors facing the press after a horrific murder who knows the case is firmly in the public eye but doesn't have a single lead. But he had to give the media something or they would just run with speculation anyway.

Plus the Scottish press were incandescent that the story – *their* story – had broken in an American newspaper. The Scottish media hadn't sat on the biggest story in the world since the bomb in the Pan Am plane over Lockerbie over twenty-five years before and deeply resented being scooped.

An hour previously, George had met with Ross and his other advisers to try to establish a 'line' before the press conference. They all agreed there was no point in denying the story, as the first rule of media management was never to tell a deliberate lie in public. All they could hope to do was to put a lid on the story until the Scottish Cabinet had been briefed and come to a decision. True to form, Ross had kept the whole Cabinet in the dark about his plans with the Russians so it was sure to be a frosty meeting.

In the meeting, Ross had been cold but professional with George, giving no hint that he suspected him of leaking the story to his favourite journalist. He had insisted that George do the press conference personally and alone, dressing the decision up by stressing that the gravity of situation required the senior special adviser for the task, but both men knew that it was revenge, pure and simple.

George stepped on to the podium and tentatively approached the microphone. He tried to recall the lessons from his media training days – avoid any particular eye contact and keep focused on the middle distance. 'Good afternoon, ladies and gentlemen, and thank you for coming at such short notice. I am delighted there is such massive media interest in our negotiations with the English this week on agricultural and fisheries policy.'

The joke only received a small ripple of laughter. A bad sign. The TV cameras kept their impassive gaze on him.

George attempted to restore his authority. He cleared his throat and began. 'I will be making a short statement then I will take a few – and I stress a *few* – questions. The Scottish government is currently meeting to discuss the situation reported by the *New York Times* yesterday morning. I can confirm that the first minister has indeed given permission to the Russian government to have a military base at Faslane in return for very significant financial backing for the new, independent Scotland.

'As President MacFarlane has now made public in his comments to the media, it is the United States' intention to impose punitive economic sanctions on Scotland if there is no promise to remove the base. The Scottish government deplores these bullying tactics and will issue a full response in due course. Thank you.'

'Are there actually Russian nuclear missiles in Scotland?' came a shouted question from the back of the room.

'I am afraid that information is classified so I can neither confirm nor deny.'

George held up a hand to still the angry muttering at this stonewalling.

'Will the Scottish government give in?' demanded the BBC political editor in the front row.

'As I said, a full response on this issue will be forthcoming shortly. Two more.'

'Why are we getting the monkey and not the organ grinder?'

George turned to the *Daily Mail* reporter. 'Thank you for your charming question, as ever, Peter. The Scottish Cabinet is currently in session. As you may have noticed, Ross Johnson is in the Cabinet and I am not.'

In the laughter, the *News of the World* reporter took his chance. 'Is it true that you were the one who leaked the story to your girlfriend Jessica Schwartz?'

Despite himself, George couldn't help but glance at Jessica in the second row. An elementary schoolboy error and one caught by the cameras. 'I'm not going to dignify that with an answer. That's all. We'll have more for you on Monday morning.'

He ignored the shouts of 'George, George!' following him and made his way to the closest exit with as much dignity as he could muster, already dreading facing this baying mob again on Monday morning. What the hell would he say to them then?

CHAPTER 9

SATURDAY, 28 JUNE — THIRTY-THREE DAYS TO INDEPENDENCE

THE IRON DUKE BAR, DENNISTOUN, GLASGOW, 2 P.M.

When he was running his PR company, George had tried, and failed, to explain to friends and clients what it was like to be in the eye of a media storm. To be 'doorstepped'; phoned at all hours; having your neighbours harassed; always watching for the lenses poking out of the windows of parked cars. You endlessly had to try to seek the agenda behind the reporters' seemingly sympathetic questions. After a while, you became defensive and cynical, incapable of seeing the good in people.

It had to be experienced to be truly known.

And this had been a storm like no other. Bigger than the 2011 election victory. Bigger than the independence referendum result. And this time, one entirely of his own making. The endless TV reruns of the press conference made him look increasingly shifty. And Jessica was also now under siege to reveal her source.

George felt pulled in two opposite directions. He craved anonymity as the world's media besieged his mobile phone, and yet he desperately felt the need for some familiar surroundings, an anchor in this media tempest.

His own personal anchor, Clare, had gone to spend the afternoon with an old college friend at the Harvey Nichols sale. She had invited him. George would rather have driven red-hot pokers through his testicles. Much as he loved her, he knew there were so many aspects of him she would never understand, including his aversion to aimless browsing in shops.

But the gulf went deeper than that. His upbringing in Dennistoun was so far removed from hers in Bearsden as to render comparison meaningless, like saying a Zulu and a Boer were both just South Africans. Glasgow: one city, two classes.

George had jumped on the new twenty-minute Superspeeder fast train to Glasgow and then walked due east all the way from Queen Street Station, along George Street until it turned into Duke Street at the junction of High Street. He looked along this urban canyon, which stretched east as far as the eye could see, to where he had grown up.

The part of Duke Street nearest the city centre was all refurbished and sandblasted red sandstone tenements. Further east the construction for that summer's Commonwealth Games had created a gleaming complex of new buildings around the athletes' village. But as he walked on, the insistent, clinging pockets of deprivation were still all around him – islands of misery in the sea of regeneration. Full of football shirts and tattoos – and that was just the women.

He passed the vast Tennent's brewery on the left where his dad had worked as a lorry driver, less than a mile from where his mother had toiled as a cigarette packer on one of the production lines of the huge red-brick Wills Tobacco factory.

As he walked, George marvelled at the fact that, just a generation before, an entire life could be contained within a five-mile radius, with the sole exception of two weeks in Rothesay during the Glasgow Trades holiday, a thought that would be inconceivable to his well-travelled, nomadic children.

A mile further and he was on the streets where he had dodged the traffic as he played football as a boy, the major changes being the arrival of an African restaurant and a halal butcher at the turn of the century.

Finally, he stood outside the Orange Lodge building where every July he had been one of the excited kids allowed to carry a cord of the local banner at the Orange parade.

They had always been close, his mum and dad and little sister Martha. The tenement flat had always been filled with the smell of fresh gingerbread or Scotch broth and by the sounds of political argument. Indeed, when George had wanted to go into the media his dad joked he had been too happy as a child to hope to be truly creative. His dad believed that working-class Scots were the most balanced people in the world – because they had a chip on both shoulders.

His family had been a traditional, conservative one. His father's version was that he made all the big decisions – who the prime minister should be, whether China should reunite with Taiwan and how closely Britain should be integrated into the European Union. His wife made all the small ones – how much housekeeping she got, where they lived and where they went on holiday.

But despite the happiness, there was a huge tension at the heart of his family.

Like many working-class men, his father was torn between a desire for George to be proud of his roots and a hope that he could escape them.

And one of those roots was an unquestioning Protestant, British loyalism. Loyalty to the monarch. Loyalty to the Union. British first, Scottish second. The facts were simple in loyalism. Since the Glorious Revolution of 1688, the Protestant monarchy had been the guarantor of traditional British liberties, parliamentary sovereignty, the rule of law and freedom of conscience. In contrast, Catholics offered unthinking obedience to a foreign pope, therefore their loyalty was always suspect.

These were the people who had given the Conservative and Unionist Party a majority of the votes in Scotland in 1955 and kept Tory seats in proletarian Glasgow into the 1970s.

George's father had fought in Korea and in the debacle of Suez in 1956, which ended any lingering hopes of maintaining the British empire. Though disappointed by the loss of empire, his father's faith in the British state remained unshaken and unshakeable. An ideal, a nation, for which he had been prepared to fight and die. And an ideal he had expected his son to adopt unquestioningly.

The underlying, simmering tension in the family had exploded when George had met and fallen in love with Bridget when they were both working for the *Glasgow Herald*. His father had never forgiven him for turning his back on – no, 'betraying' – his traditions. The university trendiness, the socialism, they were bad enough but accepted as a teenage act of rebellion. But marrying a Catholic had been a step too far, a frontal assault on his family and its culture. This seemed confirmed when Bridget had insisted that the kids went to a Catholic school. George's long, slow conversion to the cause of Scottish nationalism deepened the wound.

The very existence of grandchildren meant the rift with his father was never complete, a truce to protect the kids they both loved, but also meant that the wound never healed. It simply lay open and bleeding every time they met. George's father never really understood why George fought him; why loyalty to his new family came before loyalty to his old one. The truce was only maintained by keeping all conversations to stilted small talk.

His dad had died of a massive stroke when Catherine was six and John four. George's grief was compounded by the fact that so much had been left unsaid, so many issues left unresolved. He was as sorry as he was angry.

His sister Martha's way of avoiding the conflict had been the traditional solution of emigration. In Sydney, no one cared what religion you followed.

When his mother followed his father to the grave two years later, George's active, formal link to Dennistoun was severed.

And yet here he was, seeking solace. Seeking comfort. Seeking home in a place he had chosen to abandon.

George thought it was funny how everything in the Loyalist tradition always came back to betrayal – a litany of infamy against God's chosen ones. 'We are the people!' was the cry. 'Sold down the river,' the conclusion. Betrayed defiant heroes in their own mythology.

George enjoyed irony. Therefore he took a perverse pleasure in the fact that he had somehow contrived to disappoint and alienate both his father and his son over a position on the constitution he now doubted himself. Quite a feat.

The heavy wooden door of The Iron Duke creaked satisfyingly as he pushed it open. It was only when he stepped inside that George realised quite how incongruous his Ralph Lauren polo shirt and chinos – his accountant-on-holiday look – appeared.

He ordered a pint of heavy then made his way over to a group of old men playing dominoes with the intensity of chess grandmasters.

George had partnered his dad when he was fifteen on the Thursday night dominoes doubles tournaments, amazed at the emotional and intellectual intensity – not to mention massive fraud – that was funnelled into winning the first prize of a steak pie.

As he approached the men, he tried to recollect if the phrase 'a big crowd at Ibrox this week' had been secret code for five sixes or six fives. 'Hello, Uncle Tommy. Still cheating at dominoes, I see.'

His father's youngest and only surviving brother looked up from his pint. 'Ah, the return of the prodigal son.'

Tommy's crumpled purple face was a testament to his long, losing battle with drink. His slow decline had seen him change from a joint owner of The Iron Duke, to its manager, then its barman, then a regular. He was irascible and dismissive, but he had always had a soft spot for George. 'Have a seat, son. What brings you to these parts? Taking a wee break from betraying king and country?'

'Jesus, Tommy, give me a break. Don't I even get the benefit of five minutes of small talk before the abuse?'

'C'mon, son, you'd be disappointed with anything else.'

As they let the gentle glow of the pints fill them, the two men talked. George always loved returning to the last remnants of the self-taught working class – the proletarian philosophers who had honed their debating skills at union meetings and in public bars. Moulded at a time when the working class cared about more than who was on the front cover of *Heat* magazine.

George had more of a love–hate relationship with, but always a wary respect for, the brutal sarcasm of Glasgow humour, where any weakness was automatically exploited for comic effect. One of The Iron Duke's current barmen was nicknamed 'Thrombosis'. When George asked why, he was told it was because he was a slow-moving clot.

When a newspaper profile of George had described him as a self-made man, his uncle Tommy had written him a note saying it was good of him to take the blame. Tommy appraised him coolly. 'Yer looking well, son, apart fae they huge bags under yer eyes.'

'Occupational hazard, Tommy. As you might have seen, I've been a tad busy recently.'

'Aye, you have done well fer yerself, George. Yer dad would ha' been really proud of you.'

George was automatically on guard, warily looking for the sarcastic sucker punch. 'Really?'

'Aye, son,' Tommy said, looking directly into George's sceptical eyes. 'Really. He would never say anything tae you – that wisnae his way – but he thought you were a great son.'

After twenty minutes of the banter that substitutes for emotional closeness for Scottish men, they grew serious over politics. 'You have tae understand that there is a lotta resentment here,' insisted Tommy. 'The only culture unacceptable in yer new shiny Scotland is working-class loyalism. Any Tom, Dick or Lithuanian lesbian can get a Scottish Arts Council grant tae explore their history, but being Orange is despised.'

'Come on,' George responded. 'You know as well as I do that these guys around here don't really care about religion. I bet most haven't darkened the door of a church in months. As my old friend Benjamin Franklin put it: "Many have quarrelled about religion that never practised it."'

'Maybe so, son, maybe so. But it's a cultural thing, isn't it? People felt betrayed when Thatcher took their jobs, now they feel betrayed because Ross Johnson plans to take their country.'

'Even if that's true, it doesn't justify support for the BLA.'

'Sure, they're hotheids,' Tommy acknowledged, 'but a lot of people around here are bitter and sympathise with them.'

'But they can't win,' George insisted. 'That old-fashioned, Protestant, British loyalism is finished, even on the Shankhill, let alone in Dennistoun.'

'But they don't have to win. All they have to do is stop *you* winning. Make independence not worth the candle. And they can – and *will* – do that. Look at the polls. Even if you stagger over the finishing line next month, will the race have been worth running?'

Even through the beer, that was a sobering thought. Woozy after three unusual afternoon pints, George rose unsteadily to his feet and shook hands with his uncle. 'Thanks for the thoughts, Tommy. Let's keep in touch.'

Tommy nodded his agreement, knowing that neither of them meant it.

As George reached the door, Tommy asked one last question. 'You're a political theorist, George. If it's true the class war is over, then tell me this. Who won?'

George stepped out into the warm summer air, chuckling.

A moment later, his phone rang. It was Jessica. 'George, have you heard the president's speech? We're looking for a swift response from the Scottish government.'

THE OVAL OFFICE, THE WHITE HOUSE, WASHINGTON DC, 8 P.M.

Todd MacFarlane took enormous pleasure in his desk. Carved from timbers from the HMS *Resolute*, it was beautifully shaped, strong, solid, shiny and long-lasting, all the attributes he thought best represented America. And himself.

The one huge difference was that the desk didn't have a flaw at its heart which could bring it crashing down at any time.

Although there was autocue, MacFarlane liked the comfort of a real paper script in front of him. He had rehearsed the speech so often with Charles Sands that afternoon, he felt he could have done it off by heart. But he still liked the backup.

The president had spent the morning locked in debate with Chalmers, Butterworth and Sands about what he should say. Sands had argued for a speech that hinted at the possibility of compromise but had been out-argued and out-voted. The three others all believed that, with the story in the public domain, there was no alternative to a hard line. The Russians had to be faced down and defeated. Sands had been despatched to get the three networks to clear their schedules for MacFarlane's emergency address to the nation.

Once the policy had been agreed MacFarlane set to work copying Ronald Reagan's great skill: making it look like he was speaking off the cuff; making it up as he went along. MacFarlane remembered the former president eloquently drawing the emotional words from the depths of his soul at this very desk as he delivered his moving tribute to the *Challenger* astronauts.

Todd could close his eyes and see it now. 'The crew of the space shuttle *Challenger* honoured us by the manner in which they lived their lives. We will never forget them, nor the last time we saw them, this morning, as they prepared for their journey and waved goodbye and slipped the surly bonds of earth to touch the face of God.'

And all delivered with a tear in his eye. Wonderful. If only MacFarlane had spent more time with a drama group and less time with those magnificent young men on the football field then this might be a whole lot easier.

The floor manager counted him in. The autocue under the camera sprang into life. 'My fellow Americans, good evening and greetings from the White House. As you all now know, yesterday morning I discovered that the Russians, with the agreement of the Scottish government, have placed nuclear weapons at Faslane Naval Base at the Gare Loch on the west coast of Scotland. These missiles – the latest Intercontinental Ballistic Missiles in the Russian armoury – represent a clear and present danger to the United States. They bring Russian weapons one thousand miles closer to our shores than they have been since the Cuban Missile Crisis in 1962. As they are in Scotland, they would not be detected or destroyed by our missile defence systems based further east, in Poland and the Czech Republic. This is not a time for partisan politics but I must tell you that the previous administration's scrapping of the Star Wars defence system, for the very laudable aim of avoiding an arms race in space, means that they also would not be detected and destroyed over the Atlantic. By the time our warning system on the coast of Maine picked them up and launched a counter-attack, these missiles would already be over Iceland. Admiral Carl Butterworth, the head of the joint chiefs of staff, has estimated that we could probably destroy most of the missiles but there is a risk that some may get through and strike the cities of Philadelphia, Boston or New York. That is not a risk I'm prepared to take.

'Yesterday morning I asked Ross Johnson, the first minister of Scotland, to agree to remove these missiles within twenty-four hours or face immediate economic sanctions. That deadline has now passed and I regret to say that no such assurance has been forthcoming. I have now ordered these economic measures to take place, including the seizure of Scottish assets and the freezing of Scottish bank accounts in the United States.

'I am dismayed to tell you that when Scotland, the land of so many of our forefathers, including my own, declares independence at midnight on the thirty-first of July, it will join North Korea and Iran on a list of rogue nations. If these economic sanctions fail to work then you have my word of honour that we will find another way to remove these missiles from Scotland. This is the greatest threat any president has had to face since President Kennedy faced down the Soviets in Cuba over fifty years ago. And tonight I would like to remind you of his pledge to the world during those desperate days: "We will pay any price, bear any burden and meet any hardship to assure the success and survival of liberty."

'That is also my pledge to you tonight. I say to the people of Scotland that the citizens of the United States are your friends. We bear you no ill will. But we will not countenance this threat to our great nation continuing. Those missiles will not be allowed to stay. Thank you and goodnight.'

SUNDAY, 29 JUNE – THIRTY-TWO DAYS TO INDEPENDENCE

NORTHUMBERLAND STREET, EDINBURGH, 2 P.M.

George ignored the clutch of reporters huddling in his doorway, turned the key and stepped, soaking, into the hall, cursing the sudden shower and his inability ever to remember an umbrella.

His mood had not been improved by the constant snapping of the photographers. God, he wished he had remembered to shave and didn't look quite so hungover.

After a morning in emergency session with Ross and his advisers, George had slipped home to grab a sandwich and clear his head. They had all agreed that Ross would address the nation on Monday night and George had taken on the task of liaising with BBC Scotland, if he could get hold of any of them on a Sunday afternoon.

The argument had raged all morning as to what the first minister should say. Some favoured capitulation, others defiance. George had led the compromise party. Given how the story had leaked, he hadn't felt able to push Ross too hard. But he knew there was no alternative. How could a nation of five million defy the world's only superpower?

Ross had silenced them by insisting he would write the first draft personally. They would reconvene at 6 p.m. to go through it one final time.

Ross had been cold but professional with George since their fight. He must have known that George was the source of the story but hadn't raised it with him either publicly or privately. George didn't know how to respond, apart from playing along until the inevitable confrontation came, as he knew it must. This was not peace, just the absence of war.

And George had a deeper, lingering, concern. Being in control had always been vitally important to him. He had managed it as a student, as a teacher, as a journalist and as chief executive of his PR company. Of course, events sometimes spiralled out of control, but in general he was setting the course and dictating the pace. In charge.

Bridget's death, his powerlessness to change that path or soften the blow, had shattered that confidence. The job in politics had helped him rebuild his life. As Ross's senior special adviser, he had always quite enjoyed his sparring with the Scottish and British press, slipping them the odd story, having a quiet word in their ear in cafés or bars about who was up and down in the SNP and always making sure they had the party line. Sometimes he won, sometimes he lost. There was a cosy abrasiveness about the game, and everyone knew the rules. He was back in control again.

This crisis, however, was not a game he felt equipped to play. He didn't know the players in the world press. He didn't know the rules. In fact, he was starting to wonder if he should even be at the table at all. As he faced the might of the American government's media machine, he felt completely out of his depth.

And, while feeling this inadequacy, he was still trying to handle the delicate negotiations on separation.

Clare handed him a bathrobe as he stepped out of his sodden clothes. 'There's some fresh coffee. I'll bring it through with a sandwich. Ham and tomato OK?'

George grunted his assent and sat with the newspapers on the sofa. The headlines were all banner variations of Armageddon and Third World War. In the posh papers there were huge thought-pieces by Latin American historians on how Ross compared with Fidel Castro.

'It's an ill wind,' thought George, remembering all the historians of the Crusades who were suddenly in huge demand after 9/11 and who made sudden fortunes from books that were usually destined for the furthest reaches of the university library.

Clare gave him his sandwich and sat across from him in the armchair, her right leg tucked under her, as usual. 'What's new?'

'Ross is going to address the nation tomorrow night. He's writing it himself but we all assume it will be some form of backing-down with an offer to negotiate. Anything else is just madness.'

'Was he OK with you this morning?' Clare asked.

'Seemed to be. But I know him of old, he's just biding his time until he strikes. He moves surprisingly quickly for a fat bloke.'

Clare's laugh emboldened him. 'Listen, darling, I was thinking, it's maybe time for me to call it a day. I don't know that I am up for, and maybe even up to, this task. You know I have doubts about the whole independence project. My American friends think I'm crazy. My relationship with Ross is fucked. The vultures in the party smell my blood. And I think this whole relationship with the Russians is just nuts. There is only so long that I can stand up in front of the world's media and defend this shit.'

Clare looked at him thoughtfully. 'I think that to resign would be a mistake. I know you now. All your life, you have wanted to be a player, to be at the heart of action. And here it is, the biggest story in a generation, and you would walk away? Really? Ross needs you, George. More than ever. Be the voice of sanity. Help him do the right thing.'

'You think so?' George sounded unconvinced.

She moved over beside him on the couch. 'Absolutely, sweetheart, I really do. You shouldn't resign, George. I am so proud of you and all you have achieved. I love you for that.'

It was first time she had used the 'L' word and both of them knew the significance of the moment. She kissed his neck tenderly, then the side of his face. Suddenly they were kissing passionately. Clare pushed the bathrobe off his shoulders and straddled him on the sofa. She giggled, teasing, tugging her T-shirt over her head.

'Come on then, show me why you were voted the second most powerful man in Scotland.'

As he looked at her flushed face and laughing blue eyes, George couldn't have cared less if that minute the American Sixth Fleet was actually sailing up the Forth playing 'Yankee Doodle Dandy'.

For a brief, joyous moment, nothing else mattered.

In the rented flat across the street, the *Sun* photographer couldn't believe his luck.

MONDAY, 30 JUNE – THIRTY-ONE DAYS TO INDEPENDENCE

KIRKLEE TERRACE, GLASGOW, 9 A.M.

Sammy Wilson watched the sun glint off the blond sandstone of the row of imposing Victorian townhouses which adjoined the city's Botanic Gardens. Built when Glasgow was the undisputed second city of the empire, these symmetrical symbols of success reflected the confidence of a people who knew God was on their side and that Mammon had naturally followed.

But Sammy was not struck by the beauty or regularity of the architecture, but rather by a new wave of the seething anger and sense of injustice which never seemed to leave him. How could people have these homes when he had nothing? Treason rewarded with luxury and loyalty with poverty. Sickening.

Number three Kirklee Terrace was the home of Maureen Cairns, the deputy leader of the SNP.

He nudged the Fiesta up on to the terrace, empty now of rush-hour cars. They had watched the nanny, Mary, leave with Maureen's three-year-old daughter, Jessie, twenty minutes earlier. They knew her routine. They knew she was alone in the house.

There was not a soul to be seen. The sun silently picked out the deep etching that surrounded each honey-coloured sandstone block. Sammy knocked on the door while the other three pressed themselves against the black wrought-iron railings at the side of the door. Sammy felt the reassuring hardness of the pistol's handle in his pocket.

As Maureen opened the door they all rushed in, bundling her back into the drawing room at the front of the house. Gordon's hand muffled her shouts as Billy started to bind her wrists. They had just completed their task when they heard a key scrape in the lock.

They all froze, looking to Sammy for guidance.

Mary breezed in from the hall, talking as she walked, holding Jessie by the hand. 'The nursery say that there is definitely chickenpox on the go so they thought it . . .'

Mary's voice tailed off as she struggled to take in the scene. Three stationary men, Maureen bound and gagged on the floor and Sammy's pistol pointing directly at her.

'Just shut up and nobody gets hurt,' Sammy said firmly.

Mary was silent but Jessie started to scream, louder and louder. Mary knelt down, trying to console and quieten her, but the screams continued, echoing around the high-ceilinged room. This totally unnerved his three companions, but drove Sammy to fury. 'Get that wean to shut the fuck up!'

Jessie gave one more huge wail then there was an enormous bang as the gun exploded, the bullet hurling Jessie against the wall, the pale yellow paintwork stained with red as she slid down it.

'You bastard!' Mary took two steps towards Sammy before a bullet felled her.

'Christ, Sammy, what the fuck!' gasped Billy Wilson.

'Don't blame me, I gave them fair warning. Now let's get out of here.'

'But what about her?' asked Billy, pointing at Maureen.

'She is a fucking witness, and a fucking traitor.'

'Sammy, no, for fuck's sake!' shouted Gordon Williams.

Maureen's body was racked with sobs. Sammy knelt down and looked into her tear-stained face. 'Maureen Cairns, you are hereby sentenced to death for treason to king and country. The sentence to be carried out with immediate effect by order of Samuel Wilson, Battalion Commander, the British Loyalist Army.'

Grabbing her hair, he turned her face away from him and fired one more time. 'A shot in the back of the head. A traitor's death.'

The intense silence after the final shot was broken only by the sound of Gordon Williams throwing up in the far corner of the living room.

OFFICE OF THE SENIOR SPECIAL ADVISER, SCOTTISH PARLIAMENT, EDINBURGH, 10.30 A.M.

George had endured the giggles as he had walked along the corridor to his office, and Morven hadn't been able to look him in the eye while they had been doing the diary for the week ahead together. And now this.

Ross's fleshy, glowering face was looking right at him. 'Since you are this government's premier press specialist, paid for at great expense by the Scottish taxpayer, I assume you noticed in passing the front page of this morning's *Sun*?'

'Christ, Ross, give me a break.'

Ross held up the front page with the banner headline 'Make Love Not War'.

'No? Then do let me read it to you. "As the world teeters on the brink of the Third World War, George Wallace, Ross Johnson's Number 2, had only one thing on his mind. As our exclusive pictures reveal, there was only one missile on show as he and luscious Clare got down to some serious negotiations. George was clearly determined to break down barriers between nations. There was no border tension as Braveheart SCOTTISH leader George bonked leggy lovely, Clare, who is an ENGLISH civil servant."'

Ross looked up from the newspaper. 'More pictures and details on pages three, four and five under the headline "Crisis? What Crisis?"'

'Look, Ross, I would complain, but it will take for ever and you know those toothless bastards at the Press Complaints Commission will do nothing. If you need me to resign, obviously I will.'

'Resign? You must be joking. This is the only story that has taken the heat off me in the last forty-eight hours. I mean, I always said you were the coming man of Scottish politics but I didn't know it was literally true.'

They laughed. For a brief, lovely moment, it felt like the old days again. 'And anyway,' Ross continued, 'I owe you. People in glass houses and all that . . .'

'Of course, we'll always have Paris.'

The famous line from *Casablanca* had been adopted by those members of the Tartan Army who had been fortunate to be in the crowd when James McFadden's magnificent strike had consigned the multi-starred French national side to defeat in Paris back in 2007.

Both George and Ross had been there. George's night had finished at 4 a.m. in the Highlander bar across from the Pont Ncuf, as the condensation ran down the walls from the partying fans. Ross's had finished a little later in the Pigalle. George had ensured that neither girl spoke and that Ross was never identified. Ross was eternally grateful, but always kept his thanks jokey.

'I seem to recall, George, that you were feverishly dancing to the Bay City Rollers' "Shang–A–Lang" as the goal was played on a loop on the TV.'

'Perhaps, but I would like to stress that I was only enjoying that song in a postmodern, ironic way.'

'Of course you were,' laughed Ross. 'But your secret is safe with me. That is what friends do for each other.'

The significance of the remark was not lost on either man.

'But seriously,' George sighed, 'poor Clare is mortified. She has spent half the morning hiding in the ladies' loo over at the Constitution Unit.'

'I am sure she's embarrassed, but she'll get over it,' Ross responded. 'More important, it does your reputation no harm. You always said to me a political career can survive anything but ridicule. You are now the "SNP Stud" – quite a compliment. Half the press thought you were a big jessie, so you should be grateful. It's the third most requested image on YouTube, so you're even doing your bit in attracting the younger generation to the party.'

Ross glanced back down at the open paper. 'Mind you, you should definitely consider getting your back waxed.'

Their joint mirth was interrupted by Morven's shocked face at the door. She stuttered, barely able to get the words out. 'That's the police on the phone. Oh, Jesus, George, it's Maureen . . .'

BBC SCOTLAND HEADQUARTERS, PACIFIC QUAY, GLASGOW, 8 P.M.

Ross and George were in the back of the black ministerial Jaguar, knowing this was the last time they would have any privacy before the broadcast. Ross was absolutely insistent to his old friend. 'Maureen's death changes everything, George, can't you see that? You saw my draft last night. I was willing to make all the soothing noises you and the others wanted – to hint at compromise. But now we have the moral high ground and we should use that relentlessly to our advantage.'

George had been completely shocked at how quickly Ross had recovered from the blow of Maureen Cairns' murder. He had hardly seemed to grieve at all before starting to analyse the political ramifications. George had struggled to keep up with Ross's thinking while dealing with his own grief. 'Christ, Ross, it's really dangerous,' George warned. 'We are pursuing a path of open resistance to the world's only superpower.'

'But a superpower that doesn't want to be on the side of murderous terrorism!' Ross was animated, almost excited. 'Every political instinct tells me I am right on this. Have you seen the blogs and the instant polls? Listened to the talk shows? The people are swinging behind me – I mean, behind us. Even CND have paused their protest at the Russian nuclear missiles being at Faslane in sympathy.'

'And you are sure the Cabinet is fully supportive of your stance?'

Ross was contemptuous. 'That useless shower? You should have seen them this afternoon: a shiver ran through the room looking for a spine to run up. They are no use at a time like this. I'll have to drive this policy on my own. Well, with your help. I know I can trust you.'

It was just as well that Ross chose that moment to heave himself out of the car without looking at his friend for a response to that statement. George was sure his face would have betrayed him.

The interim chairman of the Scottish Broadcasting Corporation, the SBC, Lewis Graham, was waiting to greet them on the steps of the glass-fronted reception at Pacific Quay. He knew the BBC, one of the last of the truly British institutions, would break up with the declaration of independence in just over four weeks' time. Plans were already highly advanced for a fully autonomous SBC, which would buy in some programming from London but run its own schedule.

Lewis Graham was really hopeful that, as a loyal nationalist, he would get the top job. Therefore, he knew exactly on which side his bread was buttered. 'First

Minister, George, a pleasure to see you both. Come on up, the studio is ready. How was the journey through? I do hope independence will improve the traffic on the M8 . . .'

As Graham chatted on as they made their way to the studio, George admired once more the way that Ross could cut out the surrounding prattle and focus on the task in hand.

TV showed Ross at his most charismatic. The camera loved his unflinching gaze. It made him seem sincere. Even his physical fleshiness seemed to lend gravitas. Ross's broadcast was stern and firm, with just the right amount of tenderness. 'People of Scotland. I would like to speak to you tonight about an issue that has dominated all our thoughts over the last few days. But before I do, I would like to pay tribute to Maureen Cairns, who tragically lost her life earlier today.'

Ross's eyes misted. 'Maureen was a gifted politician, a good friend and above all a devoted wife and mother. Our thoughts tonight go out to her husband Rob, who lost not only his wife but his beautiful little daughter, Jessie. And, of course, to Mary MacDonald's parents, whose daughter gave her life trying to protect that wee girl.

'It was typical of Maureen that she rejected extra security because she wanted to live as normal a family life as possible. But no amount of security could have protected her, or anyone, from this brutal terrorist attack.

'Maureen Cairns gave her life for Scotland, the country she loved. I say to you tonight, my fellow citizens, let her sacrifice not be in vain. Let her dream of a free Scotland become a reality. Let that be her legacy. I also say we cannot – *we will not* – give in to terrorism. These vicious, cold-blooded murders must reinforce our commitment to the path of democracy. The Scottish people have spoken. They have voted for self-determination. They will not be denied.

'It is true that I have offered military facilities to Russia. That is because the Russians – unlike the English and Americans – have offered to support us in our difficult transition to nationhood. In just a month's time, we will finally be a sovereign nation. We can withdraw these military facilities at any time we choose. Our Russian friends are no threat to our democracy and way of life. Their generosity and support have been in stark contrast to the bullying behaviour of the United States.

'We Scots have no quarrel with the American people. But I have worked all my life to see Scotland free and I will not allow it to be pushed around by any nation, no matter how powerful. The motto of the ancient Scottish kings was *Nemo me impune lacessit* – "No one attacks me with impunity" – or, as we would say more colloquially, "Who dares meddle wi' me?" I want that spirit to continue in the new Scotland. Our new Scotland. My message to the United States government is the same as my message to the British Loyalist Army. In the words of one of America's greatest spirituals, "We shall not be moved." Thank you for listening. Goodnight.'

George eventually prised Ross away from the congratulatory crowd, headed by the oily Lewis Graham, and they descended the wide sandstone stairs of the atrium to the reception hall.

They stopped to say their farewells. The two men hugged – that awkward male hug which includes slapping on the back so that no form of intimacy is suspected. 'Sometimes you're just the best, Ross. A fantastic broadcast. Let's hope it gives the Americans pause for thought. Are you going straight to the Scottish CBI dinner?'

'Yes, I have ten minutes of deathless prose composed for our captains of industry,' replied Ross with deep sarcasm.

'Be nice, Ross, we need all the friends we can get.'

'OK, no problem. What about you?'

'I have the joys of the American media now. At least you have given them a great story, so we won't lack for things to talk about.'

'Ah, the press, just be sure to let lying dogs sleep. See you later.'

'Cheers, Ross.'

George took a deep breath of the soft summer air as he headed to the pedestrian Millennium Bridge which spanned the River Clyde fifty metres from the front entrance of the BBC. Just on the other side was the Crowne Plaza Hotel, where he had arranged to meet key American journalists after the broadcast. Straight ahead of him, the floodlit Victorian Gothic tower of the University of Glasgow dominated the skyline.

He stopped in the middle of the bridge to collect his thoughts and to admire the regeneration on both banks of the river. After decades of turning its back on the source of so much of its character and wealth, the city had finally brought the Clyde back to life. He loved the contrast of the new aluminium and steel with the Victorian rotundas which marked the entry and exit of the nineteenth-century tunnel under the Clyde and the industrial masculinity of the vast Finneston crane.

The evening sun played across the stainless steel silver skin of the Armadillo concert hall and illuminated the imposing struts of the Clyde Arc. George loved the fact that Glaswegians had refused to call this piece of modern engineering anything but the 'Squinty Bridge'. So much so that the traffic bulletins on commercial radio had been forced to do the same.

The power of public opinion at work. Maybe it was going to be OK for Scotland after all.

He glanced down at his watch. Nine o'clock. Never pays to be late for the fourth estate. Lost in his thoughts, George barely noticed the black Cherokee Jeep coming up the road which separated the end of the Millennium Bridge from the Crowne Plaza reception.

He stopped as it slowed down for the speed bump, ready to step behind it to cross the road. The back door swung open and two smartly-dressed men jumped out. Ignoring his protests they manhandled him expertly into the back seat, all in twenty seconds.

'Oh, Christ,' thought George, as they squeezed in on either side of him.

They were speaking Russian.

CHAPTER 10

MONDAY, 30 JUNE — THIRTY-ONE DAYS TO INDEPENDENCE

THE SCOTTISH CBI DINNER, THE HILTON HOTEL, GLASGOW, 9 P.M.

The Scottish CBI's annual dinner was always the highlight of the business calendar. Although the organisation had lost many of its younger and more radical members to the Entrepreneurial Exchange, it was still seen as the voice of industry and carried great weight with the government. Due to these defections, the Scottish CBI was more conservative than its English counterpart and loathed Scottish nationalism with a passion.

That was what made tonight's event truly extraordinary. As Ross Johnson entered the room and walked to join the top table, he was met by thunderous applause. Some of the tables even gave him a standing ovation. As he passed through the crowd, Ross beamed his pleasure at this remarkable turnaround.

But no one at the Cowan Construction table was applauding. Robert Cowan surveyed the scene with barely concealed disgust. What a shower of spineless scum. Cowan could not deny that the murder of Maureen Cairns and her daughter had been a blow to the Unionist cause, but this response was ridiculous. How could sensible businessmen allow emotion over one regrettable incident to cloud their rational judgement on where their best interests truly lay? It would require a substantial propaganda effort on the part of the SUR to combat this nonsense.

For once, he wasn't at all satisfied. And neither was the man sitting at his right-hand side, his friend Alistair Stroud, the chief constable of Strathclyde Police Force.

THE OVAL OFFICE, THE WHITE HOUSE, WASHINGTON DC, 6 P.M.

Todd MacFarlane sat alone on the bench outside the Oval Office which faced the Rose Garden, deep in thought. He silently surveyed the small but beautifully kept plot, now a riot of colour: pink, white and red blooms on every bush, bathed in early evening sun.

He knew this was a defining moment in his presidency, just as the Depression had been for FDR and 9/11 had been for George W. Bush. He had to be strong: resolute, tough, a man. He had to fight the self-loathing that constantly gnawed at him.

The one accusation MacFarlane could not bear to hear was that he was weak – a wimp. That brought back too many painful memories. It reminded him of a secret he had never discussed with another human being. A secret memory he recalled every day of his life. A memory that defined him, then and now.

MacFarlane had been an 'army brat', never settling in any place for more than a couple of years as he and his family joined his Marine colonel father in postings in Germany and all across America.

A sensitive boy, MacFarlane could not recall ever having a close school friend. He hated becoming close to someone just to be wrenched apart, so chose not to make the effort at all. The relentless moving made him lonely and introspective, absorbed in his own private world.

The incident that changed his life happened in high school in North Carolina when his father's regiment was stationed there. MacFarlane was a ninth-grader, just fourteen, tall, skinny and gangly. But he had fantastic hand–eye co-ordination, and he knew how to catch a football.

He had been trying out as a wide receiver for the junior varsity football team and had lingered in the locker room after his shower trying to analyse the weaknesses in his performance – even then, a perfectionist about everything he did, and eager to live up to the relentless expectations of his father.

He had heard four varsity seniors, all starting linebackers, horsing around in the next aisle. Curious, he pressed himself against the end of the row of green metal lockers and peered round.

He could still picture the scene now. Four beautiful, sculpted naked bodies leaping around, flicking short white towels at each other. Four laughing gods. Todd was entranced. He felt his penis swell with desire.

Suddenly one of the four noticed him. 'Hey, you, boy, come here.'

MacFarlane feverishly looked round for escape. There was none. Terrified, he stepped out from behind the locker. There could be no disguising the bulge in his shorts.

'Well, boys, we seem to have found us a genuine little faggot. Now what do you think we should do about that?'

'We should kill the disgusting little fucker,' sneered one.

'No, wait, I have a better idea,' responded another.

Then it happened.

The four rapidly pinned MacFarlane to the floor. One went to his locker and came back with a box of matches. He carefully selected one. MacFarlane would never forget the image of his cruel, handsome face, his brow furrowed in concentration.

He carefully inserted a match into the end of MacFarlane's penis and kept pushing down. The pain was excruciating.

Then he lit it.

Their laughter as his screams echoed through the locker room haunted him still. The physical disfigurement from the burn was still evident nearly forty years later.

MacFarlane had been too ashamed to go to the doctor. Equally unthinkable was confiding in his God-fearing father. So he dealt with his pain and humiliation alone and resolved that he would never allow himself to be so weak again.

Six months later, the family moved to Georgia and MacFarlane started a new high school. He redoubled his efforts to be perfect. He developed his mind, devouring every book he could find, and graduated *summa cum laude* and top of his class.

Equally important to him, he worked relentlessly to build his body through punishing sessions in the gym, surreptitiously admiring the bodies on the machines beside him, but making sure he was never caught staring.

As he acquired muscle, he switched from wide receiver to quarterback and won Most Valuable Player in his senior year, paving the way for a full football scholarship at the University of Georgia, making his father the proudest man in the state.

A naturally talented actor, MacFarlane adopted the hyper-masculinity of the Southern good ol' boy, learning to hunt and to talk about car engines, despite both subjects boring him senseless.

Throughout this transformation of mind and muscle, MacFarlane, knowing he was destined for great things, had been incredibly discreet about his sexuality. There had been only two male lovers in his life, one in his fraternity at the

University of Georgia, the other at law school at Yale. The former was now a senior circuit judge in the state of Georgia, the latter a leading light at Goldman Sachs on Wall Street. Both, like MacFarlane, now married with children. Neither, like MacFarlane, had any incentive to discuss the past – a perfect pact of mutual prevented destruction.

In 1994, MacFarlane had married Janice Fulton, a New York heiress from the liberal Rockefeller wing of the Republican Party he had met at law school. This had successfully quashed the growing rumours around his confirmed bachelor status. They had two beautifully groomed adolescent sons.

Todd had chosen ambition over sexual freedom. Now in a position of public prominence, he had no option but to forego any homosexual activity. He had to satisfy himself by remembering those sculpted youths – that fed his masturbatory fantasies and helped him to get through the chore of fathering children with his wife.

She had accepted the situation very early on in their marriage, a deal never discussed, though completely understood by them both. Janice devoted herself to her duties as First Lady, a position she adored, and her charity work. And she continued a very discreet affair with her old college sweetheart from Yale. She and MacFarlane hadn't shared a bedroom for most of the last decade.

MacFarlane's rise up the Republican Party had been remarkable. With his marriage, he had been able to reunite the party in a way not seen since Ronald Reagan's heyday in the 1980s. He brought the 'guns and God' Southern wing, Fulton's family the small-government but socially liberal party of the north-eastern states. Together, the two wings of the Grand Old Party had sought salvation in MacFarlane, a classic all-American boy who combined brains and brawn.

MacFarlane's father had left the Marines in the late 1990s and set up a hugely successful business manufacturing bulletproof vests for the armed forces, another beneficiary of the golden revolving door between the Pentagon and the US defence industries. His money and the network of Southern businessmen led by Jane Chalmers' father combined with the Fulton family's New York property empire had provided the seed finance for MacFarlane's bid for the White House.

Then MacFarlane had copied Barack Obama's tactics to defeat him, raising huge sums through millions of small donations in church collections and Internet click-and-donate offerings from people galvanised by his passionate brand of Christian populism.

But now he was here in the White House, there was no one to turn to. No one he could completely trust. Though he knew he was gay and accepted that, MacFarlane

----

constantly had to battle against the society around him with its jokes about fags and its clearly defined ideas about what constituted masculinity. This left him with the nagging doubt that he was not a proper man in the eyes of his father and the people he had grown up with, an anxiety compounded by the constant fear that he might be exposed by someone with a highly tuned 'gaydar'.

Although MacFarlane was the most powerful man in the world, an insistent part of him still felt himself to be the shameful faggot of that day in the locker room. The twin drives of this self-loathing and determination not to be weak battled constantly in MacFarlane's delicate psyche. His physical scarring was a constant reminder of the perils of weakness, so he struggled to contain and control his self-loathing. He could not be a wimp. He always needed to prove himself. The fate of the world rested on his flawed shoulders.

MacFarlane stood with a sigh and headed inside. He knew what he had to do. What the situation – and *his* situation – demanded.

Jane Chalmers, Charles Sands and Carl Butterworth all stood as the president entered the Oval Office. 'Do, please, sit,' he commanded. 'OK, you have all heard what First Minister Johnson said in his broadcast three hours ago. He has made his decision and so have I. Those missiles will have to go. As Iraq and Zimbabwe have shown in the past, economic sanctions will take years to force change, so it is time for alternatives. Operational update, please.'

Butterworth spoke first. 'As you requested, Jane and I have been working closely on the plans, as we believe it will require both military and intelligence personnel to be successful. We aim to strike at midnight on the thirty-first of July, at the very moment Scotland declares independence.

'We're working on a series of destabilising measures against the SNP government, culminating in a dramatic signal which will set off the actions of the three key players. They are our own forces, the political movement called the Scottish Unionist Resistance and,' Butterworth paused, trying to disguise his distaste, 'the irregular units of the British Loyalist Army.'

MacFarlane frowned. 'Can they be controlled, given the evidence of this morning's atrocity? Linking up with child-killers is not going to play well with middle America.'

Jane Chalmers cut in before Butterworth could respond. 'We're working on that, Mr President. The CIA is confident it can, um, *align* the conduct of the SUR and BLA so that they will operate professionally and in the interests of the United States. I have a crack team working on that as we speak.'

'OK, then what?'

Butterworth resumed his briefing with the briefest of glares at Chalmers. 'The BLA will be well provided with weapons.'

'Can those weapons be traced back to us?' MacFarlane asked anxiously.

'No, Mr President, they have come from stockpiles of IRA weapons that were supposed to have been put "beyond use" after peace came to Northern Ireland, but were siphoned off during the decommissioning process and secretly kept under our control in dumps on the Antrim coast.

'The BLA and US Special Operations troops will seize key government buildings in Edinburgh, Glasgow, Aberdeen and Dundee. Navy Seals will land at the Gare Loch and storm Faslane Naval Base, wresting control back from the Russians and destroying their offensive missiles before they can be made operational.'

'Are you sure of the timing on this, Carl?' probed MacFarlane. 'There's no danger they will be in a position to fire the missiles when we attack?'

'I'm pretty certain, sir. We have the base under constant surveillance. We know the missiles are Topol-Ms, the best the Russians have; they don't require silos to be launched. At the moment, protected by Special Ops troops, Russian technicians are working around the clock to install some of the missiles in the old Cold War silos in the hills above Faslane for maximum protection. They are also building some launch pads and a command and control centre within the base itself. Basically, they are spreading the target as wide as possible. But our experts believe it will be at least five more weeks before they're ready.'

'That seems incredibly tight to me, only a week's grace. I hope you're right, for all our sakes,' replied MacFarlane. 'Do, please, continue.'

'In addition, Special Ops agents from the CIA will seize control of BBC Scotland and Scottish Television's headquarters on Pacific Quay in Glasgow, which will give us control over the broadcast media. At five past midnight, Robert Cowan, the head of the Scottish Unionist Resistance, will address the nation on the two main TV channels. He will say that he has taken power to restore order and to avoid a catastrophe for Scotland. He will announce that he has taken immediate steps to remove the Russian missiles and also promise a new referendum within six months.'

'Can we rely on Cowan's loyalty?'

Again Chalmers jumped in. 'Absolutely, sir. The Scottish Unionist Resistance is well funded and well organised, but it is a movement of chiefs without Indians. It has skilfully taken advantage of the collapse of the traditional Unionist parties into squabbling factions, but it has no grassroots organisation of its own.

'Cowan will hope to win the referendum and any subsequent election to the Scottish Parliament – and we can help make sure he does, so his loyalty is assured. He needs us. Desperately. He may be a son-of-a-bitch, but at least he is our son-of-a-bitch.'

MacFarlane nodded his understanding and turned back to Butterworth. 'How many US personnel will be needed, Carl?'

'I reckon around seven hundred, Mr President. Two hundred and fifty Navy Seals in the Gare Loch. Two hundred CIA and army Special Ops secretly put ashore at Leith and based in safe houses in Edinburgh, and around two hundred and fifty CIA Special Ops, including communications specialists, to organise the TV broadcasts.

'The destroyer USS *Roosevelt* from the Sixth Fleet based in the Mediterranean will sail up from the English Channel and anchor in the Firth of Forth if backup is required, but I don't anticipate that happening. Finally, we have had two senior employees of Prestwick Airport on the payroll since the rendition flights of the early 2000s. I would propose that we have three hundred Marines in a tourist charter plane on the tarmac in reserve. They could be in Glasgow in half an hour if there is any form of civil disorder, but, again, we don't foresee that. There hasn't been violent political turbulence in Scotland since the days of the Red Clydesiders after the First World War. It is not in the Scots' political DNA any more. By way of comparison, Mr President, the last major regime change we engaged in, Operation Enduring Freedom to topple the Taliban in Afghanistan in 2001, involved around four hundred personnel, one hundred CIA and three hundred military Special Operations.'

'Possible resistance?'

'The main force that will come under Scottish government command on the first of August is the Royal Regiment of Scotland. It has five regular and two territorial battalions, around six thousand men in total.'

'That sounds a hell of a lot against seven hundred, Carl,' said MacFarlane doubtfully.

Butterworth, as always, was persuasive and articulate. 'In normal circumstances, we would want and expect our attacking forces to have a three-to-one superiority, sir, but these are not normal circumstances. First, the regiment will not yet be under the Scottish government's control. It's scheduled to take a new oath of loyalty on the afternoon of Friday the first of August at a ceremony at Edinburgh Castle, twelve hours after the coup. Most of the soldiers will be in their barracks on the Thursday night, polishing their boots for the big day. Second, morale has been low since the forced amalgamation of the historic Scottish regiments in 2006 and it is not the fighting force it once was. Third, we believe the soldiers' loyalties will be split. As the name suggests, their traditional allegiance has been to the monarchy, and the new king replaced his mother as colonel-in-chief. Would they rise against a new Scottish Unionist regime which is specifically monarchist in defence of an SNP government which is committed to abolishing the role of the monarchy in Scotland?'

The president looked intently at the admiral, clearly still unconvinced. 'I'm afraid it seems a big risk to me, Carl, for an operation we cannot permit to fail.'

'I understand, sir. Therefore, if the operation is given the go-ahead tonight, we plan to ensure that the officers of the regiment, who we believe are sympathetic to the SUR to a man, are worked on to bring them round. At the very least that should ensure all the battalions are confined to barracks on the night of the thirty-first of July. And once the coup is a fait accompli, we are sure they will fall in line.

'I'm not sure if Leon Trotsky has ever been quoted in the Oval Office before, Mr President, but I was really struck by one of his sayings I heard when I was doing my international relations Master's at Penn. He was undoubtedly right when he said, "A revolution is not so much against the army as for the army." Quite simply, if we have control of the Royal Regiment, then we have control of Scotland. The Communists weren't wrong about everything.'

MacFarlane laughed. He was becoming more and more impressed with his joint chief. And his rivalry with Jane and Charles was useful: easier for him to keep control by playing them off against each other.

'And remember, sir,' Butterworth continued, 'as well as the men in Prestwick, the Sixth Fleet destroyer has around three hundred Marines available as a back-up if my analysis is overly optimistic and we do face sporadic resistance in the capital.'

'Potential casualties?'

'Hard to say, Mr President. Our intelligence suggests there are around fifty Russian combat troops dug in with their technicians at Faslane, with another one hundred or so guarding the silos in the hills, so it depends if they put up a fight or not. That could get messy, as the base has excellent natural defences, ones we helped to enhance. Possibly isolated Scottish resistance apart from that, but there are no armed groups on the nationalist side so they can be as angry as they like, but they can't harm us. I would estimate no more than fifty killed and wounded at best, two hundred at worst.'

'And Russia?'

'Furious but impotent, sir. Our missile defence systems in Poland and the Czech Republic are primed. If they are stupid enough to try to launch a strike, we will take out all of their nuclear missiles. We now have a lock on three of their Borei nuclear subs and I hope to have the fourth pegged this week so we can neutralise any sea-based attack.'

'OK, good. Jane, anything to add?'

Chalmers was delighted to return to the conversation after that smooth bastard Butterworth had hogged the limelight for so long, trying to be so smart with his fancy historical quotations. She tried hard not to let her irritation show by being as businesslike as possible. 'Just that we plan to help the BLA to take out some of the key leaders of the SNP on that day, to decapitate any resistance to the coup. I would like your explicit authority for that.'

'More state-sponsored assassination, Jane? I would have thought the Chavez affair would have sated your appetite for that.'

Chalmers blushed deeply. Praise for Butterworth and criticism for her, her worst nightmare. But she was determined to persist. 'I think it is absolutely essential here to give the Cowan regime a fair wind. I am talking about no more than two or three people.'

'Let's pick that up later. Politics, Chuck.'

Todd glanced round at his chief of staff, who had visibly paled as this conversation had progressed. His mind had been constantly switching between the nightmare scenario unfolding in front of him and the more mundane issue of how he could manage to find more time to spend with Maryanne, his sweet young assistant. He forced himself to focus. 'Well, I guess I don't have to spell out to you what a political disaster this is, Mr President, and I think only the most extreme threat to our national security would make it worth even considering. On the plus side, if the coup is a bloodless success, then you should, and will, take credit for it. If it fails or involves significant casualties, in spite of Carl's optimistic analysis, then the fact that we have kept it to just this small group gives you deniability.'

Sands carefully refrained from saying what everyone in the room knew. In that event, one of the three of them would have to take the bullet for the president. But no one knew which one. 'However, even if you are completely victorious and vindicated, we'll still be crucified at the United Nations from the Security Council downwards. It's certainly possible that some of the smaller European Union countries will break off diplomatic relations in solidarity with Scotland. The whole Islamic world will see it as one more example of heavy-handed American bullying after Iraq. And we will drive the Russians into the warm embrace of the Chinese in a way we haven't seen since the high point of the Sino–Soviet alliance of the 1960s.

'The Chinese might decide to sell more dollars as a sign of disapproval, which will further weaken our currency. The dollar is only just recovering from the decision of the Arab countries to ditch it as a reserve currency and to price oil in euros. I'm not sure it could stand another major shock. So pretty much as bad as it could be, Mr President.'

The whole room paused to consider this sobering analysis. MacFarlane broke the silence. 'I think we are all aware of the potential dangers, Chuck, but I have made my decision. I, and America, need to be completely resolute on this issue.'

After a brief pause, which MacFarlane intended to underline his authority, he added, 'Anything else?'

Butterworth responded. 'Yes, Mr President. You need to speak to the prime minister. We don't need – or expect – English military assistance, but we do need their understanding. There may well be ramifications from a coup on their doorstep – financial issues and refugees through to internal anger from expatriate Scots. I'd like them on board.'

'I'll certainly do that. It's always a real pleasure to speak to Mr Jones,' responded the president sarcastically. 'OK, I think that is everything I need to know apart from one fact. What's the name of this operation?'

Butterworth didn't give Chalmers a chance to butt in this time. 'We were thinking Operation Righteous Wrath, if you agree, sir.'

'Very biblical, Carl, I like that.'

'So, sir, we need a formal "go" to start our detailed planning. Even if there are no official minutes of this meeting, this needs to come directly from the commander-in-chief.'

Like all presidents at moments like these, Todd's thoughts turned automatically to his place in history. He was aware this decision could make him a hero in the mould of Woodrow Wilson in the First World War or John Kennedy over the Cuban Missile Crisis, or a villain like Lyndon B. Johnson over Vietnam or George W. Bush in Iraq.

The leader of the free world looked at the three expectant faces and nodded. 'It's a "go".'

MELVILLE'S LOCK-UP GARAGES, PAISLEY ROAD WEST, GLASGOW, 10 P.M.

Colonel Karimov sat in the airless and windowless garage waiting for the arrival of George Wallace, silently rehearsing what he was going to say and do, and reflecting on how often he had been in situations like this in his life.

Karimov had always enjoyed exercising power over people, bending them to his will. But always with just cause. Always to advance the interests of Russia.

He took pride in the fact that he wasn't a butcher like so many of the former KGB men who made up the bulk of the current FSB. He was a professional, an artist. On occasion, of course, brute force was required, but usually the anticipation of it was sufficient to persuade people. Much more effective, and long-lasting, was a psychological victory. Bruises healed, but fear of a secret exposed or a family member threatened kept their power for ever.

Karimov had reached the height of his powers in Poland in the early 1980s after the Solidarity movement had briefly threatened to topple the Communist government. He had been a member of the elite KGB unit sent in to restore control. One trade unionist had been turned by a scholarship for his only child to study in London, one priest swayed by a threat to expose his paedophilia. The carrot and the stick: the oldest and most effective tools of his psychological trade.

If Poland had been the high point, then East Germany in the autumn of 1989 had been the nadir. He had sat in the back of the lorry with his Stasi colleagues, Kalashnikov cocked, watching the crowds blow whistles and bang pots as they marched through East Berlin demanding freedom.

Even today, Karimov was still convinced the rabble, after forty years of living in fear, would have dispersed at the first volley. But neither Gorbachev nor the old man Honecker had had the balls to give the order. The useless, spineless bastards.

And so they had fled before so-called 'people power', like common criminals in the night. And the world had seen the results of such cowardice – the collapse of the Berlin Wall and the Communist governments which sheltered behind it, the impoverishment and humiliation of Russia and the advancement of the NATO enemy to Kiev and beyond. Shameful, deeply shameful.

Even worse was to follow when the KGB was disbanded after the hard-line coup against Yeltsin in August 1991. Slowly and surely, they had rebuilt their influence. Karimov was made head of the British section of the FSB when it was established in 1995. Different initials, same people.

Like most Russians, Karimov deeply resented the loss of Eastern Europe, which they always referred to as the 'near abroad'. He had welcomed the restoration of Russian power fuelled by oil at 250 euros a barrel and Western Europe's crippling dependence on Russian natural gas.

And he had relished leading an FSB squad which had cleared South Ossetia of Georgian-sympathising scum in the summer of 2008, delighted to see the West humbled and helpless.

Now, if Operation Braveheart succeeded, Russian influence would reach to the Atlantic for the first time in recorded history. This would be an achievement greater than Peter the Great's, when he opened St Petersburg to the Baltic, greater than Tsar Alexander II's, when he defeated Napoleon and marched in triumph through Paris. And greater even than Stalin's, when he placed the red flag on top of the Reichstag.

And, he, Sergei Karimov, would be at the heart of this history. Twenty years of spying, lobbying and intelligence analysis behind the scenes were going to pay off in spectacular style. He was going to lead Russia to victory.

Not some tawdry torturer, but the man who made it happen.

Karimov turned his thoughts back to George. This would be an interesting man to control. Honest and intelligent, but vain and ambitious. George was in good physical condition but not combat-hardened like him. Not too much of a challenge – this was not going to be an artistic victory, just a necessary chore.

Raised voices at the door signalled George's arrival. Karimov rose to greet him. George was not very pleased to see him.

'What the hell do you think you are doing? Have you any idea how much trouble you are in, you shit? I am the second most important . . .'

George's words trailed off as he realised the absurdity of what he was saying, given that Karimov was flanked by four of the meanest-looking men he had ever seen. Four of the meanest-looking *armed* men he had ever seen.

Karimov greeted George's outburst with only an amused raised eyebrow, then spoke briskly. 'Please forgive the slightly unorthodox meeting, George, but it was essential that I speak to you in private and uninterrupted.'

Karimov closed off further protests from George with a raised hand. 'It's of no importance what you think of me, or indeed what I think of you. You need to calm down and you need to listen to me. Right now. So, please sit down.'

Realising there was little alternative, George sat in a tatty old dining-room chair in the centre of the garage and looked expectantly at the Russian. Karimov was cool, clear and contained. It was essential to the plan that George believed everything he said. 'I am perfectly aware that you were the source of Jessica

Schwartz's story in the *New York Times* which has caused me and my political bosses no little difficulty in the last few days.'

'You can't know it was me,' protested George.

'Oh, I do know it was you. And the reason I do is that one of our agents has informed me that the story was passed to you by MI6, who knew you would be too weak to keep it to yourself. They knew you would seek the security of the moral high ground.

'And also, George, we have been following you for the last eight weeks, including to your cosy tête-à-tête with Jessica Schwartz at her flat in London. Lovely red dress she was wearing, incidentally.'

George desperately tried to think of a response which would protect Clare as the source of his information. She had obviously been used by her friend at the Ministry of Defence. 'No, no, you're wrong. It was a leak from inside the Russian side,' was the best he could muster. He didn't even think it sounded convincing himself.

Colonel Karimov advanced towards him. George's body tensed, anticipating the blow. Instead he reached into his jacket pocket and handed him a personnel record, identifying Clare Stephenson as an agent of MI6. George speed-read the opening page then threw the folder back at the Russian. 'What is this bollocks, Karimov? You don't impress me with your cheap forgeries. Clare is a civil servant, pure and simple. She has clearly been exploited by the powers that be.'

'Oh, really?'

Colonel Karimov went to the table and extracted a large Manila envelope from his briefcase.

The photographs were the kind that had date and time stamps in the bottom right-hand corner. They showed Clare meeting the same man in a variety of locations in Edinburgh, including the Harvey Nichols terrace café on Saturday afternoon, when she was supposed to have been shopping with a friend, the same Saturday George had been drinking in The Iron Duke with his uncle Tommy. 'This man is David Smart, Clare's handler at MI6. He is number three in the hierarchy at Vauxhall Cross.'

George could feel his certainty draining away.

'Still not convinced?' questioned Karimov. 'Then maybe this will help.'

Karimov brought out an iPod and a set of mini-speakers. He carefully selected a downloaded file. It was a recording of a conversation and one of the voices was unquestionably Clare's. She was on a mobile phone. 'Yeah, he took it hook, line and sinker. The silly old bastard behaved like a wee boy. I thought he was going to burst into tears at one point. I mean, honestly. Lots of stuff about Ross trusting him and not starting a Third World War. How he would know if Ross was planning something, and that they were great friends. And how he was too important to have been kept out of the loop. The old fool.'

Then she laughed. She actually laughed. And of all he had heard, nothing tore at George's heart like that laugh.

He was vaguely aware of Karimov speaking: the words slowly swam into focus. Once he was sure George was paying attention, Karimov began again. 'Now, George, here's what I need you to do. I know you are friendly with the Americans but I need you to see the new reality. The Russians are the allies of the Scots now. I need you to be working to deepen and consolidate that alliance in all our interests. Do you understand?'

George stared at Karimov and nodded dumbly.

TUESDAY, 1 JULY — THIRTY DAYS TO INDEPENDENCE

COWAN CONSTRUCTION HEADQUARTERS, WEST REGENT STREET, GLASGOW, 10 A.M.

Robert Cowan stood at the massive, full-length window that made up the front wall of his office, surveying the city centre laid out before him. He was not normally a demonstrative man, regarding a display of emotion as a sign of weakness, but he was at this moment desperately trying to contain his excitement at what he had just been told. He knew it was important to appear statesmanlike at all costs.

He turned back to face his guest, Thomas Atkinson, the UK bureau chief of the CIA. 'When we last met, Thomas, you were only making contingency plans. Now you tell me that regime change *is* going to happen. What convinced you?'

'After Johnson's TV speech, we felt we had no option. He clearly – and publicly – committed himself to letting the Russians and their missiles stay, and we will not permit that. It is a disaster, not only for the United States, but for Scotland. I have spent some time in Soviet satellite states and, let me tell you, there are not many laughs in life controlled by the Russians.'

Cowan wisely restrained himself from enquiring exactly what it was that Atkinson had been doing in Eastern Europe that was so unamusing and resumed the conversation. 'So, on the night of the thirty-first, you need me to go to BBC Scotland at Pacific Quay and make a televised address?'

'Exactly,' confirmed Atkinson. 'Our guys will have the satellites linked so that it simultaneously appears on STV, too.'

'And if there is resistance?'

'You will have a hand-picked group of Special Operations soldiers with you at all times. The BBC only has two unarmed and ageing security guards on at that time on a Sunday night, so I don't anticipate any problems. I am assuming you would rather have our men than the BLA.'

Cowan grimaced. 'Yes, of course. I take on board what you said earlier about our friends in the BLA. The murder of Maureen Cairns was clearly a spectacular own goal. But I think, as you do, that the temptation of the money and arms will be sufficient to bring them under our control. I will make that an immediate priority.'

'Yes, please do. I am relying on you.'

Cowan acknowledged his responsibility with a nod, then continued. 'And afterwards?'

'As the Soviets knew, in politics it is not the people who vote who count, but rather those who count the votes, if you follow my drift. I am sure that you won't have any problems legitimately winning the referendum this time round, but if you do fail, well, that can be managed, too.'

With that cynical remark, Atkinson rose to leave. He shook Cowan warmly by the hand. 'And, may I say, on a personal level I'm absolutely delighted that this is the path we're taking, Robert. Or should I say, *First Minister*?'

Cowan blushed. 'Well, Thomas, as Winston Churchill said, "You can always count on the Americans to do the right thing."'

'Thank you, Robert,' replied Atkinson warmly. 'I really appreciate that.'

Robert was glad that Thomas didn't know the rest of Churchill's dictum: 'Once they have exhausted all the other alternatives.'

NORTHUMBERLAND STREET, EDINBURGH, 11 A.M.

George hadn't really known what to expect. Denial? Guilt? Tears?

Anything but this cold hardness. This calculated indifference.

He had returned to the flat from Glasgow to find her finishing her packing. Her eyes emotionless, Clare listened to George's outpouring of anger and anguish in silence.

Finally she spoke, plainly and without emotion. 'For Christ's sake, George, grow up. What did you think was going on here? That I had been bowled over by your eloquence and charisma, like some lovestruck teenager? It wasn't personal, just a job that had to be done. My mission was to protect the British state. Living with you was just a price that had to be paid, as my boyfriend in London knew.

I've been exposed as an agent by the Russians, so now it's all over.'

'But you told me you loved me.' George was aware how pathetic this sounded, his natural sarcasm shredded by his raw pain.

'I told you that to stop you resigning. You were no use to me if you didn't have access to information. Simple as that.'

George felt his whole world crash around him as Clare trailed her suitcase to the front door. It was impossible. Unreal. Agony. He shook his head as if trying to expel the very idea of her departure from his mind.

George started to cry. Tears of pain and humiliation. He hadn't done that since Bridget's funeral. Clare turned round one last time and cast a pitying glance at the sobbing figure on the sofa.

'I'm sorry, George, but it was all fake. Especially the orgasms.'

CHAPTER 11

TUESDAY, 1 JULY — THIRTY DAYS TO INDEPENDENCE

NUMBER 10 DOWNING STREET, LONDON, 11 A.M.

Prime Minister Nick Jones hadn't spoken to President MacFarlane since he had told him about the Russian plans to put offensive missiles in Scotland over a week before. When his assistant told him MacFarlane was on the line on an E428 secure personal call, he was intrigued to know what the American response would be.

The truth staggered him.

Jones listened intently as the president outlined his audacious plans for a US-backed coup in Scotland which would place Robert Cowan and the SUR in government on the first of August. His mind raced as he tried to work out the political implications for his government.

Like most politicians, Nick's immediate response to a major crisis was to look for any potential personal pitfalls and his second was to think how the history books would judge him. On both grounds, the plan for a coup looked a very bad idea.

After a pause to let the idea sink in, the president resumed speaking. He tried to be at his most charming. 'I thought it was important to give you a heads-up, Prime Minister. Obviously, our plan has major ramifications for England, from financial services to potential refugee issues, but I can assure you it is our intention for the coup to be both quick and bloodless. We have plans in place to ensure the forces of law and order are on our side.'

Though Nick was horrified, he knew he needed to be measured in tone with England's most important ally. 'Thank you for updating me, Mr President, I really appreciate it. Obviously, it is a high-risk strategy but if you think you have no alternative then I suppose you must do what you think is right. Personally, I cannot believe it is proper to flout the democratic will of the Scottish people and I would prefer a continuation of economic and diplomatic pressure. But that must be a decision for you.'

Not for the first time, Todd MacFarlane was deeply irked by the tone taken by his English counterpart. He responded tartly. 'Well, Prime Minister, given the clear and present danger to the USA's vital national interests, I am afraid I don't have the luxury of your moral stance. The missiles, as you may have noticed, are not pointing at you. If, as it appears from your tone, I don't have your backing, it would be good to know I at least have your understanding for what we need to do.'

'The English are a tolerant and decent people, Mr President,' said Jones, trying to explain his way out of an argument, trying to be firm, but fair. 'This whole situation arose because of the disaster of devolution, a disaster many in my party predicted. The English like and admire the Scots, but they increasingly resented the Scots getting more than their fair share of public spending, despite Scotland being one of the poorest parts of the United Kingdom and contributing the least in taxation.

'English parents struggling to pay university fees couldn't understand why Scottish teenagers went free. English children struggling with infirm elderly parents couldn't understand why they paid for personal care while Scots got it free. The introduction of subsidised petrol three years ago by the SNP was the last straw for many. And when this gross unfairness was compounded by the constant whingeing of Scottish politicians, English patience snapped.

'Having said all that, you must understand that there is no hatred for Scotland and her people in England. We were all repulsed by the murder of Maureen Cairns and her little daughter. I cannot sell help for her killers. That's political suicide for me. There can be no question of English support, either military or political, for this *coup d'état*.'

MacFarlane tried to control his growing annoyance with Jones, but failed to keep the irritation out of his voice. 'As I said, Prime Minister, I don't need your support, merely your understanding. We believe that any use of English forces would be counterproductive, because it would stir up Scottish resistance. I don't need you to welcome the enforced change of government, just don't condemn it publicly. The most important issue from our perspective is that you seal the border to catch any potentially dangerous elements trying to escape. We particularly want to capture the SNP leadership. Those that survive, anyway.'

MacFarlane realised immediately that he had said too much. He had placed the possibility of assassination on the agenda. He silently cursed his foolishness.

Nick chose his next words carefully, not wanting to be complicit in a clear breach of international law. 'I am sorry, Mr President, but anyone fleeing here would have the right to claim political asylum and the English courts would not countenance returning them to a new, possibly illegitimate, Scottish regime or to the United States itself. You surely can't have forgotten the fuss over rendition flights eight years ago? And how would such actions play with the half a million Scots who live here? I would remind you that more Scots live in England than live in Edinburgh. The political union may be broken, but the social union lives on.'

MacFarlane sighed. As usual with Jones, he was making no progress. This prime minister was certainly no Thatcher or Blair. He saw little point in persisting with that argument so tried another tack. 'What do you think of Robert Cowan?'

'I've met Cowan a number of times,' Jones replied. 'I even spent the night on his estate once. He's intelligent, very ambitious and not overburdened with scruples, in my view. I am not sure his right-wing agenda will play in Scotland in the long term – the people are too left-wing for that. But I'm not clear what strategy you are trying to pursue here, Mr President. I need to make clear to you that, even if the Scottish Unionist Resistance succeed in their coup and win a new referendum, we don't want the Scots back. Not under any circumstances. England has moved on.'

MacFarlane was brutally frank in response. 'I don't think the fate of Robert Cowan is the critical issue here. His long-term survival is not a strategic necessity for the United States. The most important thing is that nuclear weapons are removed from Scotland by a friendly administration. If the English won't have the Scots back, then Mr Cowan will just have to settle for ruling an independent Scotland. From what I hear of his ambition, I am sure it is an idea he could get used to, no matter his current views on the Union.'

MacFarlane's final comment could not have been more pointed. 'And the United States will have an ally it can completely trust in the British Isles.'

Jones wisely bit his tongue and said a curt goodbye. He replaced the handset and leaned back in his chair. Worries crowded in on him. He was deeply concerned about the implications of having a failed state, wracked with civil disorder, on his border. Had the Americans learned nothing from Iraq?

Even worse, Jones was now in possession of information he wished he didn't have. He felt implicated in the illegal overthrow of a legitimate government and probably state-sponsored assassination, tainted by a policy he abhorred.

He also knew one thing for sure after that telephone call: Robert Cowan was not the only man he knew who was not overburdened with scruples.

Jones was struck by a sudden, heretical thought. Despite England's alliance with the US, did he have an obligation to warn Ross Johnson? He was a political opponent, but still a human being. Could he live with condoning Ross's possible murder by his silence?

He buzzed Tony Hodge. 'Come on up. We need to talk.'

THURSDAY, 3 JULY — TWENTY-EIGHT DAYS TO INDEPENDENCE

GLASGOW CATHEDRAL, 11 A.M.

George cursed when he saw the long queue of traffic on the High Street, one being constantly topped up by traffic streaming off the motorway. This was not a day to be late. He gave the taxi driver a tenner, told him to keep the change and jumped out at the ruined old Royal Infirmary building. Catherine made a rather more tentative exit from the taxi.

George made one final attempt to persuade his daughter to come to the service but she was adamant that she wanted to stay outside. She absolutely could not bear the thought of seeing young Jessie Cairns' coffin laid out in the cathedral. She preferred to listen to the service being relayed by loudspeakers in St Andrew's Square.

They agreed to meet in front of the Provand's Lordship building straight after the funeral and George hurried on through the crowd. He tried his best not to be rude as he squeezed past people in the open plaza in front of the cathedral, acutely aware that many had recognised him from the recent pictures in the *Sun*.

He had spent the last two nights at Catherine's flat in Glasgow, desperate to see only a friendly, non-judgemental face in the morning. Clare's departure was not yet widely known but George knew the English government would leak it when it best suited them. He dreaded the public humiliation.

He knew what was coming. The laughter. The finger-pointing. 'There's no fool like an old fool.'

Losing Clare had almost felt like another bereavement to him. When Bridget had died, Catherine had insisted that he go to see a therapist, knowing that her father's natural tendency would be to seek counselling of the liquid variety.

George had made a poor patient. Every part of his macho belief system was resistant to the very idea of therapy. He didn't recall much of the three frustrating sessions he had had with the irritatingly sympathetic young man with the overpowering aftershave before they had both agreed there was little point in continuing. In George's view, sympathy was what one woman gave another in return for information. He wanted to deal with his grief alone.

But George did remember him outlining Elisabeth Kübler-Ross's model of the stages of grief – denial, anger, bargaining, depression and acceptance. He said that you wouldn't necessarily experience all of them, or even have them in that order, but that you would go through at least two. That, at least, made sense to George.

With Bridget's death, he had gone through them all, in classic order. Denial: how could his lovely wife, who looked so healthy, be terminally ill? Anger: why was this happening to them, just as they were planning a life of travel and companionship once the kids had left home? Bargaining: please let her live long enough to see her daughter married. Depression: give me another drink. And finally, acceptance. The whole process had taken three years but even now there wasn't a day that passed that he didn't think about Bridget at some point, triggered by anything from a familiar phrase to a favourite flower. Grief was a life sentence without remission.

Clare's betrayal was different. It was still too raw for all the stages. Denial had been cut short by her brutal behaviour. He was incredibly angry and knew that only the continuing relentless pace of his political life was keeping him from depression. And the only acceptance he was ever likely to have was that he had been an idiot. A blind old fool.

George quickened his pace towards the studded wooden doors of the imposing cathedral, framed by the vast Victorian necropolis on the hill behind, a lasting monument to that society's obsession with the rituals of death.

The cathedral was located in the oldest part of the city, Glasgow's heart before the Victorians spread south and west in search of space and respite from the industrial pollution and misery. Now the cathedral lay between the gentrified yuppie flats of the Merchant City and the grinding poverty of the Gallowgate.

Perspiring slightly, George entered the cool semi-darkness and made his way to his seat in the second pew, where the senior politicians were seated behind the Cairns family. George hadn't been inside the cathedral since Donald Dewar's funeral, thirteen years before. How he could do with a measure of Donald's wily political wisdom now.

He was at the end of the row, beside a massive bunch of white lilies. The sweet, cloying, sickly smell was a horrible reminder of Bridget's funeral. The flowers of death.

George and Bridget had been married for nearly nineteen years when she died. They had met at the *Herald* newspaper in 1990, when George joined as a trainee journalist after returning from the States. After a whirlwind romance, she moved into his flat. They had married three months later. She was pregnant three months after that.

George had been welcomed into the heart of Bridget's large, noisy Irish-Catholic family. At first that seemed a liberation and a stark contrast to the rejection from his own family for marrying outside the faith.

He slowly realised it all came at a cost. As his children grew, they were expected to join in the rituals of a faith he found alien. And although he had put the interests of Bridget and the kids – *his* family – in front of the desires of his parents, he soon realised this would never be reciprocated.

Bridget would simply never make the same sacrifice – her family and faith were too important to her. Although she agreed he was rationally correct in his criticisms of Catholicism, she stayed true to the Mother Church. George was infuriated and resentful at the indulgence of beliefs as deeply reactionary as his own family's Orangeism.

Despite this fissure, they had enjoyed a successful marriage, with the all-consuming task of children leaving little time for deeper analysis. Like many couples, they were often guilty of believing that the absence of conflict equalled happiness. At the point when they had the time to explore these issues, Bridget was already dying, compounding George's grief.

Both had prospered in their careers. Bridget had left *The Herald* to become Scotland and Northern Ireland correspondent of *The Guardian* and had won awards for her sensitive coverage of the re-emergence of these two nations.

George had set up his PR company with two colleagues in 1994, specialising in high-end political lobbying and media advice for blue chip clients in both Scotland and England. In a business where personal relationships were everything, George had the best contacts book in the industry. He had finally sold the company early in 2009, securing his family's financial future. Two weeks after the celebratory party, Bridget was diagnosed with breast cancer.

He tried to close out the memory of his marriage and focus on the sermon, but couldn't stand the platitudes of a minister who had barely known Maureen. She had been a wonderful woman, the conscience of the party: loyal, thoughtful, warm, but not ruthless. Therefore, always the deputy.

He and Bridget had occasionally gone round to Maureen and Rob's for Sunday tea. After Bridget's death, George had often sought sanctuary there. Their house was always filled with warmth, especially when little Jessie had come along, when Maureen was forty-five, a gift she had almost given up hope of receiving. Both of George's children had been willing babysitters, which was why Catherine couldn't bear to see her coffin this morning.

As the words 'decency' and 'motherhood' drifted in the air, he looked up instead at the coffins twenty metres ahead of him. He felt the tears well in his eyes as he looked at Jessie's tiny white coffin lying like a toy beside her mother's and Mary's. Like all parents in the congregation, he was thinking of his own kids at that age. He remembered how sweet Catherine had been, an endlessly bubbly, cheery wee soul, with a mass of blonde curls. Jessie had been the same.

How could anyone have shot her?

He looked over at the reduced, crumpled figure of Rob Cairns in front of him and felt ashamed for grieving at Clare's behaviour. This was real bereavement. He really needed to pull himself together.

After the service, Maureen's coffin, with Ross Johnson taking one of the cords, was piped down the steps. Even though he wasn't religious, George loved the soaring beauty of 'Amazing Grace', especially played on the bagpipes. All around him people were weeping openly, unashamedly.

Outside, George saw to his astonishment that the crowd had swollen further. It filled the plaza to the Museum of Religion on the left and spilled out on to the High Street. A number of youths had clambered on to the statue of David Livingstone to get a better view, one adventurous youth precariously balanced on the stone Bible clutched in the missionary's marble left hand. Above the crowd fluttered a sea of Saltires and Lions Rampant. It looked more like a football game than a funeral.

Then he witnessed a phenomenon he hadn't seen since Princess Diana's funeral seventeen years before. People started to applaud the cortège as it passed, tentative at first, then more confident.

Something had stirred in the soul of Scotland.

FRIDAY, 4 JULY — TWENTY-SEVEN DAYS TO INDEPENDENCE

THE MILLENNIUM BRIDGE, GLASGOW, 9 A.M.

Sammy Wilson was silently seething. This was his gang. He didn't mind agreeing tactics with other guys in the BLA, but this was different. Some posh cunt and a fucking Yank telling him what to do. It just wasn't right. Taking orders. Guns for fucking hire.

But Sammy wasn't stupid. He had watched the boys' faces when they had seen the money. Seen their eyes when they had unwrapped the new gear: Kalashnikovs and Semtex. There were times you had to fight, but that hadn't been one of them. He would have lost: lost the vote, lost face, lost respect. That could not be permitted.

So, now they had their orders. The Americans wanted three weeks of destabilising action to prove that Scotland was ungovernable. Then the big day – a new government to stop the slide to anarchy and restore order. Solving a problem they had created themselves. Perfect. And the boys all walk away with ten grand each with the Union saved. Couldn't argue with that.

There had been a lot of talk in the pub from the new paymasters about no more cock-ups and Sammy had been sure they had been looking at him when they said that. Cheeky cunts. Anyway, he knew he had to be careful. No more mistakes. A true settling of scores with his enemies could wait. Let's see them try to control him and the BLA when the Unionists took over. 'That will be right.'

At least this operation was more straightforward. They had been watching the flat for two days solid. Her husband always left at 8 a.m. and drove into the city centre. She left around 8.40 and cycled over the Millennium Bridge, arriving at BBC Headquarters just before 9 a.m.

But not today.

Catherine Wallace whistled to herself as she followed the cycle path alongside the massive Glasgow Harbour development. After three months of constant sickness she knew she would never again take feeling well for granted.

At twenty-five weeks, she was just entering the blooming phase of pregnancy: shining hair, glowing skin and firming breasts. At work she constantly had to stop herself cupping her hand round her swelling bump, endlessly fascinated by the changes in her body, loving every tiny movement.

She had been shocked at the hormonal mood swings. She fancied herself a hardened journalist, but the pregnancy had made her incredibly emotional,

---

especially about anything to do with children. She found herself crying at documentaries about famine and simply could not have faced the funeral of a baby she had cradled in her own arms.

Unexpected and unplanned, the pregnancy had been a real quandary for Catherine. At twenty-three, she secretly feared she was too young for motherhood, though the more people pointed that out, the more she talked about the health benefits of having a baby early and how she would be 'free at forty' to travel the world. Though she hadn't convinced even herself that was true, she now couldn't believe she had considered an abortion early on. This baby felt like the most precious thing in the world to her.

Catherine had also been worried about her dad in the last few days, but pleased he had felt able to return to his Edinburgh flat yesterday after the funeral. It felt odd, out of sequence somehow, to be looking after him again. First, after her mother's death and, now, after Clare's shocking revelation. Maybe men were always babies at heart, no matter their age: always seeking succour, always needing support.

Still, good practice for motherhood, she mused, as she swung the bike to the right and on to the Millennium Bridge.

Gordon Williams was sitting at the far end of the bridge, holding his ankle, his toppled bike lying at his feet.

Catherine dismounted beside him. 'Are you hurt?' she asked anxiously.

As she knelt down beside Gordon, Sammy, who had been leaning nonchalantly against the rail, stepped forward and placed his pistol against her neck, just beneath her blonde ponytail. 'OK, Catherine, I need you to stand up slowly, your hands by your side, and walk quietly over to that white van parked in the loading area. Do exactly as I say and no one gets hurt.'

As the odd-looking couple approached the van the back doors were thrown open. Two men in balaclavas crouched in the back. Catherine and Sammy stepped gingerly inside. The two bikes and Gordon followed.

Before they put the blindfold on, the last thing she noticed was that Gordon was deliberately avoiding looking at her.

Then she heard Sammy's distinctive rasp. 'Catherine Wallace, you are now a prisoner of the British Loyalist Army.'

THE HEADQUARTERS OF THE ARMY IN SCOTLAND. EDINBURGH CASTLE. 9.15 A.M.

Major-General Rory Stewart, commander of the army in Scotland, was not a happy man.

He loved the army and was the fifth generation of his family to serve. Stewarts had fought bayonet to bayonet against the Old Guard at Waterloo, stood in the Thin Red Line in the Crimea, braved machine guns on the Somme and landed at Omaha Beach on D-Day, and he himself had led his troops into Basra in a Chieftain tank.

But none of his family had ever faced a situation as desperate as this.

Every physical part of Rory Stewart – his crisp kilt, his cropped, greying hair, his perfectly polished boots – was a reflection of the fact that the army was everything to him. It provided shelter, warmth and purpose. It was the only life he had ever known. The highest a Stewart before him had ever risen was colonel, so he was immensely proud to have reached the exalted rank of major-general and last year to have been made commander of the army in Scotland. It should have been the happiest time of his life, yet these bloody politicos had spoiled it all.

As a professional soldier, Rory valued order and discipline above all other qualities in life. Recently, both had been in pretty short supply. In his view, the whole world had gone to hell in a handcart. Even more infuriating, he was powerless to stop it. No simple order could stem the tide.

Instead of spending his summer entertaining guests over a gin and tonic at the military tattoo on the castle esplanade, he was mired in the British army's greatest crisis since the Battle of Culloden.

In less than four weeks, the Royal Regiment of Scotland would turn its back on three hundred years of proud service to the British Crown and take an oath to the newly independent Scotland. The king would no longer be the head of state in Scotland. No longer head of the army. They would be swearing loyalty to 'the people', whatever the hell that was supposed to mean.

Well, some might swear the oath, but not him. Not a man used to either intellectual or emotional debates, he had found the whole issue of deciding loyalty deeply perplexing. He found no difficulty in being proudly Scottish and proudly British. Why on earth was it so hard for others?

Faced with the choice between sticking with his men and his loyalty to the king, he had unequivocally decided on the latter. He would resign before the oath had to be taken and find a position in the English Army. Much to his chagrin, he knew this would not be as a major-general but, as an exiled Scot, more likely to be a captain in the catering corps in some godforsaken corner of Hampshire. As he looked out of his office at the magnificent view of St Mary's Cathedral, with the Forth Rail Bridge in the distance, that was a prospect which made him want to weep.

Rory knew that most of the officers felt the same as he did, but he also knew the overwhelming majority of the other ranks would take the oath. How in God's name was he meant to impose discipline in a situation like that? You couldn't have an army run by bloody committee.

Scottish nationalism had been like a wasting disease eating away at the regiment. He had hated the fact that his tanks in Iraq had sported Saltires along with Union Jacks. Fine on the rugby field, but not on the battlefield. Battalions such as the Black Watch and the Argyll and Sutherland Highlanders had become riddled with the nationalist virus: Scottish first, British a distant second. An absolute bloody disgrace in his view.

His reverie was interrupted by a knock at the door. His adjutant entered and saluted briskly. 'Letter came for you, sir. Gentleman said it was for your eyes only.'

NORTHUMBERLAND STREET, EDINBURGH, 9.30 A.M.

George normally loved his flat – what the estate agents called an upper townhouse – with its high-ceilinged rooms and spectacular views from the kitchen over the Firth of Forth. But this morning he was blind to its charms.

Groaning, he switched over from the Radio Scotland phone-in, which was full of people complaining about the weakness of the Scottish commissioners and how they were being pushed about by their English counterparts, to Real Radio. For years it had played a guess-the-year game between 9 and 10 a.m. and George loved the warm bath of nostalgic music after the bleakness of the news.

'Clearly, 1994,' he muttered to himself as a caller failed to recognise the year the USA had staged the World Cup.

George felt really dreadful. He had been up most of the night then had fallen asleep as the sun came up, emerging feeling groggy and slightly faint at 8.15 a.m. A shower and shave had only scratched the surface of his headache. The two paracetamol had not yet kicked in.

George had always suffered from insomnia when he was stressed. He hated that feeling of being wide awake at 4 a.m. while the rest of the world slept. He had tried everything over the years: warm bath, warm milk, masturbation, counting to a thousand, reading. Nothing had ever really worked. All those wonderful months with Clare he had slept brilliantly. But when she departed, the insomnia returned – with a vengeance.

Coming back to the flat yesterday had been so much harder than he had expected, but for a reason he had not anticipated. Clare's smell was everywhere: on the bed, on the towels, on the sofa. Everywhere. There was no escape from the light musk of her perfume.

He had made himself his favourite comfort food, pasta with pesto and bacon, then sat on the couch with a fine bottle of Barolo, Maria Callas on the iPod and a new history of the Byzantine empire. Normally, a perfect night in for him, but this evening it had brought him no solace at all.

Then another night of staring into the darkness.

He double-checked his keys and wallet, then headed out, welcoming the twenty-minute uphill walk to the castle to clear his head before the negotiations with the English commissioners began in earnest again. Despite his throbbing head, he knew he had to remain focused. Less than four weeks to go until the final treaty had to be signed and so much still to resolve. Today, it was the proportionate share of the national debt.

Christ Almighty, what had he done in a previous life to deserve ten hours discussing that?

THE OVAL OFFICE, THE WHITE HOUSE, WASHINGTON DC, NOON

Jane Chalmers was in a jaunty mood as she walked the short distance along the busy corridor from her office to the very heart of American government. She felt she was now driving the Scottish strategy. In a world where she feared that most decisions were taken by men on golf courses and in cocktail bars, this was a source of particular satisfaction.

She considered herself a great success in a man's world, living proof that pretty girls don't try as hard. Though she was acutely attuned to any form of sexism against her, Chalmers had a political tin ear for the resentment caused by her own poisonous mix of charm and emotional blackmail. She was intent only on having the ear of the President – from time immemorial, the only thing that really mattered at any imperial court.

She knocked and entered. 'Good afternoon, Mr President. A very happy Independence Day to you. I believe you wanted to see me?'

Chalmers was at her oily best as she entered the Oval Office. Her smile froze on her lips when she saw that Butterworth and Sands were already sitting in the office.

She knew that the three of them were already locked in an iron triangle of distrust on the Scottish issue. Whatever the outcome of the strategy – either a failure or a success – one of them would win, one would survive and one would be sacrificed. She was determined it wouldn't be her head on the block.

'Yes, Jane, come on in. Grab a seat.'

MacFarlane was his usual businesslike self, as Chalmers settled herself in an overstuffed, mustard-coloured armchair. 'I wanted to talk to you all about Jane's proposed decapitation policy for the SNP leadership. Jane, do you want to outline your reasoning?'

'Well, Mr President, my worry is that, if people like Ross Johnson and George Wallace survive the coup, they will be a rallying point for any opposition to the Cowan government. Gone are the days when we could act in secret and keep it that way. We believe there could be a grassroots online organisation against the new regime. The nationalists have no physical weapons but could perhaps organise boycotts or industrial action through political blogs and e-rallies. That's much harder to do without leaders.'

'Carl?'

'Well, sir, even if we put aside the thorny issue of international law and the risk of American personnel being hauled up in front of a war crimes tribunal at The Hague, which would be embarrassing to say the least, I believe such a strategy would be counterproductive.'

Chalmers' eyes flitted between the two men, trying to gauge the mood. The admiral continued. 'The Cowan regime is going to struggle for legitimacy, that is for sure. But the one way we can guarantee its unpopularity – and ours – is to link the new government to state-sponsored assassination. The murder of Maureen Cairns and her daughter has revitalised the collapsing support for the SNP. More murder would mean more nationalism, and more nationalists. That is undeniable. Furthermore, there is the small matter of US law. I am sure I don't have to remind a law graduate as distinguished as Jane that President Reagan's Executive Order 12333 explicitly bans any person employed by, or acting on behalf of, the United States from engaging in assassination. Such a move had complete bipartisan support and updated previous executive orders signed by Presidents Carter and Ford after CIA excesses in the 1970s. It is also why her deputy had to resign after those, how shall I say, unfortunate events in Venezuela.'

Chalmers shifted uneasily. She hated being reminded of the killing of President Hugo Chavez, which had so dominated the first six months of MacFarlane's presidency. More important, she knew MacFarlane did, too. Butterworth was such a dick.

Sands sat in silence, for once happy not hearing his own voice. He knew, if the worst came to the worst – as it often did in politics – he would be able to swear on oath that he took no part in this discussion or any subsequent decision.

He avoided the president's eye. So MacFarlane turned back to Chalmers. 'Well, Jane?'

'Mr President, as you know Marty took full responsibility for the Venezuelan affair and fell on his sword. But since that has been brought up again, I will point out that, no matter the international criticism the US received, the result was a pro-American government in a country sitting on the largest oil reserves in the southern hemisphere. And the message went out to the world that the USA had a tough man in charge again.'

Chalmers paused to let her flattery take full effect. She didn't know why, but she knew for sure that praise for MacFarlane's masculinity always worked a treat in any argument. 'I accept the Maureen Cairns killing was unfortunate,' Chalmers continued. 'It was due to some local operatives – how should I put this? – going freelance. That problem has now been rectified. These rogue elements have been reined in.

'I can guarantee you that the decapitation policy will be carried out by members of the BLA and they will claim responsibility for it. No one will ever be able to prove the links between them and us. There will be no "smoking gun" written command. The shots will not be fired by US-made weapons. We will be in the clear and not technically in breach of the letter of Executive Order 12333. As Carl well knows, in these matters it is the letter not the spirit of the law that matters.'

MacFarlane was silent for a moment. 'OK, I have decided. Jane, you can have your limited decapitation policy, no more than four, provided that our fingerprints are not on it. I don't want any congressional hearings or threats of impeachment. Anything else?'

'No, Mr President,' chorused Butterworth, Chalmers and Sands in unison.

Chalmers' face wore that tiny smirk of satisfaction she couldn't disguise when she got her own way. It made Sands feel physically ill. As a man schooled deeply in the importance of rational thought, he hated her emotional manipulation and her foot-stamping petulance when crossed. It made people reluctant to argue against her, even when she was wrong, and deeply offended Sands' sense of reason.

'OK, that is all. Carl, could I have a minute?'

After the other two had closed the door behind them, Todd put his arm round the admiral's shoulders. 'Listen, Carl, I don't want you to take this as a defeat.

The Scottish strategy is a high-risk one. Now it has a definite author. If the plot goes wrong, then there will be only one person to blame and it won't be you or me.'

MacFarlane waited until Butterworth had opened the door to leave. 'Oh, and a happy fourth of July to you. God bless America.'

Butterworth walked back to his office deep in thought. Nothing in his military life had prepared him for the level of duplicity and cynicism he had found in the White House. An old-fashioned career navy man, he had worked his way up through the ranks of the senior, but least sexy, branch of the military. From Vietnam to Venezuela, he had simply done his duty and served to the best of his ability. But everyone knew all the really heavy lifting in the big conflicts of Iraq and Afghanistan had been done by the army and the air force, not the navy.

Ironically, this had worked in his favour and he had been appointed head of the joint chiefs of staff when the new administration came in. His promotion was widely welcomed precisely because he was not seen as a politically aligned serviceman and was untainted by any of the controversial decisions of previous presidents, unlike many in the two other services.

Since then, he had been on a steep learning curve and Scotland undoubtedly represented his greatest challenge. Well, he had risen to them all so far and he was fucked if he was going to lose this one to an over-privileged preppy poseur and a queen bitch who considered the lives of his men as merely stepping stones for her own ambition.

BBC SCOTLAND HEADQUARTERS, PACIFIC QUAY, GLASGOW, 5 P.M.

The three figures watched the footage on the disc in absolute silence.

As it finished, Caitlin O'Connor, the head of news and current affairs, clicked 'Play' again.

Catherine Wallace's blindfolded face filled the screen, followed by a wider shot of her tied to a chair flanked by four figures in fatigues with broad white belts and black balaclavas. Each held a Kalashnikov automatic rifle.

The disembodied voice on the audio track couldn't have been clearer. 'Catherine Wallace is a prisoner of the British Loyalist Army. If the Scottish government does not drop the current negotiations being led by her father, George Wallace, to destroy the United Kingdom, which is completely against the wishes of the Scottish people, and offer a new referendum instead, then we will have no alternative but to execute her two weeks from today. Ross Johnson has until midnight on Friday the eighteenth of July to respond.'

O'Connor looked at the two men in the room, Lewis Graham, the interim chairman of the new Scottish Broadcasting Corporation, and her boss, Blair Hamilton, the controller of BBC Scotland.

Graham spoke first. 'Well, we can't broadcast that, it's blackmail pure and simple. If we do, we're giving them the oxygen of publicity they crave.'

Hamilton shot him a look of contempt. As a Unionist and a BBC lifer, he regarded the forthcoming dismantling of the corporation by the Scottish government as an act of cultural vandalism and Graham as nothing more than a nationalist placeman put in to establish political control of the new organisation. If Graham had said milk was white, Hamilton would have found a way to disagree with him. As it happened, he did actually think he was wrong in principle here. 'It is news, Lewis. We have to broadcast it. The Scottish people have a right to know.'

O'Connor cut in, 'But what about her family? What about the effect on them? And younger viewers? Christ, half the population will be having nightmares about men in hoods turning up on their doorstep. And what about poor Catherine? She is one of us, one of our staff. Are we putting her in greater danger if we show this? And she's pregnant, for God's sake.'

Hamilton was adamant. 'If you remember from the hostages in Iraq, the BBC guidelines allow the screening of such footage if there is a compelling public interest, and—'

'But,' Graham protested, 'there will be no BBC – and no BBC guidelines – in three weeks' time.'

'But there are now,' insisted Hamilton, 'and I say, play it. Not the spoken demand, but the pictures. If we hurry, we can make the six o'clock. Caitlin, tell Sandy and Sally to be gentle and to do lots of context. But play it.'

Graham glared at his rival. 'Well, it is your decision, Blair. For now.'

He left the room with the threat still hanging.

THE GREAT HALL, EDINBURGH CASTLE, 5.10 P.M.

George's head ached.

The Commissioners were now arguing over whether Scotland's share of the national debt should be on the basis of current population – 8.7 per cent – or have some element linked to the share of population at the time the debt was incurred.

He looked at his watch. Time for the last coffee of the day. If he stopped after this one, then he might sleep tonight. George had nearly embarrassed himself

----

by nodding off on the large oak table around 3 p.m., his head falling deskward before he woke with a jolt. This could not continue. He needed to pull himself together.

He looked around the room for inspiration. Straight across from him the wall was dominated by heraldic shields and the large, detailed stained-glass windows that blocked the superb view to the south. Not much help there.

To his right, the far end of the hall was dominated by a huge painting of Ensign Ewart, the officer of the Scots Greys who had ridden through the Gordon Highlanders' line shouting 'Scotland Forever!' and snatched the Napoleonic Eagle of the French 45th Regiment of Foot at the Battle of Waterloo.

Now the ensign gazed impassively down on the fourteen commissioners quietly ripping apart with spreadsheets and calculators a Britain for which he had been prepared to risk his life.

That thought didn't inspire George either, so he looked across to his left at the massive, double-handed broadsword displayed against the oak panelling and fantasised about driving it through the heart of the English commissioner who was droning on about population density. That definitely lifted his mood for a few minutes.

One of the white-gloved castle assistants came to the table and whispered in his ear. He nodded and said, 'Please excuse me, something has come up. I will be right back.'

Two men were waiting for him at the studded wooden door. 'Mr Wallace? I am Detective Inspector Bruce Saunderson of Strathclyde Police and this is my colleague, Detective Sergeant Peter Lawson. I am afraid I have some bad news . . .'

CHAPTER 12

FRIDAY, 4 JULY — TWENTY-SEVEN DAYS TO INDEPENDENCE

OFFICE OF THE FIRST MINISTER, SCOTTISH PARLIAMENT, EDINBURGH, 9 P.M.

Ross had tried his best to console George as he paced relentlessly backwards and forwards across the carpeted floor like a caged animal, but he knew nothing he had said had been of any comfort at all.

A relationship based on laddish banter simply had no language for a situation like this. With Bridget's death, Ross could just murmur the usual meaningless platitudes and then look for the quickest reasonably respectable time to exit, knowing that George would rather bottle up his grief than break down in front of him.

But this situation was different. It demanded action. Ross realised even his legendary charm was of no use at a time like this. Wisely, he now chose silence.

George struggled to order his thoughts as he paced, but rational answers, his normal default position, escaped him. He would not have believed there could be worse pain than Bridget's death, but this easily surpassed it. When he closed his eyes, all he could picture in his mind was Jessie Cairns' tiny white coffin with Catherine, as a toddler, inside it.

With none of the BBC's moral qualms, Sky News was playing the hostage tape in full, including the original menacing voice-over. He looked again at the TV in the corner of Ross's office.

That was his Catherine. His baby girl. His baby.

It was his primary duty to protect her and he had failed. He understood now why it was always men who lost daughters in tragedies who led campaigns for justice. The fundamental, primal urge of protection had been breached.

But it was even worse than that for George. Not only had he failed to protect her, she was a target *because* of him. Because he was her father.

She wasn't suffering through some random event, like a car crash, or catching MRSA, she was suffering because of him, because his vanity, boredom and determination to be a player had made him accept the job as Ross's senior special adviser.

Because of him.

He finished watching the tape for the fortieth time and turned to his friend. 'What the fuck am I going to do, Ross?'

'I've spoken to Alistair Stroud,' replied Ross evenly, 'and he assured me he had ordered every available officer on to the search for Catherine. The police are doing all they can. They are interviewing every BLA suspect and potential recruit they know. But these things take time. It has only been twelve hours.'

George wasn't mollified in the slightest. 'But these are the animals who killed wee Jessie Cairns. I can't let that happen to Catherine. We have to do what they say. We have to call off the negotiations.'

'George, you know I can't do that,' said Ross, trying to be gentle but firm. 'You know that. I can take you off the negotiating team, but I absolutely cannot halt the process. We're up against the wire as it is. The whole independence process would collapse.'

'But it's *Catherine*,' George pleaded, almost in despair.

'I understand.' Ross's voice was full of sympathy. 'This is a wee girl I wheeled in her pram, took to the Christmas carnival, bought her first glass of wine, I'm "Uncle Ross" to her. But you know I can't give in to this blackmail. There can be no surrender to terrorism. *Especially* because it's someone I know and love.'

Through his despair, George knew this was true. He tried again to be rational, to be strong. He failed. He could think of nothing more to say. 'Listen, Ross, I need to go. John is on his way back to Scotland. And I need to speak to Geoff again. He's beside himself with worry.'

Awkwardly, the two men hugged, with George leaning his head against the shoulder of the taller man, a sign of vulnerability he had never shown before in their relationship.

Ross watched him leave the office, then leaned back in his chair. He had never had children, so couldn't fully understand the fierce urgency of George's love for Catherine, a love more powerful and enduring than any other. But though he had never given that kind of love, he had certainly received it.

Ross had grown up as the only child of smallholders on the Black Isle, just outside Cromarty. His parents had struggled to get by, combining work on the croft with other jobs to supplement their meagre living. His mother was a cleaner in several of the larger sandstone houses in the village and his father rented himself out as a handyman, with the refurbishment of a local kitchen making the difference between having a Christmas and not.

But for all the poverty, it was a house full of love and affection. Ross's parents completely doted on their clever, witty son and poured every ounce of their frustrations into his ever-developing desire to succeed. For another child, this all-encompassing care would have made them feel warm and secure, or perhaps smothered. Instead, it made Ross selfish. He knew from an early age that he was the only person who mattered in his family and he milked that fact relentlessly.

Ross learned two lessons from his childhood. First, he would never allow himself to be trapped in the back-breaking toil that had blighted his parents' existence. He vividly remembered being nine and secretly watching his mother weeping in the kitchen because his Christmas presents had been a bag of satsumas, some sweets and a single Subbuteo team. No football boots, no bike, no Scalextric. He had vowed then that he would never be a victim of such poverty.

Second, he learned that charm was an indispensable weapon for success. From the age of ten, Ross's great skill had been an ability to make people like him. That ability won him election to the school council and got him the starring role in the school play over better-qualified actors. At university, it won him easy extensions on difficult essays and allowed him to plough all his energy into his real passion: debating. As he matured, he added knowledge and wit to charm in his armoury.

Ross acquired male acquaintances effortlessly. Some of these relationships deepened into friendships. But it was only ever one-way. Ross could pretend closeness perfectly, but knew he had to save his real emotional energy to advance his political career.

If all these male friends had ever gathered in a single room, they would have noticed that they had one thing in common: they were all useful to Ross. In George's case, it was his invaluable insight into the workings of the media and his contact book. Others were top-notch academics or leading trade unionists and businessmen. All offered Ross either a skill he didn't have or access to a place he couldn't reach.

Acquaintances who fell from power found themselves slowly squeezed out of the circle. Fewer invitations to play golf or meet for a beer or go to the big match. This never happened immediately or suddenly – Ross was too clever to cause a fuss or create an unnecessary enemy – but slowly and inevitably.

With women, it was different. Pretending emotional engagement over a longer, more intimate period was too much even for someone as skilled as Ross. One by one, these women had reached the correct conclusion: they would always come a poor second to his political ambition.

He was sorry about that, but not sorry enough to change it. He liked the sex, but no orgasm could match a rapturously received speech. No private pleasure could equal the public vindication of a popular vote. As he grew older, the ambition grew keener. The true curse of politics was that, from the age of twenty-one, time had been running out for Ross, each election lost meaning four more years away from the levers of power. By the age of forty-nine, it was win or bust. It was more and more a young man's game – there would be no second chance after this one.

Because he was a man who had never truly loved any woman or child, ambition had filled that part of his soul; being the first first minister of an independent Scotland was the thing he craved more than any other, sought to the exclusion of all other goals. It was what he lived for. The closer he got, the worse the longing became.

That driving ambition had steadily eroded his morality, the inevitable way water smooths rock. All his calculations fed that single aim. He would do anything to achieve it. Because of that ambition, a tiny part of his mind could think that, if anything happened to Catherine, the backlash would be even greater than that which followed the deaths of Maureen and Jessie Cairns.

And then his lifetime's ambition would be one step closer.

At first, even Ross felt a sense of shame at that thought and tried to suppress it. But it would not leave him. This is who he now was.

He felt pity for Catherine, remembering her bouncing on the trampoline in the Wallace garden as he and George drank beer and argued about politics over the barbecue; he recalled her beautiful ivory dress swinging as she danced at her wedding.

But a small part of him, deep inside, was thinking, 'You can't make an omelette without breaking eggs.'

This is who he now was.

SATURDAY, 5 JULY — TWENTY-SIX DAYS TO INDEPENDENCE

ROOM 322, THE HILTON HOTEL, GLASGOW, 11 A.M.

Major-General Rory Stewart's overwhelming feeling was that this was most *irregular*. After a lifetime suppressing every imaginative thought in the pursuit of perfect discipline, this was the most extreme adjective his brain would allow him. *Irregular. Most irregular.*

Facing him across the tray of coffee and biscuits were Robert Cowan, the leader of the Scottish Unionist Resistance, and Thomas Atkinson, an American who said he was with the US Embassy. This certainly was the most irregular thing Rory had ever done in his perfectly ordered life.

Robert Cowan spoke first, in his usual direct, slightly formal manner. Because of the incestuous nature of Scotland's overlapping political, social and cultural elites, where the clichéd six degrees of separation were reduced to two, he had met the major-general a number of times at social events and had played with him on a golf outing, though he couldn't claim to know him well.

Cowan was certain this was going to be a very difficult conversation, but time constraints demanded it had to be a frank one. At least his handwritten, cryptic note had brought Rory Stewart here. That was a promising start. 'Major-General Stewart, we really appreciate you coming at such short notice and at what must be a very hectic time for you. I also must apologise for the unusual location but, as I'm sure you are aware, the need for discretion is paramount.'

'Of course, I understand,' Stewart responded. Then he added, with a nervous smile, 'It is most unusual, but then we live in very unusual times.'

'Indeed we do, Rory, if I may call you Rory?'

The major-general nodded. Cowan resumed, going through the argument that he had rehearsed the night before. 'As you know, Rory, Scotland faces the greatest crisis in her history. The Scottish government intends to rip apart the most successful political union in world history on the basis of one narrow vote, despite overwhelming evidence that the Scottish people now regret that decision. As you also know, Ross Johnson intends to replace a partnership of equals with England with military subservience to the Russians. Rory, we cannot, we will not, allow this to happen. We owe it to history and to future generations of Scots. We in the Scottish Unionist Resistance, along with our American friends, intend to strike a blow for liberty. And we need the army's help.'

The room was totally silent as Rory Stewart struggled with the implications

----

of Cowan's request. Though he lacked imagination, even he could see the issues around a serving officer discussing a conspiracy against the state with an opposition politician and what was most likely a secret agent of a foreign country.

Suddenly, *irregular* didn't seem sufficient, even to the restrained major-general. 'Robert, I hear what you are saying,' said Stewart cautiously, 'but you must understand the gravity of what you are proposing. You're asking me to commit treason.'

'No, Rory, quite the reverse. I'm asking you to commit *loyalty*. Loyalty to king and country. Loyalty to all the things you and your family have held dear for centuries. It's Ross Johnson who is asking you to commit treason.'

Stewart's mind was working overtime, trying to grapple with these fundamental philosophical questions, extremely unwelcome intrusions into his well-ordered life.

Cowan tried to take advantage of his doubts. 'There are historic precedents for this. When Bonnie Prince Charlie and his Jacobite rebels swept across Scotland, men like the Clan Campbell and the valorous Royal Scots stayed loyal to the Hanoverian Protestant succession and the Union, the cornerstones of our current religion, freedom and laws.

'These men, who braved the Highland charge at Culloden, preserved Great Britain and set in train a process of intellectual and industrial development that created the greatest empire the world has ever seen. An empire in which the Scots played a glorious part.'

Robert Cowan's out-of-character enthusiasm was powerful and infectious. He watched Stewart nod gravely and knew he was tapping into a deeply held belief system.

Now it was time to go for broke. 'That's why, in just over three weeks' time, the Scottish Unionist Resistance will launch a coup against the current regime. We will stop independence negotiations immediately and set a timetable for another referendum and fresh elections. If the Scottish people then choose the path of separation again, so be it. We would respect that decision. But you and I know that will not happen. And whatever Prime Minister Jones says at the moment, we know our English brothers would welcome us back with open arms after three hundred years of standing shoulder to shoulder. If we stop the process now, the United Kingdom will be easy to put back together again. Nothing irretrievable has happened to the financial system, the monarchy or – as yet – the army. We have the men, Rory. We don't need you to fire a shot in anger. All we need is your pledge of support and a commitment to keep the Royal Regiment of Scotland confined to barracks that night.'

And then the carrot. 'Also, we would need someone to lead the armed forces in Scotland as they were reintegrated into the British Army and purged of nationalist elements. And we would be honoured if you would take the post.'

Ambition and morality battled furiously in Stewart's brain. 'But what about the new oath?'

'The oath is not due to be taken by the whole Royal Regiment of Scotland until noon on Friday the first of August. By that time, we will be in complete control of Scotland. The very first act of my government will be to cancel that ceremony. On that you have my word. Therefore, no man would have to go back on a promise of loyalty.'

Stewart searched his mind for other possible objections. 'And there will be no attack on any Scottish service personnel?'

'Absolutely not. Again, you have my word. No Scottish soldiers will be harmed. The coup will be bloodless, unless any of the Russian Special Operations forces stationed at Faslane make a fight of it. But if so, they will be taken out by US Navy Seals. I assume you would not grieve for them?'

Stewart silently shook his head. Cowan continued. 'Nearer the time, you will need to take your senior officers into your confidence and, most importantly, make sure that only hand-picked and totally trusted men are on ceremonial duty at Edinburgh Castle the night we strike. And remember, the more you keep your men in barracks then the less they will be at risk.'

Rory Stewart couldn't think of any more questions. This was the lifeline he had dreamt of. A chance to be somebody again in Scotland, instead of a nobody posted to some backwater of the new English Army. A chance to do the right thing. A chance to be loyal.

'So, Rory, can we count on you?'

'Yes, gentlemen, you can count on me,' replied Stewart emphatically.

'Excellent, now let me run through our plans for you,' responded a deeply relieved Cowan.

Once the intellectual turmoil was over, Stewart relaxed. He understood plans. He liked plans. Plans made sense.

This time Atkinson, whose knowledge of Scottish history had been thoroughly stretched by the previous conversation, took the lead. He pushed the coffee cups to one side and spread a map of Scotland on the table. He outlined the targets and the number of military personnel that would be involved.

An hour later, Stewart was completely satisfied. Cowan produced a bottle of Laphroaig and poured three generous measures.

They clinked glasses.

'God save the king,' Cowan declared, for Atkinson's sake adding, 'and the president of the United States.'

The men left the hotel separately at five-minute intervals. As they exited through the large revolving door that dominated the front of the hotel, none of them noticed the man in the dark-blue anorak standing by the concrete wall that marked the entrance to the underground car park. Nor that he had a camera in his hand.

NORTHUMBERLAND STREET, EDINBURGH, 11 A.M.

As the three men in Glasgow began their conversation, George was sitting in his flat with John, an empty coffee flask between them. They were drained, talked out – shells of a sleepless night.

John had always been an affectionate boy, and holding his son that night had been a huge physical comfort to George. They had slept in the same bed, snuggled together like spoons, in a way they hadn't done since John was ten and in agony with growing pains.

It was also a huge reminder to both of them how much they missed Bridget, whose physical warmth had lit up their home and whose automatic remedy to pretty much any problem had been a cuddle.

They talked through the issue of Catherine over and over, but both knew there was no obvious solution. Once they had exhausted that topic for the fifth time, George asked John a question. 'I suppose you heard about Clare?'

'Yes, Catherine told me.'

George had thought as much. He had toyed with the idea of calling his son to tell him directly but thought his fragile ego couldn't have withstood an *I told you so*. Not then.

Now, with Catherine's life in the balance, all that seemed so childish and irrelevant. And so long ago, even though it had only been a week. 'Well, I guess you never liked her anyway. Too young for me?'

'No, it was nothing like that, Dad. In spite of what you thought, I wanted you to be happy again. But I knew something was wrong. I had no idea she was an English spy, but I could see she was at it. I assumed she was after your money or some kind of power groupie. Something just wasn't right. She was playing a role. I'm an actor, Dad. Sometimes it takes one to know one.'

George sighed. His son was so right. Again. 'You know, son, if there is any tiny chink of light in this situation, it has been to make me realise how little Clare really mattered. It's awful that it takes something like this to remind me what really counts.'

'It's OK, Dad, you're better off out of it. I just wish you could have found out sooner.'

The two men slumped back into silence, trying to think what they possibly could do to help Catherine. Trying to do the right thing.

Suddenly, that thought sparked off an idea in George. He could save his daughter, but it would most definitely involve doing the opposite. Doing completely the wrong thing.

THE ALBION STEELWORKS, EASTERHOUSE, GLASGOW, 11 A.M.

For the hundredth time, Catherine Wallace tried the ropes tying her wrists, but they would not budge. Her wrists were chafed and sore, but the bindings on her ankles, which were already swollen in pregnancy, were complete agony. Her burnt-orange linen top was caked with dried sweat and her elasticated-waist trousers were riding high. She lay in the foetal position on the grimy floor and tried her best to think.

Ever her father's daughter, she worked her way logically through what had happened to her. After a bumpy ride in the van, she had arrived at her current location fifteen minutes after she had been snatched at the Millennium Bridge. Given the average urban speed of twenty miles per hour, that meant she had travelled no more than four or five miles from the city centre. Given that the BLA's stronghold was in the east of Glasgow, she reckoned that put her in either Craigend or Easterhouse, rather than in some remote country cottage; she was therefore probably within shouting distance of help if she could wriggle free.

She had also been aware of being hauled up on a chair and hearing some swearing as her abductors tried to work a camera yesterday morning, which meant she was a hostage and some sort of ransom had been demanded. That gave her an odd sense of comfort, as it at least meant she wasn't going to be executed immediately.

Catherine had also worked out that silence meant the foul-tasting gag was left out, while talking restored it. In that process, one of her captors was noticeably gentler than the others. Though she had remained blindfolded throughout, she felt sure it must be the boy she had bent down to help on the bridge.

So far, her rational nature had helped her cope, but now it meant there was no avoiding the logical conclusion. Catherine knew that the Scottish government couldn't be seen to be giving in to terrorism and that her value as a hostage ended once independence was declared. That meant she had just over three weeks to live.

Catherine worked hard to suppress her rising panic at that terrifying thought and forced herself to concentrate. In her anguish, she had learnt something remarkable in the last twenty-six hours. Though she thought of all her loved ones, she found herself astonished that her deepest concern was not for her father or her husband, or even for herself, but rather for the bundle of life currently kicking its silent protest inside her.

She would survive. She had to. She could not fail her baby.

CHAPTER 13

- -

SUNDAY, 6 JULY — TWENTY-FIVE DAYS TO INDEPENDENCE

THE BAR OF THE BALMORAL HOTEL, EDINBURGH, 9 P.M.

George sat in the deep, red-leather armchair, nursing his malt like a comfort blanket. Not for the first time in his life, alcohol was providing a crutch at a time of crisis. He had abandoned his no-alcohol-during-the-week rule; it just seemed utterly irrelevant at the moment.

His guest spotted him and strode over with his usual confidence. 'So nice to see you, George, and quite a surprise given our last meeting. Can I get you a drink?'

Once the waiter had left, having deposited two Arran malts on the polished mahogany side table, George raised his glass to his companion. '*Slainte mhath.*'

'*Za vashe zdorovje,*' was the reply from Colonel Karimov's cruel, smiling mouth.

Karimov spoke first, breaking the awkward silence and as smooth as ever. 'So, George, how can I help you, given the last time we spoke, you suggested – how did you put it, please forgive me if my English is not perfect – that I could stick my nuclear missiles up my arse? I did get the correct orifice, didn't I?'

'OK, Karimov. Have your fun if you wish, but you must understand it was an exceptionally stressful time for me. I had just been manhandled by your goons and told I was sleeping with an English spy. Forgive me if I wasn't at my most courteous.'

'I'm sure your young girlfriend's betrayal was hard to take, but to blame the messenger rather than the message is childish. A schoolboy error in politics. I think you need to understand that you are playing in a different league now. The stakes are far bigger than the future of your tiny nation and certainly far bigger than one man's fragile ego.'

'The abuse was uncalled for,' George acknowledged, before adding with feeling, 'and trust me, I really do realise now that this is a different game, with different rules.'

'So, I repeat, how can I help you?'

George paused. 'It's my daughter, Catherine.'

'Yes, I heard of her kidnap. Most regrettable.'

George had a sneaking feeling that Colonel Karimov was enjoying himself immensely. And that this was not the first time in his life that he had taken pleasure in having complete power over another human being. He had not the remotest intention of making this easy. 'Look, Karimov, I know the Russians must have lots of Special Operations troops in Scotland. I have seen their work at first hand.'

Karimov appraised George coolly. 'It is possible, but obviously I couldn't confirm officially.'

'I want . . . I need . . . their help in finding Catherine.'

Colonel Karimov paused and took a sip of his whisky. 'Why?'

'I think our police have little expertise in dealing with hostage situations and . . .' George hesitated. 'And . . . I have no proof, but I know that many in the forces of law and order are politically opposed to us and may be compromised by that. Bluntly, I'm not sure they are looking for Catherine as hard as they could.'

Karimov considered this calmly. 'I think you could be right on both counts.'

'So, will you help me?' George said, trying to control his impatience.

'That could be arranged.'

George's heart leapt. This was the first glimmer of hope he had been offered in a miserable two days.

Both men were experienced enough to know that hope was the most dangerous and addictive of the emotions. George tried to quell his mounting excitement. 'And would they be successful?'

'I cannot guarantee it, of course, but I would certainly place a small wager on it.'

George wanted to scream at him, 'This is my daughter's life you are talking about, you callous bastard, not some two-bit horse race!' but he knew he had to play the game. And to play it Karimov's way. So he spoke calmly. 'How can you be so sure?'

'How can I put this, George? My men have been in places much rougher than your salubrious Glasgow housing estates. Tough as they think they are, I am sure the BLA doesn't measure up to the Chechen warlords or the Afghan *mujahideen*.

More important, my operatives are not as squeamish as your Strathclyde Police in how they extract information. There used to be a saying in Soviet times: "In America you can always find the party; in Russia the Party can always find you." We will find the kidnappers.'

George smiled at the joke, despite himself. But he knew straight away he had just condoned the use of torture. As he knew he would be when he had arranged this drink with Karimov, he was now inevitably committed to doing the wrong thing.

'And what, may I ask, George, are you proposing to do in return?'

'I will do what you asked me that night in the garages in Glasgow, Karimov. I'll bolster Ross's decision to put the nuclear warheads in Faslane and I'll redouble my efforts to make that acceptable to the Scottish public and the international media.'

'And in the future?'

George hesitated, but knew there was no turning back now. 'For as long as I am Ross's senior special adviser, I'll work in the interests of the Russian state. You have my word.'

'Then, it is agreed.'

The two men clinked glasses and drank.

George's emotions were a mixture of relief and gnawing doubt. Relief that he had finally managed to do something for his imprisoned daughter. Doubt at the price.

The Faustian pact. Her life for his integrity. Doing the wrong thing. Again.

THE MEMBERS' BAR, THE CORINTHIAN, INGRAM STREET, GLASGOW, 10 P.M.

Robert Cowan sat on one of the ample sofas of the discreet upstairs bar of Glasgow's leading club for businessmen and waited for his guest. Normally, he liked to conduct these conversations in his home, but time was of the essence. And his guest was a busy man these days.

Cowan smiled broadly as he saw Alistair Stroud, the chief constable of Strathclyde Police, enter the room. 'Alistair, so good to see you again. I took the liberty of ordering you a Bowmore with ice. I recall you are very partial to the Islay malts.'

'Thanks, Robert, much appreciated. I'm sorry I'm late but the first minister has insisted I take personal charge of the Catherine Wallace case and is looking for updates every three hours, the cheeky bastard. It takes all my self-discipline to stay civil to that man. But needs must where this particular devil drives.'

'Interestingly enough, it is precisely that subject I wish to discuss with you.'

'Oh, really?' Stroud shot a quizzical look at Cowan.

Cowan cleared his throat. 'Well, the broader defence of the Union may be at issue in this case, Brother Stroud.'

Alistair Stroud sat up, nervous and expectant at the use of the Masonic address. Both he and Cowan were members of Glasgow's elite lodge but it was most unlike Cowan to use the term in public, even in a quiet bar. 'I don't quite follow, Brother Cowan. What do you mean?'

'Very shortly, Alistair, I will take the other seven chief constables into our confidence on our plans to save Scotland from the disaster of separatism. But other building blocks must be in place first. However, I can tell you that we are determined to defeat the menace of separatism at all costs. I believe that will involve an armed coup in alliance with our American friends. And . . .' Cowan paused and looked directly into Stroud's incredulous eyes, 'it is likely that the BLA will have a role in this operation.'

Cowan held up a hand to halt Stroud's protest. 'I accept that this is regrettable, Alistair, but I am afraid it is necessary. Therefore, it would assist me greatly if your investigation into the BLA's kidnapping of Catherine Wallace gave the impression of activity, but did nothing which could damage that organisation's operational capacity. It is vital in particular that nothing befalls Sammy Wilson, the leader of the Glasgow East BLA. The man is a menace and a common lout, but we need him, for the time being anyway. Once our task is completed, you can deal with him as harshly as you like.'

Stroud paused, trying to choose his words carefully. 'Robert, you know I share your views on the Union absolutely, but I have sworn to uphold the law. A young woman is facing execution. Even the national interest—'

Cowan cut across him. 'Even if you won't do it for Britain, then you must do it for the brotherhood. The same way our brothers stopped those pictures of the children of a senior police officer doing lines of cocaine at a student party ever reaching the tabloids.'

Stroud blanched. 'I was incredibly grateful for that, but—'

Cowan cut in again. 'No buts. I'm afraid you have no choice.'

The two men's eyes locked. Stroud knew then he was defeated. 'Of course, Robert, I will see to it.'

'Thank you, Alistair. I knew I could count on you. It goes without saying that this must be approached with the utmost discretion.' Cowan smiled and continued, 'Fortunately, we brethren know a thing or two about keeping secrets.'

With that remark, Cowan stood to leave. Stroud felt his ring finger squeezed in the traditional Masonic handshake as he passed, then was left alone to ponder the meaning of loyalty.

SATURDAY, 12 JULY — NINETEEN DAYS TO INDEPENDENCE

THE IRON DUKE BAR, DENNISTOUN, GLASGOW, 3 P.M.

The sound of the Orange bands as they returned from the parade in Alexandria Park was absolutely deafening, even in the upstairs function suite, where curling white-bread sandwiches and soft sausage rolls awaited the returning marchers. And where Sammy sat, with his brother Billy.

The Iron Duke was always heaving on this day, the drinking centre of the Protestant community of the East End of Glasgow. On one memorable occasion an Orange band had actually marched in the door of the lounge bar, through the public bar and back out to Duke Street to rejoin the parade.

The big Scottish parade to celebrate the victory of William of Orange at the Battle of the Boyne on 12 July 1690 was always the Saturday before the actual date, the big Ulster one the Saturday after. This year, given the imminent threat to the Union, they had reversed the order and made Glasgow the bigger demonstration. As usual, the members of the bands and lodges would cram the Stranraer–Larne ferries in both directions over that week.

At this point, Protestants on both side of the Irish Sea felt as one. Not Irish or Scottish, but Orange. 'Hands across the water.'

They knew they were the same stock, a people divided by the accidents of history and geography. Scottish Presbyterians had settled Ulster in the seventeenth-century 'plantation' of the Province, ever-present sentries against rebellious Irish Catholics.

Industrialisation had reversed the process, sucking in thousands of Irish Catholic migrants to Scotland, but also bringing a significant minority of Ulster Protestants to the coal mines and shipyards. They brought their Orange lodges with them, which found a fertile soil in Protestant Scotland.

These Protestants who followed Rangers and sang 'The Sash' were the mirror image of Glasgow Catholics who drank in pubs called The Blarney Stone and wore Republic of Ireland tops, even though their families had lived in Scotland for a hundred and seventy years.

The reason Glasgow did not become a tinderbox like Belfast was that, although there had been no-go areas in employment for Catholics from banking to shipbuilding, job segregation was not absolute and residential apartheid was largely avoided. Bridgeton was never the Shankhill, the Gorbals never the Falls Road.

The annual summer marching season had been in decline for decades, as Scottish society became more secular and nationalist and the Ulster peace process removed the traditional enemy. But this year, there was a last-stand defiance of a people under threat. Having succumbed to Irish nationalism, they felt they were now about to lose to its Scottish version. The bands played as though drumming alone could halt this process.

George had come through to Glasgow with John and they were watching the parade pass along Duke Street. Something tribal in George had always made him bring his son here every year, even though Bridget had brought him up a Catholic. In the end, John had become an atheist like George – an extra-time winner for George in their score draw of a marriage.

As he surveyed the marchers, George wondered, as he often had in the past, how the bold, democratic and revolutionary creed of Calvinism, which had made Scotland the most educated and literate society in eighteenth-century Europe, had come to be this grotesque caricature of orange and purple.

A Protestant faith which had built a school every time it built a church, a priesthood of all believers that maintained everyone had a direct relationship with God, an ideology that insisted women must be able to read and write, had allowed itself to become inextricably bound to the most reactionary form of British nationalism.

As a student of history, George found it incredible that this faith, the faith of his fathers, which had done so much to forge Scottish identity from the 'killing times' of the Scottish Covenanters to the intellectual glory of the Scottish Enlightenment, was now the cutting edge of the British Unionist backlash.

In this case, Karl Marx had been wrong to say history repeats itself, first as tragedy, then as farce. In Scotland, they were combined. Tragedy lay in the farcical finery on display in Duke Street. Tragedy lay in a good people led astray.

As the last of the bands marched past, whistling out its traditional defiance, George and John turned away. They had enjoyed the spectacle of the parade, as ever. But their real reason for being in Glasgow was entirely different.

A quarter of a mile away, upstairs in the Iron Duke function room, Sammy watched the last of the banners flutter past. As much as his shrivelled heart would allow, he loved The Twelfth. It was a day when everyone around believed in the same things he did, a day when he could delude himself that these marchers represented the real, true, Scotland. It made him feel part of something bigger: special, significant.

But, this Twelfth, he was troubled. Though, oddly, he himself had escaped questioning, the heat was definitely on the British Loyalist Army from the police in their hunt to find Catherine Wallace. He turned away from the window as the parade finished and spoke to his brother, Billy. 'Look, I know the cops are putting the fucking squeeze on the boys, but a' they need to do is to keep their traps shut and there's fuck a' the polis can do. That Fenian bitch is a huge pain in the arse, but there's only another week to go, then we're shot of her for good, if you get my meaning. You can even do the deed yourself, if it makes you feel any better.'

Billy had made his point on behalf of the boys on the ground and knew better than to argue further with Sammy. So he grinned his assent. 'It wid be ma pleasure.'

THE BANKS OF THE RIVER KELVIN, GLASGOW, 5 P.M.

When she was alive, Bridget Kelly had always enjoyed the irony that her birthday fell around the day of the big Orange march in Scotland.

When she was four, her dad had taken her on his shoulders to watch it and had convinced her that he had organised it especially for her birthday. It had taken years for her to forgive him for that.

As *Guardian* correspondent for Scotland and Northern Ireland, she had often spent her birthday covering marches or protests against marches, hunkered down beside an RUC armoured Land Rover, pen and pad in hand, trying to avoid the missiles raining down. One of the great pleasures of Bridget's life had been to contrast her role as a serious journalist with George's job in PR. His riposte was to point to their house in Portugal and enquire if *The Guardian* had paid for it. Another score draw.

Every year since her death, George, Catherine and John had come on her birthday to lay fresh flowers and to clean the bench they had erected in her memory by the banks of the River Kelvin, where she had enjoyed so many Sunday family walks.

As the two men scrubbed in silence at the graffiti that covered the wood, they felt the constant pain of Catherine's absence. They had hoped the physical activity would take their mind off the kidnapping. It hadn't worked.

George stretched his back with a groan and surveyed his handiwork. The bronze plaque gleamed against the dark wood.

The inscription read: 'Bridget Kelly, 1965–2009. Inspirational Journalist. Loving Wife. Devoted Mother.'

A life in six words.

They were all true, George thought, but did little to capture Bridget's huge, warm, fiery, challenging personality. He smiled at the memory of her and at the incredible courage and humour with which she had fought the cancer.

Having seen the damage that religion had wrought on his nation, George was a convinced atheist but knew that Bridget had never quite managed to escape her faith and he grudgingly acknowledged the comfort it had given her in the end. As the priest at the wake had said to him, 'It is just how it is, George. That's why our Church endures. Once a Catholic, always a Catholic.'

Bridget would have been both terrified and furious about Catherine's kidnapping. George was glad she had been spared that. He feared to think what Karimov's men were doing but whatever it was he hoped they were doing it fast.

In the family's last conversation with Bridget as they gathered round her bed before she slipped into final unconsciousness, she had characteristically been worried for the children rather than herself, trying to reassure them how much she loved them. As if there could be any doubt.

Fighting back the tears as he recalled that last moment, he knelt down at the bench and whispered, 'I will find your baby, sweetheart. I will keep her safe, I promise you. No matter the cost.'

SUNDAY, 13 JULY — EIGHTEEN DAYS TO INDEPENDENCE

THE ALBION STEELWORKS, EASTERHOUSE, GLASGOW, 11 P.M.

A single point of light shone out in the ten dark acres of the abandoned steelworks. A prefabricated security cabin was the only sign of life in a complex that had once employed six hundred men. It was hard to see what it was protecting in the jumble of rusting, rotting buildings.

But no security guards were inside the prefab. It had been made perfectly clear to them it would be better for their health if they didn't clock in for work. Instead, lit by a single 60-watt bulb and a two-bar electric fire, it housed the gagged and bound figure of Catherine Wallace and the smirking figure of Billy Wilson.

Billy was taking turns at guarding Catherine with Jack and Gordon Williams on an eight-hour shift pattern. In spite of her predicament, Catherine found them a fascinating mix. Billy sneered. Jack said absolutely nothing. Gordon didn't say much at first, but she could tell he was really troubled by the whole situation. When he removed her gag to feed her he allowed her to talk a little. And spoke back.

Gordon talked about his family and growing up in the East End. He knew it was a little careless and that Sammy would be furious if he found out, but reckoned it didn't matter much, as she would soon be dead. He was only glad he wouldn't have to be the one who pulled the trigger. Everyone in the BLA knew the Scottish government could not give in to their demands and they would have to shoot her, but she seemed really nice and not like the girls on the estate. And no woman had ever listened very much to him before. So, where was the harm?

She talked about her very different life, growing up in the West End and the fact she was going to have a baby – anything that might win her sympathy, anything that might give her an edge. She also probed at Gordon's beliefs, searching for an opening. Two days before, she had pushed it too far by talking about the murders of Maureen and Jessie Cairns and he had angrily stuffed the gag back in her mouth. But he had relented on his next visit, only making sure the gag was securely in place before Billy turned up.

Billy was a very different proposition, taking great pleasure in taunting her at every opportunity. Tonight was no different. He was feeding her some disgusting Pot Noodle off a grimy spoon. 'So, you're pregnant then. That's brilliant.'

'Why?'

'We get two Fenians for the price of one bullet.' Billy laughed out loud.

'You absolute heartless bastard.'

'That's me, doll, and don't you ever forget it. You are nothing but another republican whore tae me.'

'And you are a knuckle-dragging disgrace to your cause, you—'

'Now, now, hen. Dinnae lose yer head. Let's save that for next week.'

Billy was still chuckling at his own wit when the single 9-mm bullet blew his head apart, spattering Catherine's face with brains and blood. The plastic Pot Noodle container spun in the air and rolled in a gooey mess on the grimy floor.

ROGUE NATION

Three Russian Special Forces troops in black fatigues and balaclavas cautiously entered the cabin and untied the sobbing young woman.

Before they left the cabin, one of the Russians picked up Billy's Kalashnikov in his gloved hands and fired five rounds with a practised familiarity at the door. He then replaced it in Billy's still grasp and carefully closed his fingers around it.

CHAPTER 14

FRIDAY, 18 JULY — THIRTEEN DAYS TO INDEPENDENCE

CHARLOTTE STREET HOTEL, LONDON, 10 P.M.

George winced at the price of the two glasses of red wine, then carried them carefully through the trendy crowd of gel-haired men and pouting women to the table in the corner where Jessica Schwartz sat waiting for him.

She looked particularly lovely tonight, in a red polka-dot summer dress that accentuated her curves and highlighted her long brown hair and olive skin. She smiled warmly as he approached. Perfect American teeth.

They had had a warm, laughing, intimate late supper at Bertorelli's, a spicy mushroom risotto and a bottle of Chianti Classico, then had popped into the hotel for a nightcap.

This was the first day that week that George had dared to leave Catherine's side and the first day he had rejoined the team of commissioners negotiating independence at Lancaster House in London. He was in a great mood, high with the sheer exhilaration of normality after the burden of Catherine's kidnap had been lifted. At the moment, he believed he would never complain about any everyday ache and pain again. He was certainly enjoying his night out, especially sharing it with the best-looking journalist he knew.

'Cheers,' he said to Jessica, with a wide grin.

'Cheers to you, too, George. Lovely to see you so well.' She took a healthy mouthful of the wine. 'So, you're absolutely sure Catherine is OK?'

'She seems to be. John and I have been with her and Geoff non-stop since last Tuesday night. She has no physical pain apart from some bruising at the ankles where the ropes cut into her. And she seems cheery enough, though the doctor warned us there could be some post-traumatic flashbacks later on. We're all so incredibly relieved.'

'And the baby?'

'Still thriving, touch wood – all the tests were clear. She has her final scan in two weeks' time, the day after the independence ceremony.'

'I was sick with worry for you. It's fantastic that the police managed to track her down so quickly.'

'Yes . . .' George hesitated.

Catherine had been left sedated but safe outside Stewart Street police station with a note pinned to her blouse directing the police to the Albion Steelworks. To save everyone embarrassment – the police for their failure to find Catherine and the government and the Russians for the existence of Russian agents in Scotland – the official line was that the police had rescued Catherine and that Billy Wilson had been killed resisting arrest, the five spent Kalashnikov bullets lodged in the door of the security cabin being offered as evidence for that.

He longed to tell Jessica the truth. That he wasn't such a good man. He longed to share the fact that he had sold his soul. He longed to unburden himself, but knew he could not. He would have to be strong. Confession was a luxury that would have to wait.

Jessica, sensing his unease, tried to lighten the mood. 'So, who would have believed it – Brentlake School's young stud, Mr Wallace, a grandfather. Middle-aged women all over Beverly Hills will be heartbroken!'

'Pack it in,' protested George, 'you don't want to ruin the first relaxing night I've had in weeks.'

George and Jessica fell into reminiscing about the school where she had been a senior pupil and he a rookie teacher and coach. He had been twenty-three, the girls in his senior class mostly seventeen-year-olds, all of them dating guys older than him.

The school had been a wealthy private school, filled with the daughters of film and TV moguls. And full of JAPs like Jessica.

When George first heard the term, he couldn't understand why people were being racist about the handful of Asian girls at the school. Then the headmaster explained to him that JAP really meant Jewish American Princess.

Jessica had been at the intellectual end of that particular spectrum, George recalled. He had always really liked her brightness and drive.

'I remember my favourite joke. What does a JAP make for dinner?'

'Reservations.'

They laughed as they finished the punch line together.

'And do you remember Melanie Goldfarb, who used to drive to the school in her Mercedes convertible with the licence plate JLB8?'

'Yes. And she was, too!'

'What I most remember, George, is your half-time team talk when we were two–nothing down to Saint Margaret's in the play-offs. You got us together in the huddle and said, "Remember, these people are Catholics and they hold your people personally responsible for the Crucifixion so go out there and kick their ass."'

'In my defence, you did win three–two.'

'You always reminded us about how similar Jews and Protestants were. People of the book. People of the Old Testament. Argumentative absolutists in everything they do.'

'But that's true. You know we even have the same story about ourselves as you. One Scot in a room equals happiness. Two Scots means an argument. Three, a schism.'

Their laughter, comfortable and familiar, continued over two more glasses of wine. Jessica had been the only person outside his family that George had told about Clare. The warm glow of the wine granted Jessica permission to ask how he felt about Clare now.

George shook his head wearily. 'I was a blind old fool. If I hadn't been so arrogant and vain, I would have seen there was something wrong in a beautiful young woman adoring someone like me.'

'Don't be hard on yourself, George, it's not *so* impossible to imagine a woman fancying you.'

Jessica stopped, sensing she had been too suggestive. There was an awkward pause which she filled herself. 'Anyway, I should head home. I'm exhausted and I'm covering the prime minister's monthly press conference tomorrow morning. He'll be reminding us yet again of how lucky England is to be rid of Scotland, to become once more a land of village cricket games and bicycling old maids.'

George laughed. 'Aye, good idea to call it a night, especially as my country needs me tomorrow too. Let's grab a taxi. I'll drop you off.'

When the taxi pulled up at Jessica's flat, she asked him in for coffee. George didn't need much persuasion. The combination of the wine and the warm summer air made following Jessica climbing the stairs even more pleasurable than usual, the outline of her calf flexing with each step.

George sat on the designer sofa in the combined living area and kitchen as Jessica brewed some decaffeinated espresso. He wondered how smart people could design such uncomfortable furniture.

He apologised once more for dragging her into the leaking scandal over the

----

nuclear weapons story, which had led to the tabloids raking over her private life, probing every connection between her and George.

'Don't worry about it, George, it was worth every minute to break the biggest story of the year, and . . .' she looked coquettishly over her shoulder from the kitchen, 'anyway, it is never bad for my reputation to be linked to a powerful man.'

She brought the two tiny cups of coffee over to the couch. 'And what about you, George, what do you think you will do for a date now?'

'I think I'll stick to the promise I made after Bridget died. No more difficult or challenging women for me. Low on intellect and firm of thigh, that's what I want.'

She playfully slapped his arm. 'You are a disgrace!'

'Well, you know what they say about men living lives of quiet desperation.'

Jessica hooted, 'Yeah right, the way women clearly lead lives of noisy fulfilment.'

They both laughed. They sat on the couch together: comfortable; intimate; right.

George couldn't help noticing that, like Clare, Jessica tucked one leg under her as they faced each other. One of the straps of her summer dress had slipped down her arm, echoing a loose strand of hair across her face. She looked absolutely ravishing.

Emboldened by the wine, he moistened his lips and leaned forward, whispering as he did, 'So, I was thinking I was getting too old to play hard to get . . .'

Jessica met him halfway.

The first kiss was tentative and gentle. The second, deeper and more urgent. George felt the swell of Jessica's breasts against his chest. His hand was on her unresisting thigh. His penis strained against his suit trousers.

Suddenly, Jessica broke off, panting slightly. 'George, I'm sorry, I'm not sure this . . .'

'No, it's me who should be sorry, Jessica. It was presumptuous of me. I should go.'

'George, it's just . . .' She paused, then rushed on. 'Look, I've often wondered if we should be together. I really like you, we share so much in common. Both before you met Bridget and after she died, it nearly happened, and one day it might. But . . .'

'But what?'

'But not like this. I have to tell you one fact. I may be many things, but I will never be a sympathy shag. If you want me, then you have to woo me. Properly.'

SATURDAY, 19 JULY — TWELVE DAYS TO INDEPENDENCE

THE OVAL OFFICE, THE WHITE HOUSE, WASHINGTON DC, 8 A.M.

Todd MacFarlane took a bite of his Krispy Kreme breakfast donut and looked round his three advisers in anticipation. 'OK, team, let's go. Update on Operation Righteous Wrath, please.'

Much to Carl Butterworth's fury, Jane Chalmers didn't give him the chance to go first, despite his seniority. She felt this was now her operation and she wanted everyone in the room to know it. 'Everything is proceeding very smoothly, sir. The British Loyalist Army has been reined in and is now under our direct control. Major-General Rory Stewart and the senior officer class of the Royal Regiment of Scotland are prepared to support the coup. Alistair Stroud, the chief constable of Strathclyde, by far the biggest police force in Scotland, is also on board and the other seven chief constables in Scotland will be briefed next week, ensuring the police are neutralised. One of our most experienced agents, the UK CIA chief Thomas Atkinson, is running the operation on the ground and controlling Robert Cowan's political plans. And we are flying in all our top counter-insurgency operators from Langley. I'm confident we will be ready on the thirty-first.

'Fortunately, Cowan has been invited to the BBC that night. They think he is coming as a panellist on their coverage of the independence ceremony at Edinburgh Castle, which means he has a natural cover for being in the building – perfectly placed to make the broadcast announcing the formation of a new government.'

Chalmers sat back smugly.

'Carl?'

'The USS *Roosevelt* from the Sixth Fleet is on its way from the Mediterranean to the Firth of Forth as we speak, sir, with the Marines we need on board. A smaller frigate carrying the Navy Seals is sailing up the west coast and will be anchored off the Gare Loch by the twenty-ninth. Everything we need at Prestwick Airport has been put in place.'

'And the signal we discussed?'

Chalmers jumped in again. 'The coup will be set off by a bomb in the gatehouse of Edinburgh Castle just as the independence ceremony is about to start.' She noticed the president's puzzled expression and added, 'Let me show you, sir.'

Chalmers spread a plan of Edinburgh Castle on the coffee table which sat beside the presidential seal in the carpet at the heart of the Oval Office. She

----

leaned over it and started to point for emphasis. 'Just like Guy Fawkes planned with the Gunpowder Plot four hundred years ago, Mr President, this explosion will remove the political leadership of a country and usher in a change in regime. Except, we'll make sure our bomb goes off.'

She pointed at the map with a bony white finger. 'The explosion in the gatehouse *here* will take out Ross Johnson, George Wallace and their team, who will be preparing for his speech at the independence ceremony in this room *here* directly above the archway. This has the added benefit of ensuring that there's no danger to any of the foreign dignitaries who will be gathered *here*, at the far end of the Esplanade, where the royal box and corporate boxes for the military tattoo normally stand.'

'Will the king be there?'

'He has refused to attend the ceremony. He says it is inappropriate because the new Scottish government is planning to declare a republic and therefore he will no longer be head of state. Others say he is simply in a huff because the Scottish government intends to take over Balmoral and turn it into a public museum. His brother will represent the royal family. The king is currently staying at Holyrood Palace, waiting to sign the treaty once it is finalised at the end of next week and enjoying its splendours for the last time before it is returned to the state. He plans to travel back to England on Friday the first of August once the Royal Regiment of Scotland has taken the oath to the new Scottish republic and thus severed the last bond with the monarchy.'

'Does he know anything about these plans?'

'No, sir. Given that the SUR intends to ask the king to return as a head of state, we thought it better if he could act as an innocent honest broker. If the eventual compromise outcome for Scotland once the dust settles is some kind of maximum autonomy under the British Crown then he'll have a pivotal role to play, and it's important all sides can trust him in the task of nation-building, the way King Juan Carlos did in Spain after the death of General Franco.'

MacFarlane paused for a moment, aware once more of the enormity of what was being planned but determined not to show weakness. He reminded himself this was his time. He was the man. 'OK, Jane, sounds like a plan. Any other comments?'

Sands coughed. 'I feel I must put on the record one more time, Mr President, the catastrophic effect this action is going to have on the reputation of the United States. To be quite blunt, sir, we're making enemies faster than we can kill them.'

'What do you suggest, Chuck?'

'Please let me have one last attempt to talk some sense into George Wallace. I can fly to London tonight to see him and combine that with a visit to Prime Minister Jones to keep him on side, especially given the reservations he has expressed directly to you.'

The president considered for a moment, ignoring Chalmers' very obvious sigh. There was nothing to lose, and perhaps something to gain. 'OK, Chuck. Go for it. But be quick.'

They all stood and left the Oval Office, chorusing as they did, 'Thank you, Mr President.'

Chalmers seethed silently as she walked along the corridor. If Sands' last-minute attempt to deal with the issue peacefully succeeded, then he would get all the credit for resolving the Scottish situation and she would be further marginalised in the White House.

She was sure he would fail, but there was nothing wrong with taking out an insurance policy. She would make sure the bomb was in place in the gatehouse and if it went off against orders she could always blame the local operative, Thomas Atkinson.

That was Chalmers' guiding principle: 'Deputy heads will roll.'

And if the bomb killed Ross Johnson, then the president would be bounced into action and she would get the credit for his decisive action.

Just maybe he might be looking for a woman vice-presidential candidate next time round – one with significant national security credentials. Chalmers' true ambition: to be a heartbeat away from the presidency. Then, who knows?

She went straight to her office and picked up the phone. 'Get me Thomas Atkinson in the UK.'

After three rings, he was on the line. 'Thomas. It is a "yes" on the package and on Johnson. Yes, directly from the commander-in-chief himself. You can inform the leadership of the SUR and BLA. It's all systems go.'

SUNDAY, 20 JULY – ELEVEN DAYS TO INDEPENDENCE

ROOM 611, THE SHERATON HOTEL, EDINBURGH, 11 A.M.

The window of this top-floor hotel room had a magnificent view of the north face of the castle, but it was one completely unappreciated by the two occupants of the room, who were deeply engaged in an intense, but strangely pleasurable, conversation.

Major-General Rory Stewart and Robert Cowan were both planners by nature.

They recognised and respected each other's strengths. They enjoyed working towards a common goal.

Cowan was outlining his final plans. 'I've already spoken to Alistair Stroud and he's on board. I don't anticipate any problems with the police.'

'And the Americans?'

'They are being incredibly helpful, especially about making sure we get the broadcast on air perfectly. As you will know from dealing with them at NATO, Rory, the key to working successfully with the Americans is the same as dealing with one's wife. Just let them think they are in charge.'

Both men laughed. Then Cowan resumed. 'And I got your message saying you were successful with your colleagues. Were they easy to persuade?'

'Absolutely,' replied Stewart enthusiastically. 'I spoke to all ranks, from captain upwards, and they were completely supportive to a man. None of them was planning to take the oath anyway. There will be no issue with the army's loyalty to the new regime. There are a few Scottish nationalist elements in the ranks – they have already been identified and will be removed, in due course.'

'Excellent work, Rory. Now, there was one final issue we need to discuss, the signal for the coup.'

'Yes, I wondered what you had in mind.'

Cowan hesitated for a moment. This had to be handled delicately, but firmly. 'The signal will be an explosion.'

'Where?'

'In the gatehouse of Edinburgh Castle, at five to midnight.'

'But the first minister will be preparing his speech there at that time, you can't . . .'

Stewart stopped as the full implication of Cowan's proposal hit him. He lacked imagination, but he wasn't stupid. All of a sudden, the conversation wasn't so pleasurable. Stewart spoke quietly, his voice shaking slightly. 'When I signed up for this project, you gave me your word that this would be a bloodless coup. No one apart from any resisting Russians at Faslane would be harmed.'

'No,' replied Cowan firmly. 'I remember precisely what I said. I told you that no serving Scottish serviceman would be harmed and the last time I looked Ross Johnson had no rank in the Royal Regiment of Scotland.'

Stewart was shocked at the change in Cowan. 'That's a politician's answer if I ever heard one. I'm astonished that you want me to be an accomplice to cold-blooded murder and yet you still find it a suitable subject for sarcasm.'

'Forgive me, Rory, I didn't realise you were quite so squeamish, not a quality I would expect in so experienced a serviceman,' sneered Cowan.

'There is a world of difference between killing in combat in defence of your country and planning to kill an innocent man,' protested Stewart.

Cowan remained calm and in control. 'But he's not an innocent man, Rory, he is the man trying to rip up our nation, to destroy generations of shared history.'

'So you are judge, jury and executioner all in one?'

'In this case, yes. Extreme times call for extreme measures. I'm prepared to take the responsibility for this. That's what leadership is all about.'

'And if I decide not to follow you?'

'I'm afraid you don't have that luxury,' said Cowan smoothly. 'You are already deeply implicated. You've no choice but to see it through. If the coup collapsed now, it would mean personal and professional disgrace for *all* of us, including you. Not to mention a lengthy jail sentence in Barlinnie Prison. Is that your choice, Rory?'

Stewart was seeing Cowan with new eyes – the passionate Unionist idealist replaced by a cold-hearted murderer and blackmailer.

But even as Stewart tried to come to terms with the change in his partner, he knew Cowan was right. He had no choice. He would rather die than face the humiliation of disgrace. He had to go along with murder.

He could do no other.

Years of military training meant that Stewart was quickly able to regain his composure. He knew men in combat must never sense unease in their commanding officer. Control at all times and at all costs. 'No, of course not, Robert. I'm sorry. It was just the shock of hearing the . . . the assassination plan for the first time. I'll do what is required.'

Cowan smiled. 'Good chap. I knew I could rely on you.'

MONDAY, 21 JULY— TEN DAYS TO INDEPENDENCE

THE LANGHAM HOTEL, LONDON, 9 P.M.

Charles Sands sat at a table in the enormous bay window of the hotel cocktail bar sipping a glass of Albarino, the season's trendy Spanish chilled white wine, and awaited the arrival of George Wallace.

It had been a mad rush to get over to the UK and set up the required meetings, but in spite of all the hassle and the gently gnawing jet lag, Sands was feeling surprisingly relaxed and pleased with himself.

This was largely due to the fact that he had been able to bring his luscious assistant Maryanne with him on the trip, and even now she was upstairs trying on the lingerie he had bought her in Agent Provocateur, a powerful incentive to finish this last meeting as quickly as possible.

In Sands' mind, Maryanne was his reward for all his hard work. *His entitlement.* For Sands, her wonderful eagerness and expectation was such a relief from the tedium of his home life: three small children under five and his wife always exhausted, despite the best nanny and housekeeper his dollars could buy.

But before that delicious pleasure, a delicate bit of diplomacy was required.

And who better to handle that than Charles Sands III? Who could have a better CV than him? His father had been US ambassador to Germany under Ronald Reagan. A classic Republican believer in self-reliance and small government, Sands had been educated at Philips Academy, Andover, and Yale University, where he had been an active member of the exclusive Skull and Bones fraternity. He had then worked at the State Department under George W. Bush followed by four years of international analysis for the correct, not too extreme, conservative think tanks during the Democrat interregnum. He added marriage to a society heiress with impeccable Republican connections and a house in the Hamptons to the perfect mix. And now he was chief of staff to President Todd MacFarlane. In Sands' personal view, surrounded as he was by shoot-'em-up cowboys, the president was very fortunate he had someone measured and rational like him to offer advice.

This is what Sands had been born to do. *His entitlement.*

For Sands, this Scottish business was a tricky one. Personally, he was not convinced the coup would succeed in the long term, especially against the popular will of the Scottish people. Even if it did, the political consequences for the reputation of the United States would be disastrous, worse even than the fallout from Iraq. The most important outcome of the whole affair was that he himself should emerge unscathed. He wasn't too worried about Butterworth – a decent enough patriot, but a dullard. A jobsworth. But Chalmers needed careful watching. Five foot four inches of bitter bitch from her dyed black hair to her kitten heels, Chalmers would do anything to get, and keep, power.

So far, Sands thought the cards were falling kindly for him. If the coup succeeded wonderfully, then Chalmers would unquestionably advance, but he would be undamaged. If he could negotiate an eleventh-hour diplomatic solution to the crisis with George tonight, then he would win, Butterworth would survive and Chalmers would lose. If the coup failed politically, then Chalmers would lose and he would survive. If it failed militarily, then Butterworth lost and he survived. So far, he had protected himself well.

Even if all his calculations were wrong, he had one trump card left to play. Faced with ruin, he would have to have a little chat to the president about a story one of his Yale friends had blurted out at a drunken reunion party in New York. He was sure he would have MacFarlane's full and undivided attention for that particular tale.

Sands knew this story was an atomic weapon, only to be used once – and one which laid waste to everyone around it, including possibly the person who dropped it – but it was his insurance policy, a sure-fire way of maintaining his entitlement. In politics, as when being chased by a lion, you didn't always have to finish first, but you had to ensure you didn't finish last.

As Sands pondered these issues, George came in through the revolving door, crossed the imposing lobby and turned left into the semi-circular cocktail bar. He felt great: after a punishing session in the gym, he was glowing all over and knew he cut a dash in his new bespoke suit and crisp light blue Armani shirt.

Entering the Langham Hotel bar made George smile. Last time he had nearly been thrown out. When the waiter brought the bill for the four glasses of wine he and Jessica had drunk, he had said, 'I'm sorry, I meant the bill for this table, not the whole bar.'

Jessica had laughed. The waiter had not. Neither had the duty manager.

Now he was facing a tricky meeting with the second most powerful man in America, and thus in the world. Given the urgency of the message, the White House chief of staff wanted a favour. How his dad would have enjoyed telling his domino partners in The Iron Duke about this scenario.

A perfectly groomed Sands rose to meet him, extending a hand. 'George, so good to see you again. I am only sorry the circumstances are not happier.'

'I agree, Charles. In another situation, we might have been friends.' George

----

meant it. On the surface, Charles reminded him of all the decent, clever Americans – Democrats and Republicans alike – who had made his years there so wonderful. The Americans of the Marshall Plan, who had rebuilt Europe after the war. The Americans of enlightened self-interest. The Americans he wanted as friends to the country he cared about so passionately.

After ordering George a lime and soda, Sands made his opening gambit. 'So, how are the independence negotiations progressing?'

'Fine,' George responded cheerfully. 'We're up against the wire, but I think we'll get finished by next Friday's deadline.'

'Good, good.' Sands paused. 'Forgive me cutting to the chase, but I wanted to meet you to ask if there was any possibility of a change in your stance on the Russian ICBMs in Faslane.'

'None whatsoever,' was the clear and definite reply.

Sands looked around to check they couldn't be overheard and leaned forward, earnest and encouraging. 'George, even at this late stage, there is still time. I know Ross listens to you. You can persuade him that this path is madness. Scotland can only be the loser.'

George knew that made sense, but was acutely aware of the constant presence of his promise to Colonel Karimov. He knew he could not break the oath that had saved Catherine's life. 'I understand what you are saying, Charles,' he acknowledged, 'but the first minister has made his position clear and has done so in such a public way that it is hard to imagine the circumstances in which he could climb down. The humiliation would destroy his career.'

He didn't have to add that his political career was the most important thing to Ross. As second in commands, both men instinctively understood that.

'But this is now about much more than one man's career,' Sands persisted. 'This is about the future of the world. With all due respect, you need to lift your head up and see the true significance of this.'

However much he feared it might be correct, George was getting a little tired of being told he was out of his depth. He swallowed his irritation. 'I understand only too well, but Ross is determined. And the bullying tactics of the USA have only made him more so. Scotland can look after itself, don't you worry. And persuasion is a two-edged sword. Why can you not persuade the president to step back from his hard line?'

Sands snorted then leaned forward again, this time grave and intense. 'Don't be foolish, George. You know that the president's stance is only a product of Ross's reckless behaviour. You can't blame the blamer here.'

Sands grew even more solemn. 'You are a student of history. So, tell me this. Can you name one country the Russians have ever left voluntarily? We forced them out of Cuba, the Afghans sickened them with guerrilla warfare, economic collapse and popular revolt made them leave Eastern Europe. You've lived in the States, George, you know you are better off with us. We have our faults, but, ultimately, we do the right thing. You know we will provide the money to ease the transition to independence. Persuade Ross, George. Make him do it. For your sake. For Scotland's sake.'

George hesitated. The prospect was tantalising, both for him and his nation. But he answered, remembering his promise. 'I'm sorry, Charles. For good or ill, we are now partners of the Russians. The missiles are staying.'

Sands changed tack, realising he had lost and calculating immediately what that meant for him in the triangular White House power struggle. He replaced his pleading with cold arrogance. 'You are a fool. This is stupid, immoral, the wrong thing.'

A combination of that particular phrase and weeks of relentless tension was too much for George. He completely lost his temper. 'I can't believe you have the fucking audacity to lecture me on morality. My daughter was on the point of being butchered like a piece of meat by men on your side and, for all I know, on your payroll. When the Founding Fathers wrote about the right to life, liberty and the pursuit of happiness, do you think they had in mind kidnap and execution?'

Sands bristled. 'Spare me the history lesson. Of course we make mistakes, but a lot fewer than the Russians. Do you really believe these missiles will be the last demand the Russians make of you? Do you think they will respect your democracy?'

Sands' resistance drove George to even greater levels of fury. 'Democracy? Democracy? You dare mention democracy? Do you think when Lincoln stood on the blood-soaked battlefield of Gettysburg and promised that government of the people, by the people, for the people would not perish from this earth, he had in mind Guantánamo Bay and CIA torture?'

George stood up and looked at the preppy figure across from him with contempt. 'Do those words stir anything in your shrivelled, cynical soul, Charles? I suggest you take your polished Timberlands, your perfectly pressed chinos and your Brooks Brothers shirt, roll them tightly up together and stick them right up your arse. Scotland will be free and will not be taking orders from you.'

George stood up and headed for the door, knocking over his chair as he went.

Sands watched him go and sighed. He had failed. Another political moralist who failed to see how the game was played. So unlike a professional like himself.

More importantly, he knew he was looking at a man who had just signed his own death warrant.

CHAPTER 15

SATURDAY, 26 JULY — FIVE DAYS TO INDEPENDENCE

THE SENTRY BOX, THE ESPLANADE, EDINBURGH CASTLE, 10 A.M.

Lance-Corporal Brian McTavish was not having a good day. Only five days to the biggest ceremony ever held in the castle, beamed live on TV around the world, and the place looked like a dog's fucking breakfast.

Morale had gone to fuck as squaddies spent more time arguing about taking the oath on Friday than they did getting their arses in gear.

Everything was behind schedule. The three stands had been erected on the broad esplanade but all the detailed work remained to be done. The electricians were getting in the way of the scaffolders and the TV people were, as usual, getting on everyone's tits.

And now this lot.

Lance-Corporal McTavish eyed the four men in the white van suspiciously. These were the burliest-looking heating engineers he had ever seen in his life. After campaigns in Northern Ireland, Kosovo, Afghanistan and Iraq, McTavish reckoned he had a pretty good nose for a fighter. And these smelled like soldiers to him.

He looked again at their pass, signed personally by Major-General Stewart. Now, why would the commander of the army in Scotland be signing chits personally? And, as duty security NCO, why didn't he know there was a problem with the radiators in the gatehouse and that someone was scheduled to come to fix them?

The driver was a Jock, all right, but those other three didn't look like they had grown up any place in Edinburgh he knew.

He was just about to get them all out of the van to question them further when Captain Paul Murray marched smartly up. 'What seems to be the problem, McTavish?'

'It's this lot, sir, something about the radiators needing fixed in the gatehouse. Seemed a bit odd to me. There's nothing in the plan of works that says that is to be done, and I don't like the look of—'

The captain cut across him. 'Don't worry. The problem has just come up. Seemingly the radiators need to be bled or there is a danger a pipe might burst upstairs. Can't have our glorious first minister getting his bollocks wet on his big day, can we? Let them on through.'

The lance-corporal gave the men one last disparaging look, then waved them forward. The van drove through the gap left under the main stand, weaved its way between the figures on the busy esplanade and disappeared through the gatehouse arch into the castle.

Now he had to go and deal with that big poof from the BBC and his moaning about camera angles. Christ, and he had thought fighting the Taliban was bad.

OFFICE OF THE FIRST MINISTER, SCOTTISH PARLIAMENT, EDINBURGH, 10 A.M.

The first minister's assistant, Jean, wearily wondering if she would ever get a weekend off again in her life, popped her head round the door. 'Ross, President Churov on line one.'

Ross picked up the receiver of the newly secured line from Moscow. 'President Churov, very nice to hear from you. And I very much look forward to welcoming you to Scotland in person this week.'

'Thank you, First Minister, I'm excited about seeing your beautiful country for the first time. I've seen the castle on television and it looks magnificent. I also think your office was wise to have us do the Burns Country tour in Ayrshire next week. Inspiring for me and very good picture opportunities for us both. A shared love of poetry will play well against all this nonsense talk of Third World War.'

Churov paused. 'Is everything else proceeding according to plan?'

'Yes. Colonel Karimov has made sure George is well and truly on board. George is not the most sophisticated politician, but he's a decent man and will be true to his word, which is useful to us in so many ways.'

'And you are happy about the Americans?'

Ross hesitated, reluctant to seem weak. 'It appears they have taken the bait. The USS *Roosevelt* from the Sixth Fleet is anchored in the Firth of Forth. I can't say I am not nervous about what they might do. I'm not certain we have called this one right.'

'Don't worry, First Minister,' Churov replied with confidence. 'They are old adversaries of ours, I know their psychology. Trust me, the Americans will do as we think. The plan is working. We just have to hold our nerve. Remember, timing is everything. If we get it right, we win. Of course, if we get it wrong, we are finished. But we'll win.'

'Of course. I understand. I'll make sure there are no mistakes. You have my word.'

NUMBER 10 DOWNING STREET, LONDON, 10 A.M.

As President Churov and Ross Johnson spoke, Prime Minister Nick Jones was sharing a sober coffee with Charles Sands, discussing a plan both men believed in their hearts to be disastrous. Jones had thought of little else since President MacFarlane had revealed the plot to him. And the more he thought about it, the worse it seemed.

The prime minister was questioning the chief of staff. 'Are you certain the United States is completely set on the military strategy?'

'It is, Prime Minister,' Sands replied wearily. 'We appear to have run out of alternatives. The plan to leak the story through George Wallace backfired. The hope was that the negative publicity would force the Russians to change tack. It only seems to have succeeded in bringing the Scots and Russians closer together. And I had one last attempt to persuade George Wallace to change path this week. I'm afraid I completely failed. It was really weird, he seemed to agree with everything I said but still would not budge on the official Scottish position. So there's now no choice. The military planning is at an advanced stage.'

'And do you think the political thinking is as advanced? Another failed state to follow the one in the Middle East?' asked Jones testily.

'If I'm honest, I don't think it is very well developed. But my hands are tied. The president feels he has no option. All I can try to do is keep casualties to a minimum and deal with the political fallout at the United Nations and beyond.'

'And the decapitation policy?'

Sands hesitated, then answered tentatively, 'You must know I can't comment on that, Prime Minister. All I can say is, given its dubious legal provenance, it's not a policy I did, or would ever, endorse.'

Jones admired Sands' adroit back-covering, should things come unstuck. He gave a grim little laugh. 'Your president likes his Bible. Did you not try the message, "Forgive them, Father, for they know not what they do" on him?'

'No, sir. But I did get to be Pontius Pilate: "I am innocent of the blood of this just person. See ye to it." Knowing it's wrong, but washing my hands of it.'

Just for a moment, and only a moment, both men completely understood each other and even had the decency to feel ashamed of themselves. Sands thrived on this fellow feeling and his desire to unburden himself had undermined his normal caution.

Nick Jones broke the silence that had fallen between them. 'My nation will have to deal with the fallout, so can you tell me exactly how you intend to put Cowan in power?'

'At a given signal, American forces along with the BLA will seize key government and media outlets, then, at midnight, Robert Cowan will make his broadcast to the nation announcing he is now in charge.'

'And the signal?'

'A bomb at Edinburgh Castle . . .'

Sands took one look at Jones's horrified face and hurriedly added, 'In the gatehouse, well away from the gathered dignitaries on the esplanade. The BLA will claim responsibility for the explosion.'

'Jesus Christ, this is madness. Where will all this end?' Jones desperately sought answers. 'And you'll be there to witness that?'

'Yes, Prime Minister. The presence of the president or even the vice president would look like a public endorsement of the new Republic of Scotland, which would be unacceptable. But obviously we need to be represented. Plus it would look suspicious if no major figure from the US was on the esplanade when the independence ceremony was, er, "interrupted". And I'm here in the UK anyway, so, the president asked me . . .'

Sands gave an apologetic shrug, suggesting he knew exactly his place in the great scheme of things. 'And you, Prime Minister?'

'Yes, I will be there. Protocol and all that.'

Jones barely had the energy to finish the sentence. He took a sip of his coffee, trying to suppress his growing feeling of nausea. 'And I assume it is vital for the USA to have someone senior on hand to endorse the new Cowan regime?'

'Absolutely. And to deal with the international media gathered in Edinburgh. It is going to be quite a story.'

'You're telling me. That is the first statement this morning with which I have wholeheartedly agreed.'

The two men slumped into silence, each lost in his own thoughts, frantically thinking of a personal exit strategy. As there was nothing more either could add, they stood, shook hands and parted in quiet despair.

Nick Jones sat down and drained his cup. His dilemma was now crystallised. The assassination of the first minister had just been as good as confirmed. Now, he had four days to decide. He could either warn Ross Johnson of his impending death and imperil England's single most important political relationship.

Or he could sit in the esplanade at Edinburgh Castle and witness state-sanctioned murder.

FASLANE NAVAL BASE, THE GARE LOCH, 7 P.M.

Major Gustov surveyed the new defences with satisfaction.

He was proud of his professional and meticulous preparation. Ten of the new Topol-M multiple-warhead intercontinental missiles were out in the old Cold War silos on the hills, each guarded by ten highly armed elite troops.

As the Topol-M fired on solid rather than liquid fuel, they didn't have to be in silos so Gustov had been able to keep five within the security of the base. Here, too, thirty technicians laboured round the clock to get the command-and-control system ready.

And he had the base almost impregnable. The extensive black boom erected by the Royal Navy across the loch to defend the base from waterborne sabotage met the major's exacting standards. It meant any assault from the water would be halted one hundred metres from the shore and the attackers would have to run along the boom to the shore or try to swim from there.

Either way, the machine guns he had placed at both ends of the boom would have sweeping arcs of fire across that whole area. It would be a killing field.

On the land side, he had snipers on each of the tall accommodation buildings and machine-gun nests at five hundred metres along the three-metre-tall wire perimeter fence.

It would take a force of over a thousand to storm his dug-in little garrison of fifty, and even then it would cost them hundreds of casualties. And Iraq had shown the West had no stomach for death, unlike the Russians, whose brutal history had readied them for sacrifice.

The chief scientist had assured him the missiles would be primed and ready by the first of August, a fitting birthday present for the new Scottish republic.

Gustov nodded to the sweating Russian soldiers, who had been filling sandbags and were now leaning on their shovels and smoking. 'Good job, lads, that'll do for tonight. Extra vodka ration on me.'

THE USHER HALL, EDINBURGH, 9 P.M.

As the soaring crescendo of the 'Hallelujah Chorus' filled the rafters Jessica took George's hand and squeezed it. George's eyes filled with tears at the beauty and emotional power of the music as the layers of voices built and swooped.

All the commissioners had been requested to attend the highly symbolic 'friendship tour' of the Moscow State Orchestra and Choir. George had always loved the *Messiah* and had welcomed the temporary suspension of the endless negotiations, even more when he had been able to blag a ticket for Jessica.

After the concert they strolled down Lothian Road and on to Princes Street, arm in arm, pausing to admire the gleaming new trams gliding along Edinburgh's main thoroughfare.

George stopped outside the Balmoral Hotel to say goodnight. He knew Jessica had to start filing her copy and the commissioners were intending to do another couple of hours of planning at the castle after the concert. The Friday night deadline to complete the treaty loomed over them all.

They stopped outside, avoiding the eye of the kilted doorman. George took Jessica in his arms and kissed her gently, lingeringly, on the lips. 'Goodnight, Jessica.'

'Goodnight, George.'

George gave her one more kiss then turned away.

'George.' He turned back towards a smiling Jessica.

'What?'

'Better. Much better.'

George headed back to the castle, whistling the 'And the Glory of the Lord' chorus as he walked. As he took the short cut through Waverley Station, he recalled with pleasure another aphorism of his hero, Benjamin Franklin: 'Neither a Fortress nor a Maidenhead will hold out long after they begin to parly.'

HAWKHILL AVENUE, EDINBURGH, 11 P.M.

The landlord of the new block of flats on Hawkhill Avenue had been delighted. In spite of all the economic gloom he had managed to get tenants for four of his buy-to-let properties in the last month. The tenants had even paid cash in advance for the whole year. Result.

The flats overlooked Easter Road, the famous old ground of Hibernian Football Club. But that hadn't been a selling point for the occupants. None of them was a Scottish football fan. Football to them was played by men in helmets with an oval ball.

Thomas Atkinson surveyed the heads of his CIA units with satisfaction. They had managed to get three hundred men into Scotland over the last month without being noticed, helped by the fact that Scotland, and especially Edinburgh, was such a cosmopolitan place in the summer. Now it was time to finalise their plans.

Atkinson was excited to be back on active duty again, and delighted he had so many of Langley's finest at his back. It felt like the old days. 'OK, let's start with you, Luca.' Atkinson looked directly at the wiry, muscular figure of Gianluca Sarti, whose swarthy face betrayed his Sicilian roots. 'So, Luca, given that George Wallace is, how can I put it, currently semi-detached from the Scottish government, we cannot be sure that he will be in the Edinburgh Castle gatehouse at twelve to midnight on Sunday with his boss, Ross Johnson. Therefore, he needs to be taken out before that. I would suggest you do it on Wednesday – less time for reaction to build before the Thursday ceremony and too close to the event for them to cancel or delay it in his memory.'

Luca nodded.

'Take Mike and Joe. Three should be plenty. And you will need to take one of those BLA nutcases, since they will be officially claiming responsibility for the assassination. It is really important that the final shot is his. Orders direct from the top.'

'Sure, boss. No problem.'

'Right, next is Pacific Quay. I need six men to accompany Robert Cowan at all times. This is not the most arduous task, but absolutely vital. One for you, Bill?'

As Atkinson issued his orders, a man in a dark-blue anorak methodically took photographs of the flats, to add to those he already had from the Hilton in Glasgow.

CHAPTER 16

-- -- -- -- -- -- -- -- -- -- -- -- -- -- -- -- -- -- --

WEDNESDAY, 30 JULY — ONE DAY TO INDEPENDENCE

EDINBURGH CASTLE, 4 A.M.

The two groups of negotiators sat at opposite ends of the Great Hall. Waiting. Endlessly waiting.

The Scottish and English commissioners had finalised the Treaty of Independence at 11 p.m. on the Tuesday night and had foolishly headed for a celebratory late supper at the Witchery restaurant, leaving a legal team of parliamentary draughtsmen to put the final agreed points into the appropriate legal language. Their plan was to return an hour later and sign the treaty, then it could be rushed to the king at the Palace of Holyroodhouse for his signature. But last-minute wrangles over the precise meaning of the language had delayed the final version. And no one could go home until it was finished.

And so they waited. And waited. Fucking lawyers.

George was now so tired his eyeballs ached. The commissioners had worked through to the early hours on Sunday and Monday morning and now were having to do an all-night shift. George's body was also filled with the restless edginess that comes with a lack of exercise.

Stupidly, after a week without a drink, he had had a celebratory bottle of wine with supper. He felt light-headed and slightly faint, and also felt the first stirrings of a hangover even though he hadn't been to bed, which was the oddest sensation. He stroked his soft two-day stubble, gave another half-hearted glance at the remaining clues in the *Guardian* crossword then tried to focus his mind on the two days ahead.

George couldn't believe how unexcited and uninspired he was with the whole process. During his career as a PR executive, constantly pitching for new business, he had trained himself not to get too excited by the wins or allow the losses to make him too despondent. That was a key survival mechanism in maintaining his sanity in a world packed full of liars and egomaniacs.

But this was different.

Here he was, a working-class boy from Dennistoun, in the magnificent Great Hall of Edinburgh Castle, which had witnessed so many amazing events in Scottish history, about to sign the most important document in British history since the Magna Carta.

And yet he felt empty.

He was finally everything he had dreamed of – a participant in history rather than a recorder of it. And yet it meant nothing. It was a victory without meaning. He just felt empty.

It was more than sheer exhaustion that made George feel this way. He was totally disillusioned with the behaviour he had witnessed, by the whole ruthless cynicism of the political process. And he was sickened by his own behaviour: his compromises, his lack of truth, his promise to Karimov.

He had failed to live by the standards he believed in, the standards he had taught his kids. He had failed to do the right thing.

His musings were interrupted by the secretary of the constitutional negotiations bustling in with copies of the treaty to be signed. They were still warm from the photocopier.

As the head of the Scottish negotiating team, George was the first to sign. As he took the top off his fountain pen, he thought of Robert Burns' song about the signing of the Treaty of Union in 1707, which had concluded with the words: 'We're bought and sold for English gold / Such a parcel o' rogues in a nation.'

He had been so proud to lead the fight for independence, like his famous namesake. Now, as he undid three hundred years of history, he, too, felt little more than a rogue. He wearily signed, posed and smiled for the obligatory photographs and left.

Empty.

Dawn was breaking over the tall grey buildings of the New Town as he walked back along a deserted Northumberland Street to his flat. As ever, the regular sandstone blocks of the flats and advocates' offices appealed to George's ordered mind.

He looked fondly at his local, The Wally Dug, as he passed, thinking longingly of a pint of its extra-cold Guinness. Its name always made him smile, as it celebrated the famous ceramic hounds, the 'wally dugs', that were a monument to Scottish kitsch. He liked nations that could laugh at themselves.

But now his life was no laughing matter. Could it only be three months ago that his biggest concern was that the use of the phrase 'new dawn' was too much of a cliché after the referendum vote? It had been a ninety-day descent from idealism to immorality.

He switched off his mobile and unplugged the main phone. Relishing the cold freshness of the white cotton sheets, he was asleep inside a minute.

Gianluca Sarti turned to the three other men in the BMW parked across from George's flat. They had watched George's weary arrival in silence. 'We do it when he comes out.'

He looked directly at the second in command of the Edinburgh BLA, Neil Robertson. 'We hold him. You fire the shot. Everybody understand?'

The three men nodded their assent.

KNOCKAVIE HOUSE, STIRLINGSHIRE, 9 A.M.

Robert Cowan and the five other leaders of the SUR sat round the breakfast table, waiting patiently for the housekeeper to clear the dishes. When she had taken the last plate, he began. 'Right, gentlemen, let me run through it one more time. At midnight, I will make the broadcast from BBC Scotland announcing the formation of the new government. Although the controller of the BBC, Blair Hamilton, is a convinced Unionist and a personal friend, I think he might be too old-school to approve of the coup, so I have deliberately kept him out of the loop. Once I have made the broadcast from the BBC at midnight, we swing into action. Fraser, you will deal with home affairs. The most important issue will be the police. I believe you know most of the eight chief constables already?'

Fraser Smith nodded.

'Good. I have already "squared off" Alistair Stroud at Strathclyde.'

The two other Masons in the room smiled.

'Please make sure the others are all in Edinburgh by Monday night. The officers of the Royal Regiment of Scotland are committed to our cause and thus the power of the other ranks has been effectively neutralised. The police are the only potential organised force of resistance to our new government. I cannot imagine, knowing their political views, that the other chief constables will be any danger to us, but we need them to spell out the new realities to the rank and file.

'Fraser, you need to give them the agreed line on Monday for them to spin to their forces. Remember, keep it simple: business as usual and elections to follow.'

Robert Cowan was enjoying himself enormously. He knew how to do this – how to plan a major project. He had all the business skills. He knew he could run a country. This was his moment.

As a calculated gambler, it appealed to his nature. He had worked hard to shorten the odds. The Americans behind him, the army on board. A calculated gamble. One he couldn't lose.

He turned to Torquil Crichton. 'Right, Torquil, finance for you. The key task on Monday morning will be dealing with the three clearing banks. Clearly the launch of the Scottish pound will be cancelled, so it is critical we have enough English pounds to avoid a run on any of the banks. I suggest we shut them on Monday, ready to reopen on the Tuesday. OK?'

Crichton nodded, taking notes in a narrow, wire-bound reporter's pad.

'Jonathan, you will deal with the civil service. We know morale at Victoria Quay is at rock bottom, so reintegration into the British civil service and the potential for promotion will be popular. I suggest you talk to them all in the central atrium at lunchtime on Monday, once they have had time to absorb the news.'

Cowan continued round the table for the next hour, giving orders, assigning tasks. In charge. Satisfied.

NORTHUMBERLAND STREET, EDINBURGH, 1 P.M.

George moaned softly and turned over to look at the accusing luminous figures in the alarm clock. 13.02. 'Oh, Christ.'

He switched on his mobile for his morning fix, an addiction worse than alcohol. No wonder they were known as 'crackberries'. Sixteen voice messages, twenty-two texts and forty-two emails. All new since 4.30 a.m. Did these people have no sense of decency?

He scratched his head and sat up in bed, trying to impose order in his dishevelled mind. He needed to prioritise, the indispensable political skill. Do what is important, not what is first in the queue.

He also needed to get to the office to sort things out. He had to brief Ross, then the media team, then get a dress kilt on for dinner at the castle with the visiting heads of state tonight, then a final check of Ross's speech, then . . .

George dragged his aching body to the bathroom, swearing softly and temporarily abandoning his atheism. 'Christ Almighty, give me strength. Just let me get this week over and I promise I will be less of a sinner.'

Then he thought briefly, deliciously, of Jessica. 'Well, maybe not. More of a guideline than a rule, Lord.'

The hot jets of the shower were a blessed relief, his muscles easing and his brain anticipating the caffeine to come. It was not long disappointed.

George scanned the papers as he sipped his coffee. The treaty signing had been too late for the first editions, even in this digital age. The editorials split three ways, about a third offering a cautious welcome to the new state, a third opposed but impotent, a third refusing to recognise independence and demanding a new referendum.

Well, they could complain all they like. There was no going back now for Scotland, or for George – Karimov's poodle.

George grabbed his jacket and headed for the door. 'Destiny, here we come,' he said out loud to the empty living room.

As he walked down his hall steps George, for some absurd reason, couldn't get the Buzz Lightyear catchphrase 'To infinity and beyond' out of his head.

That was nearly his last-ever thought.

From the moment he closed his front door, all the subsequent events appeared to George to happen in slow motion. He was aware in his peripheral vision of a group of men running towards him on his right-hand side and then a punch to his face as he turned to look at them. The pain of that was overtaken by shock as his right knee landed with a thud on the unforgiving stone pavement.

His brain was just adjusting to that pain when a pistol butt was smashed against his right temple and lifted his agony to a new level.

The next sensation was one of deep shock as gunfire seemed to explode all around his head in a deafening roar. Instinctively, he threw himself to the ground as the rough hands either side of him let him slip.

After what seemed like hours, but in reality was less than ten seconds, he rolled over on his back and sat up. The scene was like something from a Tarantino movie, but this time for real.

Neil Robertson lay in front of him, a pistol in his hand and a surprised expression on his face. His chest had three bullet exit wounds in a rough triangle around his heart.

The two CIA agents, Joe and Mike, were on his right, one kneeling and bowed like a Muslim at prayer, the other splayed like a broken doll, half his face missing.

On his left Gianluca Sarti sat slumped against the carved sandstone blocks of the wall, loudly moaning. His right hand looked like it was trying to spoon the contents of his stomach back inside his body.

George panicked as he saw two black-clad figures in balaclavas run towards him but was rooted to the spot, incapable of even the most feeble defence. One rushed past him, took careful aim at Sarti's head and fired.

The casual violence of this act staggered him.

A black van screeched to a halt and two more figures joined their companions in loading the bodies into the back. As he watched, dumbfounded, George tasted blood from a trickle down his temple. Another figure stepped from the passenger seat of the van.

Karimov.

After all the violence, his voice was curiously gentle. 'George, listen to me. We need to go inside.'

George stood up unsteadily and leaned against the soot-stained stone of his wall. He watched the van leave. Karimov was more insistent this time. 'Now, George. We need to go inside now. I have some things here that will make you feel better.'

George nodded, unable to do anything more. Colonel Karimov helped him up the stairs and into the living room. Surprisingly deft for a big man, he fetched George a large brandy and some paracetamol, then tenderly cleaned and dressed his wound.

George finally felt capable of words. 'Why are you doing this?'

'Because I learned first aid, the hard way, in Afghanistan, and I really don't think we want the Scottish government's number two turning up at an Edinburgh hospital with a wounded head. Not today of all days.'

George fought back the thumping ache in his head and tried to articulate his feelings. 'No, I meant . . . I meant the stuff in the street. The killing. Christ, the murder of a defenceless man.'

'Hardly defenceless,' replied Karimov. 'Don't you get it, George? Those men were about to shoot you. I have had men following you ever since I arrived in Scotland. Luckily, they intervened in time. If the shooter had been more professional, you would be dead. But he hesitated. Fortunately for you, he felt the desire to hit you first. Perhaps to give himself time, or maybe to pluck up his courage. In any event, that saved your life.'

George struggled to take it all in. 'But why would anyone want to kill me?'

Karimov looked incredulous, but his tone was, as ever, calm and measured. 'Why do you think? Because you are a face of the Scottish government and thus an enemy of the BLA.'

Karimov's mobile interrupted their exchange. '*Da*?' He listened intently for a minute then hung up. He turned to George, frowning. 'Three of the men who

----

attacked you were not Scottish, but American. Of course, they had no ID, but all three had American boxer shorts on, and shoes with US sizes stamped on the soles. They must be CIA.'

George struggled for focus, trying to digest this new information. 'Hold on, you're saying that the American government tried to assassinate me. But I've been to the White House, met the president,' adding lamely, 'and some of my best friends are American.'

Karimov smiled pityingly. 'Grow up, George. You're not in the cosy world of Scottish politics now. The stakes could not be higher. What's one man's life in comparison to maintaining the dominance of the US over us all?'

For Karimov, it wasn't a question which required an answer. He simply didn't have the mental furniture to see things differently. He was steeped in the Russian tradition of state power, of the collective over the individual, where the Western idea of the primacy of personal rights had never taken root.

Karimov finished the dressing neatly. 'Right, I need to go, but I want you to have this.' Colonel Karimov handed him a pistol. The first thing that struck George was how heavy it was. The second was how ludicrous this situation was. 'You ever used one of these before?' questioned Karimov.

'Of course I have. No meeting in the public relations business was complete without side arms. For fuck's sake, don't be so stupid. I've never wielded anything deadlier than a biro.'

Karimov continued as if George hadn't spoken. He gestured methodically. 'It is a GSh-18 semi-automatic pistol, successor to the famous Makarov. It holds eighteen 9-mm bullets. It opens like this, and fires like this. OK?'

George's head reeled. This was Edinburgh. The New Town. And he was being armed by the Russian Secret Service to protect him from Americans. This was all wrong, all so wrong.

His sole response of 'OK' really didn't do his feelings justice.

Karimov stood up to leave. He tried to comfort George. 'When my men are finished disposing of the bodies, they'll be back to guard you. They'll be parked outside in a grey Ford if you need them. The pistol is just a little extra insurance. Once you are over the shock, you'll be fine. The first time in combat is always the same.'

'Colonel?'

'Yes.'

'Why did you do it? Save me, I mean.'

Karimov seemed puzzled by the question. 'Because I need you alive. You have an important role to fill for me: for Scotland; for Russia. I can assure you that it's nothing personal. And remember, George, first Catherine and now you. You owe me. You owe me now and for ever.'

Their conversation was interrupted by a ring at the door bell.

Karimov signalled George to follow him downstairs. He positioned himself kneeling on the polished wooden floorboards, leaning with one elbow on the hall table and training his gun on the door. 'Unlock the door but keep it closed, then get behind that chair and train your gun on the door. Only fire on my command. Understand?' he whispered.

George did as he was told and the Scot and the Russian levelled their guns at the black wooden door.

George tried to keep his voice as steady as possible. 'Come in.'

CHAPTER 17

WEDNESDAY, 30 JULY — ONE DAY TO INDEPENDENCE

NORTHUMBERLAND STREET, EDINBURGH, 2.30 P.M.

The door swung partly open and an old, purple-veined face appeared round the edge. He looked at the two pistols pointing at him. 'For fuck's sake, George, what kind of a welcome is this?'

'Jesus, Uncle Tommy, you gave me the fright of my life. What the fuck are you doing here?'

'I frightened *you*, ya cheeky cunt? I feel I need to point out to you that I am not the one with a great big fucking gun in his hand.'

George lowered his pistol. 'Christ, yes . . . sorry about that. Come on in.'

He turned to Karimov. 'It's OK, it's only my uncle.'

Karimov holstered his own weapon under his suit jacket. 'It's time for me to go, George. You take care of yourself. I'll see you soon.'

'What the fuck was that all about?' exclaimed Tommy as the door clicked shut behind the Russian. 'Who was he? And what in God's name have you done to yer heid?'

'It's a long story,' sighed George. 'He is the new Russian ambassador to Scotland.'

'Well, I cannae say I took to him,' Tommy said emphatically.

'He is definitely an acquired taste,' agreed George. 'Anyway, you had better come on up. I must say I am surprised to see you in Edinburgh.'

George's surprise was genuine. His old family all held the traditional Glaswegian prejudice that you have more fun at a Glasgow funeral than an Edinburgh wedding, and therefore were not frequent visitors to the capital. Though the cities were separated by less than the average London commute, there was a massive cultural difference and a mutual antipathy. Most Glaswegians agreed with the famous remark of one of their Lord Provosts, who declared that, 'Edinburgh is hard to ignore, but well worth the effort.'

So George understood that it must be a matter of some importance that had made Tommy travel east.

'Aye, I will come up. I could murder a cup of tea. But before I do, there is someone I want you to meet.' Tommy went to the door and motioned in a nervous-looking, dark-haired boy. 'George, this is Gordon Williams.'

EDINBURGH CASTLE, 2.59 P.M.

Captain Paul Murray marched briskly down the ancient cobbles that led from the One O'Clock Gun to the gatehouse. The two police officers and sniffer dog struggled to keep up with his energetic pace. He paused at the main entrance to the castle. 'Right, gentlemen, I believe that leaves just the esplanade and the stands to check, and then we have the all-clear.'

One of the police officers looked up at the rooms above the arched gate. 'What about above here?'

'Don't worry, that area is never open to the public. It is only the court-martial room and the small balcony where the lone piper will play "Scotland the Brave" at midnight. My men double-checked that this morning when the BBC chaps put their microphones in. It's all fine. Saves you boys the trouble.'

The police officers shrugged, then tugged their liver-and-white-coloured spaniel across the bridge over the moat and on to the esplanade itself, where he started eagerly sniffing at the large metal poles which supported the stands.

Upstairs, in a bag behind the screen that covered the radiator, a digital clock ticked over to 3 p.m.

PACIFIC QUAY, GLASGOW, 3 P.M.

Pacific Quay was one of the jewels of Glasgow's post-industrial renaissance. As well as the headquarters of BBC Scotland and Scottish Television, it boasted one of Europe's best science museums and an IMAX cinema, both encased in gleaming aluminium sheets.

Facing it, on the north bank, the new Museum of Shipbuilding was finally taking shape, with the tall-masted schooner as a permanent exhibition: Glasgow's historic industry now successfully recycled into tourist dollars.

Directly across from the Science Museum on the south bank of the Clyde, the old graving docks, where ships were once given their final fitting-out, were now restored and surrounded by hip yuppie flats. Where men in boiler suits had once smoked their fags in the biting wind and rain were a digital media quarter, a Michelin-starred restaurant and a well-maintained marina.

The marina had been created inside the old sandstone walls. It was home to the yachts of serious sailors, who used it as a base to explore the islands of western Scotland from the mouth of the Clyde – Bute, Arran and Jura. It was also a temporary refuge for the curious, idle rich, bored with the south of France, and Scottish tax exiles wanting to keep a base in the old country. Moored beside the yachts was the seaplane that flew well-heeled tourists to Tobermory harbour on day excursions.

Only the most eagle-eyed observer would have noticed the nondescript boat which had joined this bustling scene in the last two weeks. But anyone who had glanced inside the main cabin would have been amazed to see the array of technology sitting there and the silent intensity of the men working on it.

Those same ten men were now listening with the same intensity to their boss, Thomas Atkinson. 'Right, listen up. Tomorrow is the big day and you men have the absolutely key role to play. Robert Cowan's broadcast simply must happen at midnight for our plan to succeed and chaos to be avoided. There can be no fuck-ups. We have double-checked the security. Two old unarmed guys at the BBC and one beardless youth at Scottish Television should not prove much of an obstacle for America's finest.'

The men grinned back at the compliment.

'Strathclyde Police have doubled their patrols since the kidnap of Catherine Wallace at the Millennium Bridge, but you can rest assured they won't bother us on the night. They have been instructed to find themselves elsewhere at midnight.'

Atkinson gestured with his forefinger as he issued instructions. 'You two will be with me, sticking as close as possible to Robert Cowan at all times. You four will ensure the BBC broadcast goes out, using the boat's satellite as a back-up if there is a problem. You three will do the same at STV. The twenty guys based at Maryhill will ring the two buildings and provide the muscle if any is required. Questions?'

There were none.

'OK, after the midnight broadcast, you two will drive with Cowan to the parliament building in Edinburgh, which will have been secured by thirty of our men. Once on the M8, you will on no account stop for anyone not personally authorised by me . . .'

Atkinson's briefing was interrupted by his mobile phone ringing.

He listened in silence to a rapid run-down on that afternoon's botched operation. 'All dead? Are you sure?'

He sensed the men around him paying too much attention to his call and stepped out on to the deck to continue.

'OK. It is a huge pain in the ass, but not the end of the world. Make sure we are in full deny-and-destroy mode. We will just have to get him on Monday. Anything else today or tomorrow might jeopardise the ceremony and that cannot be allowed to happen.'

He hung up and looked at his watch. Just after ten in the morning in the States. Clearly someone else good was playing in this game. The ball-buster-in-chief was not going to like that. Reluctantly, he dialled Jane Chalmers' private number.

NORTHUMBERLAND STREET, EDINBURGH, 3.30 P.M.

George brought through a tray with a teapot, three mugs and some digestive biscuits of indeterminate age. 'Sorry about those, haven't been shopping in a wee while.'

They sipped their tea. George realised his hand was shaking and put his mug firmly back on the table to try to disguise it.

Tommy looked quizzically at the cut and swelling bruise on George's temple. 'So you never said what happened to yer heid.'

'I slipped in the shower and banged it.'

'Aye, well, you were certainly planning to take full revenge on the plumber,' responded Tommy, looking at the Russian revolver lying on the table.

George laughed. Even as a boy he had found it hard to get one over on his uncle. 'Look, Tommy, it's complicated and probably best if no other members of the family get involved, believe you me.'

'All right, ah get the message – *shut the fuck up*. Luckily, forty years of marriage to yer Auntie Jean was perfect preparation for it.'

George took a sip of the scalding, sweet tea. 'So tell me, Tommy, apart from sharing your sparkling wit, what are you here for?'

Tommy's face grew grave, his deep blue eyes, for once, lacking their usual twinkle. 'George, you know ah hate everything you stand for, all this Scottish

---

republican pish. It goes against everything oor family has ever believed in. But what the BLA done to Catherine, and plan ti dae in the future is jist plain wrong.'

Gordon Williams shifted awkwardly in his chair.

'Young Gordon here has something tae tell you. His da and me used to work taegether at the Albion Works.'

George gave an involuntary shiver at the mention of the place Catherine had been held captive.

'Go on, son, tell him,' Tommy said encouragingly.

The few hairs on Gordon's upper lip were spotted with beads of sweat. He looked absurdly young to George. He began reluctantly then picked up pace, as if saying it quickly would make it less bad. 'Mr Wallace, ah am a' for the cause. My family are a' diehard Loyalists. But it has a' gone tae fuck. Shooting that wee wean, that was just no' right. And ah have been thinking since then . . .'

'You were there when Jessie Cairns was murdered? It wasn't you who . . .'

'Naw, naw, it wis Sammy who done it. Honest. But ah saw it – it wis horrible. And so ah've been thinking that ah want oot, but ye dinnae cross Sammy and live.'

'Sammy who?' George asked.

'Sammy Wilson.'

George looked at Gordon thoughtfully. 'So, you want to give evidence against this man in return for a pardon. And, I guess, a new address and a new identity.'

Gordon nodded, his head bowed and his eyes fixed on the ground. Ashamed.

George continued, 'But why are you telling me this? Why don't you go to the police?'

'Because there's more,' Tommy interjected. 'Ye have tae tell him, son.'

Yet again, it all came out in a rush. 'There's a plan. Tomorra. They're gonnae take over. An' the polis know about it an' are gonnae dae nothing. They are a' in oan it.'

George felt the hairs rise on his neck. 'Who is, son? Who's going to take over?'

'It's a mix. Some posh guys from the Scottish Unionist Resistance an' the Yanks. An' us.'

'Go on.'

'There's gonnae to be some big signal to start us off, then we're gonnae seize a' they fancy buildings. Oor unit's gonnae take the City Chambers in Glesga.'

'And what is the signal?'

'Ah dinnae ken, honest, Mr Wallace. Jist that it's midnight tomorra we go intae action.'

Gordon was pale and sweating profusely now. 'Christ, Sammy would hae ma baws in a sandwich if he knew I wis here.'

George knew he had all the information he was going to get from Gordon. He had to think. And fast. 'Listen, son, thanks for that. You have been a great help. More than you can possibly imagine. I need to talk to some people. But I will see you are looked after. I can promise you that.'

Tommy stood up. 'Thanks for the cuppa, George. We'd better heid back. We dinnae want anyone to get suspicious. And if ah stay much longer in Embra ah might come oot in hives.'

George walked them down to the door. He shook Tommy's then Gordon's hand. Gordon hesitated, then asked, 'Mr Wallace, how's Catherine? Is she all right?'

It all clicked into place for George. 'You were Gordon the good guard, weren't you? The one who talked to her? Catherine told me about you.'

Gordon nodded, shamefaced. 'Ah'm sorry, Mr Wallace.'

George felt his hand curl into a fist. He didn't know whether to punch him or hug him. In the end he lamely settled for, 'She is fine, son, and the baby is, too. I'll tell her you were asking after her.'

'Thanks, Mr Wallace, ah'd appreciate that.'

George's eyes locked with Tommy's. 'I really can't thank you enough for doing this. I know how hard it must be for you. Old loyalties die hard.'

'It is a'right, George. Family comes before faith. Ye were always the nicest one in the family, not that ye had much competition, mind you. Ye deserve some help. Just stay strong and, son, do the right thing. Promise me that an' ah'll be happy.'

The door clicked softly behind them.

George stared at it, a single tear rolling down his left cheek.

CHAPTER 18

WEDNESDAY, 30 JULY — ONE DAY TO INDEPENDENCE

NORTHUMBERLAND STREET, EDINBURGH, 4 P.M.

George wearily climbed the stairs and slumped on the sofa. He tried desperately to stem the tears that were now pouring down his face. He knew this was a classic sign of delayed shock, but that knowledge didn't help him control it. He willed himself into focus.

He glanced down at his watch: 4 p.m. Christ, it was only three hours since he had woken up . . . and he had survived an assassination attempt and discovered a planned coup d'état. What the fuck was going on in his life?

He couldn't deny that people were right about one thing – he most certainly was out of his depth in this new, surreal world.

First of all, he had to work out who he could talk to. Who could he trust? Who was involved in the coup? How much did Karimov know? And Ross? Which senior policemen were aiding the rebels? Who in the army?

George's mind raced, question tumbling over question. What did he need to do to foil the coup?

Then, uninvited, came the startling, heretical thought, 'Should he even try?'

Maybe it was better that the coup happened. Maybe that was what Uncle Tommy meant about doing the right thing.

If the plot succeeded, then the American-backed SUR government would have to hold elections and a new referendum. World opinion would see to that. And what Charles Sands had said in the Langham was undoubtedly right: better American masters than Russian ones. History taught that. How long would Scotland rest under the Russian heel? Decades, like the Chechens? Centuries, like the Georgians?

And, most important to him personally, he would be free of his promise to Karimov.

But a coup victory would mean the end of the dream – his dream – of Scottish independence for a generation at least, probably longer. It would mean defeat for democracy and victory for the violence of the BLA, the people who had planned to kill his daughter, against the Russians who had saved his and her lives. And the death of many people he cared about deeply.

George loved playing chess, which he considered the intellectual cousin of dominoes. He had wholeheartedly agreed with Benjamin Franklin's analysis of the game's virtues: 'First, foresight, which looks a little into futurity, and considers the consequences that may attend an action, second, circumspection, which surveys the whole chess-board, or scene of action, the relation of the several pieces and their situation and third, caution, not to make our moves too hastily.'

Perfect skills, also, for a successful political operator. And ones George sought to use now.

As George wrestled with his terrible dilemma, he was aware more than ever that he was a pawn – this time, a pawn who could topple a king.

The ringing of his mobile broke this unresolved train of thought. It was Ross. 'George, where the fuck are you? We were meant to be here together, fine-tuning this speech, two hours ago.'

'Sorry, Ross, I fell back asleep on the sofa. The negotiations went on until the small hours.'

'I heard. Well, get your arse in gear, there is a mountain of stuff to do here.'

Ross lacked his usual charm. He was edgy, nervous. And not even a word of congratulations or thanks for all his work on the negotiations. Yet again, George felt the distance between them and deep resentment at his treatment. He wondered how long he could remain the junior partner in this particular relationship. He tried to retain some dignity after Ross's brusque command. 'I will be there as fast as I can. I just need to make a couple of calls.'

DREGHORN BARRACKS, COLINTON, EDINBURGH, 6 P.M.

Lance-Corporal Brian McTavish was a deeply aggrieved man as he polished his boots. Every rhythmic stroke of the black brush seemed to heighten his frustration.

It just wasn't fair.

He and his mates in the Black Watch were confined to barracks when the whole of Edinburgh would be on the streets partying and the whole place would be hotching with talent. Not just local, *foreign* talent, too. Girls who might well succumb to the charms of a fine-looking young soldier in a kilt.

And, even worse than that, he was missing out on the chance to strut his stuff in front of the TV cameras. His mum and dad were gutted.

The officers had picked their teacher's pets for the ceremonial duty. Not the best drill team, nor those with the longest service. Just all the usual arse-lickers. All the ones who were in with the brass. All the ones in the barracks saying they backed the officers in not taking the oath, rather than with their mates who would swear it.

It was a fucking outrage.

Personally, he couldn't give a toss for politics or politicians, but he felt as Scottish as the next man. In the field, you fought for your mates, first and foremost, but if there had to be a higher ideal he was putting his arse on the line for, he would rather it was Scotland than Britain, and he knew a lot of the boys felt the same.

But that was nothing compared to the thought of all those good-looking birds going to waste.

QUEENSBOROUGH GARDENS, GLASGOW, 7 P.M.

Catherine Wallace loved being pregnant, but after a long day in the studio she could have murdered a chilled glass of Chardonnay. She looked disapprovingly at her seven-month-old bump. 'Just as long as you remember what I sacrificed for you.'

After the drama of the kidnap and the rescue, Catherine had thrown herself into her work to try to get over the shock. Producing the live discussion on independence night was a huge career break for her and she was determined not to mess it up. Her colleagues at the BBC had urged her to take some time off and had been amazed at her resilience.

Catherine knew she was holding it together, but only just. She didn't want to worry Geoff or her dad – they had suffered enough – so she kept the dreams to herself. But every night at 3 a.m. a looming face in a balaclava came to her, followed by a shot. And then her brains, like Billy's, spread everywhere.

Her thoughts were interrupted by an insistent ringing. She heaved herself out of the armchair and reached for the phone. She was just getting to the stage of pregnancy where deep leather armchairs were starting to represent a significant challenge. She shook the memory of the dream out of her head and remembered to be cheerful. 'Hi, Dad. Lovely to hear from you. How are you?'

George felt Catherine had been through enough on his behalf and was keen to protect her from further anxiety, so skipped the story of the assassination attempt. However, there was one thing he needed to discuss. 'I'm fine, darling, and just about to head out to the big celebration dinner at the castle. But I just wanted to check that you were OK.'

'I'm fine too, Dad, getting larger by the day.'

'And are you feeling safe?'

Catherine pulled the curtain back and looked out in the early evening sunshine at the squad car across the road. 'I've two of Strathclyde Police's top officers looking after me as we speak,' she giggled. 'One is smoking, the other appears to be excavating his nose. I reckon these two could see off anything short of a full frontal assault by the Seventh Cavalry.'

George was anxious and persistent. 'Seriously, honey, I can't really go into why, but I need to know you are staying in and staying safe the rest of the weekend.'

'Honestly, Dad, you never pay attention to anything,' said Catherine in exasperation. 'You know very well I'm producing the independence ceremony debate show tomorrow. We've been rehearsing all day today, which is why I'm nursing the most fetching pair of swollen ankles. Geoff can hardly contain himself.'

George was really pleased to hear Catherine sounding so happy and relaxed, but he guessed that the BBC would be an obvious target in any coup. This complicated things. He couldn't protect Catherine without revealing the plot to her.

Yet again, he postponed the decision. 'OK, honey, you put your feet up. I had better go. I'll call tomorrow. Give my best to Geoff. I love you.'

Catherine put down the phone. The journalist in her was sure her father was not telling the whole truth. But then again, neither was she.

EDINBURGH CASTLE, 8 P.M.

George had never seen the castle look quite so wonderful. Flaming torches lined both sides of the bridge across the moat. Searchlights played across her strong, impassive stone and slate face.

George looked around the drinks reception in the Great Hall, carefully avoiding Karimov's steady gaze from the corner.

Then he saw who he was looking for. Jessica was coming towards him, wearing a stunning black cocktail dress, low cut at the back, her hair dressed high and beautifully crafted, a single diamond glittering at her throat. She looked amazing. 'And here was me thinking that the castle looked magnificent tonight.'

Jessica blushed at the compliment and returned it, surveying his Clan Wallace dress kilt of light and dark grey cut through with yellow lines. 'You are a charmer, George, and you don't scrub up too badly yourself . . . Jesus, what happened?'

For the first time, she noticed the ugly welt on his right temple left by the pistol that afternoon.

Unknowingly, George echoed Sammy's line. 'I know it looks bad, but you should see the other guy.'

Somehow, it didn't carry the same menace as when Sammy Wilson uttered it. So, to Jessica's continuing questioning gaze, George added weakly, 'I'll tell you later.'

The official dinner dragged on with a series of interminable toasts. The undoubted highlight of the night was President Churov's rendition of Burns' poetry, which went down a storm with the gathered dignitaries and the international media.

The crowd thinned at around eleven. George finished his conversation with the French consul and sought out Jessica. 'Fancy a nightcap?'

'Sure.'

'How about my place? The whisky is cheap and the welcome warm.'

Jessica put on her best faux-Southern accent. 'Why, Mr Wallace, I do believe you are trying to seduce me.'

'I promise not, though I could certainly make it worth your while, in ways you can't even imagine.'

Intrigued, Jessica followed him out of the Great Hall, down past St Margaret's Chapel, and through the gatehouse where the clock behind the radiator clicked relentlessly away.

As an LA girl, Jesssica always marvelled that it was still light at 11.30 p.m.

in Scotland in the summer. Magical. If not for her Manolo Blahniks, she would have thoroughly enjoyed the walk to George's flat. Not for the first time, she cursed the lack of taxis in Edinburgh.

As George put his key in the lock, he noticed the two figures in the grey Ford across from his flat. It brought him a strange comfort.

They settled into the sofa, two large tumblers of Arran malt in their hands. 'Do you know the ultimate irony about this debate about national identity?'

'No, George, but I've a horrible feeling you are going to enlighten me,' Jessica sighed.

Like all men with what they consider a pressing piece of knowledge to impart, George was not put off by the lack of female encouragement. 'The name Wallace actually means "foreign" in Old English, that is why Wales is called Wales. Somewhere in the mists of time I was a stranger in this land – as we all were in this mongrel nation. Scotland's greatest-ever hero was actually a foreigner. I kind of like that idea.'

'George, all that I know about William Wallace is what I learned when you dragged me to see *Braveheart*. I seem to recall you were the only one cheering in the Leicester Square Odeon.'

'You see! Good, decent people, the English, but no sense of humour. Freedom, Australian-style, who couldn't enjoy the irony in that?'

'Listen, it may be the whisky or the fact I'm not steeped in your national myths, but what exactly is your point?' Jessica's tone was playful, with just the merest hint of impatience.

'Our clan motto is *Pro libertate* – "For liberty".'

'So?'

George's mind fought against the alcohol and the shock of the day. He wanted to throw caution to the wind and tell Jessica everything, but knew he couldn't. 'So, my point is that is a lot to live up to – especially as everyone seems to think I am swimming in the shallow end of the Wallace gene pool.'

Jessica laughed. 'My mom was right, never underestimate a man's ability to feel sorry for himself!'

'Too cruel.'

'Why don't you tell me what really happened today?'

George considered briefly. Whisky triumphed over caution. 'I will. On one condition.'

'What's that?'

'I'm talking to you as Jessica the human being, not Jessica the journalist.'

'Sure, it's a deal.'

George then told Jessica about the attempt on his life and America's backing for a coup by the Scottish Unionist Resistance, only holding back his Faustian pact with Karimov. He was slightly put out that she seemed more interested in the coup than the assassination attempt.

Every journalistic sinew in Jessica was straining. She was already regretting her rash promise to George. This was dynamite. Absolute dynamite. But to use it would betray George. And destroy the best chance of a relationship she had had in years.

Unable to stop, she eagerly pressed on with her questions. 'You are telling me that the United States is involved in state-sponsored assassination *and* toppling a democratically elected government. Have you any idea how important this is?'

'Give me some credit, Jessica.'

'What are you going to do?'

George outlined his dilemma. One of the skills he had retained from his PR days was the ability to summarise effectively. He had no problem understanding issues, just resolving them.

Jessica listened patiently, suddenly aware of how agonisingly torn George was and slightly ashamed of having immediately thought of what the best newspaper angles would be. 'Have you decided what you're going to do?'

'Not yet, no. I was going to sleep on it. What do you think?'

Jessica shook her head. 'George, darling, I'm not qualified to tell you that. One plan undermines my own government. The other gives in to terrorism. You would need the wisdom of Solomon to sort that out. I simply can't tell you what to think.'

George was silent, lost in anxious thought. So Jessica continued. 'But I will tell you how I feel. Do you remember we went to see the revival of *The Crucible* in London one of the nights you were down on business?'

'Sure.'

'Do you remember the last scene, when John Proctor is going to be hanged because he won't give them his name?'

'Of course.'

'And his wife won't make the choice for him. She says, whatever he does, she knows that a good man does it. Well, that's how I feel about it. God, George, you have your faults. You can be vain and bad-tempered. You wanted power more than you should have. Maybe more than you can deal with. But you are a good man, George, generous, thoughtful, clever, loving and decent.'

Jessica took his hands in hers. 'As Elizabeth Proctor concluded: whatever you decide, I know a good man does it. I know you will do the right thing.'

That cursed phrase again. George wanted to weep.

George hugged her and they sat for a few minutes, silent, locked in embrace. Jessica broke the moment. 'Listen, George, I must go. It's late.'

George walked her to the front door. They kissed longingly. 'Will you stay?' he asked hopefully.

'I don't think I'm ready to . . .'

'No, I understand. I just need someone to be here. Someone to hold.'

Jessica searched his face, then nodded.

Outside, the two FSB agents tried to get as comfortable as their car would allow.

In his bed, George held Jessica close, noting that his old Penn T-shirt looked a lot better on her than it ever had on him. He curled into her and fell fast asleep, overwhelmed by all the shocks of that day.

As he slept, Jessica lay awake staring into the darkness, the unaccustomed weight of his arm across her chest.

She now had her own dilemmas to resolve.

One professional. One personal.

CHAPTER 19

THURSDAY, 31 JULY — INDEPENDENCE DAY

PRINCES STREET, EDINBURGH, NOON

Inspector Jock Gibson waved the last impatient taxi through, then ordered his men to put in place the barricades which would shut off Princes Street to traffic for the next seventeen hours. Using a blueprint from the annual Hogmanay celebrations, he had it down to a fine art. The hundred thousand revellers arriving to celebrate the birth of an independent Scotland would have their fun. But in a supervised, organised way. He would see to that.

The city centre had been thoroughly swept for terrorist bombs and he had armed men on every entrance to Princes Street and the castle, so he was sure he would have no trouble from those clowns in the BLA.

Inspector Gibson was regularly the match commander at the Edinburgh derby between Hearts and Hibs, and he thought this was going to be a piece of cake compared to dealing with that afternoon of mayhem.

He had a light police presence planned for the crowd itself, reckoning there would be less drunken violence at the declaration of independence than at the average New Year. There had been a rumour that some Hearts casuals might try to cause some bother in a last-minute defence of the Union, so he had some police spotters out for them. But nothing else was causing him much concern. Plus The Proclaimers, Scotland's favourite old group, were the headline act and they always put the crowd in a great mood.

The biggest headache, as always, was making sure all the VIPs made it up to the castle esplanade on time. Funny how all problems always came back to traffic in Edinburgh, he thought, as he shouted at his team to get a bloody move on.

OFFICE OF THE FIRST MINISTER, SCOTTISH PARLIAMENT, EDINBURGH, 2 P.M.

Seated on either side of the first minister's expansive desk, Ross and George went through the speech for the third time in an hour. George had been drafting it, on and off, since the morning of the referendum result, adding a thought here and a line there as they had come to him through the weeks. Today had all been about refining and polishing the text.

George had tried hard to make it statesmanlike and thoughtful, with just the right hint of humility at the awesome responsibility Ross was about to shoulder. He had insisted that Ross reach out to the English, stressing that the social union remained even though the political one was coming to an end.

Ross read it out loud one final time and pronounced himself satisfied. 'It's great, George, one of your very best. I really don't know what I would do without you. You're such a support. Such a good friend.'

Like all intellectual and emotional bullies, Ross knew when to offer a little respite from his controlling behaviour in a relationship: a little glimpse of how good things once were and a hint that they might get better. Enough hope to keep the victim clinging to their dependency. It was one of the skills that made him such an effective leader of the party.

Ross believed it was a particularly successful control tactic with George because he felt so warmly about their relationship in the past and he needed Ross to feed his own desire to be at the centre of events. Naivety and ambition, a fatal combination.

Absorbed in his relentless quest for power, Ross hadn't fully understood the change in George in the last three months. He hadn't noticed how much he now doubted the whole project. Like some Greek tragic hero, Ross's ambition and love of power had clouded his judgement.

This time, George wasn't taking the bait of the compliment. 'Well, we'll see. But any speech is only as good as the delivery and I know you'll be wonderful tonight. Right from the very first day I met you at university I knew you had the gift of the gab.'

Ross eyed him suspiciously, not fooled by the warm sentiment. 'What do you mean, *we'll see*? Why would you not want to continue to be a support? What's wrong?'

George hesitated. He was reluctant to get into a debate, fearing that he might reveal more than he wanted to. More than was safe. He tried to delay matters. 'I just mean, Ross, when this is all over, we need to sit down and talk. I'm not sure I'm cut out for this any more.'

'Because of what happened yesterday?'

Naturally, Karimov had briefed Ross about the assassination attempt before George had even had a chance to tell him. 'No, not particularly. It's a range of things. That, Catherine's kidnap, the whole grinding negotiations for independence. I'm just not sure this is what I want any more.'

'Come on, George, I know it's been hard, but the finishing line is in sight. The worst is over. We are on the verge of delivering Scotland her freedom after three hundred years.' Ross grew more enthusiastic and tried to stir George's well-developed sense of history. 'We are midwives to the birth of a nation. Imagine what they will say in the history books about you. One day Catherine's unborn child will study in school what you achieved this week.'

George knew Ross really meant what *Ross* had achieved. George tried hard to ignore this blatant appeal to his vanity. If this last three months had taught him anything, it was what an Achilles heel his vanity had proved to be. 'Maybe I'm just exhausted, but I just don't feel the thrill that you do.'

'Look, I know you've worked so hard and suffered so much and, God knows, we have had to come the scenic route, but we are here now. This is real. I can touch it. Taste it. You *must* feel that, too.'

George looked at his old friend. Ross's eyes were literally shining with excitement. He realised he barely knew him at all, had barely known him all these years. 'I guess it just doesn't taste that sweet to me any more. The cost has been too high. For both of us.'

Ross's eyes narrowed in suspicion. 'What do you mean by that?'

George touched his bruised temple. 'It's really obvious what it has cost me, Ross, but have you ever thought what the long struggle to the top has cost you? No family. No friends who don't rely on your patronage. No life outside politics.'

George warmed to his theme. 'I've watched you. I've never seen you truly relax. You're endlessly calculating what actions mean rather than enjoying the moment. Always wondering what the agenda is, rather than just talking to somebody. When you're at a party, you're always looking over your shoulder to see if someone more important has come in. You only play golf with key journalists or influential businessmen. You only take people to the football to impress them rather than because you love the game. There has to be more to life than that.'

Ross, stung, retorted, 'Of course there is, but I had to be dedicated – dedicated to winning Scotland's freedom, no matter the personal cost.'

'Dedicated to becoming first minister, you mean.'

'Maybe so, but you have to admit I have been indispensable to the cause.'

'The graveyards are full of indispensable men, Ross.' Then, recklessly, George added, 'You need to get a life.'

As he rose to leave, he saw Ross's cheekbones clench as he tried to control his disappointment and anger at his attitude. With heroic self-restraint, Ross kept his voice calm. 'Don't do anything rash, George. You're just worn out. The work on the treaty, then Catherine's abduction. It's all bound to take a toll. But I know you of old, you just need a holiday then you'll be ready for the fray once more, trust me.'

One look at George's face told Ross that trust was the last feeling on his mind, so he warned him. 'Just promise me one thing . . .'

George for once held Ross's intimidating gaze.

'Promise me that you won't do anything to spoil tonight.'

George considered for a moment. Then he answered, perfectly truthfully, 'You have my word that I won't do anything to spoil tonight.'

Once George had left, Ross made the changes to the speech he knew he had to – the ones which George could never be allowed to see – in his own distinctive, angular handwriting.

THE HEADQUARTERS OF THE ARMY IN SCOTLAND, EDINBURGH CASTLE, 4 P.M.

Major-General Rory Stewart finished his last tour of the castle, checking the preparations for the independence ceremony, reflecting on what a hollow pretence it was as he tugged at scaffolding poles and inspected a random sentry's rifle. Finally he returned to his spacious, well-ordered office in the governor's mansion and pondered the twinkling lights of west Edinburgh.

For a man who had never flinched in the face of enemy fire, he was uncharacteristically nervous. An honest and straightforward man, he had thoroughly detested the last month of secrecy and subterfuge since he had met Robert Cowan and Thomas Atkinson at the Hilton. It was totally alien, both to his nature and his training.

As he had promised, he had taken all the officers of the rank of captain and above into his confidence. They had all supported him without question and none of them had talked, thank God. He had then hand-picked the honour guard for tonight's ceremony from the most loyal men in the regiment. He knew they had an inkling something was up from his unusual selection process, but he was sure none suspected the real reason they were on duty that night.

He had hated all that, but worse was to follow.

After Robert Cowan had met him in the Sheraton and told him about the bomb in the gatehouse that would both signal the start of the coup and kill Ross Johnson, he had barely slept. It felt like a desecration, an act of violence in the castle it was his *duty* to defend.

He knew it was immoral, but he had been cornered – made to accept Cowan's argument that the only alternative was failure and that disgrace and dishonour would inevitably follow. There could be no turning back.

Rory had been forced to take Captain Murray, the duty officer at the castle, into his confidence in order to ensure that the bomb was safely delivered – to ensure that Ross Johnson was killed. He could no longer evade responsibility for his actions. He was an accomplice to murder, pure and simple. Even worse, he had made Paul Murray one, too.

There was only one consolation. His king was only a mile away in the Palace of Holyroodhouse. Once this was all over he would get to see him: to demonstrate his loyalty; to pledge his allegiance in person; to receive absolution for his crime.

Rory knew he was going to do something very wrong in the pursuit of a greater good. It was a bitter necessity. All he had had to do was convince his conscience that he was doing the right thing as he paced the bedroom floor at 4 a.m. He had failed.

As he leaned back in his desk chair, he recalled the words of Martin Luther which had been drummed into him at his Sunday School in Dunblane, week after week.

When faced by his accusers and charged with heresy, Luther had simply responded, 'Here I stand, I can do no other.'

Here Rory Stewart stood. *He could do no other.*

GARELOCHHEAD, SCOTLAND, 7 P.M.

Ian Carmichael, the landlord of The Anchor Inn in the sleepy little village at the top of the Gare Loch, had been delighted to be so busy this week, all his rooms full with American guests. Young, fit men, not like the usual beer-bellied contractors coming to do business with the Ministry of Defence at the base.

Not that there had been many of them recently. Custom had fallen off a cliff since the navy had moved out two months before. There were local rumours of Russian troops there, but none had ever darkened the doors of his pub in search of a pint. What use was that to the likes of him?

And there wasn't much sign of even the protestors from the peace camp, the motley collection of messy tents and colourful caravans which sat among the well-appointed detached villas on the road to Helensburgh. It seemed there wasn't the same appetite to protest against Russian missiles as there had been to protest against American ones. Carmichael didn't have much time for hippies himself, but a paying customer was a paying customer.

These Americans were great customers. They were quiet and kept themselves to themselves, but tipped well. They hadn't really wanted to talk much. When pressed, they had told him they were part of a group cycling the Clyde Sea Lochs Trail. Not that he had seen them doing much cycling. When they were not out walking round the loch, they seemed to expend most of their energy flirting with the two young waitresses in the terrace café.

Their only request was to have an early dinner tonight. They had all wanted pasta, good slow-release carbohydrates for their big cycle tomorrow. And no wine.

That was a shame, because there was a fantastic margin on the house red. Still, they were great customers, absolutely to be welcomed in these troubled political times.

GEORGE SQUARE, GLASGOW, 9 P.M.

Sammy Wilson was furious about the escape of Catherine Wallace and the killing of his brother Billy.

It wasn't so much that he loved Billy – he wouldn't have wasted time on such a pointless emotion. He hadn't lifted a finger as his father subjected his little brother to the same relentless hammerings that he had endured. In Sammy's view, Billy simply had to learn life's harsh lessons. Much more important was the fact that Billy's murder was an affront to Sammy's dignity, his leadership of the group. That was painful. That could not be allowed to continue. That had to be rectified.

Sammy leaned against one of the massive granite lion statues that flanked Glasgow's imposing war memorial and gazed up at the facade of the Victorian City Chambers. His eye travelled from the soft yellow light cast by the seven massive bulbs at the front door up to the largest balcony thirty metres above.

Behind that balcony, the great and the good of Glasgow had just begun a celebration banquet to welcome the arrival of Scottish independence. Several magnums of champagne were chilling, waiting to be opened for a toast at midnight.

At that point, the Lord Provost would step on to the balcony and introduce Rob Cairns, who would then announce the birth of a new nation to the crowd on behalf of his dead wife, who had originally been due to give the speech.

Or, so he thought.

Instead, Sammy would lead twenty members of the BLA and ten Yank Special Operations troops into the City Chambers through the director of finance's office on George Street, which had been left unlocked by a sympathiser on the security staff. They would seize the building then announce the coup from the balcony. The crowd would be ordered to disperse under the new dusk-to-dawn curfew regulations.

The explicit orders to Sammy and the BLA from the SUR and the Americans had been to use minimum force and to avoid casualties at all costs. In particular, none of the dignitaries at the banquet were to be harmed.

As he fingered the hand grenade inside his pocket, Sammy thought, 'Aye, right, we'll see about that.'

He had a perfect way to give real justice to those republican scum and to restore his authority in the BLA at the same time. And who would really mourn them when they were gone?

NORTHUMBERLAND STREET, EDINBURGH, 10 P.M.

George drained his third dram and looked thoughtfully at the half-empty bottle of Arran malt. It was the seventy-seventh bottle of the cask he had laid down at Lochranza in 2002 and which had matured into three hundred and ninety bottles in 2012. After two years of restraint, he was certainly getting through them fast this week.

He had switched off his mobile and house phones in order to have complete peace and had settled in his favourite armchair with his favourite whisky.

Nothing in his forty-nine years had remotely prepared him for this. How could a completely exhausted former PR man hold not only the fate of his own nation but the future of world peace in his inadequate hands?

And why was he, once again, seeking solace and solutions in a bottle? George shook himself out of his self-loathing and stood up.

He looked at the clock on the wall. 10 p.m.

Enough. There could be no more delay. No more indecision. He had been through it all over and over again in his mind – a jumble of images from Catherine's blindfolded face to Clare's callous laugh.

He had made up his mind. He had to stop the coup. That was the right thing to do. He could not live with the guilt and shame of any other course of action. He could not break his cursed promise to Karimov.

And there was only one way to stop the coup. Luckily enough, George had been a diligent student and paid attention to his lecturers in Russian history at the University of Pennsylvania.

He reached for the mobile and switched it on to alert Catherine. Before he could dial the number, it rang in his hand. It was his Uncle Tommy. 'Christ, George, where have ye been? I have been trying to call you for hours.'

'Sorry, Tommy, my phone was off and—'

But Tommy was too impatient to listen to more. 'There's nae time for a' that. Ah've jist spoken tae Gordon. Ah now know what it is.'

'You know what *what* is, Tommy?'

'The signal, ya fucking moron. The signal for the coup.'

'What is it?'

'It's the gatehouse in the castle. There's a room above yon arch. There's a bomb there. Behind the radiator cover. George, at midnight they are planning to blow Ross Johnson tae kingdom fucking come.'

CHAPTER 20

THURSDAY, 31 JULY — INDEPENDENCE DAY

NORTHUMBERLAND STREET, EDINBURGH, 10 P.M.

As Tommy spoke those words, George's front door bell rang. He picked up the GSh-18 from the kitchen table and moved as quietly as he could downstairs to the narrow hall facing the door. He copied exactly the kneeling position he had seen Sergei Karimov adopt the previous day. He placed his elbows on the table and levelled the pistol at the door, trying his very best to clear the whisky from his brain and stop his hands from shaking. 'Who is it?'

'It's John, Dad, stop pissing about.'

George had never been so pleased to see the boyish, handsome face of his son. He opened the door and gave him a massive bear hug. His son stepped back, startled by this unexpected display of affection. 'Calm your jets, Dad, it hasn't been that long.'

'It's just great to see you, son. What are you doing here?'

'Come on, where else would I be but Edinburgh on a night like this? I know we've had our political differences, but I wanted to be in Scotland and with my dad.' Then he added, with a laugh, 'Plus, I am an actor, we love being there for the big, final scene.'

John draped an arm round his father's shoulders. 'I called your office but they said you weren't yet at the castle and your mobile was switched off, so I came here. I suppose you can blag me a ticket, can't you?'

George struggled to control his emotions. He remembered sitting with his son snuggled beside him under a duvet watching the results of the 1999 referendum coming in, the massive 'Yes' vote confirming the restoration of the Scottish Parliament. The adults drinking champagne in the living room as the boy nodded off on the sofa.

How simple it had all seemed then.

'Come on, son. We *are* going to the castle, but blagging you a ticket is the very least of our problems. We need to grab a cab. There is somewhere I must go first. I'll explain on the way. But the first thing I need to do is call your sister.'

They rushed outside and headed towards Frederick Street. After a hundred metres, George stopped, told John to wait and headed back to the flat. Once inside, he grabbed the pistol from the hall table and tucked it into the waistband of his suit trousers. Trying to ignore its unaccustomed weight, he hurried to catch up his son.

They hailed a cab and jumped in. George told the driver, 'Dreghorn Barracks, Colinton, as quick as you can, please.' He caught his son's incredulous stare out of the corner of his eye as the taxi sped off.

BBC SCOTLAND HEADQUARTERS, PACIFIC QUAY, GLASGOW, 10.15 P.M.

Catherine walked the thirty metres from the main entrance of the BBC headquarters to the railings on the banks of the Clyde. She carefully checked the thick silver metal bands for bird droppings, then leaned the back of her summer dress against them and cupped her left hand round her bump. As she cradled her mug of herbal tea in her right hand, she silently added caffeine to alcohol in the list of lost pleasures she was going to make this baby feel guilty about when it was older.

She took a welcome deep breath of the soft summer air. No matter how high-tech they were, galleries from where studio programmes were directed always reeked of sweat and coffee. Catherine was grateful of a break from that smell and the adrenalin-pumping atmosphere of live television.

She took a sip of her tea and surveyed the building in front of her. To be honest, she thought it was a bit of a modernist box in daylight, the five full-length glass floors under the massive BBC Scotland sign. At night, it had a magical atmosphere, the yellow light from the windows reflecting back off the inky blackness of the Clyde. As she was very well aware, the serenity of the facade was in stark contrast to the seething politics inside.

There was a fifteen-camera outside-broadcast unit covering the ceremony at Edinburgh Castle and Catherine was producing the studio discussion programme which would both precede the ceremony, then analyse it afterwards.

Catherine was glad to be back at her desk after the sheer terror of the kidnapping, though the continuing nightmares suggested she might be working through her reaction rather than dealing with it properly. Maybe once tonight was over she would seek some help. The whole episode had certainly put everything else in her life into perspective and had prompted a major bout of introspection.

She had always been a model child, sporty, helpful, top of her class. Then, at fifteen, partly in reaction to her parents' suffocating ambition for her, she fell off a cliff. She joined the school 'plastics', the fake-tanned and toned beauties who were way too cool for school, and embarked on a series of wild affairs with a series of men as inappropriate as she could manage. Through a panicked combination of bribery and threat, her parents had managed to get her through her exams and into university, a process that left lasting scars on them all.

At university, she rediscovered her appetite for study and hard work. Then she found journalism, her true calling. She excelled in the student newspaper and student TV, winning placements in spite of, rather than because of, her well-connected parents. Her passion propelled her on to the BBC's fast-track training scheme at just twenty-one. She had just graduated as a producer after two years and tonight was her first big challenge.

George and Bridget had been relieved when she had met Geoff: polite, caring, hard-working. And no piercings. Their approval had nearly been fatal to the relationship, but something in him – his decency and patience, perhaps – had made Catherine persist. Everything had seemed to be looking up for her.

Then her mother got sick. For all her communication skills, Catherine found it hard to articulate what losing a parent at nineteen meant. How many things left unsaid. How many experiences unlived. Most of all, Bridget's slow, agonising death made her realise, too late, how much of a child she still was. How much she still needed her mum. And how sorry she was for all she had done.

She was delighted to have sacrificed her big day for her mum, to see her face beam with pleasure as she sat in the front row, in her wheelchair with her morphine drip. She really hoped marriage was the right choice, though, like many bereaved young, she knew she had doubly welcomed the security and stability of a new home and had perhaps rushed in. She felt that fifteen years which normally might include bereavement, marriage and pregnancy had been compressed into four, and she only hoped that pressure wouldn't blow at some point. But this was the most painful time of all; she longed for her mum now, for long intimate baby talks, to share the most intense experience in a woman's life.

An even bigger shock was the realisation that, with a distraught brother and emotionally crippled father, she was expected to hold the family together. She realised she hadn't helped John much, but she had saved her dad, getting him to sell the house and encouraging him into a new career in politics. It had given him a new lease of life, a reason for living.

Given the last three months of stress, that didn't look like too smart a choice now, but she had the classic defence – it seemed like a good idea at the time. And it had undoubtedly made him happy, at least for a while, finding purpose in seeking a longed-for autonomy for his nation. Now, even her dad wasn't sure any more that independence was right for Scotland. Or that Ross was the right man to deliver it.

Though she hadn't told her father, Catherine was starting to share those doubts, too. In all the terrible terror of her kidnapping, then the mad rush of work, Catherine hadn't had much time to reflect on the implications of independence for herself and her profession – but she knew they were serious.

She had seen the tension at the top. The BBC was the last of the few genuinely British institutions left, along with the armed forces, the monarchy and the NHS, and would soon be joining them all at the knackers' yard.

All the BBC staff knew independence would mean big changes in political regulation and personal working conditions. Most welcomed the opportunity to cover the world from a Scottish rather than London perspective and the fact that they wouldn't have to move to London to further their careers. Worries remained about maintaining the BBC's traditions of impartiality in the new Scotland and rumours abounded of reporters who had been cheerleaders for independence getting the plum assignments. Sorting that out would be one of the priorities for the new leadership of the Scottish Broadcasting Corporation.

Catherine had watched all this tension come to a head at a planning meeting she had attended the week before, when there was a proposal to book the SUR leader Robert Cowan for tonight's discussion programme.

Present were Lewis Graham, Blair Hamilton and, holding the jackets for their ongoing battle, Catherine's boss, Caitlin O'Connor, executive producer of tonight's show.

Lewis Graham had been furious at the suggestion that Cowan should be on the discussion panel. 'You can't have Cowan on the show. He has no position, no electoral mandate.'

Hamilton had been equally adamant. 'But he speaks for millions of Scots who believe that independence is folly.'

'Including you, Blair,' spat Graham.

'As it happens, it does include me, Lewis. But my own views are irrelevant here. This is a matter of editorial policy. We are meant to be producing a discussion programme, not a puff for your good friend Ross Johnson. How can we have a discussion if the effective leader of the opposition is absent?'

'There are lots of other moderate people we could have, those who have adapted to the new reality. Who don't flirt with law-breaking.'

'But the traditional opposition is fractured and finished,' protested Hamilton.

That was undoubtedly true. Most of the Labour Party members had joined the new Scottish Labour Party, which accepted independence, with the diehard Unionist rump joining the SUR. The Tories had fallen in solidly behind the SUR and the Liberal Democrats had been all but wiped out at the 2011 election. They were all waiting for politics to return to its normal left–right axis after independence had been secured and there was no *raison d'être* for the SNP any more.

Hamilton pressed his point home. 'At this moment, there's only one debate in town and the BBC has a duty to reflect that.'

Frustrated by the logic of this, Lewis Graham sought broader support around the table. 'Caitlin, what do you think?'

'I'm afraid I agree with Blair. I don't particularly like Cowan, or his brand of politics, but I think it is right to have him on the show. Like it or not, he is now the public face of Unionism in Scotland.'

Graham knew George Wallace well and thought he could at least count on Cathcrine. 'And you, Catherine?'

Catherine knew she was being asked to choose between her journalistic integrity and her loyalty to her father's politics. There could only be one answer. And it was one her father would have supported wholeheartedly. 'I think he has to be on the show. Journalistically, anything else cannot be justified. We would be letting the viewers down. And we shouldn't forget that they pay our wages.'

Faced with this united front, Graham had been forced into a bad-tempered concession. Catherine was glad of the victory but worried about what the debate heralded for the future, a future where Lewis Graham would be the undisputed boss.

Her mind drifting back to the present, Catherine drained her tea, filled her lungs with fresh air one last time and waddled back to the glass building and the smelly studio gallery within.

Inside the building, the receptionist was having a heated discussion with Catherine's father. 'Well, I am sorry, sir. If you have left a message on her mobile and her voice-mail, then there is nothing else I can do. I am afraid it is BBC policy not to put calls from members of the public through to the studios and we have no facilities to put out an announcement. You will just have to call back later.'

'But I am not a member of the bloody public, I am her father.'

'I know you say that, sir, but I have no way of independently verifying it. And, given your tone, I am afraid I am going to have to say goodnight to you.'

Fortunately for George's blood pressure, Catherine chose that moment to switch on her phone to check her messages before returning upstairs to the gallery. He almost squealed with delight when he saw her number come up on his phone.

The connection was really poor, and George was aware he was almost shouting to make himself heard. 'Listen, sweetheart, I don't have much time, so please listen carefully. You're in terrible danger. The SUR are planning a coup led by Robert Cowan and backed by the Americans. I don't know for sure, but I'd imagine the BBC is a prime target. I'm sure they will try to get control of your building. The signal for the coup will be a bomb explosion at Edinburgh Castle just before midnight.'

'Oh, very funny, Dad, good one,' sighed Catherine.

'It's not a joke, darling. I have never been more serious about anything in my life,' George responded. 'You need to get the news out at your end. I'm going to do what I can here.'

'You can't be serious. A coup? Backed by Americans? That's crazy.'

'I know,' George persisted, 'but it is true. You must believe me. I am deadly serious. It's come from a BLA guy. Remember the good guard?'

'But Cowan is actually going to be in here at midnight. He's part of the panel on my show.'

'Well, watch him like a hawk, then. Please, Catherine, we don't have much time. I know it sounds mad but you must trust me on this. I nearly lost you once, and I couldn't stand that again.'

Catherine's mind whirled. She knew instinctively that he must at least believe this supposed coup was real. 'You know I trust you,' she replied. 'OK. I need to find Caitlin and tell her. And are you OK?'

'I'm fine, sweetheart, and John is here with me, but most important I need you to promise me that, whatever happens, you won't take any risks.'

'I promise, Dad.'

Catherine hung up, shaking her head, and hurried, as fast as her bump would allow, up the broad, sandstone steps in the central atrium to Caitlin O'Connor's desk on the second floor.

ROOM 327, THE BALMORAL HOTEL, EDINBURGH, 10.20 P.M.

Jessica Schwarz finished applying the last of her eye make-up and leaned back in her chair. She surveyed her intelligent, well-defined features. It was too interesting a face to qualify for the world of the blandly beautiful, but it was certainly more than handsome. 'You'll do,' she mused to herself.

She looked around. Another hotel room. Another news story. A life of exceptional glamour, but often of exceptional loneliness. Sacrifices that career women always had to make, though career men never seemed to have to.

She stood up and slipped on a red, tight-fitting Carolina Herrera dress. All these functions were costing her a fortune. The sooner Scotland was independent, the better for her credit card.

She checked herself again in the mirror, smiling as she remembered George's description: 'Not bad for an old doll.'

'Well, my friend, you may well come to rue that expression tonight.'

Jessica was feeling more relaxed. She had resolved her professional dilemma and was edging closer to a solution to her personal one.

Professionally, it hadn't been too tricky. She knew she had to keep George's secret – at least for the time being. To betray that source was professional suicide. She was covering the ceremony and would have a ringside seat for any developments. And besides, she was several hours of thinking time ahead of the competition. As soon as the coup happened, or was foiled, she had her first ten calls planned and her first ten paragraphs written in her head.

Personally, the call was tougher. She had to work out how good a long-term bet George Wallace was and whether she should gamble.

Like many women on the cusp of a relationship, Jessica had allowed herself to speculate what kind of life she and George would have together if she decided to pursue it, a speculation which would have horrified George if he had been privy to it.

At forty-three, she knew that any decisions on relationships were now life-changing and she was determined to choose wisely. On the plus side, she really cared about George and thought she could come to love him. He was a good, decent man who had kept himself in shape – undoubtedly a commodity in short supply. He clearly adored her and, crucially, made her laugh, as well as think.

But nagging doubts remained. He fell in love, or perhaps in lust, too easily. He could be vain and self-important. And she worried about how he had changed in the last few months. She had watched as the political process had crushed his idealism, leaving him cynical and exhausted. Did she want the responsibility of dealing with the fallout of that? Another man to baby? She believed his inner resolve and strength would return, but she couldn't be sure.

Other questions rushed through her mind. Given the huge breakthrough in fertility treatments since 2010, she still had time for a baby. Did she want that? Did he? Would he want to stay in politics? Could she stand the restraints and constraints of being a political wife?

On top of all this, Jessica knew George was keeping something from her. A secret. Every journalistic – and womanly – instinct told her there was a hidden dilemma he wanted to share but wouldn't. George was a bad liar, his face gave away the fact that he was holding something back. What? Did it matter if he kept some secrets?

And, God, could she ever cope with the Scottish weather?

THE OVAL OFFICE, THE WHITE HOUSE, WASHINGTON DC, 5.25 P.M.

There was an air of controlled excitement in the Oval Office, where Jane Chalmers and Admiral Carl Butterworth sat with their president. The tiny number of aides who had had to be let into the secret operation buzzed in and out with neatly folded paper messages for their bosses.

Perched on the edge of a sofa, Todd MacFarlane struggled to contain his nerves. He reflected again that this was a defining point in his presidency, as Cuba had been for Kennedy, Vietnam for Johnson, Watergate for Nixon and Iraq for Bush.

Success would mean a huge step towards a second term. Failure could hound him out of office. And, even worse, associate his name with one issue for ever, the way George W. Bush was with the disaster in Iraq.

He glanced down at his watch. An hour and a half to midnight in Scotland. 'OK, guys, can I get an update, please?'

As Chalmers looked up from her conversation with an aide, Butterworth beat her to it, for once. 'All the men have disembarked safely on the east coast of Scotland, sir, and are just awaiting the signal at Edinburgh Castle before seizing their targets, including the Scottish Parliament. There are no issues at the two main locations in Glasgow, the broadcasters and the City Chambers. Given our understanding with Strathclyde Police, we know security will be minimal at both points. The Navy Seals will be landing in the next fifteen minutes at their agreed rendezvous position with the advance forces at Garelochhead and will be in position for the assault on Faslane at midnight. And the three hundred Marines are on the tarmac at Prestwick Airport as backup, if required.'

'Jane?'

'No problems on my side, Mr President. Thomas Atkinson is with Robert Cowan in his car on the way to the BBC as we speak. All the BLA irregulars have CIA operatives guiding them to ensure there is no excessive use of violence. The army is fully onside. The bomb is in place.'

'And George Wallace?'

'Unfortunately, he now has a couple of Russian goons protecting him after the failed assassination attempt, and they will have to be taken out, too. Given the other priorities tonight, we thought we would take care of him tomorrow along with the rest of the cleaning up after the coup. It is likely to be a tragic car crash.'

It still seemed surreal to MacFarlane to be discussing the death of a man who had chatted to him about American history. A man whose hand he had shaken in this very office. But he knew this was not a moment for sentiment – or weakness. 'OK, I will be in the residence if anything urgent crops up. I will see you here at 6.50 for final orders.'

TAXI CAB, COLINTON, EDINBURGH, 10.45 P.M.

John Wallace had listened impatiently to his father's part of the conversation with Catherine, trying desperately to piece together what was going on. When George hung up, he pounced. 'All right, now you've spoken to Catherine, do you want to tell me what the fuck is going on? And why, instead of sipping champagne cocktails on the castle terrace, we are on our way to Colinton?'

'Well, son, it really all has to do with Trotsky.'

John sighed, fearing another of his dad's long history lessons rather than the straight answers he needed. 'The Russian revolutionary? What the hell do you mean by that?'

Unbeknownst to George, he and Admiral Carl Butterworth shared something in common. They had both taken the same course in Russian history and Soviet politics at the University of Pennsylvania's Graduate School of Arts and Science in the 1980s, although two years apart. George, because he was fascinated by Eastern Europe; Carl, because he wanted to understand his enemy better. Both had been struck by the remark of Trotsky taught in the first semester of seminars: 'A revolution is not so much against the army as for the army.'

George now revealed this phrase to his son.

'Dad, I know I might be being a bit dim, but what does he mean by that and what the hell has it got to do with us?'

George tried to explain clearly and patiently to his son what he had learned from Tommy and what was happening with the coup, but without raising his voice. He was already aware that the taxi driver had turned around a number of times during his shouted exchange with Catherine.

Then he explained the phrase. 'During the 1905 revolution in Russia, the revolutionaries had everyone on their side in their struggle against Tsar Nicholas II – industrial workers, the peasantry, the intelligentsia. Everyone but the army. So the Tsar survived when the army shot down the protestors on Bloody Sunday on his orders.

'In the popular revolt of February 1917, the difference was that the army backed the people and stopped the Tsar's train from returning to the capital. So the Communists learned the lesson for their revolution in October that year. As Trotsky said, "A revolution is not so much against the army as for the army."'

'So, in the Scottish revolution, whoever controls the army wins?'

'Exactly, and the only army in Scotland is the Royal Regiment of Scotland. I am assuming that the officers and the men at the castle must be on the side of the coup – that is how the bomb got planted safely in the gatehouse. So we need to find ourselves another army.'

BBC SCOTLAND HEADQUARTERS, PACIFIC QUAY, GLASGOW, 10.45 P.M.

Robert Cowan's car swept through the open barrier and into the BBC's VIP car park. Robert sat in the back with Thomas Atkinson, with two CIA agents in the front.

Atkinson unbuckled his seat belt, then turned to Cowan and asked him to run through his speech one more time before they went inside.

'Remember, Robert, it has to be short, sharp and to the point, as we may not have time to sort out autocue and looking down at cards makes you seem shifty.'

'Of course.' Cowan managed to sound calm despite his mounting excitement. 'I have already committed it to memory.' He cleared his throat.

'My fellow Scots, my name is Robert Cowan and I am the leader of the Scottish Unionist Resistance. Tonight the SUR has taken power in Scotland in order to stop the nation we love going down the disastrous path of separation from the rest of the United Kingdom. This decision to rip apart three hundred years of shared glorious history has been taken on the basis of one snapshot referendum result – a result that opinion poll after opinion poll show that you – we – now regret and reject. Despite this lack of popular support, the Scottish government has recklessly pushed ahead with its fatal plans for independence. Tonight we have called a halt to those.

'The nationalists have also imperilled our nation by allowing Russian nuclear weapons on our soil. I will ensure our safety by removing those immediately. But this is no blow to democracy. You have my word that within six months there will be fresh elections and a fresh referendum. I seek power not for myself or my movement, but only to save Scotland from this disaster. Until the situation has stabilised, I must ask you to follow the instructions of the forces of law and order and observe the new dusk-to-dawn curfew which we are implementing with immediate effect. Thank you for listening. God save the king.'

'Perfect, Robert,' Atkinson enthused. 'We will broadcast from Studio A, where you'll already be seated for the discussion programme. My men will clear the others from the area and keep one cameraman to do the job.'

He tapped the shoulders of the two men in the front of the car to bring them into the conversation. 'We will make our move at 11.45 p.m., when the BBC breaks from the discussion to go to live coverage from Edinburgh Castle, so that we will definitely be ready to broadcast at midnight. Everybody understand?'

The other three men in the car nodded gravely.

GARELOCHHEAD, SCOTLAND, 10.55 P.M.

The dinghy splashed softly ashore on the shingle and rocks at the top of the loch, and the ten men expertly disembarked, exactly as they had rehearsed hundreds of times before. But this time it was for real. Behind them, another two dozen identical boats sailed in and followed the same manoeuvre.

The two spaniels in the garden of the large villa where the pebbly beach met the road barked their discontent. Two men slipped away to silence them.

Captain Hugh O'Donnell greeted Lieutenant Ralph Parker of the advance guard with a brisk salute. There was no time for pleasantries. 'Operational update.'

'No change since the radio report at 21.00 hours, captain.'

The lieutenant spread out a detailed map of Faslane Naval Base on the bow of the dinghy. His sergeant lit it with a torch, casting an eerie glow on the faces of the two officers.

Behind them, the two hundred and forty other black-clad men who had landed went about their preparations efficiently and in silence.

The lieutenant pointed at the map. 'We have been watching them all week. The Russians are dug in here on the landward side and here facing the loch. We think there are maybe fifty of them. No mortars or bazookas, but they have heavy machine guns at these four points and lots of small arms and ample ammunition to survive a siege, let alone a rapid assault. I think you could say that they are expecting us.'

Captain O'Donnell sighed. The requirement to take the base quickly meant that heavy casualties were inevitable. He looked round his busy men. How many of them would survive to see the dawn, he wondered glumly. 'OK, lieutenant, let's get this show on the road. I want all the men in position by 23.45 hours, ready for my signal. Three boats from here, six from Roseneath and three from Mambeg in a co-ordinated attack. Our only hope is to storm across the boom in a mass assault and try to overwhelm the machine-gun positions.

'Lieutenant Parker, I need you and twenty men to launch a simultaneous attack on the main gate from the land side as a diversion. Take your initial position at the bottom of the Glen Fruin road. The key is to await my signal, which will be a red flare. Clear?'

Parker nodded.

'After that diversionary attack, you need to turn your men around to protect access to the gate in case any of the hundred Russians guarding the silos try to come down to aid their comrades. Otherwise, we will deal with them tomorrow, after we have secured the base.'

'Understood, sir.'

Captain O'Donnell looked at the royal blue sky above the black of the hillside, and silently cursed the Scottish light, thinking to himself, 'For fuck's sake, eleven o'clock at night and I can still see the zit on Parker's chin. This is going to be a massacre.'

A mile away, Major Andriy Gustov listened on his walkie-talkie to his spotter on the hill outlining the preparations of the American troops. 'Dinghies. That means Navy Seals or Marines. Good.'

Gustov had fought in Afghanistan and Chechnya against what he saw as ragheads and murderous terrorist scum. But this was different. This was proper warfare. He had ached to match himself against the very best. He had never got a chance during the Cold War.

Now, this was his moment. 'Good. Very good indeed.'

ROGUE NATION

EDINBURGH CASTLE, 10.55 P.M.

Sergei Karimov marched confidently into the castle esplanade in the full dress uniform of a colonel of the FSB. He appreciated the importance of putting on a good show.

Inside he was shredded by uncharacteristic nervousness. He looked again at his watch: less than an hour until the critical phone call. He had to keep his cool. He just hoped Ross Johnson could, too. He hated having to rely on weaker, lesser men rather than just himself, but he had no option tonight.

As he entered the courtyard, he saw President Churov in the corner, talking to the rest of the extensive Russian delegation. One look at that menacing face reminded him there would be no second chances. No forgiveness for failure.

BBC SCOTLAND HEADQUARTERS, PACIFIC QUAY, GLASGOW, 11 P.M.

The same four senior managers who had discussed Robert Cowan's participation in tonight's discussion show gathered again in controller Blair Hamilton's office. Hamilton, O'Connor and Graham listened in increasing amazement as Catherine recounted her conversation with her father.

O'Connor was the first to speak. 'A coup, led by Robert Cowan? You can't be serious. This is Scotland, not some banana republic. I'm sorry, but the whole idea is just absurd.'

'Is it?' asked Graham. 'Is it really? I think the Unionists and their business backers would go to any lengths to stop independence. And look at the American record of regime change in the last fifty years. If Grenada, Nicaragua and Venezuela can happen, then why not Scotland?'

Hamilton cut in, 'Because we're a functioning Western European democracy, that's why. I agree with Caitlin, the whole idea is preposterous. I'm sorry, Catherine, I know how close you are to your father, but I can't – won't – accept the idea of some kind of vast conspiracy against the government, one the SUR has managed to keep secret.'

Graham was furious. 'I think that's criminally complacent, Blair. At the very least you must stop that man Cowan from coming into the building.'

'I'm sorry, Lewis. I must insist, indeed I order, that the programme go ahead as planned. With the original line-up in place.'

Graham regarded Hamilton suspiciously. 'It's almost as if you want this coup to succeed.'

'That's an outrageous suggestion. If it makes you feel better, Catherine, I know Alistair Stroud at Strathclyde Police and I can give him a call to let him know about the rumour. But the show will go on. It's my duty to do what is right for the viewing public in Scotland. We can't go cancelling programmes on the basis of unsubstantiated hearsay.'

Lewis Graham looked at him with a cold fury, then turned on his heel and left the room, slamming the door behind him.

DREGHORN BARRACKS, COLINTON, EDINBURGH. 11 P.M.

The taxi screeched to a halt at the large metal front gates. George and John jumped out and the taxi driver sped away.

George ran up to the sentry on duty. 'I'm George Wallace. I need to speak to your ranking NCO immediately.'

The soldier coolly eyed him up and down. 'Listen, mate, I don't care if you are William fucking Wallace, you don't get in here without a pass.'

After the endless tension of the last two days, the soldier's attitude was the last straw. George was so sick of being told what to do by everyone. Adding a pimply twenty-year-old to the list was just unbearable.

To his surprise his fury came out as cold, calculating anger. He shoved his parliamentary pass under the private's nose. 'Listen, son, read that carefully. I am George Wallace, the second most important man in the Scottish government. A government, incidentally, that you will be swearing undying loyalty to in just over twelve hours. Now, if you don't want to be cleaning parade grounds with a toothbrush for the rest of your career, you'll get me the fucking ranking NCO and you'll do it now.'

The private took one look at George's face, then scurried off to C Block.

John looked at his father with a mixture of surprise and new-found respect. Less than a minute later, the sentry returned with the upright and imposing figure of Lance-Corporal Brian McTavish. 'Good evening, sir, I'm Lance-Corporal McTavish. What seems to be the problem?'

'Are you the ranking NCO here?'

'I am, indeed.'

'Then I need to speak to you on a matter of urgent national importance.' George glanced at the sentry. 'Preferably inside, if possible.'

John and George followed McTavish into the cold walls and high meshed windows of C Block barracks. The curious and bored soldiers of Black Watch

----

B Company, who had been confined to barracks all weekend, gathered behind McTavish as he turned to listen to George. 'Now then, sir, what's all this about?'

George took a deep breath. He thought of all the hundreds of speeches he had made in his life and knew this one had to be the best. There was absolutely no room for error. 'I am George Wallace. I'm the senior special adviser to the first minister, Ross Johnson. The story I am about to tell you may sound incredible but it is true. I swear to you.'

'Hey, aren't you the guy who was caught shagging by the papers?'

George ignored the interruption by one of the young squaddies and the laughter that followed. He had to keep focused. Despite his churning stomach, he managed to speak calmly and evenly. 'Tonight, the Scottish Unionist Resistance, backed by the terrorists of the British Loyalist Army and American Special Forces, are going to launch a coup against the legitimately elected government of Scotland.'

A surprised murmur swept the room. George now had the soldiers' undivided attention. 'The signal for the coup will be the explosion of a bomb in the gatehouse of the castle . . .'

'A what?' exclaimed McTavish, as the memory of the four men in the white van suddenly struck him.

'A bomb.'

'Christ! Those guys in the white van. Fuck's sake, I knew there was something dodgy about them.'

McTavish's mind whirled, trying to follow through the appalling consequences of that thought. They were absolutely devastating. He spoke his conclusions as he thought them. 'Fuck's sake, that means Captain Murray is in on it. He ordered me to let them through. *And* the order was signed by the major-general himself.'

His mind forced him to the only logical conclusion. 'And that is why all the arse-lickers are on ceremonial duty tonight.'

George knew it was now or never. 'Gentlemen, we must stop this coup. Whatever your personal views on independence, the people of Scotland have voted for it in a free and fair referendum. I need you tonight to look beyond your orders to stay in barracks. I need you to find a deeper loyalty to Scotland. To the Scottish people. That is the oath you will take tomorrow. I need you to act on it tonight. I need you to come to Edinburgh Castle with me right now to stop these people. And to save Scotland.'

Lance-Corporal McTavish turned round to the silent soldiers behind him. 'Well, boys, you have heard what the man has to say. What do you think? Do we follow Mr Wallace or not?'

CHAPTER 21

THURSDAY, 31 JULY — INDEPENDENCE DAY

STRATHCLYDE POLICE HEADQUARTERS, PITT STREET, GLASGOW, 11 P.M.

Chief Constable Alistair Stroud sat alone in his top-floor office, silently surveying the lit Victorian towers of the West End. He had come in to work to ensure that the handover to the new regime went smoothly.

He was usually delighted to speak to his old friend, and sometime golf partner, Blair Hamilton. But not tonight. In a very disturbing phone call, Hamilton had just told him that the BBC had heard a rumour that there was going to be a coup against the SNP government.

Naturally, Stroud had reassured him that he had no information to suggest anything was amiss but that he would check it out right away. As he put the phone down, he was a deeply troubled man. If there was any danger that the coup might be foiled, he had to ensure he had an exit strategy in place.

THE ESPLANADE, EDINBURGH CASTLE, 11.45 P.M.

As the massed ranks of the Pipes and Drums played 'The Black Bear', Charles Sands squeezed past two African prime ministers and their aides to his seat at the end of the back row on the north stand. In normal circumstances he would have been furious at the diplomatic slap in the face to the USA this marginalised seat represented. But these were not normal circumstances. Personally, he was delighted to be as far away from the gatehouse as possible.

He tried his best not to think about Ross Johnson in that room, putting the finishing touches to his speech just a few feet away from the bomb that would end his life. He hated the fact that it had to be this way, but one man's life could not stand in the way of the vital national interests of the United States.

Sands' conscience would have to accept that.

As he looked down on the magnificent, torch-lit esplanade, he caught the eye of Nick Jones, who was seated eight rows in front of him and was looking round at the gathered VIPs. The two men shared a silent, significant look.

Jones turned back round and looked at the ancient castle. He, too, a classic one-nation Tory and decent, moral man, had come to terms with his conscience.

BBC SCOTLAND HEADQUARTERS, PACIFIC QUAY, GLASGOW, 11.45 P.M.

Catherine Wallace opened talkback to the presenter, Sandy Martin. She spoke confidently, directly into his earpiece. 'Two minutes until we switch to live coverage from the castle, Sandy. Push the SNP on the disastrous financial consequences of independence one last time. She's getting away with murder in this debate.'

As Sandy vainly tried to get a straight answer on devaluation of the Scottish pound from the Nationalist MSP, Catherine listened to the PA count the director into the switch to the live coverage from Edinburgh Castle. She warned Sandy at a minute, then again at thirty seconds.

Sandy broke from his questioning and looked directly at camera three. 'Well, that is all from the Glasgow studio for the moment. You will be hearing more from me and my guests at quarter past midnight. But now it's over to Sally at Edinburgh Castle, where the excitement is mounting on this historic evening. Goodbye for now.'

'And we are out,' Catherine instructed the gallery. 'Back on air in half an hour. Ten-minute pee and tea break, and back at your desks to run through the top of the show at midnight. Sandy, I'm coming down to have a word about pinning down that slippery nationalist.'

As the night had continued to progress without incident, Catherine started to wonder if perhaps her father had been misinformed about the coup. Maybe it was just a wild rumour he had picked up – without substance, like so many political stories. And she had done her task. She had alerted Blair and he had informed the police. If there was any trouble, they surely would be able to nip it in the bud.

In any event, as many women had found to their cost, she had a more pressing issue. Being seven months pregnant meant never being further than two minutes from a loo.

Catherine emerged from the toilet and went to the studio floor to talk to her presenter. As she did so she watched Robert Cowan's three guests emerge from the green room and also head to the studio. She noticed the three men simultaneously reach into their jackets and produce handguns. 'Christ, Dad must be right!'

Thomas Atkinson reached the studio doors first and spoke to the small knot of people gathered. They stared in amazement at the snub-nosed Colt. He felt empowered and excited at being back on active service. 'OK, I need everyone to be quiet and listen real close. In just under fifteen minutes' time your new first minister, Robert Cowan, is going to broadcast to the nation from this studio to announce the formation of a Scottish Unionist Resistance interim government. The satellite is already aligned and once the signal is given at Edinburgh Castle we will switch to this feed.'

He gestured towards the production team and the guests. 'My men will take you to the green room and guard you until this is all over.'

'You,' he said, pointing at one of the cameramen, 'you will record the message on camera three. As for the rest of you, as long as you co-operate then no one will get hurt. Please do not consider causing any trouble. Your security guards are already our prisoners and my men have this building, and the Scottish Television building, completely surrounded. Any resistance would be futile.'

Blair Hamilton was the only one of the stunned group to speak. 'I am the controller of BBC Scotland and I will not permit my organisation to be a party to this despicable action.'

'Please step aside, Mr Hamilton, and don't be foolish,' Atkinson responded.

But Blair continued, shooting an accusing look at his old friend, Robert Cowan. 'I am a British Unionist, but this is a disgrace to democracy, and I won't stand for it. Robert, I can't believe you intend to be a party to this outrage.'

Hamilton took a deliberate step in front of the studio door. Atkinson looked at his watch. He had no time for this shit. He acted now as he had before, in cities from Pretoria to Prague. He struck Hamilton viciously across the face with his pistol, knocking him to the ground. He then put two bullets expertly into the kneecap of his prone victim.

Ignoring the screams and gasps, he turned to the rest of the shocked group and said calmly, 'Now, if we've quite finished here, let's get this show on the road.'

He gestured to his two companions. 'Take them to the green room now and make sure there's no more nonsense.'

Atkinson's earpiece crackled to let him know that his agents had secured both broadcasting buildings on Pacific Quay and the satellite was ready to go.

Catherine knelt and cradled Blair's bloodied head. She thought of her father's advice, and her unborn child, and decided to do no more.

Atkinson looked at the pale and shaken face of Robert Cowan, who had just witnessed the deliberate maiming of a man he had known for thirty years. 'OK, First Minister, let's do it.'

THE GATEHOUSE, EDINBURGH CASTLE, 11.45 P.M.

Ross walked on to the narrow balcony which led out from the court-martial room in the castle gatehouse and looked over at the crowded stands of the esplanade, the colourful flags of sixty nations fluttering above them.

He had finished the final words of his speech, and his aides had made sure he was immaculately dressed in full Highland regalia, set off by the blue and dark green Gunn tartan worn by the Johnsons.

The balcony was empty apart from the microphone, for the lone piper would play 'Scotland the Brave' at midnight to signal the arrival of the world's newest nation.

Ross looked straight up at the flagpole above him at the very top of the castle, where the Union Jack would be lowered and the Saltire raised in just fifteen minutes. His flag. His nation. His victory. This was *his* moment.

Ross double-checked his watch. It was time to make the most important phone call of his life. He dialled his PA. 'OK, Jean, it is time, as planned. Patch me through to the Oval Office.'

He listened to the two rings, then spoke. 'Good evening, Mr President, it is Ross Johnson. We need to talk.'

Ross completely missed the irony that this call was taking place beside the room where so many soldiers had once been tried for disloyalty.

THE ESPLANADE, EDINBURGH CASTLE, 11.50 P.M.

George Wallace dodged his way round the poles which held up the stands on the esplanade and raced past the imposing equestrian statue of Earl Haig.

He desperately tried to suck as much air as possible into his aching lungs, glad

---

now of all those sessions in the gym. Twenty men of B Company of the Black Watch seemed to jog effortlessly behind him.

As he ran up towards the drawbridge, every muscle in George's legs screamed their complaint at this unexpected exercise and his whisky-filled stomach contracted with a stitch. With one last effort, he pushed himself to the wide arch of the gatehouse. He felt every one of his forty-nine years as he raced across the cobbles.

It had been a hair-raising trip across Edinburgh in the two commandeered army trucks, with George bouncing about in the back as he shouted encouragement to the driver.

Lance-Corporal Brian McTavish's authority had got them through the army checkpoint at the first barricade across from Deacon Brodies' pub, where Castle Hill gives way to the Lawnmarket.

Inspector Jock Gibson had been a tougher proposition but a combination of George's parliamentary pass and clear, driving concern had been enough to persuade the inspector that he was serious. Gibson had rounded up half a dozen cops and was five hundred metres behind George and his pursuing troops.

George crossed the bridge over the dry moat, passing the silent stone statues of William Wallace and Robert Bruce carved on either side of the arch, and reached the door to the gatehouse on the left-hand side.

The squat, muscular figure of Captain Paul Murray barred his path.

George caught his breath as the Black Watch squaddies fell in behind him. They saw Captain Murray and hesitated. Years of military discipline made them pause.

George felt no such barrier. 'In the name of the Scottish government, I must ask you to let me pass. There is a bomb upstairs which will kill innocent people and set off a civil war in our nation. I am going up there to stop that. Right now.'

Captain Murray grabbed a rifle from one of the startled sentries. 'Over my dead body, you do. I have my orders. And that fucking rabble behind you will all be court-martialled for disobedience.'

He levelled the rifle at George. 'Not one step further, Mr Wallace.'

George found an inner strength and courage he didn't know he possessed. 'I know for a fact you don't have live rounds in that gun. That is not permitted at ceremonies at the castle. The plot has been discovered. The police are on their way. It's all over, Captain. Don't be stupid. You don't want to add a charge of murder to your current problems.'

With that, George, followed by John, walked calmly towards the troubled figure of Captain Murray, who had let his rifle drop. Lance-Corporal McTavish and the other squaddies made to follow.

But watching this collapse of military discipline snapped something deep inside the captain. This affront to his authority was just too much to bear. 'No you don't, you bastard!'

Murray lunged towards George, the sharpened bayonet on the rifle glinting in the fire of the torches on the wall. Before George could react, McTavish threw himself to his left to block the blow. There was a sickening squelch as the bayonet buried itself deep in his chest. McTavish grunted and crumpled.

Without thinking, George pulled the Russian revolver out of his waistband and fired once, shocked at the unexpected power of the recoil. Murray screamed and sprung back, clutching his shoulder. He was quickly overpowered by the other men of the Black Watch.

George once more willed himself into focus. He didn't have time to think about having fired a gun in anger for the first time in his life. He rushed up the stairs and burst into the court-martial room.

He went straight to the radiator and ripped away the decorative wooden screen that covered it. Behind lay a ticking, khaki bag.

Hearing the commotion, Ross finished his phone call to the president and stepped in from the balcony. With one look, he took in George's mad, dishevelled air and the grey pistol in his right hand. 'George, what in God's name are you doing?'

'I'm sorry,' George gasped, 'but there's no time for explanations.'

John and George carefully extracted the bag from beside the radiator and carried it gingerly between them down the stone spiral staircase. In George's imagination the ticking got louder with every step.

At the bottom, they ignored the melee of cops and squaddies and headed up to the ramparts. The hundred metres from the gatehouse door to the six massive black guns of the Argyle battery on the walls stretched, seemingly endlessly, before them.

Panting, the two men lifted the bag up the cobbled incline, torn between the desire to hurry and the desire to be safe. They passed tentatively under the menacing eight metal spikes of the portcullis gate and then climbed the ten smooth stone steps to the ramparts beside the audio-guide store.

George and John looked over the sheer drop then, with one mighty shove, they hurled the khaki bag down and watched it slowly disintegrate as it crashed its way down Castle Rock.

CHAPTER 22

THURSDAY, 31 JULY — INDEPENDENCE DAY

THE OVAL OFFICE, THE WHITE HOUSE, WASHINGTON DC, 6.55 P.M.

The president walked the two hundred metres from the residence to the Oval Office as briskly as he could. As he entered, he waved them all to sit. This time, he didn't even pause to consider Jane's feelings about the use of sexist language. 'Gentlemen, I've just spoken to the first minister of Scotland. In under five minutes' time he'll make a speech from the ramparts of Edinburgh Castle announcing that the Russian nuclear missiles are being withdrawn from Scotland with immediate effect.

'In return, I have agreed that I will attend a conference in Edinburgh later this month on behalf of the United States on the need for disarmament raised by this crisis. I'm delighted to say that the USA, through the judicious use of pressure, has managed to win a complete victory without firing a single shot. Therefore I'm ordering the termination of Operation Righteous Wrath. That is an abort, repeat that is an abort.'

There was a split-second of stunned silence then a rush for the phones. In the turmoil the president approached one person in the room and whispered, 'Could I have a word outside, please, Jane?'

The pair stepped out in the covered colonnade that looked over the Rose Garden. MacFarlane cut straight to the chase. 'I'm afraid it's all over, Jane. You gambled and lost. You'll be taking the hit for this so that the administration – my administration – is not damaged. I need your resignation letter on my desk in an hour. Just think of it as a surgical procedure. The diseased part has to be cut out to save the healthy body. I'm sorry, Jane, but it is just politics. Nothing personal. Please excuse me now. I need to get back in there to sort things out.'

MacFarlane left Chalmers standing stunned, all her hopes and ambitions melting like spring snow. All her years of service to MacFarlane rendered meaningless. Not a word of kindness. Not a word of thanks.

As her life crumbled around her, Chalmers faced one savage but unavoidable truth.

She had absolutely no one to talk to about it.

BBC SCOTLAND HEADQUARTERS, PACIFIC QUAY, GLASGOW, 11.58 P.M.

Robert Cowan looked at the sweating figure of the cameraman then at the CIA agent, pistol cocked, beside him.

He forced himself to shut out the image of Blair Hamilton's bloody leg and to go through the speech on the cards one more time. Everything he had ever dreamed of was finally within his grasp – from the mean streets of Dennistoun to leadership of his nation. He had to stay strong. He had to stay focused.

Cowan was dimly aware of Thomas Atkinson's phone ringing behind him and thought, just as they say in cinemas, that he would need to switch that off during his broadcast. Then he felt Atkinson's hand on his shoulder. 'Robert, it's all over. The coup is off. Come on, we have no time to waste. We need to get to Prestwick Airport. Now.'

Atkinson helped Cowan to his feet as the bulbs inside his head shattered one after another. Noisily, he vomited over his polished black shoes.

FASLANE NAVAL BASE, THE GARE LOCH, 11.58 P.M.

Captain O'Donnell looked down at his watch. Two minutes to go. Every natural instinct he possessed tried to drive his body closer to the black rubber of the dinghy and the gently lapping waves at the edge of the loch.

He could see the lights of the Russian machine-gun positions less than two hundred metres away on the other side of the boom. In less than three minutes, he would have to lead his men in a suicidal dash across that boom to the naval base.

Men hadn't fought like that since the First World War and he knew the consequences would be the same. Slaughter. Warm and silent, urine ran down his leg.

His walkie-talkie crackled into life. It was the ship: 'We have an abort. Repeat, we have an abort. Return to base immediately.'

Two tears of relief joined his piss in the bottom of the boat.

THE CITY CHAMBERS, GEORGE SQUARE, GLASGOW, 11.58 P.M.

Sammy Wilson and the rest of the BLA men had waited for the barman in the Merchant City pub to call time, then walked across the broad flagstones of the Italian Centre to the east end of George Square and the rendezvous point at the war memorial. Sammy was sexually excited at the prospect of the violence to come. He lovingly stroked the grenade in his pocket.

The CIA men crossed through the expectant and happy crowd from the Millennium Hotel on the opposite corner of the square, trying to look as unobtrusive as possible. The lead agent approached Sammy and took him aside as the other CIA men expertly circled the other BLA men. 'Listen, Sammy, I need you and your guys to beat it, pronto. The operation has just been called off.'

Sammy stared at him, uncomprehending. 'Fuck off. That's not possible. These bastards are due their comeuppance. Right now.'

The CIA man grabbed his arm with a grip that brooked no dissent. 'Listen to me, Sammy, and listen good. It's over. Now go home before you do something stupid. My orders are that there's to be no violence and I'm going to make sure that happens.'

Sammy now felt powerless. The sexual surge left him. He felt empty, used. Never in his life had he moved so rapidly from one emotion to another. He staggered out of the square, pushing revellers out of his way, and headed east along Duke Street, desperately trying to gather his thoughts.

Behind him, Rob Cairns took a sip of water and prepared to go on to the balcony to announce the birth of the Scottish nation to the people of Glasgow, completely oblivious to how close he had come to joining his wife and daughter in the graveyard.

THE HEADQUARTERS OF THE ARMY IN SCOTLAND, EDINBURGH CASTLE, 11.58 P.M.

Unlike many on the esplanade, Major-General Rory Stewart knew exactly what a pistol shot sounded like. When he heard the noise of George's pistol wounding Captain Murray, he immediately hurried to the gatehouse. Whatever this was, it wasn't part of the plot.

When he arrived, his eyes in one swoop took in the Black Watch soldiers who had pinned Captain Murray to the ground and the others who had gathered round the dying figure of Lance-Corporal McTavish. He knew the game was up when not a single soldier snapped to attention when they saw him. Instead, they all met him with a cold, defiant stare.

Stewart lost the staring match. With as much dignity as he could muster, he turned on his heel and smartly marched up the cobbled path to his office, not even noticing George and John locked in embrace on the ramparts.

Major-General Rory Stewart walked to his room and locked the door behind him. He sat at his desk and surveyed the photos there. His parents beaming beside him when he became a commissioned officer. His graduation class at Sandhurst. His sister with his nephew wearing his Glengarry. Him taking the salute at the tattoo last year. And him in a tank leading his troops into Basra.

So many achievements. So much pride. And now only shame.

Decisive to the end, he opened the desk drawer, pulled out his regulation revolver. Placed it in his mouth. And fired.

He could do no other.

CHAPTER 23

THURSDAY, 31 JULY — INDEPENDENCE DAY

EDINBURGH CASTLE, 11.59 P.M.

Ross Johnson strode to the microphone in the centre of the esplanade with all the confidence of a man who knew he had gambled and won. Big time.

In the north stand, Charles Sands looked on amazed and desperately scanned his mobile for text messages. Prime Minister Nick Jones looked down with relief.

The last strains of 'Amazing Grace' from the massed ranks of the Pipes and Drums faded away and Ross began. 'Tonight, it's my great honour and pleasure to welcome the ancient and proud nation of Scotland back into the world family. I want us to be a positive and productive member of that family. We Scots have contributed so much in the past, from the wonderful literature of Burns and Stevenson to the incredible inventions of the telephone and the television.

'We need to – we will – do the same in the future. But there has been a shadow over these celebrations. A shadow of war. We've seen the doomsday clock move back to two minutes to midnight. We have once more faced a nuclear holocaust, a threat my generation had believed we had consigned to history.

'This is not what I want for Scotland. That is why I am delighted to announce that, after discussions with presidents Churov and MacFarlane tonight, we have all agreed to remove the Russian nuclear missiles from Faslane Naval Base on the Gare Loch in the interests of world peace.'

Ross's speech was interrupted by thunderous applause from the stands and from the vast throng watching on big screens on Princes Street below. Charles Sands and Nick Jones looked on in astonishment. Ross paused and rode the applause.

'Both presidents have agreed to join me here in Edinburgh in August for a major conference on disarmament. Our aim is to preserve peace for this generation and for many to come. I ask you now to join me in celebrating Scotland's rightful return to independence after three hundred years of union with England. Though the political union is ending, I look forward to the social union continuing, with all the peoples of these islands working together in peace and prosperity.'

More heartfelt applause greeted this remark. Ross, aware of the cameras, as always, raised and deepened his voice for his final remark. 'Ladies and gentlemen, honoured guests, please welcome back Scotland the Brave.'

At exactly midnight, lit by a giant searchlight, the Union Jack was lowered and the Saltire was raised on the main flagpole on top of Edinburgh Castle. On the balcony outside the court-martial room where Ross had made his telephone call to Todd MacFarlane, a lone piper played 'Scotland the Brave'.

Many wept openly, having believed that they would never see this day in their lifetime. Once the Saltire finished its ascent, one hundred thousand voices in Princes Street joined as one as the massed ranks of the Pipes and Drums began the new national anthem of 'Flower of Scotland'. The song rose to a thunderous climax at the prophetic final verse.

George put his arm round his son's shoulders and looked down at the crowd from the ramparts of Edinburgh Castle and thought, 'Please let this be the right thing.'

THE OVAL OFFICE, THE WHITE HOUSE, WASHINGTON DC, 7.10 P.M.

Admiral Carl Butterworth and a handful of aides had watched Ross Johnson's speech on television in absolute silence. Butterworth shook his head in wonder as the singing began and the fireworks exploded over Edinburgh Castle.

The president spoke from his desk. 'OK, guys, that is a wrap. Gentlemen, you have all done brilliantly and I thank you on behalf of the people of the United States for all your efforts. Carl, my office at 7 a.m. tomorrow to start planning our strategy for the peace talks. Please call Chuck and tell him to stay in Scotland to begin the liaison work for the conference.

'It has been quite a day for us all and I, for one, need a large beer. And, given the country we have been dealing with, maybe a whisky, too.'

Todd relished the laugh his remark received from the gathered men. His presidency would be associated with success. He had proved himself in the toughest of circumstances. Not a wimp, a real man.

Four hundred metres away Jane Chalmers wept bitter, silent tears in her office as she handwrote her resignation letter.

FRIDAY, 1 AUGUST

STRATHCLYDE POLICE HEADQUARTERS, PITT STREET, GLASGOW, 00.10 A.M.

Chief Constable Stroud watched the TV screen intently and knew right away the coup had failed. He also knew right away what he had to do.

He phoned the chief inspector in charge of E Division, which covered the city centre and the East End. 'Hi, Alan, it's Alistair here. Just wanted to give you a quick heads-up. There is a dangerous character called Sammy Wilson I want you to pick up ASAP. He lives in Dennistoun and my tip-off is that he heads the BLA terrorists out there. Approach him with caution, but make sure you get him. Thanks.'

NUMBER 10 DOWNING STREET, LONDON, 00.10 A.M.

Tony Hodge finally got through to Prime Minister Nick Jones on his mobile. 'Well, I'll be fucked. The lucky, lucky bastard.'

'Ross certainly is, Tony, but then the same could be said of us. This way we get everything we want and need.'

'Indeed we do,' grinned Hodge. 'I will get those messages of condolence changed to one of congratulation. And start preparing for the conference. Have a good night, Nick, and don't drink too much whisky.'

THE GREAT HALL, EDINBURGH CASTLE, 00.30 A.M.

George grabbed Jessica's arm and steered her out of the celebratory drinks. She spoke first. 'George, darling, I'm so pleased to see you. I have been thinking a lot about us and need to talk to you.'

'That's great, Jessica, and I very much look forward to it. But first I need to tell you some things and then I'm afraid you are going to have to go straight to work. All I told you in my flat is no longer off the record. Publish, and let me be damned.'

THE A7, 00.30 A.M.

The CIA driver swung at 80 miles per hour into the Prestwick Airport exit at the massive Ayrshire roundabout, having ignored the looming speed cameras the whole journey down from Glasgow.

In the back of the car, Robert Cowan finished the mobile phone conversation with his wife. She was on her way with the contents of the safe – the passports, the share certificates and the dozen gold bars. And the children.

It was all over: a disaster. Everything he had worked for, snatched from him at the last moment. As he leaned back in the car's leather seat, Robert tried to make sense of it all. As he contemplated the wreckage of his life, he was struck by one thought. Unlike Blair Hamilton, at least he would walk again.

And that was some small cause of satisfaction.

DUKE STREET, DENNISTOUN, GLASGOW, 00.40 A.M.

Sammy turned off Duke Street and walked towards his tenement flat, still trying to work out what had happened. He halted, all his senses suddenly alert.

There was a police squad car parked outside his home.

Sammy slipped into a close and pressed himself against the rough sandstone. His confusion turned to cold fury. He knew one thing for sure. He had been betrayed once more.

Fucked over again.

CHAPTER 24

SUNDAY, 3 AUGUST

ROOM 327, THE BALMORAL HOTEL, EDINBURGH, 5 A.M.

Jessica was beaming as she spoke to her boss, Frances Copeland, editor of the *New York Times*. She had the front page of that morning's paper up on her laptop screen. She and Copeland had been working on it for the last hour, doing the final edit together in real time.

For the second day running, her byline dominated the front page as the paper followed up the previous day's scoop about the aborted coup.

They agreed the final sentence, then uploaded it directly to the presses. Copeland was delighted. 'I mean it, Jessica, these articles have been the most important sustained pieces of political journalism since Woodward and Bernstein on Watergate forty years ago. You are an absolute shoo-in for this year's Pulitzer Prize. I'm so proud of you.'

Jessica tried hard to keep the pleasure out of her voice. 'Why, thank you, Frances, that is most appreciated.'

'Jonathan is following up the CIA angle here with a big profile of Jane Chalmers. He's struggling to find anyone with a nice word to say about her. The White House has disowned her totally. She's on her own.'

'Couldn't happen to a nicer woman,' Jessica said, with feeling.

'What's next for you?'

'I want to do a piece on where now for the Royal Regiment of Scotland and I'm hoping Rory Stewart's sister might eventually open up about him. The family is a bit sensitive at the moment but keen to defend its name and history. Maybe after the funeral.'

'What about Johnson?'

'He has promised a proper sit-down on his plans next week – the only US interview, exclusive to us.'

'And George Wallace?'

Jessica paused and smiled to herself. 'Don't worry, Frances, I have something special in mind for him.'

'Well, great work again, Jessica. Try to get some sleep and we will pick up again this afternoon, your time. By the way, I hope you are planning to take a well-earned vacation?'

'I'm hoping to have a couple of days off to enjoy the Edinburgh Festival once the follow-up work is finished in the next week or so, then I'll stay on to cover the peace conference. Speak soon.'

Jessica hung up the hotel phone, then picked up her mobile. She composed a short text message, but hesitated over the 'Send' button.

She looked at her watch and decided a couple of hours of sleep first would be the better option. She plumped up the luxurious pillow and was fast asleep less than five minutes later.

OFFICE OF THE FIRST MINISTER, SCOTTISH PARLIAMENT, EDINBURGH, 10 A.M.

The two cups of coffee lay untouched between them, as cold as the atmosphere. Yesterday's *New York Times* lay on the table. Its banner headline screamed: 'US-Backed Coup in Scotland Foiled'. Just below the fold was a second headline: 'CIA Director Resigns in Assassination Scandal'.

George and Ross sat on armchairs either side of the coffee table. George realised it was only six weeks ago that he and Ross had had a fist fight beside these very chairs. A lifetime ago.

Ross finally broke the silence. 'There is going to be a state funeral on Friday for Lance-Corporal Brian McTavish, with full military honours. And I propose to call the new Scottish bravery award in the new Scottish honours system the McTavish medal in his memory.'

'He deserves no less. He was an incredibly brave man. He saved your life as well as mine.'

Ross gave a dry laugh. 'Well, that is where you are mistaken, George. He was a brave man but he most definitely did not save my life.'

'What do you mean? That man went—'

Ross cut across him, coldly, cruelly. 'It's now time for some honest talking,

George. I do owe you that – though, I have to say, not much else. You think you have been extraordinarily brave and principled. But actually, you have been extremely stupid. You fancy yourself as a student of Russian history. You must remember what Lenin called Westerners who praised and supported his regime?'

'Yes, of course. Useful idiots.'

'Well, that's the role you have played in this whole business. A useful idiot. You were played like the proverbial violin.'

George sat up straight in his chair, curious, edgy.

'You see,' Ross continued, 'the bomb had already been made safe. Didn't you think it was odd it didn't explode as it crashed against the Castle Rock?'

George's mind was reeling, trying to come to terms with the enormity of what he was being told. 'I guess I just assumed the fall smashed the link between the detonator and the explosive.'

Ross laughed out loud. 'The bomb had been made safe days before. We knew about the coup all the time. Russian intelligence had been following all the main plotters. We have photographs of their meetings at the Glasgow Hilton, full records of their so-called safe houses in Edinburgh. The Russians and I knew all along. You revealed no secrets, George. You foiled nothing. We wanted them – we needed them – to attempt a coup.'

George's head ached as he tried to process all this new information.

'And even if we hadn't been following them, I would have known. The prime minister phoned me last week to tell me about the bomb. It seems Nick Jones's delicate conscience couldn't stand the thought of my innards peppering the Edinburgh Castle gatehouse.

'If one were cynical – and you know I don't like to be, George – one might also note that having the coup foiled means there is no danger the Unionists will win, and thus no chance the English would have to take the Scots back, and therefore his precious Tory majority is safe for a generation. But let's be generous and give credit to his conscience.'

George sat with his head in his hands, rubbing his temples as if trying to erase what he was being told.

'Your mistake was to forget the golden question of politics. Always ask, "Cui bono?" – who benefits? You see, this way, George, everyone wins – well, apart from you. Jessica Schwartz will win the Pulitzer Prize for her two scoops for the *New York Times* with, I am sure, much more to follow. Your former young love, Clare Stephenson, has returned to London to a big promotion – and clearly should win the Oscar for Best Actress, if there is any justice. Nick Jones gets rid of us and has the thanks of a grateful party and people – and remains in power. Robert Cowan has been offered political asylum in the United States and will no doubt see out his retirement on the beaches of Florida with his trophy wife.'

George felt his anger vein start to pulse. He hated the fact that Ross was relishing telling him how clever he had been – and how stupidly he himself had behaved.

But Ross had an even more astonishing revelation. 'And, George, just as there was no bomb, there never were any warheads. Those missiles your girlfriend Jessica saw trundling into the Gare Loch were empty. The Russians never wanted warheads pointing at the heart of America.

'You see, they can't afford a new arms race, especially with fears over both the huge growth of the Chinese economy and its rapid military development. So the plan is that the international disarmament conference in Edinburgh later this month, held under UN auspices, will agree to a satellite monitoring system open to all. No one will have the advantage of their own early-warning system because the technology will be made available to everyone. UN bases at strategic points of the globe will have the ability to shoot down any aggressive missile fired by any state. The current American system in Poland and the Czech Republic will be scrapped. It will be the greatest step forward for world peace since the Treaty of Versailles in 1919. And Scotland – and I – will get much of the credit.'

George stared at him, too stunned to speak.

'Churov outlined it all to me when we walked along that corridor in the Kremlin,' Ross went on. 'They needed a major crisis to bring the Americans to the negotiating table. Now the Americans are happily going to accept a position they would have rejected three months ago. And, by backing down, the Russians have regained the moral high ground and won the gratitude of the international community for avoiding war.

'The Russians knew that Clare was a spy. They used the deputy minister that MI6 think is their source inside the Kremlin to feed the story of the missiles to British intelligence. Clare, in turn, fed it to you. We knew you were weak, George, full of so-called moral scruples and insufficiently committed to the nationalist cause. We knew you would run to your little friend Jessica. So, *voilà*, we had our very own, artificially created international crisis. You were played, George – nothing but a useful pawn.'

George felt like he was above this scene, looking down at two actors playing roles in a movie he couldn't understand. He tried to stay focused. He swallowed hard then wet his lips. He croaked, 'But what about MacFarlane?'

'I phoned him just before I made my speech at Edinburgh Castle. We understood each other perfectly. I told him that I knew about the planned coup and wanted him to call it off to avoid bloodshed. In return, I would order the nuclear missiles out. He would have his public victory. He accepted that he would have to desert the SUR and the BLA – a small price to pay for a man like him. Now his approval ratings are over 70 per cent. He is likely to go into the Republican primary season in Iowa and New Hampshire unopposed, while the Democrats tear themselves apart, unsure whether to call him a hero or a warmonger.

'He knows the real threat to America is not Russian missiles but the fact that the Chinese own so much of the American national debt that they could cripple the economy overnight just by selling their dollars en masse. This solution lets him focus on that problem and on cutting the defence spending which is crippling the US economy.'

Ross picked up the *New York Times* from the coffee table and contemptuously tossed it over to George. 'Oh, and as you have seen in your girlfriend's paper, Jane Chalmers will take the rap for the foiled coup in Scotland. After the fuck-up in Venezuela, she was a dead woman walking anyway. She goes and none of the shit sticks to MacFarlane. Perfect.'

George stared at his former friend, as if seeing him for the first time.

'And you see, George, the biggest winner of all is me. We Scots are a deeply divided people: Highlanders and Lowlanders, Catholics and Protestants, Unionists and Nationalists. This crisis has made us realise what unites us rather than divides us. There will be trials for the worst of the BLA terrorists, but I will ensure that the leaders of the SUR, apart from Robert Cowan, are pardoned in the interest of national unity. Chief Constable Stroud has been very active and helpful in the round-up of suspects. The crisis has pulled the nation together behind the idea of independence. It has saved Scotland. Oh, yes, and it has guaranteed me at least another full term in office.'

George didn't even have the strength to be angry. He was suddenly so dog-tired and mired in confusion, sorrow and self-pity. 'I can't believe you could betray me like that, Ross.'

'The truth is you betrayed yourself, George.'

'What about our friendship?'

'Oh, please,' Ross sneered, 'don't be a sentimental fool. We're not in the playground now. We were once useful to each other, no more than that. I put Scotland and, yes, my ambition before you. But you put your desire for honesty and moral purity before your duty to me. So don't play the martyr now. We'll

----

keep it polite, though. There will be no unnecessary unpleasantness. There's a typed resignation letter already on your desk. The official reason is that you are leaving to spend more time with your family. Please sign it on your way out.'

Oddly, George's immediate reaction was one of relief. His resignation absolved him of his debt of honour to Colonel Karimov and Russia.

Then other feelings hit him: anger, humiliation, exhaustion. He stood to leave, abject, defeated. As he reached the door, Ross spoke again. 'What you have to understand, George, and what you have never understood, is that it's just politics. Nothing personal.'

EPILOGUE

SUNDAY, 3 AUGUST

THE TUN BAR, HOLYROOD ROAD, EDINBURGH, 12.30 P.M.

George stepped into The Tun as it opened its doors for the first time that day. He was not blind to the irony that this was the very bar he had drunk in the first night he kissed Clare.

Much to the surprise of the young Pole behind the bar, he ordered not an espresso but a pint and a double Arran malt on the rocks. As the first burn of the whisky hit his throat George sought consolation in the same places he had always sought inspiration: poetry and history. He couldn't get out of his head the thought of Yeats' Irish airman's reflection on nationalism as he faced death in the First World War: 'Those that I fight I do not hate, / Those that I guard I do not love.'

How true that was for him. But Scotland now had her freedom, a freedom he still wanted, still believed in, in spite of all that had happened. Yeats had been right again when he wrote about the Easter Rising of 1916, which had forged the modern Irish nation, 'A terrible beauty is born.'

Maybe that was how it had to be. The deaths of Maureen and Jessie Cairns and the aborted coup uniting Scotland the way the execution of the leaders of the 1916 Rising had united the Irish in the south. Scotland, with its complex divides and tangled history, was finally one – born among unnecessary death and shattered lives.

Born bloody, not beautiful.

George had been the unwitting midwife. And Scotland had her freedom.

'Here's to bad people who do good things,' he announced out loud to a bemused barman and an empty bar, before draining the whisky.

His brain winced at the kick of alcohol so early in the day.

He had switched his mobile off before he went in to see Ross. It was not a conversation he had wanted to be interrupted. When he turned it back on, there were three text messages.

The first was from John, saying he had seen a great flat in the Cowgate and he had an audition for one of the squaddies in the National Theatre of Scotland's revival of *Black Watch*.

The second was from Catherine, saying the final scan was all clear and that the delivery date had been confirmed as the last week of September.

The third was from Jessica. It simply said: Woo me. Properly. Room 327, Balmoral Hotel. 1 p.m. One condition. Never call me an old doll again. Jessica xx

He smiled at the phone then looked at the half-finished pint intently.

It was a decision but not really a choice.

So what if he had been betrayed? So what if people weren't as good as he wanted them to be? He could not surrender to self-pity. There was so much to live for. So much to do in the new Scotland.

Abandoning his drink, he walked towards the sunlit door, stepped out and started to hail a taxi for the Balmoral Hotel. Deciding he would prefer the exercise, he took a deep breath of the summer air and headed up Holyrood Road.

He was smiling broadly and his anger vein no longer throbbed.

As George left the bar, Sammy Wilson strode purposefully down the Royal Mile to the Holyrood parliament's entrance hall.

Ross Johnson's last feeling as he strolled towards the doorman holding open the back door of the ministerial Jaguar was one of deep and complete satisfaction.

Sammy's four bullets hit him so rapidly that he barely registered any pain, just a sensation of toppling, then the plunge into infinite blackness.

Unlike most politicians, Ross Johnson died a happy man.

ACKNOWLEDGEMENTS

I would like to thank a number of people who read this book in various drafts and provided encouragement and invaluable advice: John Boyle, Jean Carwood, Bill Clements, James Clements, Liam Hamilton, Paul Heaney, Dan Korn, Allan Little, Lorna Maloney, Bridget McCann, Hamish Mykura, Stephan Pahides, Ian Sherwood, David Smart and Kirsty Wark.

I would also like to thank Mainstream for their support, especially Bill Campbell, Graeme Blaikie and Jennie Renton for her expert editing. Above all, I would like to thank my agent, Andrew Gordon of David Higham Associates. I truly appreciated his unfaltering belief, his judicious editing and his patient guidance through the new world of novel writing.

Any remaining errors and failings are my own.